MOTOR CITY BURNING

ALSO BY BILL MORRIS

Motor City

All Souls' Day

MOTOR CITY BURNING

BILL MORRIS

PEGASUS BOOKS
NEW YORK LONDON

MOTOR CITY BURNING

Pegasus Books LLC
80 Broad Street, 5th Floor
New York, NY 10004

Copyright © 2014 by Bill Morris

First Pegasus Books cloth edition July 2014

Interior design by Maria Fernandez

Library of Congress Cataloging-in-Publication Data is available.

ISBN: 978-1-60598-573-2

10 9 8 7 6 5 4 3 2 1

Printed in the United States of America
Distributed by W. W. Norton & Company

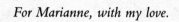

For Marianne, with my love.

Oh, the Motor City's burnin',
It ain't no thing in the world that I can do.
Don't ya know, don't ya know, the Big D is burnin',
Ain't no thing in the world that Johnny can do.
My hometown is burnin' down to the ground,
Worster than Vietnam.

—from "The Motor City Is Burning"
by John Lee Hooker

Our interest's on the dangerous edge of things.
The honest thief, the tender murderer, the superstitious atheist.
—Robert Browning

MOTOR CITY BURNING

PART ONE

OPENING DAY

1

UNCLE BOB WASN'T LYING. CAN'T MISS IT, HE'D SAID OF THE hippie house on Plum Street where it would be safe for Willie to park his baby, his immaculate classic Buick. And there it was now, right side, halfway down the block, painted up like a bad acid trip—orange walls, purple trim, some of the windows missing and others cracked and milky, the front door covered by an American flag with a peace symbol on the blue field where the fifty stars were supposed to be. A kid with stringy blond hair halfway down his back was waving cars onto the back yard. Music poured from an upstairs window, jangling electric guitars and a woman wailing, *"Go ask Alice when she's ten feet taaaaaaaaall. . . ."*

The driveway was pocked and cracked so Willie took it slow. He had the Sonomatic radio tuned to the pre-game show on WJR—Uncle

Bob told him he absolutely must not miss it—and a guy with a folksy southern drawl was reciting some kind of poem:

> *For, lo, the winter is past,*
> *The rain is over and gone;*
> *The flowers appear on the earth,*
> *The time of the singing birds is come*
> *And the voice of the turtle is heard on the land . . .*

Voice of the *turtle*? Man, that cracker must've been smoking something good, Willie thought as he switched off the radio, parked and locked the car.

He paid two dollars to a chubby girl wearing bell-bottom jeans and a tight sweater, no shoes, no brassiere. She flashed him a smile and the peace sign and said, "That's a pretty far-out car you got there. What is it?"

"It's a '54 Buick Century."

"Wow, looks brand new. I love that trippy pink-and-black paintjob."

"Thanks. So do I."

"Looks like something Elvis would drive." She noticed the license plate. "You really from Alabama?"

"Yes, ma'am."

"Ma'am!" She laughed so hard her breasts jiggled under the nubby sweater. It was the sort of thing he would not have dared to notice back home—until the day he did dare to notice, and then proceeded to learn the high price of noticing. The girl said, "You don't gotta call me ma'am. My name's Sunshine."

"And I'm Willie." He shook the offered hand. Her fingernails were painted turquoise and they were gnawed down to the quicks. Weren't her feet cold?

"How come you're way up north here, Willie?"

"That's a long story . . ." He caught himself before he called her ma'am again. "Got some family up here. Thought I might find a better job."

"So did you?"

"Not really." He managed a chuckle. It was a reflex. He knew how important it was not to let white people see his pain, not to even let them suspect that he might be in pain.

"Um, Willie . . . ?" She touched his arm and looked into his eyes. He noticed for the first time that her eyes were glassy and pink. Must be nice, smoking reefer before noon. "Listen, I'm . . . we're . . . everyone here in the house, we're, like, all real sorry about what happened to Dr. King."

He stiffened. "You're very kind to say so, Sunshine, but there's no need to be sorry."

"There's not?" She looked confused. "How come?"

"Cause you didn't kill him."

"Of *course* not, but. . . ."

"Sides, there's a lot of us brothers think the man was a sell-out."

"Dr. King? A *sell-out*?" Satisfied when Sunshine's jaw dropped—he loved to fuck with white people, especially the ones who believed their hearts were full of good intentions—he turned and left without another word.

The neighborhood was shabby—glass glittering on the sidewalks, houses in need of paint, black bruises on the street where cars had leaked their vital fluids. In the shadows between houses there were still gray slag heaps of unmelted snow. In *April*. Surviving his first Detroit winter was not something Willie was going to forget anytime soon. One day he was sitting in buttery sunshine in Palmer Park reading *The Autobiography of Malcolm X*, watching swans glide across the pond, marveling at the palette of the trees, the bloody reds, the juicy oranges, the richest colors he'd ever seen. The next morning he awoke to a blizzard, the first of his life, a storm that had come howling down out of Canada in the night and dumped a foot of snow on the city.

This neighborhood, the shabbiness of it, reminded Willie of something he picked up from a Chicago brother named Clifford Jenks who'd shared a cell with him at Parchman Farm in Mississippi back in '61, during Snick's "jail, no bail" phase. Unlike the other Freedom

5

Riders, Clifford and Willie weren't big on singing or Scripture. They spent most of that long night talking about sports and girls. They were still wet from the hosing they'd been given, shivering from the chill breath of the fans the guards had trained on them.

What Clifford said was: "Must be some kinda unwritten law that all stadiums is in shitty neighborhoods. Look at my hometown. Comiskey Park's on the South Side, in a black ghetto. Look at Yankee Stadium, South Bronx, a Puerto Rican ghetto. And look at D-troit. Tiger Stadium, in a white ghetto—which is the worst kind a ghetto they is." Clifford Jenks was something, a man who could make you laugh inside a cage in Parchman Farm.

As Willie joined the river of fans flowing toward the ballpark, he felt the familiar tingling. He'd always loved crowds, their anonymity, their electricity, their animal warmth. This mostly white crowd was in high spirits, like they hadn't heard the news about Martin Luther King—or didn't care. For the past week there'd been riots in Washington, D.C., San Francisco and dozens of cities in between, but Detroit had remained almost eerily quiet. Just one death, two cops wounded, a few student walkouts and assembly line shutdowns. Nothing like last summer, when a routine police raid on an illegal after-hours liquor house set the city off, a week of burning and looting and shooting that Willie and a lot of other people had spent the past nine months trying to forget.

And now, just after Willie's riot nightmares had finally stopped, Martin Luther King Jr. gets himself killed by a white man in Memphis. At least, everyone said it was a white man did it. Almost a week after the shooting they still hadn't found the gunman, and Willie was convinced they never would. He didn't think he was being cynical, just realistic. When it was announced that the funeral would be held in Atlanta on April 9, President Johnson, that lame white duck, decreed that the opening day of baseball season would be postponed from the 8th to the 10th, and he ordered all flags flown at half-mast. The Academy Awards show was also postponed by two days. Willie greeted these tokens with a shrug.

Though he had given up on King years ago, the details about the assassination fascinated him. For days he devoured newspapers and magazines and lived in front of his television set. He learned that the embalmers had to spend long hours working on King's corpse because the whole right side of his face was shot away, the jaw barely dangling. They had to rebuild the face with plaster. In Atlanta the coffin was placed on a crude farm wagon that was pulled through the throngs of mourners by two Georgia mules. This attempt to dress the patrician King in the trappings of the common man struck Willie as calculated and deeply dishonest, downright shameful. But hardly surprising. That, after all, was what mythmakers did. Given some of the things he'd heard King say, Willie even believed the man had pursued martyrdom.

Willie devoured such news not because he was shocked or even particularly dismayed by the killing, but because all the images of King had reawakened something in him. Hard as he'd tried to forget what happened during the riot, now he felt a need to remember something that happened long before the riot. Something he thought he'd buried forever. Something he would need to remember—and confront—if he ever hoped to escape from the purgatory he was living in.

All he had to go on was two little words: *de Lawd.*

His memory, clouded by the poisons he'd ingested during the past year, could tell him only that he first heard those words somewhere in Alabama and that they were uttered by a girl with a voice as soft as satin. He could still hear her voice but could no longer picture her face or remember her name. He had forgotten so much. The one other thing he knew about the girl's words was that they were dripping with acid and they were directed at King. Hearing a sister deride King as *de Lawd* had made the floor fall out of Willie's world, like a trap door had opened beneath him. Everything in his carefully constructed life fell through that trap door—all his beliefs, his ideals, his idols, his faith that the world could be made to change and that he could play some small part in changing it—everything started falling that day. And on the day after King's funeral, years after he heard those two killing little words, Willie could see with fresh eyes that he was still falling and he wanted to stop.

Watching those ridiculous Georgia mules pull King's coffin through the wailing mob in Atlanta, Willie understood that if he could recapture the moment when he first heard those two words—if he could relive that moment—he might be able to reassemble the life that fell through that trap door. Then he might be able to tell the story of that life. For the first time in years, thanks to Martin Luther King's murder, that was what he wanted to do.

He was jolted from his reverie by the shriek of a traffic cop's whistle. This edition of Detroit's finest, an Irishman with a cranberry nose, was holding up traffic with a big white-gloved paw so pedestrians could cross Trumbull. Even now, the sight of a Detroit cop sent a hot flash of terror through Willie. He hunched his shoulders and kept his eyes down as he hurried across the street.

When he made it safely to the other side he exhaled, then looked up and saw the great sooty iceberg of Tiger Stadium looming in front of him. It was lovely. Then came the smell of a charcoal fire warming bags of peanuts, tended by a whiskery old man in a hooded sweatshirt. "Roasted peanuts here!" he barked, bouncing from foot to foot to keep warm. "Gitcher hot peanuts!" The man was wearing gloves with the fingertips cut away, just like the gloves people wore to pick cotton back home.

As Willie waited in line at the ticket window, new smells came to him—wind-borne ash and cinders from the city's smokestacks, a vaguely briny smell off the river, diesel exhaust from idling buses. And then, after he paid fifty cents for a bleacher seat and began ascending the switchbacks that carried fans from the street to the upper deck, he realized he was climbing into a symphony of smells, a single complex aroma that had been composing itself since the first baseball game was played fifty-six Aprils ago in this, America's oldest big-league ballpark.

It was equal parts mustard, sweat, stale beer, urine, popcorn, wet wool, vomit, perfume, cigar smoke and boiled pork. It was that musty smell iron gives off after it has stood in one place through fifty-six scorching summers and fifty-six Arctic winters and an unknowable number of sleet storms and baseball games and football games, half-time pageants and fistfights and pennant drives, after it has absorbed the shuffling of millions of pairs of feet, heard the guttural animal roar of cheers and boos and taunts, after it has housed the whole range of human emotions, from ecstasy to scorn to despair, that touch the lives of people who live in a sports-mad city like Detroit.

He was winded when he reached the upper deck. Pausing to catch his breath, he told himself winter was over and he needed to get back out on the basketball court. He noticed something on the concession stand menus called "Red Hots," and the cryptic words CRUSH ALL CUPS stenciled on the walls at regular intervals. He had entered a house of mysteries and secret codes. The bleachers were reached by long catwalks suspended by cables from riveted iron girders. Looking down gave him a mild sense of vertigo, so he lifted his eyes to the rectangle of blue sky before him. He saw seagulls. And then he stepped into the sunshine.

Arrayed before him was the most beautiful room he'd ever seen. It was painted green, this irregular open-air room, its upper-deck seats sheltered by a tarpaper roof, the field a luxuriously cross-hatched emerald carpet. The infield dirt was tinged with something black. Coal dust? The bases glowed like sugar cubes.

He climbed toward the big black scoreboard at the top of the bleachers, toward the huge A.C. spark plug shooting through a ring of fire. From up there he could see the spires of downtown, but he turned his back on the skyline and studied this lovely open-air room. The longer he gazed out at the park, the smaller it seemed to become. It was hard to believe the place could hold upwards of 50,000 people. It was so . . . so intimate.

The American flag on the roof behind home plate was at half-mast, as he'd expected, and the pennants of the American League teams rimming the roof were all crisply horizontal from the river wind that cleared the roof on the first base side and galloped across the outfield. He was glad he'd worn a sweater under his nylon windbreaker. He wondered how it was humanly possible to watch the Lions play football in this place in the middle of December.

By the time a fat man in a tuxedo stood behind home plate and sang the National Anthem, the bleachers were nearly full. It was not going to be a sellout, but it was a fine surly crowd. After a minute of itchy silence for Martin Luther King, everyone stood and roared as the Tigers were introduced and sprinted out to their positions. The loudest cheers were for Al Kaline, the veteran right fielder, and Willie Horton, a home-grown hero, a powerful black slugger who tipped his cap as he jogged to his position in left.

A black pitcher named Earl Wilson strode to the mound and began warming up. Of course Willie knew there were black pitchers in the major leagues. He'd listened to St. Louis Cardinals games on KMOX radio since he was a boy, and he would never forget the seventh game of the 1964 World Series. He had just returned to his apartment in Tuskegee to write about the fires he'd walked through during that so-called Freedom Summer, and the Series came as a welcome distraction. A bunch of his old college buddies crowded into his apartment for the seventh game because he had the best radio reception and the coldest beer in town and because Bob Gibson, the intimidating black pitcher, was starting the game for the Cardinals. Surely Gibson understood that there were brothers crowded around radios like this all over the country, hanging on his every pitch, hoping he could put down the vaunted Yankees, the whitest of dynasties, and lay to rest the myth that black people were lazy, that they weren't as mentally tough as whites, that they couldn't be trusted with jobs as momentous as pitching the deciding game of the World Series. Gibson pitched brilliantly, then gave up two runs in a tense ninth inning before getting the Yankees' dangerous second baseman, Bobby Richardson, to pop up, sealing the Cardinals' victory.

Sitting in the Tiger Stadium bleachers now, watching Earl Wilson throw his last warm-up pitches, Willie remembered feeling a flood of elation and relief when Bob Gibson got that last out. So he was aware that there were black pitchers—black stars at every position—in the major leagues. But knowing this and seeing it with his own eyes for the first time were two very different things.

Just before Earl Wilson threw the first pitch of the 1968 season, two brothers came up the aisle and sat on the bench in front of Willie. One was middle-aged, very dark-skinned, almost blue, what Willie called "African black." White hair boiled out from under the upturned brim of his Panama hat. He was sucking on a toothpick. He nodded to Willie, who felt an instant kinship with this man, his deep blackness, his warm-weather hat, his silent gesture of greeting. Without thinking, Willie let slip a southernism: "Hey now."

"A'ight—and y'sef?" the man said.

"Fine, thanks. Got Earl Wilson on the mound."

"I seen that," said the other man, who was younger, fairer, tea-colored. He wore a tan trench coat with epaulets over a brown pin-striped suit, his yellow necktie loose, his shirt collar unbuttoned. His brown oxfords were laced tight, deeply creased but polished to a high shine. They looked elegant and businesslike and comfortable, three things that rarely went together. He looked like one of those rich oats you see in Esquire magazine, a successful businessman who could afford to duck out of the office in the middle of the day to catch a ballgame or drop in on his girlfriend.

"Ain't no flies on Earl," said the older man, motioning to a beer vendor. He turned to Willie. "Care for a Stroh's?"

"Um, sure."

"Three," the man told the vendor. He paid for all of them and passed around waxed-paper cups with foam spilling over their brims.

"Much obliged," Willie said.

"Ain't no thing." The man took a long drink of beer. "So where you from, Cuz? You ain't no Michigan boy. Your manners is too good."

"I'm from Alabama. Down around Mobile."

"No shit. My homeplace in Lurr-zee-ana, not far from Lafayette."
He let out a yelp when Earl Wilson struck out the leadoff batter.

"What brings you up here?" Willie asked.

"Work, same as everybody else. Been at Ford's the past twenty-two years. Right now I'm a second-shift foreman at the Rouge. Name's Louis Dumars." He and Willie locked thumbs, stroked each other's palms. "And this here's Clyde Holland—the famous barrister with the even more famous brothers." The two friends shared a laugh, and Willie locked thumbs with Clyde, brushed the offered palm. His hand was softer than Louis's.

"Willie Bledsoe. Pleased to meet you both."

After Wilson retired the side in the top of the first and the Red Sox took the field, Willie said to Louis, "So do you always get Wednesdays off at the Rouge?"

"Fuck no, man. I called in sick—just like half the rank-and-file all over town. You know you shouldn't never buy no car made on a Monday, right?"

"No. Why's that?"

"Cause—half the guys on the line's working with a hangover and the other half's at home sleepin theirs off."

Clyde laughed.

"Same goes for the Tigers' home opener," Louis went on. "I pity the fool buys a car made today. Half the bolts is gonna be missin and the other half's gonna fall off fore the car's a month old."

Clyde roared at this. Then he said, "How bout you, Alabama? How come you so far from home?"

"Work, same as everybody else."

"So what is it you do?"

"I work in a private club." Willie was going to leave it at that, but Clyde seemed to be waiting for more. So Willie said, "Bussing tables."

"A busboy." Clyde clucked his tongue, a sound Willie knew well, the sound of the native Detroiter's scorn for all the poor unhip country hicks who kept pouring in from the South and gobbling up the lowliest jobs simply because they thought they'd arrived in the Promised Land and hadn't learned the score yet.

Reggie Smith singled and a rookie named Joe LaHoud walked to start the Boston second. When Rico Petrocelli laced a double that rolled to the wall in left-center, scoring both runners, the mood of the fans turned sour. A greasy-haired white guy, his thick arms protruding from the rolled-up sleeves of a T-shirt, leaned over the front railing of the bleachers and bellowed, "Come on, Horton! Get your fat ass in gear! You coulda cut that thing off!"

Everyone within earshot guffawed.

"Damn," Willie said. "Fans're tough up here."

"Ficklest motherfuckers in the world," agreed Clyde, draining his beer and crushing the cup with the heel of an oxford. Watching him, Willie remembered the stenciled command on the walls. Clyde, seeming to read his mind, said, "Easier to sweep up after the game if they flat."

"Ahh." One mystery solved.

Boston added a run in the third, which ignited fresh grumbling about the quality of Earl Wilson's pitching. He won a brief reprieve by lofting a high fly to left in the bottom of the third, a ball that looked like a routine out until the wind off the river caught it. The crowd erupted when the ball sailed over the fence into the lower-deck seats.

"Earl my main man!" Clyde shouted, standing to applaud with everyone else as the pitcher trotted around the bases. "Motherfucker can stone *play!*"

But in the sixth inning the wheels came off for Earl Wilson. The Red Sox loaded the bases with nobody out. Even way up in the bleachers, some 500 feet from home plate, Willie could taste the doom in the air.

"Take him out," Louis pleaded softly when the Tigers' manager, Mayo Smith, marched out to the mound. The greasy-haired heckler was joined now by a small gang, including one guy who'd stripped off his shirt. He was as pink as a Smithfield ham. Obviously fueled by vast doses of Stroh's, they began to chant, "Lift the bum! Lift the bum! Lift the bum!"

But Smith left Wilson in, and the next batter, pesky little Rico Petrocelli, hit a sharp single, scoring one run and sending Earl Wilson to an early shower. As he trudged off the field, boos cascaded down from the stands in physical waves.

"Shoulda took him out," Louis said, shaking his head.

"That shit-ass had no bidness leavin him in," Clyde agreed. "His arm obviously tired. Any soda cracker could see that—even one named after *may*onnaise."

By the seventh-inning stretch Boston was ahead 6–1 and fans were beginning to shuffle to the exits. But Louis and Clyde were staying put, and so was Willie. Despite the racial tension, Willie wanted this game, this moment, to last forever, just as he'd wanted Earl Wilson's lazy home run to stay airborne forever. He realized this was the first time he'd felt truly at ease since arriving in Detroit.

He was looking at the scoreboard when a roar went up from the crowd. A muscular black player had stepped out of the Tigers' dugout and started twirling a cluster of bats like they were toothpicks. The hecklers sprang back to life.

"Hey, Gates! You remember to visit your parole officer this week?"

"Gates! Looks like you got along pretty good with that prison food!"

Willie turned to Louis. "What're those freckle bellies bellering about now?"

"That's Gates Brown coming in to pinch-hit. Best in the game, you ax me. Them crackers is giving him shit cause he did a little time. The joint's where he got the nickname Gates."

"What'd he do time for?"

"Burglary," Clyde said. "I represented him."

"And you didn't do a very good motherfuckin job!" Louis said, and the two friends laughed and slapped hands.

Damn, Willie was thinking, the Tigers even had black ex-cons on their roster. His love for this team was growing deeper by the minute.

Gates Brown yanked the first pitch into the right-field corner and sauntered into second base with a double. Didn't even break a sweat or get his uniform dirty. That took care of the hecklers. But the mention of prison had reminded Clyde of something.

"Du, check this out," he said to Louis. "Got a call this morning from a client a mine, name of Alphonso Johnson. Po-lice woke him out of a dead sleep and hauled him downtown for questioning."

"What for?"

"That's the amazing thing—for an unsolved murder during the riot. That's been almost a whole year ago. I didn't know the D-troit po-lice worked on nothin for a year."

"Ain't a continental thing those fools do that surprises me no more. They get away with murder any day a the week they want to."

"So did your client kill somebody?" Willie said.

Clyde shot him a withering look. "How the hell'm I suppose to know that, Alabama? You think a man kills somebody and goes around braggin on it?"

"No."

"Hell no. I don't know if he's guilty and I don't care. He's my client. What I'm tryin to tell you is that the po-lice is still workin shit from the riot. That was news to me."

It was news to Willie, too. The very worst news he could possibly have heard.

After the final out of the game, a 7-3 loss for the Tigers, Willie stood and took a last long look at the park, trying to commit it to memory. Then he followed Louis and Clyde and the rest of the hard-core fans down the switchbacks to the street. The two friends made plans to meet for Saturday's game against the White Sox, and they asked Willie if he was planning to come.

"Depends on my work schedule," he said. They posted the schedules on Thursdays, and there was a chance he would have to work on Saturday afternoon. "If I've got the day off I'll definitely be here."

"Here, Alabama," Clyde said, handing him a business card. The embossed letters, gold on black, said *Clyde Holland, Attorney at Law.* Then *Penobscot Building* and a phone number. "A brother never knows when he's gonna need a lawyer in this man's town."

"Amen," Louis said.

"Thanks, Clyde." Willie slipped the card into his wallet and said his goodbyes.

There was no sign of life at the hippie house on Plum Street, and his Buick was the only car left in the back yard. Driving up Cass, Willie tuned in WJLB and got the new one by Stevie Wonder, "You Met Your Match." Great bass line and a nice jump to the beat, Willie thought, another sure hit for a kid who'd been cranking them out for years and wasn't even out of his teens yet. Just thinking about Little Stevie Wonder made Willie feel old. Then came the signature sign-off of his favorite deejay, Ernie Durham, velvet-tongued "Ernie D," who delivered his farewell over a drenched blue bed of horns: *"I'm rough and I'm tough and I know my stuff . . . and you're lucky you live in a town where you can hear the Rockin' Mr. D. before the sun goes down . . . goodbye for now, D-troit, I LOVE ya! Now git yo'selves ready for Martha Jean the Queen!"*

But Willie barely heard it. He couldn't stop thinking about Clyde's client getting hauled downtown for questioning in a murder from the riot, a murder that was nearly a year old. Willie realized he'd allowed himself to get lulled into a false sense of security. Just because the riot was ancient history didn't mean the cops had forgotten about the last few unsolved murders. Far from it.

He realized the first thing he needed to do was get this Buick off the street. Again. It was the only thing that could possibly be his undoing. So instead of parking in his usual spot—out in the open at the curb near the corner of Pallister and Poe—he guided the Buick up the narrow driveway that ran between his apartment building and the scorched shell next door. He had to move some tires and old paint cans to make room in the garage. Then he pulled the Buick in and covered it with a tarp and closed the garage door.

He didn't want to give the cops a thing. And he damn sure didn't want to find out—from them or anyone else—exactly what had happened on the night he'd spent the past nine months trying to forget. But the world wouldn't let him forget. It was like a stone in his guts— the killing guilt that lurked there, waiting to pounce if it turned out he had killed a woman in cold blood.

2

SATURDAY MORNING NOT QUITE TEN O'CLOCK AND FRANK DOYLE
had the Homicide squad room to himself. The place was quiet, flushed
with spring sunshine. If he didn't know better, he might have believed
the city of Detroit was at peace with itself.

When he sat down at his big ugly brown metal desk with the *Free
Press* sports page and a fresh cup of forty-weight from the Bunn-
O-Matic, the first thing Doyle noticed was the manila envelope in
his IN box. It said INTEROFFICE and CONFIDENTIAL. That sounded
promising, but before he could open it his telephone rang. Not even
ten o'clock on a Saturday morning and already the calls had started
coming. What was he thinking? This was Detroit. The calls never
stopped coming.

Though he'd come in to clear up some paperwork and was, technically, off the clock, Doyle picked up the receiver. You never know. Police work is all about luck and squealers, and maybe this call would bring him luck. The good kind, for a change.

"Homicide, Doyle." More than a year on the job and he still got a little jolt every time he heard himself say the words.

"Frankie, it's Henry Hull calling from the Harlan House. Sorry to bother you on the weekend like this."

"No problem, Mr. Hull. You know I'm always glad to hear from you." It was true, sort of. Whenever Doyle heard that familiar squawk, his first thought was, *The little bug-eyed bastard's never going to give up, God bless him*. Doyle put a smile in his voice and said, "Before we go on, Mr. Hull, I've got to tell you something. You're the last person in the world who still calls me Frankie, and if you don't knock it off I'm going to drop this investigation."

"Hold on one minute, young fella. You drop this investigation and I'm going to report you to Sgt. Schroeder. You and your brother both."

"Report us? For what?"

"Shoplifting. Every day on your way home from school you and Rod stopped by the market. I mighta been behind the meat counter but Helen was behind the cash register and old Hawkeye never missed a trick. Every day, she saw you pinch a Bazooka Joe bubble gum and your brother snagged a Tootsie Roll. Every day—for years."

"You knew? Why didn't you say anything?"

"Because the Doyles were good people. It doesn't hurt a boy if he believes he's slick—so long as he doesn't take it too far. Which you and your brother didn't do, obviously."

The Hulls' Greenleaf Market was the unofficial social hub of the Jefferson-Chalmers neighborhood, the place everyone went for bread and milk, for cigarettes and candy and gossip, to argue politics or talk sports. The Hulls were generous with credit, especially if a customer was visited by hardship, which was a regular occurrence in a city that lived and died with the boom-and-bust cycles of the auto industry.

They were also, as Doyle had just learned, lenient with the right kind of shoplifters.

"Frankie, you're not gonna believe it," Henry said, "but I found something we missed!"

He was right. Doyle didn't believe it because Henry left no stone unturned. For the past nine months he'd been amassing a small mountain of evidence in a fourth-floor room at the Harlan House Motel on West Grand Boulevard at the John Lodge Freeway, where Henry now lived and where his wife had died on the morning of July 26, 1967, with a single .30-caliber bullet from a sniper's rifle lodged in her liver.

Or was the fatal bullet fired by someone other than a sniper?

A lot of black people in this town—from rabble-rousing Rev. Albert Cleage to Congressman John Conyers to the editors of the Michigan *Chronicle* to some of the cats way out on the revolutionary fringe—were convinced that the fatal shot was fired not by a sniper (that is, a *black* man) but by a National Guardsman (that is, a *white* man). Given the chaos on West Grand Boulevard that night and the Guard's horrendous performance during the riot, Doyle knew it was not a far-fetched theory. And there had been many times—usually when his boss, Sgt. Harry Schroeder, was pushing him to make that fucking Hull case go down—that he would have been delighted to buy the theory himself. But Doyle didn't buy theories because they suited his desires or someone else's political agenda. He bought theories and made arrests based on physical evidence, witnesses, confessions, and, sometimes, luck and squealers. And he knew he was nowhere close to making an arrest in the Hull case. The name stared down at him from the squad room wall, written in red grease pencil on a sheet of clear acetate: VIC #43 HELEN HULL. Just above it was the name of the only other riot victim whose killer was still at large—VIC #42 CARLO SMITH—a firefighter who got shot through the head while he was organizing units outside a burning warehouse on the East Side. The Hull and Smith cases, like all unsolved homicides, grew colder by the day. They were an insult. A torment. A homicide cop's worst nightmare.

But there was something that gnawed at Doyle even worse than seeing Helen Hull's name in blood-red block letters every time he came to work: the two snapshots of Helen Hull he kept on the corkboard partition that separated his desk from Jimmy Robuck's. Doyle was a sucker for snapshots, especially family snapshots, no doubt because he didn't have a family of his own other than one workaholic brother, an alcoholic sister-in-law, and their two daughters, who grew more ungodly gorgeous by the day and believed, for some strange reason, that their Uncle Frank had personally hung the moon.

Of course there were a dozen pictures of the girls, Lizzie and Val, pinned to the corkboard, along with a picture of his brother the day he'd made captain, a picture of his parents on their wedding day, a picture the Doyle family in front of the Christmas tree taken during the twilight of the Truman administration.

All those pictures orbited around the two pictures of Helen Hull. The bigger one, in full color, showed Henry and Helen surrounded by the Doyle brothers and a couple dozen neighborhood kids, everyone roaring full-throat, arms around each other's shoulders, black kids, white kids, Arab kids, a couple of Hispanic kids, even Henry Wong the Chinese kid, all scabby knees and missing teeth and PF Flyers, one big happy family standing at the top of the center-field bleachers in Tiger Stadium. Doyle loved that picture. Henry and Helen rented a bus every summer and took all the neighborhood kids to a Tigers' game, even sprang for hot dogs and peanuts and Cokes. It was, without fail, the best day of every summer in a boyhood that now seemed like it was nothing but a long string of cloudless summer days.

The other picture of Helen Hull was much smaller, black and white. It was a crime-scene photo taken in the fourth-floor hallway of the Harlan House Motel on the night she died. It was a brutal thing, which was why Doyle kept it pinned to the partition. He would not allow himself to forget what had happened to Helen Hull.

In the photo she was lying on her back on the hallway floor with shards of glass all around her. But it was her expression and her body language that got to Doyle every time he looked at that picture. Her eyes were wide open, like she had just seen something unimaginably horrible, and she was holding up her hands, as though pleading with someone or trying to ward off a blow. There was a dark stain just above the belt of her creamy dress. That's where the bullet went in and her life-blood poured out. Whoever pulled the trigger was one hell of a shot.

The scene was starkly lit. The police photographer had to use a flash because the cops had shot out all the lights as soon as they arrived on the fourth floor. The last thing you noticed was the uniform standing off to the side of the frame holding a flashlight and looking down at Helen Hull with an expression that was hard to read. Was it pity? Or was it scorn that anyone could be stupid enough to stand in a brightly lit picture window while a war was being fought down on the street? The uniform was Charlie Dixon, a classmate of Doyle's from the police academy. One day, when this was all over, Doyle planned to ask Charlie what was on his mind when that flashbulb went off.

"You say we missed something, Mr. Hull?" Doyle said now, sipping coffee and trying to sound excited. He wasn't awake yet.

"Something that was right under our noses the whole time! It's a miracle we missed it!"

His excitement was more contagious than the measles, and Doyle found himself waking up a little. "What is it, Mr. Hull?"

"I can't explain over the phone, Frankie. You gotta come see it with your own eyes. It's unbelievable!"

Doyle woke up a little more. Henry said "unbelievable" only when he had something good. "I'll drop by soon as I clear up some paperwork, Mr. Hull. Give me, oh, a couple hours."

"No rush. I'll be right here."

Doyle thanked him for calling and tore open the manila envelope. It contained a pair of tickets to tomorrow afternoon's game between the Tigers and the Chicago White Sox. The tickets were tucked inside a note that read *You don't know where these came from. Enjoy the game. Rod.* Doyle had planned to spend Sunday weeding his vegetable garden, but those weeds weren't going anywhere.

He studied the tickets. They were upper-deck box seats on the first base side, his favorite spot in the park, and the first pitch was at 1:05 P.M. Perfect. He was enough of a traditionalist to believe that baseball was meant to be played in sunshine, not under the hot white glare of those lamps they'd bolted to the stadium's tarpaper roof. And he knew from careful reading of box scores in the *Free Press* that the fever of Opening Day had already cooled. After drawing more than 40,000 fans for the opener, the team pulled in only about 10,000 the next day. It was still early, of course, but a lot of people were saying that these Tigers had a legitimate chance to win the pennant and atone for losing it to Boston on the last day of the '67 season. That would be nice. This city could sure as hell use a little cheering up.

Doyle was glad his brother hadn't sent tickets for Opening Day. He hated Opening Day, which he called Fair-Weather-Fan Day, and he avoided it for the same reason he stayed home on New Year's Eve, which he called Amateur Night. Noise-makers and stupid hats and champagne expensive enough to make you act like an asshole but cheap enough to give you a head like a dirigible the next morning. All that forced gaiety. The only thing Doyle hated worse than being told when to have a good time was being told he wasn't allowed to have a good time.

The question now was: Who to invite to the game? He wanted to ask a woman, but the right kind of woman, one who would be interested in what took place on the field. He couldn't stand going to the ballpark with someone who didn't care about the game, who was just there to show off the new wardrobe or blow off a little steam. Let the Grosse Pointe swells sit down behind the dugout looking like a million bucks, and let the brothers and the longhairs and the rivet-heads from Hamtramck sit out there in the bleachers and take their shirts off and get rowdy and loud. Doyle went to ballparks to watch ballgames.

The choice was obvious. Cecelia, the bartender at the Riverboat out on East Jefferson, had started calling him "Hon" and touching the back of his hand when he dropped in on his way home to drink a few beers and admire the view. Not the river view out the window, the view across the bar. He could watch her for hours, the way her brassy hair flashed in the dim light, the way her hips swiveled as she marched back and forth behind the long U-shaped bar. She would probably have tomorrow off. Just as he made up his mind to swing by the Riverboat after visiting Henry Hull, his phone rang again.

"Homicide, Doyle."

"Francis Albert Doyle—shame on you, me boy, for working on your day of rest," came the falsely sugared brogue of his brother, who was the only person in the world who still called him Francis. Rod knew Frank hated it, but that's how it works between brothers. One is forever the big brother and one is forever the kid brother and the former never stops reminding the latter of this unchanging fact of life. Doyle was pushing thirty, which meant he was still too young to enjoy it but way too old to fight it.

Doyle knew his brother wasn't calling to chastise him for breaking union regs. He was calling to make sure the Tigers' tickets had arrived safely and that the gift had been registered in the debit column of their brotherly ledger. Rod had been like this since they were shoplifting Bazooka Joe and Tootsie Rolls, but his native skill at calibrating favors and debts had acquired a razor sharpness two years ago when he made captain. He got the promotion after leading the Vice raid on the Grecian Gardens restaurant, where he personally discovered four little black books that recorded a series of bribes paid to uniformed police officers for ignoring liquor and gambling violations. Twenty-one cops were indicted, a bit of overdue house-cleaning that did not go unnoticed by the man whose image it burnished most, Jerome P. Cavanagh, Detroit's liberal Democratic mayor who, back in 1966, still fancied himself destined for the U.S. Senate at the very least, maybe a Cabinet post, possibly even the White House itself. And why not? The sky hadn't fallen yet in 1966. In the eyes of the national press back then, Cavanagh was still "The Dynamo in Detroit," the man who'd funneled millions of War on Poverty dollars to his city, which boasted the nation's largest NAACP chapter, low unemployment and high wages, the only city in America with two black Congressmen and a thriving auto industry and a home-grown, black-owned record company called Motown that cranked out the finger-popping hits as fast as the factories cranked out the gas-guzzling cars.

Rod Doyle saw to it that he not only got a captain's chair for his role in the Grecian Gardens case, but that his kid brother stopped patrolling the gritty streets of the Tenth Precinct and started breathing the relatively rarefied air of the fifth-floor Homicide bullpen at 1300 Beaubien Street. Thanks to his brother, Frank even got to skip the detective's standard apprenticeship in Vice, Burglary and Violent Crimes, and he got teamed with Rod's old partner, the Homicide squad's leathery legend, Jimmy Robuck.

Doyle thanked his brother for the Tigers' tickets. Then, since he wasn't supposed to ask, he asked, "So where'd they come from?"

"Believe it or not, I appointed one of Reverend Cleage's cronies to the Citizens Review Board—guy has the beer concession at Tiger Stadium—and suddenly I'm getting deluged with Tigers tickets. Just remember, you'll be watching Al Kaline compliments of the Church of the Black Madonna and the Stroh Brewery Company."

They shared a laugh at the way the world works.

"All seriousness aside," Rod said, "what're you doing down there on a Saturday morning?"

"Paperwork. And I just got a call on the Hull case."

"The Hull case?"

"Helen Hull. You know, Henry's wife—from the old Greenleaf Market."

"So who was the call from?"

"Henry, of course."

"Jesus, he still tending the flame?"

"Afraid so." Doyle paused. He didn't like the sound of what he'd just said. "Actually, I'm glad he is. Mrs. Hull didn't deserve what she got. Neither did Henry."

"I hear you. I can't believe you boys're still working shit from the riot, though."

"Well, believe it. One went down last week, but we've still got two unsolved. And your friend on the eleventh floor of the City-County Building wants them to disappear in the worst way. He's even started calling Sarge to check our progress in the case."

"Cavanagh's been calling Schroeder?"

"Afraid so." This time he didn't mind the sound of what he'd just said.

"So why don't you figure out a way to pin it on the State Police— or better yet, the National Guard—and make everyone happy? Cavanagh, you, me, and every black-power wacko this side of the Ohio state line."

"Believe me, the thought's crossed my mind more than once."

They shared another laugh. This one was shorter than the first.

"I'll let you go," Rod said. "Kat made me promise to pin you down on that dinner invite. She says you're working too hard—but mainly she wants you to come visit . . ."

I'll bet she wants me to come visit, Doyle thought.

". . . and the girls want to see their favorite uncle."

"I'm their only uncle, Rod."

"True, but they still ask. Christ, you wouldn't believe how fast they're growing up! Liz just got her first pair of toe shoes and we bought a horse for Val."

"You bought a *horse*?"

"A pony, actually. And we didn't buy it, strictly speaking. Kat did."

"Oh." Alcohol makes people do strange things, though Doyle guessed it probably wasn't all that strange for a teenage girl in Bloomfield Hills to have her own pony. What was strange to Doyle was that his brother had actually left the city, had let his wife's family money talk him into a four-bedroom Dutch colonial on an acre of suburban lawn that looked more like a putting green than most putting greens. The hardwood trees that towered over that lawn had been around longer than the Model T. Yes, it made perfect sense for a girl in that world to have her own pony.

"So when can I tell Kat and the girls you'll be out?" Rod said.

25

"Tell them I'll be out as soon as I clear a few things up. Maybe next week."

"Promise?"

"Promise. And thanks again for the tickets."

"Don't thank me. Thank Rev. Cleage."

"I'll do that next time I see him."

Doyle's coffee cup was empty and he was awake at last. Talking to his brother—thinking about his life out there in the suburbs—did what it always did. It made Doyle itch to show the world that there was still hope for the Motor City. He got up from the desk without touching the stack of paperwork. He couldn't wait to get to the Harlan House and hear Henry Hull tell him about the unbelievable thing they'd missed.

3

THERE WAS A WEDDING RECEPTION AT OAKLAND HILLS COUNTRY Club that Saturday, so instead of spending the afternoon sitting in the bleachers at Tiger Stadium drinking beer with Louis and Clyde, Willie spent it wandering through the mob in the clubhouse's cavernous ballroom, carrying tray after tray of glasses brimming with cheap champagne.

It wasn't a bad gig. The bar boys and Chi Chi, the Mex bartender, set up rows of glasses on the horseshoe-shaped bar in the downstairs lounge, and they popped corks and poured as fast as they could. Every time a busboy came in to refill his tray, custom dictated that he toss off a glass himself. By the end of every wedding reception, a couple of busboys wound up out on the tennis courts on their hands and knees, coughing up everything they'd eaten in the past twenty-four hours.

Willie drank a couple, three glasses, didn't blow his cool. As the reception was winding down and the guests were heading up the broad curving staircase to the banquet room, he loaded up one last tray and made a pass through the hangers-on who weren't eager to have solid food interfere with their mid-afternoon buzz.

"I'll take a couple of those, son."

Willie bristled. Son—it was half a notch above boy. He turned and faced a barrel-chested man with bright yellow hair. The guy stubbed his cigarette in an ashtray and lifted two glasses off Willie's tray. "Last call for alcohol," he said, laughing moistly. "Thanks a million."

"Yes sir." The man was standing off by himself pounding down a couple of final jolts. His skin was pitted and flushed, his necktie loose. Willie smelled loneliness coming off him, and started to move away.

"Tell me something, son," the man said.

Willie turned back toward him. "Sir?"

"I've never seen you before. Are you new here?"

"Yes sir. I started about a month ago."

"I'm Chick Murphy. I'd shake your hand but—" He lifted the two glasses and sipped from one, then the other.

"And I'm Willie Bledsoe, sir. Pleasure to meet you." Again he started to move away, and again the man drew him back.

"You from Detroit, Willie?"

"No sir, I'm from Alabama originally."

"No shit. Got a mechanic working for me who's from Alabama— Tuscaloosa, I believe it is. Name's Gaylord Banks. Ever hear of him?"

"No sir, can't say that I have." What was it with white people up here? They all seemed to think that every black person in Alabama knew every other black person, like it was one big happy jungle village.

"Best damn mechanic ever worked for me," Chick Murphy went on. His words were a little slushy, his eyes a little hot, but Willie could tell the man knew how to hold his booze. He drained both glasses, returned them to the tray, and took one more.

Willie noticed then that something was wrong with the man's left hand. He looked closer, trying not to stare, and realized the pinkie was missing. Chick Murphy said, "So what brings you way up here, Willie?"

"I've got some family here. Bob Brewer's my uncle and—"

"Bob's your uncle! He's the best damn waiter we've ever had here! Pure class!"

"Thank you, sir."

"I'll be honest with you." He leaned close, close enough for Willie to smell nicotine and sour wine and breath mints. "Some of the guys on the staff here aren't worth two shits. But Bob Brewer—he's class all the way." He drank, then glanced out the tall windows at the golf course. "Christ, I hate weddings," he muttered. "I had box seats for the Tigers game today, and here I sit because one of my best customers is marrying off his daughter. You been to a game yet?"

"Went to my first one on Opening Day, as a matter of fact."

"What'd you think?"

"I loved it, especially the park. Only trouble was, they got beat."

"They're gonna be okay." The change of subject seemed to revive him. His hot eyes were dancing now. "If their pitching holds up, I don't see how anybody's gonna be able to stay with them this year. They've got too much firepower. Plus they owe the fans one for blowing the pennant on the last day of last season."

"I saw Earl Wilson hit a home run—and he's a pitcher."

"Wait'll you see Kaline and Horton and Cash get loose. Those guys can murder the ball."

Willie noticed Dick Kowalski, the club manager, standing by the doorway to the lounge drawing a finger across his throat, the signal that the bar was closed and it was time to start picking up all empty glasses and dirty ashtrays.

"Well, Mr. Murphy, it's been nice meeting you. We've got to clean up now. Would you care for another before I go?"

"I'm good, thanks." He drained the glass he was holding and set it on the tray. "Say, I was just thinking . . . I've got a couple of tickets to tomorrow's Tigers game, but I've got to play golf. Any chance you could use them?"

"Afraid I've got to work a double shift again tomorrow. But thanks anyhow."

"Well, maybe next time."

As Willie started picking up empty glasses he watched Chick Murphy stride toward the men's room. The man had to be high as a Georgia pine, yet he was able to walk in a straight line. These Detroit guys, their livers must've been made of cast iron.

When the ballroom was cleaned up, Willie decided to head down to the Quarters, the impromptu bunkhouse in the basement where the black waiters and busboys took breaks and sometimes spent the night if they got stuck working late and didn't want to drive all the way back into the city. The champagne was wearing off, and he could feel the first faint throb of a headache. A nap might be just the thing to get him ready for the dinner shift.

When he entered the Quarters, Hudson and Wiggins were locked in one of their epic poker games. They'd taken off their ocher jackets and white shirts and clip-on bow ties and were playing in their T-shirts, suspenders dangling from the sides of their tuxedo pants. They both wore alligator loafers over thick 'n' thins—sheer silk socks with black stripes. They wore gaudy pinkie rings, too, touches that announced to the world that no uniform could bleach the blackness out of them. Just to make sure the message hit home, Wiggins wore his hair in a greasy conk and Hudson shaved his skull.

There was a mountain of dollar bills on the table, and neither man looked up when Willie hung his white jacket and dress shirt on a hanger and hopped up onto one of the top bunks and opened his book. But he was too sleepy to read. The Tigers game was on the radio, and as he drifted off he heard a roar and the voice of Ernie Harwell, the turtle guy: *"Going . . . going . . . long gone! Willie Horton just hit one clean out of the park! That thing might never come down!"*

Willie was smiling when he fell asleep.

❖

Laughter woke him. Then Hudson's bullfrog voice: "You still see Luvel Broadnax round?"

"Luvel?" Wiggins said. "Shit. That nigger been sleepin underground prit near three years now."

"What happened?"

"Got shot during a craps game in the parking lot outside Olympia after a boxing match. Shot through the chest. Never did catch the nigger who did it. Cat from Toledo, way I heard it."

"So what you got?"

"You really wanna see what I got?"

"Lay you damn cards down."

Willie heard the snap of cards. Then a moment of silence. Then Hudson roaring, "A motherfuckin *flush!*" And he was banging his fist on the table and hurling his cards at the wall.

Still groggy, Willie looked down at them. Wiggins was cackling and scooping a pile of bills off the table. Couple of old-fashioned, slavery-time handkerchief heads, Willie thought, as lazy as the day is long and ready to blame everything on The Man, acting like brothers shooting brothers during a craps game was business as usual, so thoroughly trapped they didn't even realize there was a trap. Willie thought of them as Sambo and Quimbo, Simon Legree's two brutal slaves in *Uncle Tom's Cabin*, who proved that no one makes better tyrants than the tyrannized. He supposed Chick Murphy had guys like Hudson and Wiggins in mind when he'd confided that some of the waiters in this place weren't worth two shits. In addition to their shared love of drinking and gambling, they both had quick tempers and mean streaks and they stole anything that wasn't bolted down.

Hudson stood up from the card table, stretched, yawned. He had liver lips and rhinoceros ears. His gleaming skull was dented in several places, and Willie had often wondered what had caused those dents. Wrenches? Bottles? Cops' nightsticks? Maybe they were just badges of a childhood spent in Paradise Valley, the inevitable marks left on the son of an autoworker who, according to Hudson, liked nothing better than to get drunk and beat on people, especially his wife and children. As often as he'd puzzled over those dents on Hudson's skull, Willie wasn't about to ask how they got there.

"Whatchoo readin now, Professor?" Hudson said, looking up at Willie. The nickname was not meant to be flattering. Hudson had dropped out of the sixth grade, and he had no use for knowledge that came from anywhere other than the street. More than once he'd expressed the opinion that a fair-skinned bookworm like Willie would have made a perfect poster boy for the United Negro College Fund. Willie didn't take it personally. He'd learned long ago that black people who can't get at the real oppressor wind up lashing out at one another.

He looked at the book lying open on his chest. "It's called *Black Like Me*."

"What's it about?" Hudson asked without interest. He was watching his ace boon coon Wiggins stack his winnings in a very neat, very tall pile. Hudson was smiling. Losing was delicious torture for him. It was his way of life.

"It's about this white dude who dyes his skin and travels around the Deep South passing for a brother."

"No shit," Wiggins said, licking his thumb as he counted his pot. "Why some honky do a fool thing like that?"

"To find out first-hand what prejudice feels like. The book's not bad. Only trouble is, the writer buys into that jive about race relations down South being a blot on the whole country. Like whitey's treating us like princes up here."

Hudson actually chuckled. "What this gray dude do bout his hair, Professor?"

"He shaved his head."

"Ah."

"Well," Wiggins said, adding his winnings to his roll and tucking it into his tuxedo pants, "that ofay wanted to know about prejudice, he shoulda come see me. I could write a motherfuckin book about prejudice."

He and Hudson guffawed and slapped hands, the poker game already a dim memory. Willie watched them, thinking that James Wiggins, with his fried hair, rhiney skin and bloodshot eyes, had probably never read a book from cover to cover in his life. The man couldn't string two grammatical sentences together, let alone write a book. The whites of his eyes were the color of cold piss, and Willie guessed it was from something much worse than drinking.

Just then the swinging doors squealed open and Bob Brewer strode in, carrying his ocher waiter's jacket, a white shirt and a pair of tuxedo pants in a dry-cleaner's plastic bag. "Gentlemen, gentlemen," he said, hanging the clothes in a locker. When he noticed Willie on the top bunk he said, "What up, Cuz?"

"Not much, Uncle Bob. What's up with you?"

"If you get your narrow ass down off that bed and come outside, I'll show you."

Willie yawned and hopped down off the bed. He put his white shirt back on and, smoothing his hair, followed his uncle out the door and down the scabbed concrete hallway. This netherworld, the service end of the rambling clubhouse, smelled of rotten fruit and ammonia, stale beer and starch and steam. Willie thought of it as the second worst thing that had ever touched his nostrils: the stench of servitude. Bad as it was, though, it couldn't touch the smell inside that garage at police headquarters last summer. That was in a league of its own: the stench of degradation.

As he passed the clattering ice machines, one of the bar boys went by pushing a cart stacked with cases of top-shelf liquor—Canadian Club, Cutty Sark, Beefeaters—the fuel for tonight's festivities. All the busboys and waiters at Oakland Hills were black and all the bar boys and bartenders were white. The reason was obvious to Willie. Dick Kowalski didn't think niggers could be trusted around all that pricey booze.

Willie was still yawning when he and his uncle stepped out of the clubhouse and into hazy sunshine. The day had turned almost hot and the trees beyond the caddy shack were bearded with green buds, aching to burst. Maybe winter really was over.

Uncle Bob led the way across the members' parking lot to the employees' lot. From fifty yards away Willie saw it, tucked off in the corner by itself. He knew right away it was his uncle's car because of the way it gleamed, because everything about Uncle Bob was clean. He dressed conservatively and he was always freshly shaven, impeccably groomed, didn't even have razor bumps. He wore his hair short and natural, like Willie's, in that tasteful middle zone between Wiggins's conk and Angela Davis's big-ass black power Afro. It was obvious from the way Bob had parked the car off in the corner that he was gripped by the new car owner's terror of sideswipes, door dings and bird droppings.

The car was a fully loaded, two-door 1968 Buick Electra 225 with a muted bronze paintjob and creamy vinyl top, elegant and understated, a far cry from the loud color schemes Willie was accustomed to seeing on cars in the city: lizard green, salmon pink, fire-engine red, burnt orange. And then, for good measure, some gaudy, fake-gold shit around the license plate, wide whitewall tires, spoke wheels, curb feelers, the finishing touches that announced to the world that this car was owned by a man who was black and damn proud of it. When Willie first got to town he thought those city brothers were unaware that the bulbous lines and gumball paintjobs that distinguished cars like his pink-and-black '54 Buick had given way to something more subdued. Oh sure, the muscle cars drag racing up and down Woodward were a blur of candy-apple red and canary yellow. But those cars were driven by greasers, who weren't even all the way white. It didn't take Willie long to realize that the Detroit brothers had indeed heard the news. They simply chose to ignore it.

But Uncle Bob was different. His life was dedicated to blending in. He was as proud as any black man Willie had ever met, but he refused to give the white man fuel for the stereotypes that fed his racism. There was nothing flashy about Bob Brewer—the only jewelry he wore was a Timex watch and his wedding band. He rarely drank, and he didn't gamble or smoke or take anything stronger than aspirin. So it was no surprise to Willie that his uncle's new Buick would have been right at home in the members' parking lot at Oakland Hills, alongside all the conservative, late-model Cadillacs and Lincolns and the hulking, wood-paneled station wagons favored by suburban housewives.

"Well, what do you think?" Bob asked, beaming.

"She's a beauty, Uncle Bob."

"You like the color?"

"Actually, I think you should've gone for chartreuse. Woulda fit your personality a lot better."

Bob laughed at the jibe. "Guy on the lot where I bought it told me something interesting. You know where the name comes from?"

"Sure. Everybody with half an education knows Electra was a Greek chick from a messed-up family whose momma—"

"No, no, not the Electra part. The Two-Twenty-Five part."

"Oh. Beats me. Is it the horsepower?"

"That's what I thought, too. Come to find out that when Buick started using the Electra name back in '59, the thing was two hundred and twenty-five inches long. Think about it—that's damn near twenty feet long."

This car wasn't quite that long, but it was close. The relative lack of chrome and the sharp lines made it seem even bigger and longer than it was. There were four chrome notches in the front fender, which marked it a "four-holer," a top-of-the-line Buick. The hood was huge, much flatter and longer and wider than the bulbous hood on Willie's '54 "three-holer," and the trunk looked big enough to hold a Volkswagen. Or a couple dozen assault rifles.

"Hop in, let's take her for a spin," Bob said. It was the first time Willie had heard something like childish excitement in the man's voice.

They headed east on Maple Road, then left at Lahser. At the touch of Bob's foot the Buick shot into the warm afternoon, just ate up the

road. Willie watched the orange speedometer needle climb effort-
lessly past 40, 50, 60, up to 70. Bob had the windows rolled up and
the air-conditioning on, and Willie wondered if this wasn't another
of his strategies, like the muted paintjob, to keep from drawing attention to himself. This far north in the suburbs, a black elbow sticking
out of an expensive new car's window could attract something a lot
worse than stares.

"Hope you don't mind the AC," Bob said, fiddling with the
controls.

"No, it's fine. Feels good. Man, this thing rides smooth."

"What'd you expect? It's an Electra."

There it was again. He called the car an Electra, the way a white
man would. To all the brothers in Detroit, the 225 was a Deuce and a
Quarter, or simply a Deuce, a term of great reverence, for this car was
the pinnacle of status in the inner city, even higher than a Cadillac.
Cadillacs were for preachers and pimps and the rich honkies out in
Grosse Pointe and Bloomfield Hills. The Deuce and a Quarter was
the hip Detroit ride.

"You need to get you one a these," Bob said. "You still driving
that old Buick?"

Willie took a deep breath and got ready to tell the lie for the first
time. He thought of his mother's sister, Aunt Nezzie, that great reposi-
tory of mother wit, telling him years ago that if you're going to lie
you'd better have a good memory. He'd been rehearsing this lie ever
since the Tigers' game, when he stowed his Buick in the garage after
hearing about Clyde Holland's client getting taken downtown for
questioning. That was Willie's wake-up call, his return to a world of
worry he thought he'd escaped. Now he could see that there would be
no escape from that world until the murder was solved. And even that
prospect merely tightened the bind he was in. He wanted to learn he
was innocent, of course, but what about the unthinkable—what about
learning he was not? So he wanted the cops to remain in the dark
because as long as the case remained unsolved he could tell himself
that he was innocent—and that his brother was innocent, too. Not

knowing might be even better than knowing, but uncertainty was its own kind of purgatory, one he was not eager to re-enter. Yet he had no choice. So here he was, getting ready to tell the well-rehearsed lie for the first time. He glanced at his Uncle Bob and said, "Yes and no."

"What's that suppose to mean?"

"Means I can still drive it, but I'm afraid to. The transmission's leaking like a faucet, so I parked it in the garage till I save up enough to get it fixed."

"How much you pay for that thing?"

"Nothing. It was a gift."

"No shit. From who?"

"A Navy buddy of my brother's, a white guy named Sam Malloy. He and his long-legged blonde wife showed up at my place in Tuskegee in late '63, right after President Kennedy got shot, and handed me the keys and the title."

"Just like that?"

"Just like that. I couldn't believe it either." Five years later, Willie still couldn't believe it. He'd spent his boyhood learning to make do with the second-hand and the second-rate—hand-me-down clothes and shoes from his brother, hand-me-down textbooks from the white schools, with all the important stuff already underlined, the covers falling off, entire pages missing. At the colored playground the basketball court was cracked and uneven, the rims bent and rusty, the balls smooth as cue balls. The baseball diamond was pocked, baked dirt with a few shoots of crab grass. He didn't give these things a second thought, nobody did. And then, when he was a young man putting his body on the line to change the world he'd once accepted as a given, a friend of his brother's drove up and gave him the most beautiful car he'd ever seen. *Gave* it to him. It was so miraculous it was almost an insult to the monastic life he was living at the time. But on that day Willie came to understand something that his fellow Snick foot soldiers, those austere warriors, never acknowledged or discussed—that there was another world out there, a world of shiny things that weren't cracked or bent or used-up, and those things were within reach, even for a black man, and there wasn't a damn thing wrong with wanting them. Willie loved that Buick shamelessly, and of course he pampered it.

Uncle Bob said, "So why'd this white dude give you a car?"

"He told me Wes saved his life on a patrol one night in Vietnam, and he wanted to repay the favor. So Wes told him to give me the car."

"Well, get that tranny fixed and sell the thing and get you an Electra. All you gotta do is play your cards right."

"My cards, Uncle Bob? What cards?"

"I been watching you. Your mother was right about you."

"She's your big sister. She's always right."

"Listen to me. You aren't like the rest of the Negroes up here. You got a brain and you aren't afraid to work. Plus, you're articulate and you know how to talk to all kindsa people. Those things right there can take a man a long way up here. Even a black man."

"Uncle Bob, I've got a year of college under my belt and I'm working as a busboy at a honky golf club in the suburbs of—"

"If you didn't want to wind up bussing tables, then maybe you shoulda stayed in college like your daddy and I told you to."

Willie should have known that was coming. His uncle, like his father, bought into the myth that something as flimsy as a college degree could actually make a difference in a black man's life. On the other hand, Willie's mother, the best educated person in the family, had urged him to listen to the voice in his head and drop out of Tuskegee and join the movement. And she'd never second-guessed him when it all fell apart. Ma BeBe was a rock.

Bob said, "Is there something wrong with bussing tables?"

"No, Uncle Bob. Not a goddam thing. I love it."

"You're saving money, aren't you?"

"A little." He wanted to add that he wasn't saving it nearly as fast as he'd squandered it over the past year, but he was too ashamed to admit that to his uncle or anyone else.

"You aren't working in no car factory or turpentine still or cotton patch, are you?"

"Hell no."

Uncle Bob shifted in his seat, and Willie could feel it coming: The Lecture, The Black Bourgeoisie Pep Talk. He didn't want to hear it again, and suddenly he was angry. Angry at his uncle for buying into all that up-by-the-bootstraps, Booker T. Washington horseshit. Angry at himself for getting painted into a corner and having to take the lowly busboy job. Angry at the white man for setting up the game so the black man's only choices were between bad and worse, between wrong, wronger and wrongest. Yes, he was back in that familiar purgatory.

Before his uncle could launch into The Lecture, Willie cut him off. "You ever read Paul Laurence Dunbar by any chance?" Willie assumed he had, for as much as Uncle Bob was a driven man and a believer in the system, he was no black Babbitt. He'd put himself through night school at Wayne State and he still found time to read serious books, attend symphony concerts, visit the Institute of Arts. He was active in Detroit's Democratic Party and had just been named a delegate to the upcoming convention in Chicago. Bob Brewer's biggest worry was not that President Johnson's Great Society was an expensive joke, but that by choosing not to seek re-election Johnson had ceded the White House to the Republicans. It had long ago stopped mattering to Willie which white man lived in the White House.

"Sure," Bob said. "*Lyrics of a Lowly Life*. All those stories in dialect." Suddenly he slipped into a respectable darkie-on-the-plantation dialect: "'An' ez fur boss, I'll be my own, I like to jest be let alone . . .' Dunbar was a man after my own heart."

"And look at him," Willie said. "Cat as gifted as that, wanted to go to Harvard Law School, wound up as an elevator operator in Dayton, Ohio, making four dollars a week. I think of a guy like Paul Laurence Dunbar and I ask myself what's the use of dreaming?"

"You think he let that elevator job stop him from dreaming? And writing?"

"I got no idea."

"You know damn well he didn't. You want to know what's the use of dreaming? I'll tell you. Once you stop doing it, you're a dead man."

"Well then, I guess that means I'm a dead man."

But his uncle didn't hear him. He was already delivering The Lecture. "How you think I managed to pay cash for this Electra? By saving my tips and playing the numbers? Hell no. I had a dream, and even more important I had a plan—and I stuck to it. I bought up apartment buildings dirt-cheap when the white folks got scared and started moving away from the West Side. Then I rented them to Negroes. That riot was the best thing ever happened to me. All my buildings were fully insured, and with the money I got on the four that burned down I turned around and bought six more. And this car."

It was madness, Willie thought. Even Mr. Clean here was unclean, feeding off the fears of the white man while bleeding the black man. "If you're so flush, Uncle Bob, why don't you lower my rent? And quit that boge waiter's job while you're at it?"

He ignored this too. He was talking about his friend Berry Gordy, who was minting money at his record company on West Grand Boulevard. Then he talked about another friend, the black Congressman John Conyers, smart as a whip, a man going places. Then he talked about the classes he was taking at U. of D. toward getting his own real estate license so he could start buying and selling property without giving a cut to Mr. Charlie. Be his own boss, just like Paul Laurence Dunbar.

But Willie had tuned him out. He was thinking about how to get rid of his '54 Buick. Maybe he should take the Alabama plates off it and just leave it in the garage and take a bus out of town. But what if the police found the car? Surely they could use the serial number to trace it to Alabama. Maybe he should put a brick on the gas pedal and let it take a swim in the Detroit River.

Then a better idea came to him. Maybe he should do exactly what his uncle was suggesting—paint the Buick and trade it in for a used Deuce and a Quarter. Then he could forget the cops and point his new car away from Detroit and just let it take him away from all this bad air and worse history.

But first he would have to get some money together. Again he thought of all the bread he and his brother had made selling those guns when they first hit town, and again he cursed himself for pissing away every last dime of it. He'd lost track of all the stories he'd told himself to justify his behavior. He told himself his brother had leaned on him to make the run from Alabama to Detroit—though Willie was secretly glad for an excuse to get away from the ghosts of the South. He told himself he needed a change of air if he was ever going to get back to work on his book—but the words hadn't come in Detroit any more than they'd come in Alabama. He told himself the world owed him a little fun—and so he gave himself over to pleasure for the first time in his life. He had money to burn, and he burned it. Saw Edwin Starr at the Twenty Grand, Etta James at Baker's Keyboard Lounge, Freddie Hubbard at the Drome, went all the way out to a VFW hall in Mt. Clemens to hear Bobby Blue Bland. After the bars closed at three o'clock he might hit a blind pig for a nightcap or load up on barbecued pigs' feet at the Log Cabin. Everywhere he went he was the life of the party, always a roll in his pocket and a girl on his arm, everyone's stick buddy.

It was the very sort of behavior that made his parents and Uncle Bob see red. They even had an expression for it—"nigger rich"—and it was the most scathing put-down they could utter about a member of their own race. Their scorn applied to all forms of wasteful behavior, the tendency to squander not only money but health, opportunity, good luck, anything acquired through hard work or simple fate. Squandering invariably led to need, and a needy man had an instinctive urge to seek a scapegoat. Willie's parents and his uncle would not abide this yearning for a scapegoat because they believed that all people achieve their own failures as well as their own successes, and the only way to attain true dignity is to accept responsibility for those failures and successes without complaint or false pride. As much as Willie hated to admit it, he knew they were right. This fix he was in was his own damn fault. He'd finally come to understand that the world doesn't owe a thing to any man.

Uncle Bob was saying something about Chick Murphy.

"I'm sorry," Willie said. "What was that?"

"I said Chick Murphy made me a nice price on this car. He beat Krajenke by almost five hundred bucks."

"Chick Murphy sold you this car?"

"Yeah, you met him?"

"He was at the wedding reception I worked this afternoon. Man drinks like a fish."

"Well, he might be a boozer but he's the biggest Buick dealer in Michigan and he damn sure did right by me on this deal. You oughta talk to him. I'm sure he'd take your old Buick in trade."

It was such a beautiful idea that Willie couldn't get it out of his head. He was in a daze all through the dinner shift that night, unable to stop working and reworking the angles. If he got a cheap paintjob on his '54 Buick and unloaded it on a dealer with a huge lot, the car would as good as disappear. Once it was resold, the cops would never be able to trace it back to him. And once he got behind the wheel of his own Deuce and a Quarter, all his problems would be solved.

He told himself these things so many times that by the time he fell asleep on his bunk in the Quarters, well past midnight, he had actually come to believe they were true.

4

As soon as Doyle opened the door to the basement garage, the smell hit him. It was a layered, physical thing, the smell of ammonia and lye and disinfectant and their failure to conquer the far more powerful smells of human shit and piss and sweat and rage that had stewed in that garage since last July, when it was pressed into service as an impromptu holding tank for hundreds of people who'd been arrested on charges of curfew violation and looting and arson and were waiting their turn to stand before an over-worked, short-fused Recorder's Court judge and learn that their bail was up there in fantasy land, in the neighborhood of ten grand. Doyle guessed the stench would linger in this garage forever.

He climbed into a Plymouth and headed north on Woodward. It amused him that these cars were considered "unmarked." With their cheap hubcaps, long radio antennas and identical chocolate paintjobs, they might as well have had bull's-eyes on the doors. Couldn't the brass at least spring for a few different shades of paint, maybe a Chevy or a Ford every once in a while just to keep the bad guys guessing?

He took Woodward instead of the Lodge Freeway because he preferred surface streets. For one thing, you were less likely to get a brick dropped through your windshield by some prankster who'd cut a hole in the cage on an overpass. For another, you were more likely to pick up on new strains of street life.

As he passed the Fox Theatre he saw that another Motown Revue was coming. His eye caught a few names on the marquee—Martha & the Vandellas, the Miracles, Marvin Gaye and Tammi Terrell. "The Sound of Young America" sounded like fun, but he knew it wasn't available to him. He was much closer to his thirties than his teens, and he wasn't about to pretend he didn't know it. Besides, he preferred jazz.

When he crossed over the Ford Freeway, the atmosphere changed. It wasn't anything on the street; it was something in his stomach, a sudden tightness. Instead of turning left on Grand Boulevard and going straight to the Harlan House, he kept heading north, guided by the tightness in his stomach. He knew where it came from: It came from the neon sign and his need to see it. And suddenly there it was up ahead, on the left side of the street, waiting to remind him of so many bad things. The palm tree with its green neon fronds, unlit at this time of day, topped the familiar metal rectangle. What he saw next came as too much of a shock to be a relief.

They'd changed the name.

What had once been the Algiers Motel was now the Desert Inn. They'd changed the name but they hadn't bothered to take down the sign and get rid of that fucking neon palm tree. The place was a blot on the entire police force, on the city itself.

Doyle slowed the Plymouth as he passed. There were a few black guys drinking out of paper bags in the parking lot beyond the swimming pool, out by the annex building. That was the killing floor. That was where cops killed unarmed civilians in cold blood. He was so mesmerized he almost missed "her"—the six-foot Negro with the copper wig and the hot pink mini-skirt and high heels who was hip-swiveling along the sidewalk in front of the motel, dangling a big white purse and checking each car as it passed. Christ, Doyle thought, now they've got trannies doing the hooking up here—in broad daylight.

He turned left onto Boston, a boulevard of fading but still-grand mansions. The grandest of them all was off to his right, a three-story palace roosting on a green carpet that was being groomed by black men riding a fleet of little tractors. Country living right here in the heart of the Motor City. Berry Gordy, the founder of Motown records, had paid a million for the place last year, and the understanding around town was that he'd done so to squelch rumors that the company was planning to move to L.A. But Doyle had his doubts, and he wasn't alone. A million bucks was beer money to a guy like Berry Gordy. Besides, why shouldn't a thriving record company join the exodus? Did it have an obligation to hang on just because it happened to be owned by a black man? Did Ford Motor Company have a similar obligation just because old Henry made his pots of money here? Nobody squawked when he took his show out to snow-white Dearborn.

After crossing over the Lodge Freeway, Doyle turned left onto Twelfth Street, where it had all started. The gutted buildings still looked warm to the touch, like the fires had stopped burning nine hours and not nine months ago. Very few of them had been torn down yet, as though someone—insurance companies? the white power structure?—had left them standing as perverse monuments to the madness that had swept this city. Those that had been torn down had usually been replaced by nothing at all, just pebbly, weed-choked lots that glittered more brightly every day with smashed wine and liquor bottles. Ragweed Acres, Doyle called these vistas. Businesses along Twelfth that were untouched or only brushed by the flames had usually been modified—windows filled in with bullet-proof bricks or cinderblocks, a hideous but necessary architectural trend known locally as "Riot Renaissance."

Driving through his old precinct never failed to depress Doyle. He'd spent three of his seven years in uniform patrolling this neighborhood and he'd grown fond of it. It had never been plush but it was always solid, working-class, and there were still many blocks where people owned their homes, trimmed their hedges and lawns, went to church, belonged to the block association, the U.A.W., the N.A.A.C.P. But they were being nibbled away. Since the riot, whites and many better-off blacks hadn't been able to get out fast enough.

Now he was passing the shoe repair shop where the first person died during the riot. That case was Doyle's baptism by fire. The shop was empty now but the red neon shoe was still in the window, unlit, as dead as Krikor Messerlian himself. He was the Armenian immigrant who ran the place, a sweet shriveled old goat who always offered Doyle strong coffee and strong opinions whenever he stopped by to chat. When the neighborhood started to burn last July, Krikor stayed in his shop around the clock, armed only with a fireplace poker and the immigrant's determination not to back down, not to cede his little patch of the American dream.

When a gang of black kids gathered outside and threatened him through the locked door, Messerlian cursed them and told them to get off his property. Their response was to kick down the door and beat him to death. The police dispatcher used the word "mob," and when Doyle arrived at the scene Krikor Messerlian was lying inside the shop in a sticky pond of blood alongside a fireplace poker. His face was gone.

Doyle did what Jimmy Robuck had taught him to do at a murder scene: He followed his gut. He told the two uniforms to secure the building and not touch anything while he went knocking on doors in search of a witness because his gut told him they would never have anything on this one without an eyewit. As he turned to go, one of the uniforms, a black rookie, nodded toward a big stucco house across the street and suggested he might want to talk to an elderly lady in a blue dress who lived on the ground floor.

Doyle always did his own door-to-doors because he didn't trust uniforms with something so important and he'd discovered in his first week on the job that he could get people to tell him things. Mamas, widows, ex-husbands, eyewitnesses, sometimes even the killers themselves—they seemed to want to tell him things. Jimmy Robuck said it was a homicide cop's greatest gift.

Doyle knocked on a dozen doors before he got to the lady in the stucco house across the street. Her name was Clara Waters and she told Doyle she was on her front porch watering her geraniums when the boys kicked down the door and started beating the old man. She knew the boy who took the pipe, or whatever it was, and used it to smash Mr. Messerlian's face. She even told Doyle where the boy stayed—"corner apartment in that little two-story brick across from Roosevelt Field."

The kid was eating a bag of Frito's and watching "I Love Lucy" when Doyle and Jimmy knocked on his door. He had fresh blood on his sneakers and his fingerprints matched those on the fireplace poker next to Krikor Messerlian's body. They had the kid locked up, his confession signed and the paperwork on its way upstairs before the Medical Examiner started dismantling Krikor Messerlian's corpse in the white-tiled autopsy room in the basement.

Yes, this job was all about luck and squealers—and getting people to tell you things.

When Doyle reached Clairmount now he pulled the Plymouth to the curb and shut off the engine. To his right was the building where it had all started. The print shop on the ground floor was still vacant. He wondered if the blind pig upstairs, the United Community League for Civic Action—or was it the United Civic League for Community Action?—was back in business, serving illegal after-hours booze. It wouldn't have surprised him. Very little surprised him anymore.

The street looked shabby, sadder than ever. People called it "Sin Street" or simply "The Strip," and during the riot one poet at the *Free Press* had described this stretch of Twelfth Street as "an ugly neon scar running up the center of a Negro slum." Doyle didn't think it was ugly. He thought it was alive. It contained the usual gallery of pawn shops and furniture stores, record shops, soul food restaurants and discount liquor stores, a religious artifacts shop that offered statues of the Virgin Mary, money-drawing oil, skin-whitening ointments. The street was always buzzing. Now he could see the fading words SOUL BROTHER and NEGRO OWNED and AFRO ALL THE WAY spray-painted on certain windows and walls, the black owners' way of pleading with arsonists and looters to pass them by. Zuroff Furniture Co., once one of the busiest enterprises on the street, was boarded up, a FOR RENT sign out front. It was hard to blame old Abe Zuroff for packing it in. The Jewish merchants had gotten hit especially hard during the riot, and Doyle had often wondered why. Was it simple bad luck, a case of being caught in the wrong place at the wrong time? Or was it something darker, something tribal, a settling of scores for slights, real or imagined, that blacks had been feeling for years in every inner-city in America, Detroit included? Doyle had given up on believing he would ever know the answers to such questions.

Across the street from Zuroff's there was a storefront church, its name painted crudely around a big red cross: *Truth and Light Free Will Deliverance Tabernacle.* A junkie was nodding in the doorway. Thank God for churches and junkies, Doyle thought, imagine the hell we'd have to pay without them to take some of the edge off. Two men were sprawled on the hood of a Cadillac in front of the church, passing a quart bottle of Colt .45 malt liquor—a completely unique experience, if you believed the popular ad campaign, which Doyle did not. An enormous radio on the roof of the Caddy was blasting Smokey Robinson: *"If you feel like giving me a lifetime of de-vo-o-tion, I second that emotion. . . ."* Ten-dollar flatback hookers sashayed back and forth across the street, brazenly waving down cars. Doyle easily knew half of them by name.

He'd seen enough. He started the Plymouth and eased down Twelfth Street. The brothers and sisters on the sidewalks all stopped what they were doing and gave the unmarked their very best Motor City hate stares. There was heat in those stares. Doyle turned left at Grand Boulevard, ending his little trip down Memory Lane and turning his thoughts to what Henry Hull could possibly have for him on this fine spring morning.

❖

As always, the door to Room 450 was ajar and Henry Hull was sitting alone on the sofa. Henry's skull was as smooth and white as an onion. He was barely sixty years old but looked eighty, the flesh on his face sagging. His eyes, once so bright, were now lifeless and dull, the light gone out of them. Doyle knew the man well enough to know that his sorrow went even deeper than his personal losses, for Henry Hull, like most native Detroiters, was immensely proud of his hometown, of its swagger, its work ethic, its dirty fingernails and thick wrists, its ability to accommodate a crazy quilt of races and ethnic groups, shoulder to shoulder. Sure, there had always been tension—labor organizers were regularly beaten during the Depression, and thirty-four people died in a vicious race riot that started on Belle Isle in 1943—but in Henry Hull's eyes such flare-ups were inevitable in such a big rough city, and they were the exception, not the rule. Detroit had always been a city that worked, in both senses of the word. Now, for the first time in Henry Hull's life, there were disturbing signs that it had stumbled so badly it might never pick itself up.

"Knock, knock," Doyle said, pushing the door open.

"Come in, Frankie," Henry said, rising from the sofa. "I just brewed a fresh pot. You want a cup?"

"Silly question."

There was nowhere to set their mugs on the coffee table because it was buried under drifts of paperwork—the autopsy, Doyle's typed report of the crime scene, newspaper accounts of the killing and the ongoing investigation. Pinned to the room's walls were blown-up maps of the blocks surrounding the motel, and Henry's endless lists of addresses and phone numbers and names, all the far-fetched leads that had failed to locate Helen Hull's killer and, in Doyle's opinion, probably never would. He'd learned that the twelve hours after a homicide are the most crucial for a detective and that a case that stays open for a month is likely to stay open forever. That meant the Helen Hull case had been open nine times forever.

"Let me see, let me see, it's right here somewhere," Henry said, digging frantically in the pile of papers. His doggedness and the futility of his quest filled Doyle with admiration and sadness. Sometimes he found himself wishing the old guy would simply give it up, pack his belongings, check out of the motel, and get on with his life. But Doyle knew that was out of the question, and deep down he was glad it was. He'd vowed to find Helen Hull's killer the day he stood at the corner of Jefferson and Piper looking at the burned-out shell that had been the Greenleaf Market. Henry had just come back from identifying his wife's body at the morgue. Watching him spray-paint the words THANKS FOR WHAT YOU'VE DONE on the market's charred walls, Doyle broke down and wept.

"Here it is!" Henry cried, unearthing a photocopied map. "I don't know how we could've missed it." He had drawn a dotted line in red ink from the motel to a street corner behind Henry Ford Hospital on the far side of the Lodge Freeway.

Henry stood up and grabbed his binoculars. "Come on, Frankie," he said, starting for the door, "I've got something to show you. Let's walk through what happened again."

For the thousandth time, Doyle thought, following him out the door.

"Okay," Henry said, turning right in the hallway, Doyle on his heels. "Helen can't sleep because of all the noise down on the street, so she walks out into the hall. She passes Lisa Perot's room and sees that the door's open and the lights are on." Henry jerked a thumb at the door to Room 433. "Helen walks all the way to the window."

They had reached the picture window at the north end of the hallway. Henry pulled the string that opened the curtain, and they were looking down at West Grand Boulevard. Doyle hated revisiting this spot, for it was written in the homicide bible that while it's possible to murder a man only once, it's possible to murder a murder scene a thousand and one times. And this one had been slaughtered.

In the early hours of last July 26, the area around the Harlan House was a war zone. All streetlights had been shot out. Sniper fire aimed at Henry Ford Hospital was so heavy that the staff had to blacken the windows in the emergency rooms so they wouldn't die while trying to save the dying. Tanks roamed on West Grand Boulevard, pouring rounds from .50-caliber machine guns at anything that moved. They were answered with tracer fire from the rooftops. National Guardsmen, poorly trained and terrified, were also shooting at anything that moved, including other Guardsmen and police. The night was thunder and chaos.

It was Helen Hull's second night at the motel. She'd checked in when the riot started spreading to the East Side, while Henry stayed behind in their apartment above the shuttered market with a loaded deer rifle. Police cruised the Jeff-Chalmers neighborhood with bullhorns, urging residents and shopkeepers to stay away from windows and doorways, reminding them about the dusk-to-dawn curfew. A National Guard unit had bivouacked in Ford Park down by the river because there were rumors that black militants were going to mount an invasion by boat from Canada, then blow up Detroit's water works. The city was jazzed with such rumors.

"Okay," Henry said now to Doyle, "so Helen calls to Lisa Perot to come look at the tank down on the street. The globe light behind her is on."

Which made her a beautifully silhouetted target. Within seconds, two bullets crashed through the window. One missed her, and one ripped into her chest, penetrating her heart and glancing downward before coming to rest in her liver. Then, according to the interviews Doyle conducted after the shooting, one of the most bizarre incidents of that bizarre week took place. A man named J.R. Glover of the U.S. Chamber of Commerce was hastily packing his bags in Room 401. When he heard the crash, he crawled out into the hallway and saw Helen Hull lying on her back. Suddenly a man with a rifle charged into Glover's open room and began firing out the window. National Guardsmen peppered the room with dozens of rounds, but the man, miraculously, was not hit.

Then the police arrived. They stormed into Glover's room and disarmed the man with the rifle and hustled him away. Someone smashed or shot out the globe light in the hallway. And someone in the hallway fired at least one bullet out through the window where the fatal bullet had entered.

By the time Doyle and Jimmy Robuck showed up, the crime scene was a disaster. Helen Hull had been taken by ambulance to Ford Hospital, where she was pronounced dead on arrival. It was impossible to examine the scene in the dark, and it was too dangerous to use flashlights for more than a few minutes. After noting the location of the three bullet holes in the window, the detectives and the rest of the police left the scene.

When Doyle returned in the morning, the plate-glass window had already been replaced and the blood-soaked carpet had been torn up and thrown away. Even the police who'd been on the scene after the shooting gave him conflicting accounts. The only good news was that the Medical Examiner had dug a fragment of a .30-caliber bullet out of Helen Hull's liver. If a weapon was found, there was a chance of matching slug with gun. A slim chance, to be sure, but it was better than nothing.

So every time Doyle revisited this end of the fourth-floor hallway, he despaired. It was a terrible crime scene. A difficult investigation had been made virtually impossible by circumstances beyond his control.

Now Henry raised the binoculars to his eyes and gazed through them to his left, toward the freeway. "There! Just past the right edge of the hospital, one block to the north. Yellow brick building. Five stories tall."

Doyle took the binoculars. A moment later he said, "What is it?"

"It's an apartment building called the Larrow Arms. You see that rooftop?"

"I see it, all right. It's . . . it's *perfect*. Mr. Hull, it's perfect! How in the—how could we have possibly missed it?"

Though it would have taken a superb shot to score a direct hit from that distance and that angle, it was not out of the question.

"It's perfect!" Doyle said again, still peering through the binoculars.

"It gets better," Henry said. "I went over there yesterday and started knocking on doors. And a lady who lives on the second floor on the east side of the building—the side facing the Lodge— says she saw some things on the morning of July 26th that I think you'll find very interesting. She said she'd be willing to talk to you and Jimmy."

"Who is she?"

"A widow lady's lived there for years."

"She black?"

"Yeah, but decent. A real lady." He reached in his pocket and handed Doyle a scrap of paper. It read: *Charlotte Armstrong. Larrow Arms, apartment 2-E. TY5-7930.*

Cecelia was tending bar that afternoon at the Riverboat, as Doyle had hoped, and she had a bottle of Stroh's and a frosted glass on the bar before he was settled on a stool. She knew he hated beer mugs. He'd told her they made him feel like he was wielding a weapon, which was the last thing he wanted to feel when he was off the clock. He'd also told her, proudly, that he'd never taken his service .38 out of its holster while on duty.

It was a nice story and it played well with the ladies. Only trouble was, it wasn't true.

When she went off to fill an order at the service bar, Doyle turned and looked out the Riverboat's picture window just as the Bob-Lo boat came chugging past the big Canadian Club sign on the far shore. That was something he'd always loved about Detroit: You were so far north you actually looked south toward Canada, toward that scintillating little eyesore known as Windsor, Ontario.

Windsor—Vicki Jones's hometown. Three weekends ago he'd gotten home at four in the morning after finishing up a double shooting at the Driftwood Lounge and discovered that Vicki had needed all of fifteen words to kiss him off. They were stuck to his refrigerator door: *I can't spend the rest of my life waiting for you to get off work.* Not even a *Sorry* or *Good luck* or *It was fun.*

Fair enough, though there was no denying he would miss Vicki's skull-popping blowjobs and those rare Sundays when he got to stay home and play jazz records for her and cook lavish Italian meals that lasted, over bottles of good Valpolicella, late into the night. Vicki loved his record collection even more than she loved his cooking. Her tastes in music ran toward Aretha, the Supremes, and Gladys Knight, but he opened her ears to new worlds, to Duke Ellington and Lester Young, to Miles and Monk and Bird. She even learned to like Chopin and Debussy. Doyle would also miss those nights they went out dancing at places like the Twenty Grand, at black clubs where the whole room lifted off together, at after-hours bars and private parties where he wouldn't have dared take a white girl. He was accepted—he was tolerated—in those places because he was with Vicki. Because Vicki was a fox with a big laugh who could dance— anything from a slow grind to a waltz to the funky chicken—like nobody else in the house.

Now Cecelia brought him a second Stroh's, touched the back of his hand and said, "There you go, hon." She was wearing a loose blue silk blouse and a tight black skirt instead of pants. It was the first time he'd seen her legs, and they were marvels. There was something else different about her look, but he couldn't figure out what it was.

By the time his second beer and the Bob-Lo boat were gone, he'd figured it out. It was her hair. There was a hint of strawberry coloring in it, less brassy than the blonde she'd been before. It still tumbled to her shoulders and it still shimmered, but now there was fire in it. It suited her milky skin and green eyes. She was standing in front of Doyle, fixing two 7-and-7's for a well-dressed black couple at the far end of the bar. "You sure are quiet," she said.

"Yeah, had a strange day."

"Strange good or strange bad?" She was squirting 7-Up into the highball glasses from a gun attached to a metal hose, another modern "improvement," like night baseball and push-button telephones, that

Doyle instinctively distrusted. What was wrong with opening a bottle of pop and pouring it in a glass?

"Actually, it was strange good, believe it or not."

He admired her legs some more as she took the drinks to the black couple. She came right back with a fresh beer and a fresh glass. "Why shouldn't I believe your day was strange good? Don't cops have good days once in a while like everybody else?"

"Sure they do. Every once in a long while." He laughed. "I love what you've done with your hair."

"You're the first person to notice. You really like it?" While she studied herself uncertainly in the mirror behind the bar he snuck another look at her legs. He felt like a dog, but he couldn't stop himself.

"I like it," he said. "A lot."

"Thanks. It's my natural color, but I still can't decide if I like it or hate it."

"Well, I like it." He took a sip of beer. "Say, I was wondering . . . you a baseball fan by any chance?"

She turned back toward him. "No, I'm a Tigers fan. There's a big difference. I *love* the Tigers. I've loved them since I was a little girl. If you're asking me to a game, the answer's yes."

That wasn't terribly complicated. You spend hours screwing up the courage to ask a woman a question, then come to find out she's been light years ahead of you the whole time. It had always been like that for Doyle. He supposed it had something to do with his Catholic upbringing. The Immaculate Heart of Mary nuns and the Jesuits didn't exactly pass along a wealth of tips on romance and courting. Father Monaghan, the priest who had the unenviable task of explaining the birds and the bees to a roomful of hormone-stoked, zit-faced jerkoffs at U. of D. High School, referred to the fuzz that was magically sprouting around their genitals as *poo*–bic hair.

"I've got a couple of nice box seats for tomorrow's game," Doyle said. "First pitch is at five past one."

"And I've got tomorrow off. I've got a paper due Monday, but I guess I'll just have to finish it after the game. My father taught me never to pass up a ticket to a Tigers game."

"A paper?"

"Yeah, on how the Cubists influenced Mexican mural painters."

"You're still in school?"

"Grad school—at Wayne State. I'm working toward a master's in art history so I can get a minimum-wage job as an assistant curator at the Institute of Arts. Then I'll work my way up from there." She waved at the liquor bottles and the beer taps. "This is just paying my tuition and rent. I tried to make it as an artist, but . . ."

"But what?"

"But nothing. I went to New York and studied at Pratt. I wanted to paint cityscapes and portraits—not soup cans. I couldn't get a gallery to show my work, so I came home and went back to school. And I love it."

This was a pleasant surprise. Detroit had never had much use for the arts or artistic types. Artists in this city didn't wear paint-spattered jeans or suffer gorgeously in grimy lofts. They wore smocks over their business suits—they were almost always men—and they worked in vast, well lit studios at places like the G.M. Tech Center, dreaming and sketching and building life-size clay models of next year's Tempest or Corvette. They did some glorious work, to Doyle's way of thinking, but there wasn't an Abstract Expressionist or Pop artist among them. As for the women in Detroit, most of them carried themselves as though their greatest ambition in life was to become a professional bowler. Doyle was about to tell Cecelia how much he loved to hate the Diego Rivera murals at the Institute of Arts when she said, "How bout I fix us a late breakfast at my place before the game? Say, eleven-thirty?"

"Sounds good."

She drew him a map on a cocktail napkin. She lived in one of those new twin high-rise apartment buildings on East Lafayette, not far from here, twenty-story slabs of glass and concrete. He'd always assumed they were put there for the benefit of swinging singles, dope dealers and the mistresses of rich auto executives. So bartending art students were allowed to live there too. He tucked the napkin in his pocket and promised to show up at her door at eleven-thirty sharp.

On his way across the parking lot he considered swinging by the Larrow Arms, but his stomach was empty and he'd gotten a surprising buzz off the three beers. He didn't want to do something stupid that might ruin the day's good luck. So he headed east on Jefferson toward the big rickety frame house where he grew up, where he still lived, and where he expected to die. The house was pale green and in bad need of a coat of paint and a new roof, but since he couldn't afford to pay someone to do the work and couldn't afford to take time off to do it himself, the house was going to stay pale green and it was going to continue to leak. He lived alone there with the ghosts of his dead parents. His mother's spirit resided mainly in the kitchen and in the vegetable garden out back, the places where she'd passed her love of cooking and gardening down to him. The old man could usually be found on the front porch, where Doyle had installed some ratty furniture from the parlor. He liked to sit out there at night and smoke a cigar and tell his father about his day. He would have plenty for the old man tonight.

So Mrs. Charlotte Armstrong could wait. Doyle wanted to be at the top of his game when he sat down and asked her what she saw and heard the night Helen Hull died.

5

THERE WAS A LATE LUNCH RUSH IN THE MEN'S GRILL AT OAKLAND Hills Country Club that Sunday afternoon when members came pouring in off the golf course to watch the climax of the Masters golf tournament on television. Willie was the only busboy working the room, and his Uncle Bob and Edgar Hudson were the only waiters. Hudson, as always, was useless. He stood around kibitzing on gin rummy games and laughing way too hard at the members' jokes, slapping a napkin on his thigh, skinning 'em back for all he was worth. Once in a while he'd saunter over to the bar to get an order of drinks from Chi Chi.

Willie didn't mind having to hustle, especially with his uncle. It made the clock move and it put money in his pocket. He was sure

Uncle Bob was the only waiter on the staff who gave busboys the full ten percent of his tips they were entitled to. Besides, Willie had no interest in kibitzing on gin rummy games or watching golf on television. The only black people on the TV screen were the ones carrying the golf bags and raking the sand traps.

All afternoon Willie kept one eye on the door where the men came in off the golf course. Finally, a little after four o'clock, Chick Murphy walked in with a transistor radio pressed to his right ear. He sat down and kicked off his golf spikes and ordered a Michelob from Hudson. He was looking at the television set but Willie could tell he was paying closer attention to what was on the radio. When he saw Willie, he waved him over.

"Yes, Mr. Murphy?"

"Just picked up the Tigers' game. Bottom of the twelfth, tied 5-5. McAuliffe's on third and Gates is coming in to pinch hit." The other men at the table, pink with sunburn and dressed in sherbet-colored clothes, ignored him.

"Gates Brown?" Willie whispered, moving closer.

"Yup. Ball one."

"How many outs?"

Chick Murphy held up two of the three fingers on his left hand. Willie could hear the fuzzy roar of the Tiger Stadium crowd, and he wondered if Louis and Clyde were in the bleachers. One of the men said to Chick Murphy, "Turn that shit down, would you please? Goalby's getting ready to putt on eighteen."

"He can't hear this, numbnuts," Chick Murphy said. "Ball two."

No sound came out of the television set, and the room was as quiet as a tomb. Willie tried to imagine a game where all the spectators had to be utterly silent and still. He thought of those gyms in Alabama where he'd played basketball, raucous cauldrons of sweat and noise, cheering and chanting, the fans dancing to saxophones, bongo drums, tambourines, syncopated clapping. On the TV screen now a lantern-jawed guy leaned over a putt for a long time, then drilled it into the hole. There were sighs of relief, palms slapping tables, a few soft whistles.

"Swing and a miss," Chick Murphy said. "Two balls and a strike." Willie was the only person listening to him. "Here's the pitch . . . he hit it up the middle . . . it's going . . . it's a single! McAuliffe scores from third! Ballgame!"

Chick Murphy sprang from his chair and wrapped an arm around Willie's shoulder, gave him a crusher squeeze. One of the men cocked an eyebrow and said, "You don't knock it off, Murphy, I'm gonna tell the wife."

Willie went back to work. Later a cry went up from the crowd when the announcer reported that the Masters had not ended in a tie, as everyone believed. A guy named Roberto De Vicenzo had signed his scorecard with a 66 instead of the 65 he shot, and the rules required him to accept the higher score. It cost him a tie. There were hoots of disbelief throughout the room, and Willie watched as Bob Goalby slipped into a green sport coat, grinning like a hyena. Win a major golf tournament and you get an ugly jacket.

"Say, Billy . . ." Chick Murphy, in plaid pants and stocking feet, was on his way to the locker room. There were bright-green grass shavings stuck to his lemon-yellow socks.

"It's *Willie*, sir. Willie Bledsoe."

"Right. Sorry. Your Uncle Bob tells me you might be in the market for a new car. Here." He handed Willie a business card. "Give me a call—or just drop by the lot. I'm always there."

"Thanks, Mr. Murphy."

As the men filed into the locker room, Willie studied Chick Murphy's business card. *Stay on the right track to 9 Mile and Mack!—for the best Buick buys in Michigan!* He knew, he just knew he was holding his one-way ticket out of purgatory.

After the dinner shift that night Bob Brewer gave Willie a ride home in his Deuce and a Quarter. The deeper they went into the city the more Willie noticed people pausing on the sidewalks to watch the big bronze boat float past. He could tell his uncle was digging the attention.

When Willie got home he was bone tired from the back-to-back double shifts, but he was too keyed up to sleep. He drank a beer and tried to watch "Mission: Impossible," but his mind kept drifting. He'd made good progress on one half of his mission; now it was time to get started on the other half.

He went into the bedroom, where his Remington typewriter sat shrouded on the desk between a stack of untouched paper and his old college reading lamp, the one with the dented brown hood over the bulb. He'd brought the typewriter and lamp with him from Alabama because he thought they would provide some vital link to the world he was leaving behind, thought they would spur his memory, make the words flow. He thought wrong.

He set Chick Murphy's business card on the desk—*Stay on the right track to 9 Mile and Mack!*—then he dug in the back of the closet and took out his Alabama box and set it on the bed. There was no doubt in his mind that the moment of his story's conception—the moment when he heard the girl hiss *de Lawd*—was inside that box. He started removing the contents and placing them on the smooth green blanket.

First came the clothes—the white T-shirt, denim bib overalls and clunky brogan shoes. By 1962 this outfit had replaced sport coats and neckties as the unofficial Snick uniform, a way to blend in with the dirt-poor locals and look more like a "been-here" than a "come-here." Most of the organizers were college kids or recent dropouts like Willie, well-read in the works of Fanon and Camus and other writers who meant absolutely nothing to a poor black sharecropper, a man who, as often as not, lived in a shack with a tarpaper roof and no running water, a number-three galvanized tub for baths, the interior walls papered with pages from an old Sears catalog. A house made of wood and wind. There would be pot-bellied children everywhere, flies, mangy dogs, clucking chickens. There would be an outhouse in the back yard, a clothesline and a vegetable patch, some ancient car hovering on cinderblocks awaiting repairs that would never come. The only book Willie ever saw in any of those houses was the Bible. The sameness of those places, the stupefying monotony—that, to Willie, was the killing thing about poverty.

He went into the kitchen to make a pot of coffee because he sensed he was in for a long night. While the coffee brewed he put his new Gerry Mulligan-Dave Brubeck album on the stereo, turned down low. Then he took off his tuxedo pants and dress shirt and put on the T-shirt and overalls, still smelling of Duz detergent. He left the brogans unlaced. He had forgotten how good the clothes felt, so loose and free.

He removed an envelope full of black-and-white snapshots from the box. The first one showed Willie holding one of the rifles his brother had shipped to him, piece by piece, from Vietnam, a Remington 700 with a Unertl scope. Wes had snapped the picture one day when they were out in the piney woods near Tuskegee blasting away at Jax beer cans. Willie was wearing shades and smoking a cigarette, trying to look like a badass, but he looked exactly the way he'd always felt around guns: scared pissless.

There were dozens of pictures of Willie in his Snick uniform, mostly taken in Alabama and Mississippi. The pictures blurred together after a while, but one jumped out. It showed Willie talking to a sharecropper named Jess Hocutt in the swept-dirt yard beside his house near Indianola. Behind them was a Stutz Bearcat with no tires. It was always a good idea to go slow with country people, so by way of breaking the ice Willie had asked about the car. Jess had laughed, glad for the chance to talk about something other than the dreaded topic of registering to vote. The last thing Jess Hocutt needed, on top of the rest of his woes, was to bring down the wrath of the white man. It took Willie a whole week of day-long visits to persuade Jess to walk into the Sunflower County courthouse and tell the startled clerk that he wanted to register to vote. It was one of the hardest and most rewarding things Willie had ever done.

When he got to the last snapshot in the envelope, he felt his first shiver. It was a picture of him in his Snick uniform, standing by the reflecting pool during the March on Washington. To complete the bumpkin effect, he was wearing a straw hat. He was deep in conversation with another Snick volunteer, a beautiful brother from New York named Bob Moses who had memorized most of the Bible and dug Camus even more than Willie did—and Bob could read Camus in French. Playing a hunch, Willie opened his journal from the summer of '63—the notebooks were dated and neatly bundled—and he soon found a long entry about the March, including this exchange with Bob Moses by the reflecting pool:

"Know what this is?" I asked Bob M.

"A couple hundred thousand freedom-high brothers and sisters is what this is," he replied.

"Yeah, but this ain't no March on Washington."

"No? Then what is it?"

"This here's the FARCE on Washington."

Bob had guffawed. He knew Willie was mimicking Malcolm X, but he happened to agree with him—and a lot of other people who'd spent years in the trenches. Most Snick foot soldiers viewed the March as nothing more than a public relations stunt scripted by the Kennedys and the F.B.I., with Martin Luther King as their star house-nigger. Their star White House-nigger. Bob and Willie had come to Washington to picket the Justice Department and, almost as an afterthought, they went to the reflecting pool to hear John Lewis, the only speaker from Snick on the day's program. John's speech wasn't bad, but when Willie learned later that the organizers had forced him to water it down, his disdain for the March grew even deeper.

Looking at the photograph of those people packed all the way to the Washington Monument, and remembering what he and Bob Moses had said, Willie realized he'd made his first small breakthrough. If he'd lost faith in King by the summer of '63, then that meant the trap door had already opened and he had already begun to fall. He kept soldiering on for another year after the March, though he could see now that he was just going through the motions. It's hard to admit you're living a lie.

So now he knew that the moment he was looking for—the moment his disillusionment was born—had happened before the Farce on Washington. That still left him with a lot of ground to cover, a little more than three years' worth, from early 1960 till the summer of '63. But suddenly he felt hopeful. He refilled his coffee cup and took the rest of his journals and files out of the box and set them on the desk. He started digging through the stack in chronological order, beginning in early 1960.

He was still digging when he heard the first birds and looked up to see that the windows were blue. The night had begun with high hopes after he matched the picture of the Farce on Washington with the corresponding journal entry, but as the night wore on he realized the journals were spotty and thin. Sometimes he wrote dense pages about a night in jail, about the lurid, almost laughable epithets of the white hecklers, about the strange tickly sensation of sitting at a lunch counter and having a white man pour sugar on top of your head and feeling the granules trickle down inside the collar of your shirt. One notation read: *Ketchup looks like blood on a starched white shirt.* These were the kinds of details he could use. But then there would be gaps where he didn't write a word for weeks.

Just before the sun came up, he finally had another breakthrough from an unexpected source: a newspaper clipping. Some of the people in the movement were crazy about collecting their press clippings, but Willie had never much cared for it even though he worked for a time in Snick's press office. Most of the reporters and photographers he dealt with were white, and while many of them were sympathetic to the cause, a few even bright and crazy brave, he didn't believe they could understand what the students were going through or tell their story straight.

But for some reason he'd saved the Atlanta *Constitution* from May 15, 1961. The badly yellowed front page was dominated by the now-famous photograph of a burning Greyhound bus outside Anniston, Alabama. The photographer must have been crouching on the shoulder of the road. In the foreground a white man and a white woman are sitting on the ground, stunned and obviously in pain. Behind them two unidentified black men are looking at the bus, their backs to the camera. They're looking at the open door of the bus with the S&H green stamps logo, at the sprinting dog that appears to be spewing smoke from its mouth, at the black smoke gushing out of the shattered windshield and the open side windows.

Willie remembered why he'd saved this newspaper: He was the unidentified black man on the far left.

Suddenly he could smell the noxious stench of burning rubber, feel the pain where his left pants' leg had caught fire. He had nearly been burned alive inside that bus. As he studied the picture he even remembered the name of the black man standing beside him: It was Moses Newsome, a gutsy reporter with the Baltimore *Afro-American* who had sat next to Willie on the bus that day, interviewing him, asking him why he'd given up his snug berth at Tuskegee to join the movement. When Willie was in mid-sentence, the driver had pulled the bus off to the side of the road and vanished into the trees. Only then did Willie see the white mob closing in.

He stood up from the desk and snapped off the lamp. His neck and back were stiff, his vision foggy. He got a beer from the refrigerator and went out onto the screened-in porch where he liked to sleep when the nights got suffocating hot. Looking down at the street, watching the first people emerge from their homes and leave for work—a mechanic, a maid, several orderlies and nurses heading to Ford Hospital—he understood that he had learned something important during that long night: What he was looking for was not in his Alabama box, his personal record of the events he had lived through; it was in the recorded history of those events, things like the picture of the burning bus in the Atlanta newspaper.

He plopped into the overstuffed chair and propped his brogans on the railing. He was exhausted but happy. He marveled at the string of little things that had happened to him in the past week—a chance meeting with two strangers at a ballpark, a chance meeting with a car dealer, a ride in his uncle's new Deuce, the discovery of a snapshot and a journal entry and a famous picture of a burning bus. It felt like a beginning.

He understood that he would have to go outside himself in order to see into himself. Oakland Hills was closed on Mondays, so he would catch a few hours of sleep and then walk over to the library on Woodward and start the monstrous job of scrolling through newspaper microfilm from early 1960 through the summer of 1963.

There was no doubt in his mind that the moment of conception he was looking for was hidden in a newspaper article or photograph, and he believed in his heart he was destined to find it. And once he found it, only one thing would be able to stop him: the Detroit police.

6

DOYLE SPENT THE MORNING IN HIS GARDEN, CAREFULLY SELECTING flowers for a bouquet. He wanted to wow Cecelia without looking like he was trying too hard. As he was on his way out the door a few minutes past eleven, his telephone rang. He considered ignoring it, but he put down the flowers and picked up the receiver. You never know.

It was Jimmy Robuck calling to say he wouldn't be able to meet Frank at the ballpark, as they'd planned, because Walt Kanka had just called in a favor—and Jimmy had to go downtown to help him bang on Alphonso Johnson, the prime suspect in the murder of Carlo Smith, Vic #42. Though Doyle wanted to get off the phone, he listened while Jimmy gave him an elaborate play-by-play of what he had in mind for Alphonso. Just before he hung up, Jimmy said, "You don't need no third wheel no how. Have fun. Hope you get lucky."

"You too, Jimmy."

As he rode the elevator to the twentieth floor in Cecelia's building, Doyle checked his watch. Fifteen minutes late, already in the dog house before the first date had even begun. Story of my life, he thought, stepping off the elevator.

Cecelia's door opened and she said, "You're late."

"I'm sorry . . . got a phone call from my partner as I was walking out the door . . . couldn't get rid of him. . . . Brought you a little something."

"For *me*?" she said, accepting the flowers. She needed both hands to hold the bouquet of black-eyed Susans, irises, snapdragons and pink peonies. From the look on her face, Doyle could tell he'd overdone it. Strike two before he got in the door.

While she was putting the flowers in a vase in the kitchen, Doyle walked straight to the picture window. He could see his reflection in the glass. He'd worn a sport coat with a houndstooth check over a green crew-neck sweater because Vicki Jones had told him the sweater picked up the green in his eyes. She wasn't the first woman to tell him his eyes were his best feature. His jeans were faded, and his oxblood loafers, polished once a week, glowed like old wood.

Cecelia came back from the kitchen and joined him by the window. He was holding on to the windowsill because the altitude was making him dizzy. "That's some view you've got," he said. There were vistas to the east, south and west. He was pointing upriver, east. "Look, there's Belcatraz!"

"That's Belle Isle."

"Yeah, but us cops call it Belcatraz. So many people got arrested during the riot that we ran out of places to put them. They wound up packed into the garage at headquarters, in school gyms, in fire stations, even in the bath houses at Belle Isle. Ergo, Belcatraz."

"That's the first time I've heard a cop say ergo." She was smiling. Maybe he hadn't overdone it with the flowers.

"It's the Jesuits' fault," he said. "They made us study Latin and logic." Now he was pointing west, toward downtown. "There's head-quarters—it looks so puny from way up here! And the Frank Murphy courthouse. And Greektown—I can almost smell the garlic. You can even see the poor man's Golden Gate."

"Is that what cops call the Ambassador Bridge?"

"No, that's just me. I spent a week in San Francisco last year—best food I ever ate. Every time I look at the Ambassador Bridge now I think of the Golden Gate, and every time I see Belle Isle I think of Alcatraz."

"Speaking of food, it's almost ready. Would you like a cup of coffee or—I'm having a Bloody Mary."

"Bloody Mary sounds good."

"Hope you like 'em spicy."

"I like everything spicy."

When she came back with the drinks, he was sitting on the chocolate-colored sofa studying the décor of this beige cocoon like it smelled bad.

"What's the matter, don't like the furniture?" she said, handing him his drink.

"No, no, no. . . ."

"Don't worry. I'm going to redecorate, get rid of all this brown crap and chrome. Place feels like a cheesy nightclub. But I had to wait for the settlement to come through."

"The settlement?" Here we go, he thought.

She clicked her glass against his. "Here's to my divorce."

"To your divorce." He held the celery stalk aside with his index finger and took a drink. He closed his eyes when he swallowed.

"You like it?" she said.

He could hear the anxiety in her voice. "No, I don't like it, I love it," he said. "The cracked pepper, the horseradish, the Worcestershire sauce. It's perfect." He took another drink. "So. You were married."

"For two years. The settlement finally came through last week. Now I get to pay the rent on this groovy pad all by myself." She waved at the room. "This is Ronnie's idea of class. You've really got to wonder about a guy whose favorite color is brown and who's got more chrome in his living room than he's got on his car."

"So what happened to the marriage?"

He was afraid he was pushing too hard, but she didn't hesitate. "For starters, I married him for all the wrong reasons. I'd just gotten back from New York, my dream of making it as an artist all shot to hell, like I told you. I was a mess. We met at a wedding—and when he asked me to dance, that was it. Guy's a great dancer. Four months later we were at another wedding. Ours."

"Then you moved here?"

"No, we lived in an apartment in Warren for a while so he could be close to work—he worked as a stylist at the G.M. Tech Center. Mostly did dashboards and door handles. We moved down here last year because Ronnie wanted to be where the action is. He actually said things like that with a straight face. He talked me into dying my hair that tacky blonde color. He started staying out later and later and got into drugs and eventually lost his job at G.M. Last I heard he was selling auto parts in Ecorse. Or maybe it's Wyandotte."

"So what does he drive?"

"Hunh?"

"You said there's more chrome in this room than there is on his car. You can tell a lot about a man in Detroit by the car he drives."

"Oh. It's bright yellow, an Oldsmobile 4-4-something. Loud as hell, and fast. One of Ronnie's favorite expressions was *You can tell the men from the boys by the size of their toys*. What a complete jerk." She sipped her drink. "So how about you?"

"I've never been married—or divorced."

"No, I meant what do you drive?"

"Oh. A baby-shit green '61 Pontiac Bonneville with a hundred and twenty thousand on the odometer. I love that old thing. You?"

"I just bought a blue Mustang convertible. First new car I've ever owned. I love that new thing."

With marital status and cars out of the way, they were quiet for a while. Frank cocked an ear, picking up the music. She'd put on a

Chopin record with the volume way down. "I could change the music if you like," she said.

"No, no, this is nice."

"I like to listen to classical on Sunday—it's so soothing. But I've got plenty of Motown. Or I could put on the new Creedence album if you're into rock—"

"No, please. I love Chopin." A shower of snowflakes washed over them. "Isn't that Scherzo No. 3?"

"I'm not sure what it's called."

"That's Van Cliburn playing though, right?"

"As a matter of fact, it is. You actually like Chopin?"

"I love him. I heard Van Cliburn play an all-Chopin program last year at Ford Auditorium. I was in pig heaven."

"You're really something, Detective Doyle."

"How's that?"

"Well, you're the first cop I've ever met who says ergo and has heard of Chopin. Let alone Van Cliburn."

He shrugged. "And you're the first bartender I've ever met who studies Mexican murals and listens to classical music at home on her day off. I can't stand it when people put each other in boxes."

She went into the kitchen to check on the food. Knowing that he'd spent a week in San Francisco eating at fancy restaurants probably wasn't doing anything for her self-confidence. He watched as she took a deep breath and started putting the food on plates. "You hungry?" she called to him.

"I'm always hungry."

"I hope you like Eggs Benedict."

"I liked them the last time I ate them."

"When was that?"

He came across the room and leaned against the bar, watched her pouring Hollandaise sauce over the eggs and ham, then spooning out roasted red potatoes with peppers and onions and garlic on the side. "Let's see—it was a little over a year ago. At the Detroit Club."

"I didn't know they allowed cops in there."

"I didn't either. But when I got promoted to Homicide last year, the shift commander and my sergeant took me to Sunday brunch there. Brunch!" He laughed softly. "It was their way of baptizing me. On street patrol they do it with Stroh's and shots of well bourbon. In Homicide, they do it with mimosas and Eggs Benedict."

"Well, I'm not making any promises that mine are as good as the Detroit Club's."

They ate at the glass-topped table with chrome legs in the corner of the L-shaped dining nook. Frank ate quickly, eagerly, with deft movements of knife and fork. He didn't keep switching the fork from his left hand to his right, the way most men in Detroit did. The fork stayed in his left hand, the knife in his right.

Cecelia was wearing a skirt and espadrilles with open toes, and she'd painted her toenails to match her fingernails, berry red. It was all visible through the glass tabletop, and none of it was lost on Doyle.

"Everything okay?" she asked, topping off their drinks from the pitcher she'd mixed earlier.

"Wonderful. You made this Hollandaise from scratch, didn't you?"

"First time. Are they as good as the Detroit Club's?"

"Way better."

"Really?"

"Swear to God. I wouldn't lie about something as important as food."

She believed him. He surprised her by asking for a second helping of potatoes. It was no great sacrifice—the food was sensational—and besides, his mother had taught him that every woman loves to watch a man devour her cooking. In time he learned that it cut both ways. He loved to watch a woman devour his cooking.

In the elevator Cecelia told him pink peonies were her favorite flower, then asked where he'd bought the bouquet.

"I didn't buy it," he said.

"Then how . . . ?"

"I grew them."

"You grew those flowers?"

"Got a garden behind my house and I built a hot house last year. Now I've got flowers and fresh herbs year round."

She was revising her earlier opinion that he was a member of that legion of men who try too hard. This man grew flowers—and he listened to Chopin and appreciated good food and had good table manners. He even stuck out an arm to hold the elevator door open for her when they reached the lobby. In two years of marriage Ronnie had never held a door open for her once.

Cecelia knew more about baseball than Doyle did. Way more. She knew when base runners were supposed to steal. She knew when managers were supposed to change pitchers. She even knew in the bottom of the 12th that it was time for Mayo Smith to send in Gates Brown to pinch hit. Which he did. Which resulted in a sharp single up the middle that scored the winning run from third base. When Doyle praised her knowledge of the game, she shrugged. "Comes with the territory when you've got six brothers."

Cecelia was so wound up after the game that she insisted they swing by the Lindell AC to decompress. It was packed with fans, roaring and boisterous. The tables were full so they stood at the bar. Doyle spotted Gates Brown and Willie Horton at a corner table, sharing a pitcher of beer with a group of fans. Cecelia pointed out her favorite piece of memorabilia on the walls—the framed jockstrap once worn by Lions linebacker Wayne Walker. When the drinks came she said, "I love coming to the place where Alex Karras got his ass kicked."

"You mean where he got busted for betting on games?"

"No, don't you remember? He came in here with a bunch of guys from the Lions and picked a fight with that pro wrestler, Dick the Bruiser. Got his clock cleaned, way I heard it."

"And people think wrestling's fake."

"Tell that to Alex Karras."

They laughed. They'd been laughing all afternoon. Doyle found her easy to be with, and even easier on the eyes. With one espadrille propped on the brass rail, she went unnoticed by no one in the largely male crowd, and she seemed right at home in the loud smoky company of men. She was aware that these men were aware of her, yet she wore the awareness with an easy grace. It was, Doyle thought, the rarest of womanly arts. Probably had something to do with those six brothers.

When the drinks were gone she offered to buy a second round but Doyle said he had a better idea. "You like jazz?"

"The only kind of music I don't like is country. Can't stand all that weepy hillbilly shit." She broke into a fair approximation of Mel Tillis's anthem for all the displaced Southern yokels marooned in the Motor City: *"Last night I went to sleep in Dee-troit city . . . By day I make the cars, and by night I'm a-makin the bars . . . I wanna go home, ohhhhhhhh Lord, I wanna go home . . ."*

Doyle said, "I know a place that has jam sessions on Sunday. I saw Charlie Parker there when I was in high school."

"I've got a paper to finish, remember?"

"We'll only stay for one set. I'll get you home early. Promise."

"Well, if you promise. . . ."

As he guided the Bonneville out Grand River, away from downtown, he asked her if her door was locked.

"No. Should it be?"

"Yes. Please lock it."

"How come?"

"Because you're a fool if you don't in this town." Even though it was Sunday. Even though the day was fair and the sun was barely brushing the treetops and he had a snub-nosed Smith & Wesson insurance policy tucked under the driver's seat.

"What's a big mean cop like you scared of, hunh?"

"I'm not big and I'm not mean and I'm not scared. I'm just being smart. Believe me, there's a big difference."

But she wouldn't let it go. "I think you're scared. Well I'm not scared—and I'm not locking my door. Can't make me." She folded her arms, stuck her lower lip out in a fake pout.

Now she was pissing him off. Most of the people he knew who thought they were fireproof had gotten burned; more than a few had gotten dead. The alcohol had helped turn Cecelia's native confidence into cockiness, but she was too pretty, too noticeable, too ripe a mark to be able to afford the luxury of cockiness in this part of Detroit. It was time to instill a little fear in her, for her own good. He said, "See that stain on the carpet, there by your feet?"

"Yeah. What is it, motor oil?"

"No, it's blood."

She moved her feet away from it. "How'd it get there?"

"Same way that dent got in the dashboard."

He gave her the short version of the night he was driving on this very stretch of Grand River three winters ago, headed to Olympia to meet his brother for a Red Wings game. While he waited at a red light, his unlocked passenger door swung open and a big black girl with a yellow wig and turquoise eye shadow slid onto the front seat beside him. He told her to get out. Hookers had long ago lost their power to rattle him. As he reached to turn down the radio he felt the tip of a knife blade pressing against his throat.

The light turned green and she told him to take the next left and suddenly they were moving away from the lights of Grand River, into a dark tunnel. As soon as he felt the knife blade leave his neck, he slammed on the brakes and jammed the gearshift into park. Her face made a loud *POP!* when it hit the dashboard and he grabbed a fistful of yellow wig and kept banging her face against the dash. Blood was pouring from her nose and mouth onto the carpet. She'd dropped the knife. He reached around her and opened the passenger door and shoved her out with his foot. He didn't bother to wash the blood out of the carpet or fix the dent in the dashboard.

When he finished telling the story, Cecelia said, "Okay, you win." She locked her door, then slid across the bench seat, pressed herself against his ribs. His anger vanished as suddenly as it had arrived. He put his arm around her and pulled her close as he made the jog at West Grand Boulevard onto Dexter, then headed north.

Dexter, like Twelfth, carried a load of memories for Doyle, and as he drove slowly up the street he pointed out the numerous shops with Jewish names on the signs—Dozodin Market, Sussman Printing, Goldman Hardware. It was an illusion, he told her, because when the Jewish merchants gave up, as often as not they sold their businesses to Arabs—A-rabs, in the lingo of the street—Syrians, Palestinians and Chaldeans.

"What're Chaldeans?" Cecelia said.

"Iraqi Catholics. Under the Chaldeans' code, a slight to any man is a slight to his entire family, and retribution has to be swift and final. Last winter this junkie with a gun held up the new Chaldean owners at Gutman Brothers Variety, a party store over on Linwood. Thought he'd made the perfect score—couple hundred in cash plus a half dozen Hershey bars for good measure, then out the door clean as a whistle. Two nights later, the junkie winds up in the basement of Gutman Brothers handcuffed to a pole with a chained German Shepherd snapping a few inches from his crotch. After a day of that, Johnny and Tommy Yacoub went down and beat the living shit out of the guy and then un-cuffed him and told him to get lost and stay lost. Next time they'd kill him. The Chaldeans' code says to hell with probable cause, to hell with search warrants, reasonable doubt, Miranda rights and all the rest of it. If you know the guy did it, you make him pay. There's more than a few cops in this town who think they're on to something."

"But not you."

"Let's put it this way. There's never been another holdup, or so much as a report of shoplifting at Gutman's. It's hard to argue with that kind of results."

They pulled up in front of the Drome Lounge at dusk, just as the pink neon martini glass in the front window started sputtering to life. Muffled jazz leaked out of the place, drowsy drinking music.

Doyle hurried around and opened Cecelia's door. She took his hand and, rising to her full height, kissed him on the lips. "Thanks for the tour," she said.

"My pleasure."

"I do believe you love this sorry old city."

"Yeah, I do. I really do."

"I promise I'll never accuse you of being scared again."

He shrugged. "Nothing wrong with being scared."

They kissed again, longer this time, then walked arm-in-arm past two sharply dressed black guys who were leaning against the club's side wall. Doyle watched them watching him. He didn't recognize them. Drug dealers or pimps, he guessed. They rattled him even less than hookers.

The place was half full, the Benny Anflick Trio on the bandstand. As though on cue, the seductive music they'd heard from the street died and Benny launched into one of his drum solos. When you own the place, you get to bang on your drums as much as you want. The other players, a sax man and a bassist, yawned and checked their watches. Doyle thought of that long-ago night when that bandstand belonged to Charlie Parker, the doomed god. Things had slid at the Drome, just like they'd slid everywhere else in this town.

Doyle guided Cecelia to the booth near the front door, as far from the bandstand as they could get. The booth was bathed in lovely pink neon from the martini glass, a light that had the power to make the world go away. Cecelia slid onto the bench facing the bandstand and ordered a whiskey sour. Doyle slid in beside her and asked for a Stroh's. Again he had a splendid view of her thighs. All through the ballgame he'd had to fight off the urge to bend down and plant his lips on the succulent slopes of those thighs. When he looked up he saw Walt Kanka waving from the far end of the bar.

"Oh shit." Doyle looked at his hands.

"What's wrong?"

"Don't look now, but that guy sitting at the end of the bar works with me. He's the last person in the world I want to see right now."

"How come?"

"Because this is my day off and I don't want to think about work." The best way to prevent a visit to the table from Walt Kanka was to go right at him. "Wait here," Doyle said. "I'll be right back." He rose and headed for the men's room.

The Drome hadn't lost all of its class, which meant there were still linen hand towels in the gents' and you still pissed on ice cubes and perfumed pucks of disinfectant in a long porcelain trough. Sure enough, as soon as Doyle started melting ice cubes, the door opened— a burst of Benny banging away at his drums—and Walt Kanka took a stance at the trough. He was wearing his favorite suit, a brown polyester job that looked like it would explode if it got within five feet of a lit match.

"Who's the redhead?" he said.

"She's a strawberry blonde."

"So who is she?"

"Friend of mine." Doyle was staring at a phone number on the knotty-pine wall that promised an unforgettable blowjob from Loretta for the unbeatable price of $5.

"Good-lookin broad," Walt Kanka said.

"Thanks, Walt. I'll be sure to tell her you think so. It'll mean a lot to her."

"How long you two been effin?"

"Jesus Christ, you married fucks are all alike, you know that?" Doyle zipped his pants and moved to the sink. "We're on our first date. I took her to the Tigers game. They won in twelve. Anything else you need to know?"

"Jeez, pardsie, no need to get your neck up. Just an innocent question."

But they both knew there was no such thing as an innocent question from a member of the Homicide squad. As one of the squad's few bachelors, Doyle was a natural target for the sexual speculations of a few dozen middle-aged men with lukewarm marriages, rotting livers, and imaginations both jaded and overheated by years of witnessing every manner of killing ever devised by man. After seeing hundreds of corpses missing limbs, eyeballs and/or genitals, after seeing the handiwork of bullets, knives, blunt objects, fists, fire, battery acid, rope and piano wire, after becoming intimate with the glazed empty stare of the dead, it was hard for a middle-aged man with an overweight wife not to wonder what a good-looking young woman—a living, breathing one—was like in bed. It was only natural, Doyle supposed, but he dried his hands briskly and dropped the towel in the hamper and moved for the door.

Then Walt Kanka, standing at the sink and studying his gorgeous Slovak face in the mirror, said, "You hear the news?"

Doyle froze. "What news?"

"My riot case went down."

"No shit. Carlo Smith went down?"

"Cross my heart." He whipped out a comb and started working it through the waves of silver hair. "Alphonso Johnson gave it up this afternoon. I'd thrown in the towel, but your buddy Robuck finally wore the little scrote down."

"Jimmy called me this morning, said he was heading downtown. How'd he do it?"

"You know how Ro is with the smokes. He started out getting real chummy—I was afraid he was gonna kneel down right there in the yellow room and give Alphonso a knob job. Then he told a few lies—about Alphonso's fingerprints being on the murder weapon, about a footprint that matched the sneakers Alphonso was wearing at that very moment. Jimmy even said he had a photograph. The usual shit. Then he offered to do Alphonso a once-in-a-lifetime favor if he would just sign the confession."

"What'd he offer?"

"He said it was a brother-to-brother offer, one the big Polack detective didn't even want to make. You know how the spades are— any white guy's automatically a Polack if he's not a Guinea."

"Or a Mick."

"Right. So anyway, Jimmy said that he and he alone could get Alphonso twenty years on a guilty plea of Man One—but if a first-degree murder charge went to trial, Alphonso be on his own in a world a shit. Said a confession now would look a whole lot better to a judge than all that incriminating evidence would look to a jury, especially those fingerprints and footprints. Christ. I beat on Alphonso for a solid fuckin week and didn't get anywhere—and Jimmy breaks the jig in four hours flat."

"He ask for a lawyer?"

"Only on the night we picked him up—that smart-mouth high-yellow Clyde Holland. Jimmy kept telling Alphonso he didn't need a lawyer. Believe it or not, Alphonso believed him."

"I'll be damned," Doyle said, not because he was surprised by his partner's interrogation skills or Alphonso Johnson's colossal stupidity, but because the realization was dawning that VIC #42 was off the squad room wall and he and Jimmy were now the proud owners of the last open murder case from the riot.

"Yeah," Walt Kanka said, putting away his comb, "Alphonso signed the confession a few minutes after three. I've been celebrating ever since. Gonna get drunk as a monkey."

"Congratulations, Walt. That's . . . great news."

"Congratulate Jimmy. He's the one made it go down. Oh Frank, there's one more thing."

"Yeah?"

"We're not going public with this yet. Sarge is convinced Alphonso's got some more stories to tell. We're gonna keep working him. Mum's the word for now."

"Sure thing."

When Doyle got back to the booth Cecelia said, "What happened?"

"Nothing."

"Bullshit. You look like your dog just died. What'd he say to you?"

"Just shop talk. Let's drop it. Work'll be there when I show up tomorrow. Finish telling me the story about how your parents met."

Walt Kanka sent a round of drinks to the table and Doyle tried to pay attention as Cecelia resumed a familiar Detroit tale, one she'd started telling back at the ballpark, about her mother's parents coming from Czechoslovakia and settling in Hamtramck, her mother working as a key punch operator and meeting Tommy Cronin, an Irishman from the West Side, a salesman with friends all over town and money to burn. . . .

But Doyle only caught scraps of the story. Walt Kanka had broken the spell with his bad good news. When the band took a break, Benny Anflick came over to the booth to squeeze Doyle's shoulder and offer his trademark greeting, "How ya doin, babe?"

Babe. When Benny finally drifted away, Doyle put a $10 bill under his empty glass and said, "Let's get out of here."

It was dark now, and though the two black guys were gone and the night was starry and soft, Cecelia locked her door without having to be reminded. They didn't say much during the drive back to her place. When Doyle pulled into the parking lot on East Lafayette, she invited him up for a nightcap.

"Thanks," he said, "but I'd better be getting home."

"Relax. I'm not asking you to spend the night. I've still got a paper to finish writing, in case you forgot."

Seen from the twentieth floor at night, Detroit was astonishingly beautiful, diamond spokes radiating through skewed grids, an orderly world where no harm could possibly come to any man. A freighter with the blue Ford oval on its smokestack was gliding downriver, riding low in the water, its belly swollen with iron ore taken on in Duluth, Minnesota. The ore would be off-loaded at the Rouge, where Doyle's father worked for thirty-five years, and where he died.

Cecelia poured a snifter of Drambuie for Doyle and a cup of coffee for herself and they sat by the window, admiring the river and the lights. They drank in silence, holding hands, both of them happy that the day's earlier ease had returned. After a long while she said, "So you still don't want to talk about what your buddy had to say back at the club?"

"He's not my buddy. And no, this is too nice."

She didn't press, and he was grateful for that. Vicki Jones never stopped peppering him with questions when he got home from work.

He still wasn't sure which she hated more—the hours he kept or his refusal to answer her questions.

"But tell me one thing," Cecelia said.

"Sure."

"Tell me you don't really approve of the way those Chaldean guys deal with things."

"No, of course I don't. It's just that sometimes this job makes me feel like we're losing the war."

"And this is one of those times?"

"Maybe. I'm not sure yet."

At the door he kissed her goodnight, a long kiss that hinted at things to come. Driving home, he could taste her lipstick, could hear her whistling like a sailor when Al Kaline drilled a home run into the upper-deck porch in right field. But as sweet as those memories were, by the time he reached his house they were crowded out by the knowledge that Helen Hull's murder was now the only one still unsolved from the riot. That meant the hot seat was hotter than ever. It was time to go talk to that Armstrong woman.

7

AFTER THE LONG NIGHT WHEN HE UNEARTHED THE PICTURES OF the Farce on Washington and the burning bus outside Anniston, Willie's life took on a sense of purpose and urgency it had lacked for years. He spent his free days in the microfilm room at the Detroit Public Library, methodically reading back issues of the *Free Press*, the *Michigan Chronicle* and the *New York Times*, beginning in January of 1960. He made photocopies of important articles and pictures, took copious notes. If he had to work a night shift at Oakland Hills, he slipped on his Snick uniform as soon as he got home and worked into the small hours at his desk, combing through the contents of his Alabama box. The harder he worked, the more energy he had and the less sleep he needed. Like his mother used to say, if you need to get a job done, give it to a busy man. He even found time to catch a few Tigers games.

Late one Saturday night Willie sat at his desk, his only companions the distant purr of the Lodge Freeway and the burble of Miles Davis's trumpet. He had just found something near the bottom of his Alabama box—a dozen neatly typed, single-spaced pages held together by a paper clip. It was the outline of the first three chapters of his book, written in Tuskegee after his return from Atlantic City in the fall of 1964. His plan was to write a memoir of his time in the movement, a foot soldier's intimate story. The only thing he knew about the book's title was that it would contain the word *whirlwind*.

He had worked on the book steadily until his departure for Detroit in the spring of 1967, yet all he had to show for two and a half years of toil was these dozen pages. He read them with a rising sense of dismay. Chapter One, "Wake-Up Call," was to tell the story of the day when, at the age of nine or ten, he walked into the Andalusia Public Library and asked for a library card and the white librarian, Mrs. Satterfield, told him, almost sadly, "I'm sorry, young man, but Nigras aren't allowed to check out books." Those were her exact words, and he would remember them as long as he lived. It was the first time he saw that white people saw him as different—that is, inferior. It was his baptism, the wake-up call that comes sooner or later to every black person in America. Chapter Two, "First Feud," was to tell the story of the first time his parents argued in his presence—over Rev. Martin Luther King's radio address supporting the Montgomery bus boycott. "Foolishness!" Willie's father had roared at the radio. His mother disagreed: "Bout time somebody in a pulpit talked about the here and now instead of all that pie in the sky in the bye-and-bye." And Chapter Three, "Taking Leave," was to tell the story of Willie's decision to leave Tuskegee Institute and walk into the whirlwind.

A dozen skimpy pages and then—nothing. Not a single scrap of flesh on the bones of that outline. Not a single page of prose despite all the notes and pictures and clippings inside the Alabama box. Why? Why had that pathetic trickle of words dried up?

He gazed out the window, listened to the traffic and the trumpet and the whisper of the trees. He started walking through those two and a half years in Tuskegee, trying to remember how a project begun with such high energy and high hopes could sputter, stall, and die.

He remembered that in Tuskegee he'd tried to take inventory of all the jails he'd been in, the beatings he'd absorbed, the fire-bomb-ings he'd survived. But he couldn't do it. His concentration and his memory were shot. He was having trouble falling asleep, and when he did sleep he had wicked nightmares. A car back-firing on the street made him jump. After finishing the outline of Chapter Three, he simply didn't have the strength to start Chapter Four. A sense of paralysis came over him. Then panic.

And then his brother came back into his life.

Wes materialized on Willie's front porch on a rainy night in the fall of 1966, dripping like a dog. Willie was shocked that the chiseled killing machine had allowed himself to get fat and sloppy. Wes said he'd come to claim the pieces of the guns he'd been mailing from Saigon, but instead of picking up the stuff and leaving town, he installed himself on the sofa in Willie's living room and proceeded to spend the winter watching TV, drinking beer, eating pork rinds and fried-oyster po' boys. He roared at the morons on "The Beverly Hillbillies" and "Gilligan's Island," he bit his fingernails during "The Wild, Wild West," and, unable to sleep, he stayed up late watching re-runs of Alfred Hitchcock and "The Twilight Zone." On Saturday mornings he watched cartoons with the rapt glee of a child.

Willie, meanwhile, went into his bedroom and closed the door and tried to keep working on his book. But the drone of the TV and his brother's laughter made it impossible for him to move beyond those dozen skimpy pages. He was still having trouble sleeping, and on many of those long nights he could hear his brother screaming as he sprang off the sofa, drenched from another jungle nightmare.

Now Willie understood that he and Wes had been crushed by the same thing. Some people called it shell shock, or battle fatigue, or stress. Willie thought of it as something else: the violent dismantling of the belief that it was possible to make a better world.

Their only relief came on the rare days when Wes rose from the sofa and loaded the trunk of Willie's '54 Buick with guns and ammunition and they rode out into the country together for a little target practice. Blasting away at Jax beer cans was the only time they were both engaged in the moment, able to concentrate, free of the numbness and the nightmares from their very different but very similar wars. It was the only time they were both fully alive. But by then Willie's book was graveyard dead.

He awoke in his desk chair at dawn. The Miles Davis record was spinning silently on the turntable. He showered and shaved and walked the four blocks to Twelfth Street to buy a *Free Press* from Aziz, the Syrian who ran the corner newsstand.

"Good news and bad news today," Aziz said, taking Willie's dollar.

"We lost."

"Yes, by a score of 8 and 4 to the Senators of Washington. Lolich does not look so sharp. But still we are in first place!"

"Got a double-header today."

"Two games for the price of one. A most excellent idea."

"I'm going to the park, Aziz. Want to come along?"

He gave Willie a look like he'd lost his mind, but there was a smile behind it. "Mister Willie, if I go to the ballgame, how do I sell my papers? How do I pay my rent, huh?"

"Well, maybe we'll go to a night game sometime. After you've closed for the day."

"That I would very much like." He handed Willie his change. "Enjoy the games. Tonight I maybe will see you at the Chit Chat?"

"I'll be there."

On his way home, Willie realized why he felt so fresh after just a couple of hours of sleep in the desk chair. It was because he was buoyed by the revelation that had come to him in the night. He and his brother were bound by shared suffering. They were both damaged warriors. That didn't excuse or guarantee anything, but it did give him hope that his damage was a way back into his story. For the first time, he understood that his story was not a civil rights story. It was a war story.

He was ravenous and when he got home he fixed a big breakfast of ham and eggs, grits, toast and coffee. As he ate he read the sports page closely, the accounts of yesterday's loss, the box score, Joe Falls's column, stories of injuries and slumps and hitting streaks. He couldn't get enough news about the Tigers.

After breakfast he tucked the newspaper under his arm and walked to Woodward and caught the DSR bus. As the bus rattled toward downtown he glanced at the front page. Same old same old. Eugene McCarthy's dark-horse presidential campaign still gaining momentum, the Vietnam war still dragging on, the Paris peace talks still going nowhere. The only thing that held his interest was a story at the bottom of the page that said H. Rap Brown, Stokely's successor as the head of Snick, was on trial in New Orleans for carrying an M-1 carbine across state lines.

Willie needed to believe he was different from H. Rap Brown. Willie did not let his brother talk him into driving those guns to Detroit because he shared Rap's enthusiasm for the looming race war. By then Willie was beyond caring whether a race war was inevitable, desirable, unthinkable, or merely the fantasy of a bunch of fanatics with big mouths and a few loose screws. He agreed to make the trip because he needed the money and he needed a change of scenery. He also needed to believe he was disengaged, above the fray, a mere mercenary. Now he was working to revive his book project not because he believed it was possible to change other people. He was doing it for a much simpler and, he thought, purer reason: because he did not want to remain invisible and he did not want his life to be pointless.

"Hey, you there! In the back!"

Willie looked up. The bus had reached downtown and the driver was eyeing him nervously in the rearview mirror. There was no one else on the bus.

"You deaf? I said last stop! Everybody off!"

Willie left the newspaper on the bus. He studied his scuffed brogans as he walked, and he realized his Snick uniform fit his mood perfectly. It was faceless, generic, ideal for a man trapped in that gray no-man's-land between the black world and the white world. Part of that gray area was his predicament—the small-town southern Negro marooned in a sprawling northern factory town, the once-proud idealist reduced to working a lowly job for The Man while worrying about the police. All that was predictable and bad enough. What made it worse was that he had nowhere to turn for refuge. The movement had proven to be a sad joke. Religion had never been an option. Other than a few beers at the Chit Chat after a Tigers game, the conventional pleasures no longer held any allure. He didn't miss the sweaty fury of the dance floor or the fuzzy buzz of a Thai stick. He'd never gotten a kick from gambling. His brother had hit the road—and may have wound up in a ditch. And working with some hard-core Stepin Fetchits at Oakland Hills had reminded Willie that he had no need whatsoever for the white man's approval or largess. He had nowhere to turn, and no one to turn to.

As he joined the line at the ballpark ticket window, Willie wondered if this no-man's-land might not be the perfect place for him to be right now. Maybe it was best that he had nowhere to turn. Like Ralph Ellison's invisible man—like all men—he had no choice but to look within himself. And thanks to the picture of the burning bus and the typed outline of his first three chapters and the revelation about war that had come to him last night—looking within himself was what he was finally beginning to do.

He bought a ticket for the bleachers and began the ascent into the familiar symphony of smells. Loudspeakers carried the pre-game show. As the city streets receded beneath him, Willie felt himself getting lighter, airier, escaping from a world of worry into a carefree world of pure play. Walking along the gangplank that led to the bleachers, he caught sight of the rectangle of sky up ahead. Again he saw seagulls, and his pulse quickened. Then he stepped into a green bowl of sunlight.

He told himself that maybe this was his new home and refuge: this feeling of release he got when he came to this magical place.

To his delight, Louis Dumars and Clyde Holland were sitting right where they'd been on Opening Day. "Well, well, well," Louis called when he saw Willie coming up the steps. "Look who's back. If it ain't Mo-fuckin-beel, Ala-goddam-bama!"

They smacked palms. Clyde repeated the greeting, then looked Willie up and down and said, "Where you pick up them vines, boy? Some watermelon patch?"

"No," Willie said, strangely pleased by the teasing. "This is what we use to wear when I worked with the Student Nonviolent Coordinating Committee down South a few years back. You know, Snick. It's helping me remember things."

"Student nonviolence my ass," Clyde said with a laugh. "You looks like a motherfuckin hick."

Clyde did not look like a hick. In his expensive sunglasses, colorful dashiki, creased slacks and sandals, he looked like what he was—a prosperous black man enjoying his day of leisure.

Earl Wilson was pitching again for the Tigers, and he took a 4-0 lead into the eighth inning. After getting one out he gave up a single and a walk, and Mayo Smith replaced him with John Warden. This time there were no boos as Wilson walked slowly off the field, his head held high. The man, Willie thought, had a long ton of poise and dignity. Louis and Clyde and Willie stood to join the cheering. Wilson tipped his cap before vanishing into the dugout.

Warden promptly gave up a walk and a grand slam and just like that the score was tied and the joy was gone and the stadium was roiling with anger.

"Dig a hole, Warden!" someone shouted.

"Yank the bum!"

"Like I say," Clyde said, shaking his head, "ficklest motherfuckers in the world."

Fred Lasher replaced Warden and promptly put the fire out. In the bottom of the ninth inning Gates Brown drove in the winning run with a pinch-hit single to left field, and the place erupted. John Warden's sins were already forgotten.

"Didn't I tell you Gates the best pinch-hitter in the game?" Louis exulted, accepting hand slaps from Clyde and half a dozen delirious strangers.

In the lull between games, Willie went exploring and returned to the bleachers with three cups of beer and a bag of peanuts in a cardboard tray just as Clyde was saying, "Alphonso done fucked up."

"Who's Alphonso?" Louis asked, thanking Willie for the beer.

"Remember on Opening Day when I tole you bout a client a mine name of Alphonso Johnson got picked up by the po-lice for questioning on a murder during the riot?" Louis and Willie nodded. "Well, turns out the po-lice got a tip, and while they had Alphonso downtown they tore up his crib. Found his gun and claimed they matched it to the bullet they took out some dude's head who died during the riot, some fireman. It was a lie, a course, but suddenly dumbass Alphonso believes he's in a world a shit."

"So what happened?" Willie said. There was a roaring in his ears.

"I'm not all the way sure," Clyde said. "What I do know is he signed a confession—after I tole him not to say a word less I was in the room with him!"

"You and me both know the po-lice done beat it outta him," Louis said.

All Willie could think about was how grateful he was that there were no more guns in his car or anywhere near his apartment. He tried to remember what Wes had done with those last three guns before leaving for Chicago, but he couldn't.

Once the second game started, Willie managed to quit worrying about the guns and the police. The day was too fair—soft sunshine, bleached white clouds marching across the sky. Gates Brown started in left field for Willie Horton, an acceptable substitution in Willie's eyes, but he was disappointed that Ed Mathews was inserted for Norm Cash at first base. Willie had played first base in high school and at Tuskegee, and he was developing great respect for Cash's fielding and hitting. It was hard to argue with the results, though. Mathews smashed a three-run homer in the fourth inning and Al Kaline added a two-run shot in the sixth.

When the score reached 7-0 in the seventh inning, fans began moving for the exits. But once again Louis and Clyde and Willie stayed put, bound together by the unspoken understanding that even watching a mop-up job here in this beautiful green room surpassed anything that awaited them down on the streets of Detroit.

Clyde bought one last round of beers, then turned to Willie. "You still workin that busboy job?"

"Fraid so."

"Where's it at?"

"Oakland Hills Country Club. Way out in honky land."

"No shit. One a my best clients is a member there. Man name of Chick Murphy."

"The Buick dealer?"

"Thas right. Man's a prince. Traded with him for a new Deuce and a Quarter just last week."

"You're Chick Murphy's lawyer?"

"Not his personal lawyer. He calls me whenever one a his nigger mechanics gets liquored up and does something stupid. I make a nice chunk a change off them fools."

Every day, it seemed, the big city got a little smaller. And Chick Murphy seemed to have satisfied customers all over this shrinking town.

The second game ended 7-0, and the day's sweep left the Tigers two games ahead of second-place Cleveland. It was a glorious day to be a Detroit Tigers fan. Willie was feeling so good he accepted Clyde's offer of a ride home in his new Deuce and a Quarter. It was fire-engine red with a white convertible top and white seats, AM-FM radio, power windows, much flashier than Uncle Bob's Deuce, and it beat the hell out of the DSR. Willie didn't want the party to end just yet, so he asked Clyde to drop him off at the Chit Chat Lounge.

❖

The place was packed, as it always was when the Tigers were in town. Aziz was sitting on a barstool drinking a Vernor's ginger ale because he was a Muslim and he never drank alcohol. Next to him sat Erkie, who was drinking a shot of Old Overholt and a Stroh's chaser because that was all he ever drank. Willie made his way through the mob toward them.

Though his bar-hopping days were past, Willie stopped by the Chit Chat from time to time because the walls were covered with Tigers memorabilia, and Izzy Gould, the three-day Jew who owned the place, always unplugged the jukebox and tuned the radio to WJR on game days. The jukebox was an old Seeburg full of great records, everything from Sarah Vaughan to Clarence Carter to Bo Diddley. To top it off, the Chit Chat was on Euclid just a few blocks from Willie's apartment, which meant he could crawl home if he had a few too many.

When he reached the bar he saw that Erkie had a Viceroy cigarette stuck in the gap where his second tooth on the lower right side used to be. His head was shrouded in so much smoke that at first Willie thought he was on fire. Normally Erkie was in high spirits when the Tigers won, but now he looked glum.

"Why the long face, Erk?" Willie said, sliding onto the empty stool next to him. Izzy Gould put a bottle of Stroh's in front of Willie and rapped the bar twice with a knuckle, his way of letting regulars know the first one was free.

"That fuckin Kaline!" Erkie moaned without removing the cigarette. It bobbed when he talked. Willie realized he was blotto, which was no surprise. Erkie spent every waking hour on that barstool, directly beneath the Hamm's beer sign, waiting for someone to buy him a drink. The Hamm's sign had a waterfall made of tinfoil that actually appeared to tumble over rocks, especially after you'd had a few.

"What's your beef with Kaline? He hit a two-run homer in the second game."

"Sonofabitch—it was the 307th of his career. Broke Hank Greenberg's club record."

Just then Izzy set a shot of brown liquor in front of Willie, a fresh shot of Old Overholt in front of Erkie and a shot of Vernor's ginger ale in front of Aziz. Izzy didn't want teetotalers to feel left out.

"This round's on the house!" Izzy shouted. "To Hammerin' Hank!"

"To Hammerin' Hank!" everyone shouted back, flipping their shot glasses.

Now Willie understood Erkie's long face. Erkie had forgotten more about the Tigers than most men would ever know. Willie had always been a sucker for old-timers, and whenever he bumped into Erkie he gladly bought him shots of Old Overholt just to keep him talking. Erkie's two favorite Tigers of all time were the "G-Men"—Charlie Gehringer, the Mechanical Man, at second base and the great Hank Greenberg at first.

Aziz said, "Finish telling the sad story about Ty Cobb after his retirement, Mr. Erk." Aziz was a sucker for old-timers, too.

"Where was I?" Erkie said, his cigarette bobbing. "Oh yeah. After he retired, this woulda been along about in the Thirties, Cobb used to go big-game hunting out West with that famous writer, you know, what's his name, the bullfight guy?"

Aziz gave him a blank look.

Willie said, "Ernest Hemingway?"

"Thas right, Hemmenway. Later on, in the Fifties, Cobb played golf with President Eisenhower hisself. But he passed a few years back, not a friend in this round world. In the end, all that fame and all that Co-Cola stock didn't do him a lick a good." He drained his beer. "You know, it's funny. I knowed the man was a red-ass first time I laid eyes on him at Halloran's, where I use to wash dishes. Man was what they called a nigger-breaker during slave times. But much as he hated us, I still felt sorry for the way he died. Ain't nobody deserves to die all alone like that."

The old man reminded Willie of his father, Reverend Otis, who was forever preaching to his sons that racism was a sickness and it was their Christian duty to love the racist just as they should love a victim of polio or cancer. Willie tried to do his Christian duty, though in the end he failed. His brother didn't even bother to try.

As Erkie launched into another Tigers story, Willie turned to watch the sports wrap-up on the TV bolted to the ceiling in the corner. They replayed Kaline's historic home run and even flashed a picture of Hank Greenberg.

Willie ended up closing the place down with a skinny white hooker from West Virginia named Ginger and Tommy Slenski, a DSR bus driver who had worked that afternoon and was still wearing his uniform. Everyone called him Ralph because he looked like Jackie Gleason on "The Honeymooners." He was telling Ginger a disjointed story about a mob setting his bus on fire during the riot, but the long day of drinking had finally caught up with Willie and he had trouble following Ralph's story.

As he weaved back to his apartment, Willie considered how rich the day had been. How many days do you learn new things about H. Rap Brown, Ernest Hemingway, Ty Cobb, Dwight Eisenhower, Hank Greenberg and Ralph Ellison? As rich as the list was, he had the nagging feeling he was forgetting something. When he got home and turned on the late news, he remembered what it was.

A Channel 2 reporter, a sharp-looking black lady with a big Afro and a red silk scarf, was interviewing two detectives in front of 1300 Beaubien Street—a fat, silver-haired white guy and a dapper black dude. They were explaining that Alphonso Johnson, a paroled felon, had confessed to the murder of Detroit fireman Carlo Smith, who was shot by a sniper during last summer's riot.

Then there was a picture on the screen of a white woman identified as Helen Hull, a lumpy old doughball with harlequin glasses, her gray hair pulled back into a bun. The reporter was saying that the Detroit grocer, shot dead while looking out a window in the Harlan House Motel, was now the victim of the last unsolved homicide from the riot. She signed off with: "Police say their investigation into her death is continuing. This is Sylvia King reporting live from Detroit police headquarters for WJBK."

Willie snapped off the TV and swallowed four aspirin and took a long hot shower. But when he lay down in bed the ceiling started spinning and he spent an hour waiting for it to stop. The whole time a question ate at him: What had become of those last three guns from the trunkload he and Wes had brought up to the city a year ago? There was only one person who knew the answer. In the morning Willie would make a long-distance phone call he dreaded.

As he lay there in the dark, he kept seeing the two detectives, the white one with the silver hair and the black one with the crisp suit, and he kept seeing the doughy dead white woman named Helen Hull. The sight of her made the stone of guilt in his gut bigger and harder and colder than ever. The tree outside his window shivered in the breeze. A siren howled. He could feel the big city getting smaller, closing in.

PART TWO
TINDERBOX

8

Doyle was gunning the Plymouth out the Lodge Freeway, weaving through traffic, honking the horn, gripping the steering wheel like he was trying to break the thing in two. Jimmy Robuck, not one to get nervous in the passenger seat of a car or anywhere else, said, "You might want to ease off that gas pedal, Frank. The lady ain't goin nowhere."

Doyle slowed the car and blinked at Jimmy, seeming to come back from another world. "That a new suit you're wearing?" Doyle said.

"Yeah, poplin. Picked it up at Brooks Brothers when Flo and I were in New York. The bow tie, too. You like?"

"Very nice. Makes you look positively pro-fuckin-fessorial."

"Pro-fuckin-fessorial." Jimmy chuckled. "You really somethin, man."

"You know you're not suppose to wear white bucks before Memorial Day, don't you?"

"Course I do, but weather this fine, I decided to bend the rules. How bout you? That silk suit don't look cheap."

"Can't afford to buy cheap clothes. I got an Italian guy out on Livernois making my suits for me now."

"Bespoke?"

"Got no choice. Nothing off the rack fits me."

"The shirt too?"

"Oh yeah. You ever seen a shirt in a store with a fifteen-inch neck and thirty-seven-inch sleeves?"

"Not as I recall."

"That's because they don't make them. I'm telling you, Jimmy, I'm a freak."

"I dig them cuff links."

"Thanks, they're opals." He shot his cuffs, pleased by the compliment. "Got to do my part to keep up our rep as the sharpest dressers on the force."

"Ain't sayin much. Most a them chumps look like they sport coats made out of car upholstery."

"Or wallpaper."

They laughed, not because it was funny but because it was so true. Most of their fellow detectives thought a sport coat was something you put on when you needed to cover the hairy forearms sticking out of your short-sleeved shirt. Not all of Doyle's shirts had French cuffs, but he wouldn't dream of wearing a short-sleeved shirt with a necktie, any more than he would dream of wearing one of those wide cop neckties made out of synthetic shit—the better to keep gravy and soup off your shirt, the better to cover your nose if you had to pop a car trunk on a hot day knowing that the body in there had been marinating at least a week.

Jimmy said, "You really think this Armstrong woman's gonna tell us somethin we don't already know?"

"I got no idea, Jimmy, but we can't afford not to check her out, can we? You heard Sarge. He's got people all the way up to Cavanagh breathing down his neck to make this case go down."

"You must think she gonna be good, way you been buggin me to ride out here with you."

They both knew why Doyle wanted Jimmy to ride along. Henry Hull said the woman was black, and the detectives knew that they were more likely to get something out of her if there was another black face—Jimmy Robuck's—in the room. It usually helped to have a black face in the room when a Detroit police interviewed a black witness or interrogated a black suspect, and it always helped when a black defendant went on trial. A black judge on the bench, a black detective on the witness stand, even a couple of black bailiffs could help put a jury at ease, give a boost to the prosecution, convince the jurors that a black defendant actually had a chance of getting justice inside the Frank Murphy Hall of Justice.

Doyle parked at the corner of Pallister and Hamilton, and the partners got out and stood looking up at a yellow brick pile with *Larrow Arms* carved in stone above the front door. They could hear the round-the-clock whoosh of the Lodge Freeway off to their right.

Doyle pushed the button marked ARMSTRONG and opened the buzzing foyer door. Jimmy followed him up one flight of stairs. The stairwell smelled like collard greens that had been boiling in fat back for years. The steam had become part of the wallpaper and carpets. While Doyle was no great fan of soul food, he found the smell reassuring, a sign of permanence. And the building was clean, in good repair. The Negro middle class, fighting the good fight.

The woman who opened the door was what Doyle had been led to expect by their phone conversation. She was all the way Southern—a rust-colored wig, flowered dress, gold-rimmed bifocals, her arms as soft as bread dough with brown flesh sagging from her biceps. She was wearing perfume, good, strong, nose-hair-curling perfume. She looked like she was on her way out to church, which was actually a possibility because this was Wednesday and Southern Baptists took Wednesdays almost as seriously as they took Sundays. She had a bosom like a queen-size mattress, and Doyle had a hunch she sang in the church choir and could really belt it out.

"Mrs. Armstrong," he said, "I'm Detective Doyle and this is Detective Robuck from the Detroit Police Department. We spoke on the phone." The men showed her their shields.

"Come in, gentlemen, come in," she said with a slight drawl, like this was a long-awaited social visit and not a homicide investigation. "You gentlemen make yourselves to home while I fix us a cup a tea. Y'all drink tea, don't you?"

"Yes, ma'am," they said in unison.

She went into the kitchen but the detectives didn't sit down. They both shuffled around the living room, looking at things, trying to read the woman. The apartment was immaculate, the rug worn but swept so hard and so often it made Doyle's arms ache just to look at it. The hardwood floor glowed. The walls and tabletops were cluttered with framed pictures of babies, old people, teenagers in caps and gowns, football players, an ironworker dancing and grinning on a skyscraper's I-beam, and then the two pictures you knew were coming: the dead saints, John F. Kennedy and Martin Luther King.

Charlotte Armstrong returned with a silver tea service and motioned for the men to sit in the matching chairs that faced across the coffee table toward the sofa, where she installed herself, regal as a queen. The chairs were wrapped in hard plastic and they crackled when the detectives sat down. There was a plate on the coffee table stacked high with bricks of fresh-baked crumb cake. The men did as they were told and helped themselves. It was delicious, still warm, loaded with brown sugar and cinnamon, and there was a long reverent silence as they ate.

Doyle got things started by asking Charlotte Armstrong if she was feeling better.

"Yes, I'm better today, praise the Lord. Like I tole you on the phone, I been in bed the past two days with a misery in my back."

"Is that your husband?" Jimmy asked, motioning toward the grinning man on the I-beam.

"Yes, that's my Charles. He passed last Christmas."

"I'm sorry for your—"

"Rose to treasurer in his ironworker's local, first time a Negro was ever elected an officer. Made good money, too, a hundred and sixty a week plus overtime, enough for me to have my own car. That picture there was taken on the twenty-first floor of the new Pontchartrain Hotel downtown. Heights didn't mean a thing to Charles. Worked forty-one years on high iron, what he did his whole life."

Jimmy was thinking about how Detroiters love to boast about their wages when Doyle said, "Looks like Charles loved his work."

It was the perfect thing to say. Charlotte Armstrong beamed at him, and again Jimmy had to marvel at his partner's knack for putting people at ease, getting them to tell him things.

Doyle pointed at two pictures of a young man in a gold frame: one a muddied but grinning football player holding his helmet against his hip, the other a beaming graduate in an indigo cap and gown.

"That your son?" he asked.

"Yes, thas my James. He's the spit and image of his father. The Lord done raised me up a holy son. He's an accountant at Ford's. Yesterday were his birthday."

"And how old he got to be yesterday?" Jimmy said.

"He done made twenty-six. Spent the whole afternoon in that chair you're sitting in. He do comfort my gray hairs."

In one smooth move Doyle shifted gears—finished his crumb cake, put down his tea cup, took out a notebook and ballpoint pen. "Now Mrs. Armstrong," he said, "Mr. Hull tells me that when he came to visit you, you told him about some things you saw last July 26th. Tell us, what exactly did you see that night?"

She put down her tea cup, pinkie extended, and patted her lips with her napkin. She was enjoying herself. Doing her civic duty.

"It must of been after midnight," she said. "Yes, it was definitely past midnight because Charles and I stayed up to watch the late news about the riot. Then he went on to bed because he had to get up early for a job he was just starting out in Troy at—"

"Yes, it was after midnight. . . ." Doyle could keep people on track without them realizing there was a track.

"I had all the lights off on account of the snipers, naturally, and I was sitting by that window there, looking out across the freeway. It looked like a war over on Grand Boulevard. Tanks and guns going off. Fire trucks and po-lice. Sirens. I probably shouldn't of been so close to the window, but it was a furnace-hot night and there was so much noise weren't no way I could sleep."

"What did you see next?"

"A car pulled up right down below that window."

"What kind of car was it?" Doyle had started writing in his notebook.

"Oh goodness, Detective, I don't know much about cars. And the street was dark on account of they shot out all the streetlights. There was a moon, though."

"Were the car's headlights on?"

"No, but when the car doors opened I could see by the inside lights that it were real pretty. Shiny like. But it weren't no new car. Had lots of chrome like cars use to have."

"Do you have any idea what kind of car it was? Was it a big car like a Cadillac? Or small like a Mustang? Or—"

"Gracious no. My eyes aren't so good anymore."

Doyle didn't write that down. He said, "How about the color?"

"Well, the seats were red and black, that much I could see by the inside lights."

Jimmy said, "You say the car doors opened, Mrs. Armstrong. Two doors, three doors, four?"

She looked at Jimmy. She seemed surprised to see him sitting there.

"Two doors," she said to Doyle. "And two men got out."

"Did you recognize them?" he said.

"No, from this angle I couldn't see their faces. And it being so dark—"

"Could you tell if they were black or white?"

"They were both Negroes, of that I'm sure."

"How can you be sure?"

"They were wearing short-sleeve shirts. One was fat, the other was much taller. And thin."

"What'd they do next?"

"They opened the trunk and stood there talking for the longest. Sounded like they were arguing. Then the fat man took something out the trunk. Looked like one a them bags soldiers carry. You know, a, a—"

"Duffel bag?"

"That's it, a duffel bag. And then he carried it cross the lawn and into the building. The other man followed him. In the moonlight I could see that the fat man, the one carrying the duffel bag, had a limp. I could still hear them talking—"

"Could you make out what they were saying?"

"No, they were talking too low. I'm sorry."

"That's fine, Mrs. Armstrong. You're doing just fine. What'd you hear next?"

"I heard the downstairs door open."

"Is that door always kept locked?"

"Oh yes. They's been a buzzer on the front door since we moved in here five years ago."

"Can you hear the buzzer from up here?"

"Yes, I can."

"Did you hear the buzzer before the men opened the door?"

"Come to think of it, no. I didn't."

"So these men had a key to the front door?" Doyle and Jimmy exchanged a smile.

"Well, yes," she said, "I suppose so. I hadn't thought about it, but I suppose you're right."

"So the men came in through the front door."

"Yes, I heard them come up the first flight of stairs—no voices, just footsteps. They passed our door, then kept on going upstairs. I heard someone knock on a door. For a while after that I didn't hear a thing. I figured they'd gone into an apartment and that was the end of it. I was fixin to go to bed—but then I heard their voices again."

"Where?"

"Coming from up above." She pointed at the ceiling. "But I don't think they were inside the building."

"Why not?"

"Well, they were laughing, talking loud. The way their voices carried, it just sounded like they were outside."

"On the roof?"

"The fifth floor's kept locked on account of that's where the residents store they spare things. But yes, it sounded like there were two men on the roof, maybe three."

"Who has a key to the fifth floor?"

"I wouldn't know. We never stored anything up there."

"Did you hear anything else?"

"Oh yes." She smoothed the lap of her dress, brushed away a crumb. Doyle and Jimmy were afraid to look at each other. They could hear the roar of the freeway, the ticking of a clock. Finally she said, "I heard gunshots."

"How many?"

"I counted nine."

"And then what?"

"Then it stopped. I heard two men talking very loud—arguing again. They might of been drunk. Before long I heard a car coming up the street—it was a po-lice."

"Yes? And then?"

"Nothing."

"No footsteps? No voices?"

"Not a thing."

"No one left the building?"

"Not that I could see or hear."

"About how much longer did you sit by the window?"

"Not long, maybe fifteen minutes. I saw another po-lice pass by real slow with its lights off, but that was all I saw. Then I went on to bed."

"Did you report this to the police?"

"I tried, but the lines were always busy. I couldn't get through."

Frank and Jimmy helped themselves to a second piece of crumb cake while Charlotte Armstrong went into the kitchen to write down her landlord's name, address and phone number on a slip of pink paper.

When they got back to 1300 Beaubien, Doyle started typing up his notes while Jimmy looked over his shoulder, occasionally making a suggestion. Doyle was a much faster typist, used all his fingers and didn't even have to look at the keys.

They knew there had been at least two shooters on the roof of the Larrow Arms and one of them lived on the building's upper floors. The timing matched the time of Helen Hull's death. The rooftop afforded a clear shot at the Harlan House. They had a rough description of a car. Jimmy reminded Doyle to type in that the fat man had a limp, that there may have been a third man on the roof, that one or more of the men might have been drunk. The top floor was locked, so they needed to find out who had the key. "And don't forget the landlord," Jimmy said.

"I haven't forgetten the landlord." Doyle removed the neatly folded pink paper from his shirt pocket. It was the last thing he typed into the file: *Bob Brewer. 3417 Normandy. GArfield 4-6743.* "I'm going out to see him tomorrow, soon as I do a little research."

"All by your lonesome?"

"If I have to. Of course I'd love for you to come along."

"Course you would. But I got to be in court all day to testify in that double at Duke's Playhouse."

"Then I'll go alone. I don't want to let this thing cool off again. I can feel it, Jimmy. This could be the one we've been waiting for." He smacked his forehead. "Damn!"

"Whatsamatter?" Jimmy said.

"I got so wound up I forgot to ask Mizz Armstrong for her crumb cake recipe."

9

WILLIE WAS DRESSED HALF AN HOUR BEFORE HIS UNCLE BOB WAS due to pick him up for work. Pacing his living room, he decided there was no sense putting it off any longer. He dialed his parents' telephone number in Andalusia. It was his second long-distance call of the morning, and he was dreading this one even more than the first. With luck he would catch his mother at home alone, keep his father out of this. She picked up after the third ring.

"Bledsoe residence."

"Hey, Ma, it's me."

"William! What a pleasant surprise. How *are* you?"

"Fine, Ma. Everything's cool."

"You still working?"

"Afraid so. Got the lunch shift today."

"You putting some money away?"

"Trying."

"Your Aunt Nezzie's here. Want to say hello?" There was a muffled sound, voices. His Aunt Nezzie hated telephones, wouldn't have one in her house. His mother came back on the line. "Well, Nezzie says hello."

"Tell her I said hey. Got some good news, Ma."

"Oh?"

"Started back working on my book."

"That's wonderful, William."

"Yeah, been going to the library to read old newspaper articles about the stuff we did. Been remembering a lot of things."

"Have you started writing again?"

"Not yet. But soon. I can feel it."

"And how's brother Bob?"

"Same old. Richer by the day."

She giggled. "Stop that, you."

"Ain't lyin. He just bought a shiny new Buick that's bigger'n my apartment."

"I know. He sent us a picture of it parked in front of their new house. It looks like a manor somewhere in England."

Willie tried for his most casual tone. "Say Ma, I was wondering, you heard from Wes lately by any chance? I just tried calling him at that number in Chicago but they said he left town. Nobody knew where he went off to."

"As a matter of fact your brother called last week."

"He did?"

"Yes. Why is that so exciting? To hear him tell it, you two had some big falling out."

"It wasn't no big falling out. It was a misunderstanding's all."

"Wesley made it sound like you two were at each other's throats."

"It wasn't like that. You know how he exaggerates everything."

"I see. Well, he's on his way to Denver."

"Denver? What's in Denver?"

"He said he has some friends there. Navy buddies. You know how he's been since he got out the service. Drifting from here to there, no direction, no ambition."

"Yeah, I know. He give you a telephone number?"

"No, he said he was calling from a pay phone at a bus station somewhere in the Midwest. St. Louis, I believe it was. But he said he'll call soon as he makes it to Denver."

"You think you could do me a favor?"

"Of course."

"When you hear from him, please ask him to call me. It's important."

"What's this all about, William? Is something wrong?"

"No Ma, I swear. I just want to straighten out the misunderstanding we had. Simple as that."

"Fine. I'll ask him to call you when I hear from him. Any other news? You find a girl?"

"Nothing serious. I have gone to a few baseball games though."

"Baseball games?"

"Yeah, the Detroit Tigers. First place in the American League. Made a couple of good friends at the ballpark, two brothers—a dude from Louisiana and a lawyer."

"Well, that's . . . nice, I suppose."

"And how's the Reverend?"

"He's fine, thank you for asking. He's down to the church. He and some of the boys from the choir are finally fixing the roof."

"Still working the Jesus thing, is he?"

"You know he is. He'll be praising the Lord when he's inside a pine box."

Willie heard his Aunt Nezzie laughing in the background. She had nothing but scorn for the Jesus racket, the way her brother-in-law, now that he'd retired from the railroad, spent all of his time at his church, Mount Olive True Holiness Baptist Tabernacle, a little white-washed box sitting up on cinderblocks in a thicket of loblolly pines just south of Andalusia. The faithful sat on folding chairs, waving paper fans from Hargett Funeral Service, worshiping by the light of a single 60-watt bulb that dangled by a wire from the ceiling. They were all ready for the rapture even though the roof leaked. Or maybe they were ready for the rapture *because* the roof leaked. Willie had to give his father credit for one thing, though. At least he wasn't one of those preachers who drove a Cadillac and kept a harem of young redbones hand-picked from the church choir. Otis Bledsoe drove an old Ford. He was a true believer, a foot-washing Baptist who dismissed Methodists and Episcopalians and the like as "shallow-water" because they did their baptizing indoors instead of where it was supposed to be done—outdoors in a snake-infested brown river, under the all-seeing eye of God. "Well, give the Reverend my best," Willie said.

"I'll do that."

"I better go, Ma. This is expensive."

"All right, William. Write me a letter."

"Will do. And don't forget to tell Wes to call me."

"I won't forget. Bye now."

As he hung up the phone Willie heard a horn honk and saw his uncle's Deuce and a Quarter glide up to the curb on Pallister. Willie hurried down the stairs, several dollars poorer but still no closer to knowing what had become of those three guns.

10

DOYLE SPENT THE MORNING RESEARCHING REAL-ESTATE RECORDS, then ate a salad and moussaka alone in Greektown before heading north. Normandy Street was flanked with solid, well-maintained houses, not far from U. of D. High School, Doyle's alma mater. He parked the unmarked Plymouth two doors down from 3417, a tidy two-story brick with a slate roof and exposed timbers, about a seven iron from the fence of the Detroit Golf Club, if Doyle remembered distances correctly from his boyhood summers spent caddying there. He hadn't called ahead—he was hoping the element of surprise would work in his favor—and he sat in the car for a while trying to read the street. There were For Sale signs on half a dozen front lawns on this block. So even out here on the leafy northern fringe of the city, miles removed from ground zero, whitey was packing it in.

A black woman answered the door. She had smooth butterscotch skin, straight hair and a toothy Diana Ross smile. Doyle showed her his shield and asked if Mr. Bob Brewer was in.

The smile disappeared. "My husband's at work," she said, hugging the door.

"You're Mrs. Brewer?"

"That's right. I'm Mary Brewer." Not cold, but a long way from warm. Like she thought he'd assumed she was the maid. Christ, he thought, you step on a land mine in this town every time you try to move.

"What time do you expect your husband?"

"Bob's not in any trouble, is he?"

"Oh no, ma'am, nothing like that." Doyle gave it a little chortle, as though the very thought was ridiculous. "I just need to ask him a few questions about one of his tenants."

"Oh." She relaxed, but only a little. About a third of Diana Ross's warmth returned. "Well, he's working late tonight. He'll probably spend the night since he has to work a double shift tomorrow. I'll tell him you came by. Do you have a card?"

"Where does he work?"

The eyes narrowed a notch, the smile disappeared again. "He's a waiter."

"I see. And where does he do his waiting?"

Now she was glaring. "At Oakland Hills."

"Oakland Hills?" He'd never heard of the place.

"The country club."

"I'm sorry, I'm drawing a—"

"It's out in Birmingham."

"Do you know *where* in Birmingham?"

"West 15 Mile, near Telegraph."

Like pulling fucking hen's teeth, Doyle thought as he nursed the Plymouth farther north out Woodward, through Ferndale and Royal

Oak, all the way to Birmingham. It was a notch below Bloomfield Hills but still plush, the sort of place where the people with For Sale signs in front of their houses on Normandy Street surely dreamed of winding up, almost a whole Detroit away from Detroit, a village of pricey shops and well-scrubbed children where it hardly seemed possible that human beings were capable of torching their own neighborhoods and climbing up on rooftops to shoot at policemen and firemen. Doyle had to remind himself that this was how America had always worked: When places like Detroit made you rich enough, you took the money and you ran and you didn't look back. The only difference nowadays was that nobody could run far enough, or fast enough.

It was late afternoon when he finally pulled onto the parking lot at Oakland Hills Country Club. The massive white clubhouse looked like something off a movie set. Gone with the Fucking Wind, Doyle thought, tuning the radio until he picked up WJR and the voice of Ernie Harwell. The first game of the Tigers' twi-night double-header had just started and the Red Sox already had two men on base. No wonder—Mickey Lolich was pitching, and he was as famous for his shaky starts as he was for his strong finishes. Carl Yastrzemski proceeded to park the next pitch in the center field bleachers, and the Red Sox owned a 3-0 lead before the Tigers had even come to bat. Better get the shower hot for Lolich, Doyle thought, snapping off the radio in disgust.

The arrival of a shit-brown Plymouth went unnoticed by the people straggling in off the golf course, by the men drinking gin and playing cards in the cozy grill, by the elegantly dressed couples pulling up under the portico in Cadillacs and Chrysler Imperials to meet other elegantly dressed couples for drinks and dinner. These people thought their money made them immune. Doyle had bad news for them.

The manager received him in his cluttered office off the front lobby. He was a harried little terrier in a cheap suit named Dick Kowalski, a St. Stanislaus grad like Cecelia Cronin, and he pleaded with Doyle to come back around ten o'clock because Bob Brewer was working a very important private cocktail party and banquet for some big shots from Ford Styling. Dick Kowalski pinched the bridge of his nose and said, "If I have to pull him off the floor now it'll fuck everything up. Believe me."

Doyle believed him. They were a couple of city boys marooned out here in far suburbia. Doyle told himself he could work with this guy, then told Kowalski he'd return around ten.

He drove farther north, all the way to Bloomfield Hills. He found Cranbrook Road without too much trouble and parked across from 1030 and cut the engine. He could hear cicadas whining in the tall trees, and he could see that his brother's house was lit up like Christmas. Every light in the place was on, upstairs and down, an extravagance that seemed designed to tell the world that the family in the big Dutch colonial didn't have to worry about electricity bills or anything else. Doyle was sure it was Kat's idea of class. His old man would have given his brother hell.

A shape passed by the window on the bottom left. One of the girls? Doyle felt a spasm in his chest and reached for the door handle, but then he remembered the last time he had come here. It was late last summer, everyone still stunned by the riot. Rod grilled steaks on the patio and they ate at the picnic table with the family from next door. The neighbor was a stockbroker who worked downtown and bragged about the three guns he'd just bought in Ohio, a common practice in the suburbs of Detroit that summer. "Just let some nigger try to carjack me," he said. It was all Doyle could do not to pimp-slap the pudgy little fuck in the pink shirt with an alligator on his left tit.

After the guests went home, Rod took the girls up to bed and Kat fixed fresh drinks—she always seemed to be fixing fresh drinks— and brought them out to the patio. Fireflies were winking above the back lawn that rolled like a carpet to the edge of the lake. Kat handed Doyle his drink—Jack Daniel's, a couple of ice cubes—then she sat on the arm of his Adirondack chair. He was instantly uncomfortable. She started in with the music about how Rod was married to his job, not to her. Doyle was thinking she should get together with Vicki

Jones and start a sob sisters club. Just then he felt Kat's fingernails gently raking his right thigh, starting at the knee and heading north. She said, "You know, Frank, sometimes I think I married the wrong brother. I went for the responsible one instead of the cute one. I can't help but wonder. . . ."

He was rescued by his brother bounding out of the house, chuckling about something the girls had said upstairs. Kat jumped to her feet and strolled back to her chair. They never said another word about it because he never went back to the house. He realized, sitting there in the Plymouth, that of all the things he despised about the woman, the worst was that she'd taken his nieces out of his life on the night of that cookout.

He waited until the lights in two of the upstairs rooms went out. The girls were safe in bed and there was no longer any reason for him to sit there alone in the dark feeling bitter. If he wanted to have the girls back in his life, he realized he would have to figure out a way to get around their mother. It shouldn't be all that complicated. Like so many things, all you had to do was want it bad enough.

He found a Big Boy on Telegraph and picked at a slice of apple pie and drank half a dozen cups of coffee while reading the Detroit *News*. He was relieved to see that they'd played Alphonso Johnson's confession on the metro page instead of the front page, but they ran a long sidebar about the ongoing Helen Hull investigation with a picture of Henry and Helen in their aprons out in front of the old familiar Greenleaf Market, back before this city lost its mind. Doyle left his half-finished pie on the counter and headed back to Oakland Hills.

He found Bob Brewer sitting alone in Dick Kowalski's office reading *Time* magazine, his bow tie loose, his waiter's jacket unbuttoned. Handsome guy, but he looked tired. Brewer stood up when the detective walked in, shook his hand, looked him in the eye. Doyle decided to open the conversation on a genial note. "Dick Kowalski tells me you're the best waiter he's got on the staff, Mr. Brewer."

"He said that for real?"

"Scout's honor. You sure do put in some long hours."

"Yeah, these private parties tend to run late. Car guys, you know."

"Right, car guys. But you work hard even when you're off the clock."

"Sir?"

"You've managed to put together quite an impressive little real-estate empire."

Bob Brewer stared at the detective. "I can see you do your homework," he said, and there was an edge to the compliment. His way of announcing that he didn't appreciate having a cop snoop around in his private affairs. So much for the genial note.

"Just doing my job," Doyle said, giving him the bland smile.

"You know, it's a funny thing," Bob Brewer said, but he wasn't smiling. "For once I feel like the world's playing right into my hands."

"How's that, Mr. Brewer?"

"Well, you've obviously researched the public records. So you know I bought up most of that real estate in the past three years—and a bunch of it since the riot. I'm picking up nice pieces of property at fire-sale prices, so to speak. And you know why?"

"Cause whitey's heading for the hills?"

The man in the starched jacket smiled for the first time, and Doyle could see that he had beautiful teeth. Black people had the best teeth and the prettiest babies. "That's exactly right," Bob Brewer said, chuckling at the irony of Detroit's panicked real-estate market and at the detective's candor about such a delicate racial topic. "Cause whitey's heading for the hills. You happen to notice all those For Sale signs on my block?"

Doyle filed this away. If the man knew he'd already been to Normandy Street, then the wife had obviously called to alert him. Wise, wary people. Doyle respected that. "As a matter of fact I did notice the signs, Mr. Brewer."

"They're not my fault."

"Your fault? I don't follow you."

"You see, I'm no pioneer. I wasn't the first black man to buy a house on Normandy Street. I was the third. I waited and went in six months after the riot. Bought that big Tudor for a song. Like I say, the world's playing right into my hands."

"That's great, Mr. Brewer." Doyle could tell the small talk was loosening him up, so he decided to keep the ball rolling. "Were you born here in Detroit?"

"No, I'm from Alabama originally. Little town called Andalusia."

"Andalusia? Never heard of it."

"Nobody has. It's a little dot on the map bout halfway between Tuskegee and Mobile. Came up here when I was nineteen and never went back. Feels like I been here my whole life."

Enough small talk. Doyle cleared his throat. "Mr. Brewer, I need to ask you a few questions about your rental property at the corner of Pallister and Hamilton, the Larrow Arms." And with that, the oxygen in the room changed, went from cool geniality to deep frost. "One of your tenants, Mrs. Charlotte Armstrong, tells me something happened in the building on the morning of July 26th last year. That was a Wednesday, during the riot."

"You spoke with Mizz Charlotte?"

"Yes."

"She's a great lady, my dream tenant. But she's getting on in years—"

"She may be getting on in years, Mr. Brewer, but she's not blind and she's not deaf. She saw two black men get out of an older model car beside the building sometime after midnight that night. One was fat, the other was tall and thin. She heard them enter the building and climb the stairs to an upper floor. Then she heard voices coming from the rooftop. Then she heard gunshots. Nine of them."

Doyle waited for this to sink in, watching Bob Brewer's expression. So far, nothing. Doyle pushed on. "You know of any tenants from last summer who might've had an older model car? One with a red-and-black interior? Lots of chrome?"

Bob Brewer ran his fingertips along his jaw. His fingernails were shiny. Doyle supposed he was lining up his lies, for the First Commandment of homicide work is that everyone, absolutely everyone, lies. There were glints in Bob Brewer's close-cropped Afro, probably from one of those sprays the brothers use. Finally he said, "No sir, I'm trying but I can't recall anyone in that building last summer who drove an older model car. I'm sorry."

"Do you have a list of your tenants from last July?"

"Aw shit, Detective, people come and go so fast in that part of town. . . ."

"But you strike me as the kind of guy who keeps pretty good records. Cancelled checks, things like that."

"Oh sure. But a lot of people pay their rent with money orders, even cash. Some have leases, some don't. Some sub-let, some let friends stay. I've got too many tenants to know exactly who was where and when they were there."

It was time to shift gears. "Mrs. Armstrong tells me the fifth floor is kept locked, that tenants store things up there."

"That's right."

"And I assume you get to the roof from the fifth floor."

"That's right. There's two doors that open onto the roof."

"Any idea who has a key to the fifth floor?"

"I got one somewhere."

"Anybody else?"

"The super's got one."

"And what's his name?"

"Thompson. Anthony Thompson."

Doyle took out his notebook and wrote the name down, nice and slow. "Anthony live in the building?"

"Ground floor, right side."

"He a good man?"

"So-so. He drinks. Sells a little burial insurance on the side. I hear he did a little time once, but he seems to've straightened out."

"You know what he did time for?"

"Can't say as I do. But I spect you could find out."

"Was Anthony in the building early in the morning last July 26th?"

"I got no idea. You'll have to ask him."

Like pulling fucking hen's teeth, Doyle thought again, and it struck him as a shame that this city's—this country's—bad history was coming between Bob Brewer and himself, two men who, despite their many differences, wanted many of the same things. But Doyle had lived through enough to know that this country's history would always tell the same story. It would always tell the black man that the policeman was the enemy, and it would always tell the policeman to suspect the black man without giving him the slightest benefit of the doubt. Honkies versus niggers, till death do us part. Two armed camps, Doyle thought sadly, with the arsenals growing bigger, the distrust growing deeper, the future growing dimmer by the day.

"Mr. Brewer, you've been a tremendous help. One last question."

"Sure thing."

It was a longshot, but it was something Doyle and Jimmy had been toying with for weeks, and Charlotte Armstrong's story about the duffel bag made Doyle think they might be on to something. "Did one of your tenants at the Larrow Arms last summer serve in Vietnam, by any chance?"

At last Doyle saw it: the slight widening of the eyes, the flinch. He'd finally hit a nerve, and the longer it took for the answer to come back the more certain he was that it was going to be a lie. After a long while Bob Brewer said, "I'm trying to think . . . I can't . . . I can't think of anyone in that building who's ever been in the service. No sir, I'm sorry." Then the clincher: "Why do you ask?"

"No special reason." And now Doyle was doing the lying, and he knew Bob Brewer knew it. It was no secret that many of the guns used in the riots in Detroit and dozens of other American cities had once been used against the Viet Cong in Southeast Asia, then smuggled stateside and sold on the black market. For now, Doyle was satisfied that he'd caught Bob Brewer in a lie. He was convinced Helen Hull was killed by a Vietnam veteran who lived at the Larrow Arms and knew how to shoot guns accurately from great distances. Now all Doyle and Jimmy had to do was find the guy.

Half an hour later Doyle was lost in thought as he sailed past Northland shopping center on the deserted Lodge Freeway, headed back downtown. He did his best thinking alone in a car late at night. The light rain helped, the monotonous slap of the windshield wipers mesmerizing him just like the metronome used to mesmerize him during his boyhood piano lessons. Four years of that torture established that he had no musical talent, but it gave him enough of an ear to recognize and appreciate genius, from Chopin to Fats Waller, Brubeck and Brahms. Thinking of Chopin reminded him he needed to get back in touch with Cecelia Cronin.

Whap, whap, whap went the wipers, lulling Doyle, urging him to make a "pickup," something that would link two seemingly unrelated fragments of the Helen Hull story. It didn't help that he was still unsure exactly what this story was about, but at least his conversations with Charlotte Armstrong and Bob Brewer had convinced him there were pickups out there, waiting to be made.

He glanced at the vast empty Northland parking lot as he passed. Northland always made Doyle think of his old patrol partner, Jerry Czapski, who'd started moonlighting as a security guard at Northland a couple of years ago and made the front page of the papers when he broke up an armed robbery by firing a single bullet into the perp's brain as the guy was exiting Kay Jewelers with a sawed-off shotgun in one hand and a gym bag full of swag in the other. Czapski, known in-house as the worst shot on the Detroit police force, was famous for a whole day. Of course it went straight to his head.

And now, as Doyle splashed toward downtown, he couldn't get Jerry Czapski out of his head. Doyle spent his last two years in a uniform stuck in a radio car with the guy. Zap branded Doyle a nigger-lover the day he broke up an armed robbery in a party store without drawing his gun. Doyle talked the perp, a black hoops prospect from Pershing High School named Reggie Boyd, into laying down his shitty little pawnshop piece. "Only a nigger-lover would do a thing like that instead of shooting the little scrote," Zap said afterwards. Hell, Doyle didn't even carry a drop piece, which was more or less standard equipment among Detroit cops at the time, a spare weapon that could be planted on a dead or wounded man to make a bad shooting look good.

Those two years riding with Jerry Czapski felt like twenty. Every day he seemed to come up with a new ethnic slur. He started with the obvious ones—nigs, jigs, smokes, spooks, spades, darkies, coons. Then he went for the slightly more exotic—spics, yids, dagos, kikes, chinks, A-rabs, wetbacks, towel-heads, camel jockeys, micks, guineas. Whites from the rural South were hillbillies, rednecks, crackers, yokels, dirt-eaters, hicks and trash. He didn't shy away from his own kind, either—polacks, bohunks, no-necks. One day he wanted to pull over a car because it had Ontario plates. When Doyle pointed out that the driver hadn't done anything wrong, Zap said, "Yeah, but he's from *Canada*. What the fuck's he doing over here?" Looking back, Doyle realized Zap was an equal-opportunity racist. He hated the human race.

He told Doyle at least once a day that his dream assignment was pulling wheel duty on a Big Four, the scourge of the Detroit ghetto, a squad car with a uniform at the wheel and three plainclothes cops packing shotguns, tear gas and a ton of bad attitude. "Ain't nobody gives any shit to a Big Four," Zap said dreamily.

As Doyle passed the West Grand Boulevard turnoff, the one he'd taken to get to the Larrow Arms, his thoughts drifted back to his last night as Zap's partner. His promotion to Homicide had come through and he was counting off his last hours in a uniform, praying for a quiet shift. They were cruising west on Davison in a radio car, Czapski at the wheel. It was muggy for a spring evening, a lot of people out. Czapski turned left on Wildemere, taking it slow, drinking in every movement on the street the way he always did, hoping something would catch his eye.

"My, my, my, what have we here?" he'd said, letting off the gas so the car was barely crawling. A young Negro male had come hurrying out of an apartment building and climbed into a car and pulled away from the curb.

"What is it, Zap?"

"That nigger."

"What about him?"

"He's got out-of-state plates."

"So?"

"So how you suppose some jig from Alabama paid for that nice cherry Buick? Chopping cotton?"

"I wouldn't know, Zap, but something tells me you're going to find out."

"Damn straight I am." He turned on the roof flasher and pulled the Buick over.

Doyle stayed in the radio car listening to the murmur of call-out codes while Czapski went to question the driver. It was only after he heard Czapski berating the guy that Doyle got out of the car and stood with his hands resting on the roof. People were coming out of buildings, standing on porches, waiting. This had become a major Motor City spectator sport—watching The Man hassle the brothers. Doyle wished Czapski would hurry up. A woman on one of the porches shouted, "What the fuck he do wrong? Leave him be!" Doyle heard a bottle break. From where he was standing he could see the driver's right arm, long and brown, resting across the top of the Buick's front seat.

And now, sailing down the deserted Lodge Freeway in the rain, Doyle saw it, the memory as vivid as a snapshot: the tops of the seats in that old Buick were red.

When he got back to headquarters he went straight to the musty records cage on the second floor and woke up the night clerk and got him to dig out the run sheets from the first week of May, 1967. Run sheets recorded every move every cop made in the course of every shift. They were not always complete or in chronological order, and Doyle couldn't remember the exact date of his last shift. But he was convinced there was a pickup waiting for him in that stack of paper.

Three hours later he found it: At 6:43 P.M. on May 4, 1967, Patrolmen G.L. Czapski and F.A. Doyle, in Car 77, made a routine traffic stop of a 1954 two-door Buick Century at the corner of Wildemere and Tuxedo. After questioning by Patrolman Czapski, according to the run sheet, motorist was allowed to go on his way. No summons was issued. The driver's name was William Brewer Bledsoe. His local address in Detroit was the Algiers Motel. His home address was 2412 Greenwood Dr. in Tuskegee, Alabama.

Doyle made a photocopy of the run sheet and circled the driver's middle name and his hometown. He could hear Bob Brewer describing Andalusia, Alabama: *It's a little dot on the map bout halfway between Tuskegee and Mobile.*

It was too good to be a coincidence. It was a pickup to end all pickups, and Doyle was so excited he went up to the fifth floor and started dialing Jimmy Robuck's home number. But he caught himself before the connection went through. It was after three o'clock in the morning and he'd just worked an eighteen-hour day. The pickup would still be there tomorrow.

By the time Doyle got home the rain had stopped and the sky had cleared. He went into the back yard to check on his garden and was surprised to find that the tomato plants already came up to his waist and the corn was knee-high. Even in the weak moonlight he could see that the garden was in bad need of weeding. The breeze brought a whispered reproach from his mother.

He poured a snifter of cognac and lit a cigar and went out onto the front porch to watch the moon and listen to the dripping night. He could see the lights of huge freighters sliding past on the river, on their way to feed the beast that never sleeps. Doyle's father, fuzzy around the edges and a little milky, was sitting in the butterscotch La-Z-Boy recliner, his old TV chair. Before Doyle could say a word, his old man said, How come you haven't brought Vicki around lately?

Because she blew me off, Doyle said. Left a note on the fridge and disappeared while I was out late working a double at the Driftwood. Well, at least Herb Silver's happy now.

What do you mean?

I heard him talking to Effie from the kitchen window one night after he saw Vicki and me walk up these porch steps holding hands. I could hear him saying, That fucking Doyle kid'll never change. First he spends all his time in Ford Park playing basketball with the coloreds. Then he goes out dancing with them. Then he gets one for a partner. And now he's screwing one. Next thing you know we're gonna have a bunch of nappy-headed thugs cutting across the front lawn and stealing our hubcaps.

Herb Silver's an asshole, the old man said. Always bragging about how many ribbons he won for his roses and how much he paid for his new Cadillac. You gotta wonder about a guy whose front lawn looks like he trims it with scissors.

Doyle laughed. Good point, he said. Herb's been talking about putting the house up for sale ever since that black couple moved in at the end of the block.

Good riddance. Let 'em move out to Southfield where they belong.

Doyle told his father about the past few days—the conversations with Charlotte Armstrong and Bob Brewer, all those For Sale signs on Normandy Street, the Vietnam angle, the picture of the Hulls in the *News*, the pickup. He didn't mention that his brother's house was lit up like Christmas. No sense pissing the old man off at this late date. Doyle said, Henry and Helen looked so happy in that picture in the paper.

They *were* happy, his father said. Two of the finest people I ever met.

We've been dead in the water for ten months, Doyle said. And now, just like that, we've got a chance.

His father asked him why things always seemed to happen *just like that*.

Beats me, Doyle said. For all he knew, his old man was thinking about the way he'd died. One minute he's eating a meatloaf sandwich on the second-shift lunch break in the stamping room at the Rouge, the next minute he's face-down on the greasy concrete floor, already dead from a heart attack that would've taken down a bull elk. Doyle said, You know what I'm always saying about detective work.

Right. Luck and squealers.

So we finally caught some lucky breaks. We were damn sure due. Now if we would just hear from some squealers.

That would be nice.

Yeah, Pop, squealers are always nice.

11

STINGERS ALWAYS TASTED BETTER TO CHICK MURPHY AFTER A
Tigers victory. He was sitting alone at the bar in the upstairs mixed
grill at Oakland Hills, getting started on his second stinger and
replaying tonight's game in his head. The Tigers fell behind early
and were down 2-0 after six, then they woke up and beat the Red
Sox going away, 7-2. Beat 'em like a dirty rug.

"You know what I was just thinking, Cheech?" Chick Murphy
said to Chi Chi, who was rubbing clean glasses with a bar cloth and
swallowing a yawn.

"What, Meester Murphy?"

"I was thinking that this Tiger team is a lot like this city."

"How you mean?"

"Well, you can get 'em down and you can keep 'em down for a long time, but somehow they always find a way to bounce back. Those sonsabitches never quit."

"Berry true," said Chi Chi, who didn't know a thing about baseball.

"These late-inning rallies aren't doing a damn thing for my blood pressure, but they sure as hell are exciting to watch."

Just then Willie Bledsoe walked into the room carrying an empty bus tray and started clearing the last dirty table. Chick had liked the kid the first time he laid eyes on him. Like his uncle, Willie was hard-working, articulate, polite. He moved with the grace of a natural athlete. Kid was handsome, too, tall and fair-skinned, sharp-jawed, well-groomed. None of that greasy shit in his hair that Wiggins and some of the others used. Even that scar on his lip looked good, like he wasn't afraid to mix it up.

"Hey, Willie," Chick called to him, stirring his brain dimmer with his right index finger, then licking the minty fingertip. "You get a chance to listen to the game tonight?"

"Naw, Mr. Murphy, we got swamped. Heard we won, though. You go?"

"Yeah, a customer gave me a coupla nice box seats down by first base. I heard every cuss word that came out of Norm's mouth. I swear to Christ, that guy never shuts up—and he could make a sailor blush!"

This, as Chick had hoped, got Willie to stop working and walk across the room. Chick knew that Norm Cash was Willie's favorite player, which was another thing he liked about the kid. While the other black guys in the clubhouse tended to favor the obvious black players, usually Willie Horton or Earl Wilson or Gates Brown, Willie developed preferences based on subtle things, like Norm Cash's soft hands and quick feet, his way of coming up with hits at the right time. The kid understood the game, and he judged players by their ability, not their race. A week or so ago Willie had told Chick he played first base in high school and college, even got a tryout with the Houston Colt .45s. When Chick had asked him what happened at the tryout,

Willie said, "Nothing. I couldn't hit a big-league curveball if they hung it in front of me with clothespins. So much for my baseball career."

Now Willie said, "How'd Cash do tonight?"

"Norm looked good. He's going to be all right soon as he stops chasing those outside curveballs. He went three-for-four, with a homer. Drove in three runs. Turned a couple of slick plays in the field, too."

"So his batting average moved in the right direction for a change."

For a change. Spoken like a true Detroit fan, Chick thought, rapping the bar, his signal for Chi Chi to hit him again. Cash drives in three runs, plays flawless defense—and all people can talk about is that his batting average is nowhere near where it's supposed to be. That was something Chick loved about Detroit, the way the fans were demanding, sour, impossible to satisfy—and yet eternally loyal. They loved you but they didn't give you anything for free.

Another thing Chick liked about Willie was that he was all ears whenever Chick talked about the old Tiger teams. Most young people nowadays don't give a rat's ass about anything that happened before last Tuesday, but Willie seemed genuinely interested when Chick told him how he'd grown up worshiping Hal Newhouser, Mickey Cochrane, Schoolboy Rowe and, above all, the G-men. And Willie seemed to believe Chick when he predicted this was going to be a memorable season, maybe right up there with the two World Series championships he'd lived through, in '35 and '45.

As Willie went back to work clearing and resetting the last table, Chick thought about how the members of Oakland Hills sometimes grew attached to people on the staff, to favored waiters and bartenders, even busboys and caddies. Many of the club's members had had humble beginnings themselves, and no matter how rich and powerful they'd become, they liked to feel they were still in touch with the common man, still knew the taste of the salt of the earth. In a lunch-pail town like Detroit, it was important to remember where you came from. Chick Murphy started out washing Packards at a dealership on

Gratiot during the Depression, then graduated to shoving booze in his father's bar on Dequindre. And he wasn't going to let himself or anyone else forget it.

Thinking about how far he'd come, Chick considered asking Willie about his life back home, what it was like being a Negro in a place like Alabama, a place that might as well have been on the cold side of Mars to a guy who'd never traveled farther south than the Notre Dame football stadium in Terre Haute, Indiana. Chick reached for his drink, missed it—and almost pitched off the barstool.

"Meester Murphy," Chi Chi said, appearing out of nowhere to grab his elbow and wrestle him back onto the stool.

"Thanks, Cheech. Musta slipped. . . ."

"Is berry late. Maybe is time to go home?"

"Righto, Cheech."

"You are dribing?"

"Actually. . . ."

That was when it hit him—one of his brilliant ideas. He turned just as Willie placed the last water goblet upside-down on the table, gave it a final inspection, and started to remove his bow tie.

"Say, Willie," Chick called to him, "you think you could do me a huge favor?"

"Uh, sure, Mr. Murphy."

"You got a driver's license?"

"Yessir."

"You think you could run me home in my car? I really don't need to be driving." He rattled the ice cubes in his glass, surprised to see it was already empty. He would run his brilliant idea by Willie on the way home. "You can bring my car back here tonight—and my wife'll bring me by to pick it up in the morning."

"Uh, sure."

"If it's too much trouble I could call a—"

"It's no trouble, Mr. Murphy. I'm spending the night here anyway. Gotta work the lunch shift tomorrow."

"Well, then, I'll have a short one for the road and we'll go." He turned toward the bar but Chi Chi had vanished. "Ah, what the hell." He set his empty glass on the bar. "Let's roll."

Minutes later Willie found himself sliding behind the wheel of a 1968 Deuce and a Quarter, silver with a black vinyl top and black leather seats that smelled like sex itself. He could see there were only 67.8 miles on the odometer, which meant the car was a demo. Chick Murphy probably drove a different one every day.

"Take a right," Chick said, lighting a cigarette. They headed east on 15 Mile, the same route Uncle Bob had taken the day he took Willie for a spin in his new Deuce. It was well past midnight, traffic was light. "Go ahead and see what she'll do," Chick Murphy said. Then, seeming to read Willie's mind, he added, "Don't worry. If a cop pulls you, I'll do the talking. Give her the gas."

Willie eased his right foot down on the big accelerator pedal and the car gathered itself and broke into a gallop, a throaty, thrilling, groin-tingling gallop. He glanced at the speedometer and was astonished to see he was doing eighty-five.

"You like that pickup?" Chick Murphy said.

"Hell yes I like it, Sur—Mr. Murphy." He'd almost slipped and called him Surf. All the clubhouse staff, even the white guys, called him Murph the Surf behind his back because his glossy yellow hair could only have come from a beach or a bottle.

It was not that Willie and the other black guys on the clubhouse staff disliked Chick Murphy. He was not one of those members who told nigger jokes in the men's grill and then lowered their voices if a black waiter or busboy approached, thinking they were being discreet. If anything, the Surf tried too hard in the opposite direction, tried to be chummy in a way that made most of the black staff uncomfortable. Willie could remember the night when the Surf came down to the basement, drink in hand, and popped his head into the Quarters to see if anyone could use four tickets to an upcoming Tigers game. Someone turned the radio down. Waiters looked up from their craps games—what they called African golf—and the dice stopped flying. Everyone was obviously uneasy, and it got worse the longer the Surf lingered, trying to make small talk and act like one of the guys. There was nothing wrong with the gesture, it was just that he had crossed the invisible line and it was obvious he was unaware that the line even existed. Like so many white people, he assumed that good intentions—in this case, an offer of free baseball tickets—was enough. Watching him there in the doorway of the Quarters, feeling how tight the air had suddenly become, Willie thought of how his mother had drilled into him never to trust white people, especially the ones who profess to have good intentions. Racist peckerwoods were easy to deal with, she said, because they were so predictable; it was the white people with good intentions who will ambush you every time.

"You need to drop by the dealership," the Surf was saying as they sailed along 15 Mile. "Take a test drive. You look real sharp behind the wheel of a Deuce, if I do say so myself."

Deuce, Willie thought. White guys never talked like that. "Aw, Mr. Murphy, no way in hell I could afford a ride this nice."

"Take a left at the light, on Lahser. Money's no problem. What're you driving now?"

"The DSR."

"The what?"

"Detroit Street Railway. The bus. Or I catch a ride to work with my uncle or one of the guys."

"You mean to tell me you live in Detroit and you don't even own a fucking car?"

Willie thought of his '54 Buick parked out of sight in the garage behind his apartment. He considered telling the Surf the standard lie about the Buick's leaky Dynaflow transmission, but that would lower the car's value at trade-in time. Besides, there was no future in letting a white man know more about yourself than he needed to know.

"Course I got a car, Mr. Murphy. Matter of fact, it's a Buick—a mint-condition '54 Century. Restored it myself." The lie began to beget more lies. "It's in the shop for a tune-up is all. The mechanic working on it's slower'n molasses in January, says he's having trouble finding a set of points. So for now I have to catch rides with friends— or take the good old DSR."

The Surf launched into a spiel about some nice clean used Skylarks he just got in, but Willie didn't hear much of it. He was too busy enjoying the power of this Buick, how easy it was to handle. He could control it with his thumb. It was like driving a 400-horsepower stick of butter.

"Okay, easy does it," the Surf was saying. "Take your next right, on Long Lake."

They took a quick left after that, onto a smooth silver street that ran between the biggest houses Willie had ever seen. They were fortresses tucked back off the road, behind stone walls and tall hedges and thickets of trees, immense houses with four-car garages. Chick told him to turn up a driveway, a long serpent of blacktop that deposited them in front of a brick mansion with exposed wooden beams and a slate roof. The word Tudor came to Willie, and he thought of his mother's description of Uncle Bob's new house. That house would fit into this place's garage. Every light was burning, which made the house seem even larger, more unreal.

"Let's go see what there is to see," the Surf said, opening his door and lifting himself out of the car with a groan.

"You want me to come in?" Willie said.

"Sure. Why the hell not?"

Halfway up the sidewalk Chick stopped and put a hand on Willie's shoulder. His breath smelled minty. "Oh, say Willie, I almost forgot. I had an idea back at the club. You ever think about selling cars for a living?"

"Nosir, can't say that I have."

"Well, I could use a sharp young guy like you on my lot. Someone who can talk to, you know, to all kinds of people."

Willie stiffened. "You mean to black people."

"I mean black people, white people, rich people, working people. I get all kinds. And I'm sure you'd make a hell of a lot more money than you're making at the club."

"I don't doubt that."

"Well, give it some thought."

"Yessir, I will."

"I'm serious."

The front door was unlocked. Willie followed him into a slate-floored foyer, through an enormous dining room lit by a chandelier, then down a long hallway that led toward the back of the house, toward muffled music.

"Where the fuck is she?" the Surf muttered as he went. Then he cried, with too much joy, "Ah, there you are, Shug! I'm home!"

The woman sitting on the sofa was reading a magazine and smoking a cigarette. She looked bored and angry, like someone who'd been waiting for a bus a long time. She was a fading beauty with dyed blonde hair that was going black at the roots. She was wearing suede high-heels the color of burgundy wine. At first Willie thought her legs were bare, but then he realized she was wearing stockings. Flesh-toned, Willie said to himself. She put down her copy of *Town & Country* and took a pull from a glass full of ice and brown fluid. Chick Murphy turned down the stereo on his way to her. Willie recognized the music—that Herb Alpert chump with his Tijuana Brass. So this was the kind of swinging shit rich white people listened to. Smoke was leaking from the woman's nostrils. "So Chick, what possessed you to buy a gun?"

"Who says I bought a gun?" he said, pecking her cheek and tearing at his necktie. "This is Willie Bledsoe from the club, darling. Willie, my bride Blythe. Willie gave me a lift home because—"

"Because you're stone drunk, as usual. I say you bought a gun. I found it in your sock drawer this morning."

"I bought it . . . I bought it for protection." He gave Willie a sheepish look. "But mainly, Shug, I bought it because I woke up the other day and realized I've got to be ready to kill any man who tries to come between you and I."

"Between you and me."

"Oh for chrissakes, Blythe, lay off the grammar lessons already and fix us a drink, wouldya. Willie, you want something?"

"Nosir, I'd better be going."

He watched the woman rise from the sofa, shakily, to her full height. With the heels she was nearly six feet tall. She must have been a fox in her day. Still not bad, but the skin was getting leathery from the sun, the hair was kind of scorched looking, and the ass was widening under the tight silk skirt. He noticed that her legs were still good—a woman's legs are the last thing to go—as she wobbled over to the bar in the corner and poured from a crystal decanter marked SCOTCH. She picked up tongs and added two ice cubes from a sweating silver bucket. "You sure you don't want something— Willie, is it?"

"No ma'am. I really need to be getting back to the club." He took in the scene. Two people with more money than they would ever be able to spend, with a gun in the sock drawer, unable to speak proper English or act civilized in front of a stranger, listening to Herb Alpert while drinking themselves blind day in and day out, the bitterness between them growing like some malignant tumor. Again Willie thought of his mother—and how this scene would confirm every suspicion she ever had about white people, especially the ones with money.

The woman handed the drink to her husband. "You need to protect me," she said, "why don't you learn how to fight?"

He collapsed on the sofa next to her magazine. "I already know how to fight. I was Golden Gloves champion of Detroit when I was sixteen, case you forgot. Let's drop it. Have a seat, Willie."

He sat in an overstuffed chair facing the sofa. Through the large bay window he could see a lopsided moon hovering above their heads. Behind them the lawn ended in a distant stand of trees. Looking around, it occurred to Willie that this room was nearly as big as the house he grew up in. Yet the room somehow felt cramped, stuffed with too much furniture, too many lamps and vases and flowerpots, too many pictures on the walls, too many winking decanters. Willie sensed desperation in all this clutter.

The Surf gave his wife a recap of the Tigers game, which clearly bored her. Finally, when she gave out a big yawn he took the hint and drained his glass and stood up. "Willie's going to take my car back to the club, Shug. Can you give me a lift over in the morning to pick it up?"

"Sure." She accepted another peck on the cheek. Willie stood up and shook Chick Murphy's hand and wished him goodnight. Instead of going upstairs Chick stepped into the half-bathroom under the staircase and, without closing the door all the way, took a stance at the toilet.

While Blythe struggled to light a fresh cigarette, Willie glanced at her husband. As he was zipping up his pants Chick gave out a little yelp of pain, then struggled to free his dick from his zipper. It was all Willie could do not to laugh out loud. Witnessing a white man's distress—without him knowing it—was without a doubt one of life's most under-rated joys.

After Chick made it up the stairs, Willie turned to say goodnight to Mrs. Murphy. But she said, "Sit down, Willie. Let me fix you a quick drink before you run off."

What the hell, he thought. He was in no hurry to get back to the Quarters for the inevitable late-night poker game and sparring session with Wiggins and Hudson. "Thank you, Mrs. Murphy. I guess I could drink a beer if you've got one."

She went to the bar and leaned over to fish in the refrigerator. Her skirt rode up far enough to reveal the tops of her stockings, the clasps of black garters, creamy slivers of thigh. Willie felt a pleasant buzzing in his groin and wondered if she was giving him this show on purpose or was just sloppy from the scotch.

She brought him a bottle of Cinci beer. "You need a glass?"

"No, ma'am," he said, reaching for the bottle.

She didn't let go of the bottle. "Cut the 'ma'am' crap, would you? We're not at the club anymore. My name's Blythe."

He thought of the hippie girl Sunshine on Plum Street giving him the same command on Opening Day. He said, "The bottle's fine, Blythe. Thank you very much."

She released the bottle and returned to the sofa. Her stockings made a crackling sound when she crossed her legs. The Herb Alpert record ended, and to Willie's relief she didn't ask him to turn it over. "So tell me, Willie, where's your home again?"

"Alabama. A little town called Andalusia, down around Mobile."

"That's right. My husband's told me a lot about you. You're Bob Brewer's nephew, aren't you?"

"Yes."

"And didn't you go to college?"

"Just one year. A little less, actually. At Tuskegee."

"Tuskegee?"

"It's a black school in Alabama."

"Oh. Our youngest boy's playing football at Notre Dame. So why didn't you graduate?" She re-crossed her legs. That crackling sound again.

Three gulps and already Willie could feel the beer going to work, thanks to fatigue and an empty stomach. "Well, Blythe, that's a long story. The short of it is that I got caught up in the movement."

"The movement?"

"The civil rights movement."

"Really? Chick never said anything—how *fascinating*." She leaned forward, like she was actually interested. "I thought Dr. King was a remarkable man. Did you know him?"

"Wouldn't say I knew him. I met him a few times. Had some dealings with him." He heard the voice again, a complete sentence this time: *Man believes he's de Lawd hisself!*

"What all did you do?"

It occurred to Willie that this was probably the first time a black person—other than maids and caterers and furniture movers—had ever set foot inside this house. He took another drink of beer. "Mostly I tried to integrate lunch counters and bus stations, get poor black sharecroppers to register to vote. Stuff like that."

"Was it hard?"

"Damn near imposs—excuse me. Yes, it was very hard. Most of them were scared to death. And with good reason."

"Was it dangerous?"

"Sometimes, sure."

"Did you ever get, you know, attacked? Or beat up?"

"Few dozen times is all." He pointed at the scar on his lip. "I got this from a beating."

"Who beat you? Rednecks?"

"Depended on the day. Rednecks. Upstanding citizens. State police. City cops. National Guard, you name it. My lip was rednecks."

"How *awful*." She held a hand to her throat, and bracelets jangled on her wrist. "Of course I've seen pictures of the fire hoses and the dogs and all. But I've never met someone who actually got beaten. I can't imagine what it must be like to live down there. For a colored person, I mean."

He had half a mind to tell her it wasn't all that different from Detroit, but white northerners never believed this. Blythe Murphy was waiting, her eyes unblinking, and Willie realized she actually thought she wanted to hear the truth. He knew better. Very slowly he said, "Let me put it to you this way, Blythe. One of the first people I met in Detroit was this old black guy from North Carolina named Erkie. He told me something that's just now beginning to make sense to me. He said, 'Down South, everybody knows where the lines are drawn. Up here in the North you got to find out as you go along. They don't Jim-Crow you up here, but making a mistake in Michigan can get a black man killed just as dead as it can get him killed in Mississippi.'"

"And you believe that's true?"

"I know it's true."

"Well!" she said, sitting up straight and removing her hand from her throat. "Of course we've got our share of racial problems up here too. After what happened in Detroit last summer, that's no big secret."

He looked at the woman and thought, *You got no idea what happened in Detroit last summer.*

She changed the subject, started talking about how much she loathed golf and everything else about the country club set. She loathed cocktail parties and bridge and car talk. She loathed her father, who'd made a fortune manufacturing ball bearings and was convinced the Detroit blacks were getting ready to rape and pillage all of Bloomfield Hills.

Willie enjoyed her little rant. Halfway through his second Cinci, he was feeling pleasantly loose, his face aglow, and Mississippi and Martin Luther King and the riot were the farthest things from his mind. Just as he was beginning to sink into the folds of the chair, Blythe stood up. "I'm going to run you back to the club now, Willie. That way Chick's car'll be here in the morning and I'll be able to sleep in. Wait here while I get the keys."

"The keys are in the ignition."

"How do you know that?" She seemed flustered.

"Cause I left them there."

"Oh, of course. You drove Chick home. Let me freshen up real quick and we'll go."

He watched her cross the room, that ass, those sculpted legs. She was not walking in a straight line, and he wondered how long she'd been drinking. All day? All her life? He watched her go into the half-bathroom. Unlike her husband, she closed the door behind her.

Willie studied the room's clutter while he waited. There was even a gazelle head with corkscrewing antlers mounted over the fireplace. Had the Surf gone big-game hunting in Africa? Or was that a prop from some furniture store in Royal Oak?

"All set!"

Blythe was standing in the doorway holding a purse that matched her shoes. Her lips were a hotter pink than before, glossier.

He followed her out the front door and down the winding brick sidewalk to the Buick. Watching her ass sway in that silk skirt, it was all he could do not to reach out and give it a squeeze. *Watch it,* he told himself, *that's trouble you don't need.*

When they reached the car she hopped up and sat on the hood, a surprisingly nimble move for a woman who'd had trouble getting up off a sofa and walking across a room. She held out her hands.

"Come here, Willie."

He didn't move.

"Don't be afraid. Come here."

The bracelets jangled again—a noise so loud he was afraid it would wake her husband, dogs, the whole neighborhood. He felt himself being tugged into the cloud of her perfume, her whiskey warmth, and then her pink lips were on his. Her tongue darted into his mouth. When his cock began to stir, he tried to pull away.

"Come back here," she said, kissing him again, more greedily, tongue swirling, fingernails raking his back. He heard her shoes drop to the driveway, *clop, clop.*

It went on until he thought he would explode in his tuxedo pants. Finally she pushed him away. They were both breathing hard. "Let's go," she said, hopping down off the hood, opening the door and sliding behind the steering wheel. He walked around behind the car, wiping his lips with the back of his wrist, hoping this nightmare was over. His cock was aching. When he slid onto the passenger's seat she was wiping lipstick from her face with a tissue. At Lahser Road she turned right.

"Um, Blythe, I believe the club's to the left."

"I know where the club is. There's something I want to show you."

Willie was thinking how bad it would look if a cop saw them. But the streets were empty, the houses all dark. He tried to relax. She had forgotten to put her shoes back on, and he could smell the hot nylon on her feet mingling with her perfume and the car's leather upholstery. That smell doubled the ache in his cock.

After a mile or so she turned left, then right onto a narrow road that curved between tall hedges. He remembered all those late-night drives on Mississippi back roads with his headlights off, the gas pedal on the floor, his heart in his mouth. Those drives had seemed as dream-like as this one. The only difference was that now he felt dread along with the fear.

In the dash lights her face was green, but softer than it had been back in the house, prettier. When her hand brushed against his stiff cock, she said, "Oh my. . . ." Squinting, she slowed the car, then turned left through a gap in a barbed-wire fence and onto a dirt lane that led down to a small lake. She pulled into a thicket of trees and zipped down the power windows before shutting off the headlights and the engine. Crickets were singing. A bullfrog burped. Through the trees Willie could see moonlight wiggling on the lake.

"Isn't it lovely?" she sighed.

"It's very pretty. Where are we?"

"It's called Orange Lake." She giggled. "My boyfriends used to bring me here to make out when I was in high school."

Suddenly, with the same agility she'd exhibited hopping onto the Buick's hood, she slipped from behind the steering wheel and slung her left leg across his lap. Now she was straddling him, kneeling, and they were kissing again. "Grab my ass," she commanded, and he obeyed. The skirt rode higher, and he realized she was not wearing panties. She was very wet.

Her hands grappled with his zipper. She moaned as she guided his cock up into her, and then her head was banging the car's roof as she pumped him. It was all he could do to hold on, just hold on and try not to think about what he was doing. Try not to think about how good it felt and how hard it was going to be to live down, how impossible it was going to be to forget.

The first birds were singing as they rode back to Oakland Hills. Neither of them spoke. She shut off the headlights as she pulled onto the club's big empty parking lot. When she stopped the car, she put it in PARK but left the engine idling.

"Can I ask you something personal before you go, Willie?"

"Uh, sure."

"Was that . . . is this . . . you know, the first—"

"The first time I've ever been with a white woman?"

She nodded. He could smell leather and perfume, sex and sweat. Again he considered telling her the truth but instantly decided to tell her the lie she wanted to hear. "Yes, this is the first time."

"Me too. I mean—"

"I know what you mean, Blythe."

"And I loved it. Every minute of it."

"Me too, Blythe." And this time, though he hated to admit it, he wasn't lying. He'd loved every sweaty thrashing vulgar taboo minute of it. He'd loved her urgency and her hunger and her lack of shame. He'd loved hearing her curse as each orgasm came on. It was perverse perfection that she was married—to a former Golden Gloves champion who had a gun in his sock drawer and was *ready to kill any man who tries to come between you and I.* That may have been the thing that had turned Willie on most—crossing a line that could get him killed.

She kissed him one last time, and then he was standing alone in the parking lot watching the Deuce and a Quarter's taillights vanish into the blue dawn, not quite believing what he had just done.

12

BOB BREWER LET THE HOT WATER WASH OVER HIS SORE NECK and shoulders. He was dead on his feet, trying to shake off the cobwebs. Without his glasses he could barely read the labels on all the products lined up on the sink next to the Quarters shower stall. Royal Crown hair relaxer. Sulfur-8 scalp conditioner. Shavine depilatory. All the empty miracles that promised to make the black man less black.

Bob had taken the past week off work so he could devote all of his time and energy to cramming for the real estate licensing exam. Nothing else mattered. He was so focused he even forgot about the visit from the sharp-dressed Detroit cop who'd come out to Oakland Hills to ask all the wrong kinds of questions. If Bob passed the exam, he would finally be able to kiss the waiter's job goodbye. If he flunked. . . . No, that was not going to happen.

Yesterday, the day after the exam, he got a call from Dick Kowalski begging him to come in and work a big private party for the top hundred Chrysler salesmen in Michigan. Since he wouldn't know the results of the exam for two weeks, Bob decided it would be unwise to burn his bridges at Oakland Hills just yet. It was while he was dropping off his last tray of dirty glasses at the dishwashing station at 2 A.M. that Bob had heard the news on the kitchen radio: Minutes after being declared winner of the California Democratic primary, Bobby Kennedy was shot in the head by a lone gunman in the kitchen of the Ambassador Hotel in Los Angeles. When Bob heard the news he sagged against the dishwashing machine and sobbed.

Now the shower was going cold. Bob shut off the water and stepped out of the stall. As he was toweling off he thought again of Bobby Kennedy and he had to hold on to the sink till the urge to cry passed. He put on his glasses and boxers and plastic shower slippers, wrapped the towel around his neck and went out to get dressed.

He was surprised to see Willie on his bunk reading *The Confessions of Nat Turner* with a flashlight. Bob walked over to him and whispered over the gentle snoring of the men, "What up, Cuz?"

Willie's head jerked up from the pillow. "Uncle Bob," he whispered back. "What you doing up so late?"

"You mean so early. Had to work a private party that went into triple overtime. Caught a few winks and now I gotta go meet my lawyer downtown, sign some papers. You weren't here when I got up. Where you been?"

"Chick Murphy got drunk and asked me to carry him home. Let me drive his Deuce—even invited me in for a drink."

"How'd you get back?"

"His wife drove me."

"Watch out for that one!" Bob said with a chuckle. "I hear she shagged the golf pro. You just now getting back?"

"No, I . . . couldn't sleep. Went for a long walk on the golf course."

MOTOR CITY BURNING

Bob started dressing. "You hear the news?"

"No. What news?"

"About Bobby Kennedy?"

"What about him?"

"He got shot."

Willie slumped into the pillow, picked up his flashlight and went back to his book.

"You ain't even gonna ask what happened?" Bob said.

"Sure. What happened?"

"Some A-rab shot Bobby in the head. He'd just given his victory speech after the California primary—and the motherfucker shot him while he was walking through the hotel kitchen. I still can't believe it. I bawled like a baby when I heard the news."

"He dead?"

"Last I heard he was in surgery—critical condition. But you figure it out. Shot in the head isn't usually good news." Bob turned on his transistor radio and held it to his ear. After a while he shut it off and put it in his locker. "No change," he said as he finished dressing.

On his way out the door Bob remembered the other thing. He walked back to Willie's bunk. "By the way, Cuz, a Detroit po-lice was here last week asking me questions."

He watched as Willie snapped into the sitting position, then took a deep breath and eased his head back down onto the pillow. "What kind of po-lice?" Willie said.

"A homicide detective."

"He white or black?"

"White."

"Big guy with white hair and bad skin?"

"No, he was kinda thin, actually. Reddish hair, tall, dressed too good to be a cop, I thought at first. But he damn sure talked like a cop."

"What all he want to know?"

"All kindsa shit about that apartment building I own down the street from you. The one where Wesley use to stay."

145

"What about it?"

"Like I say, all kindsa shit." Bob leaned in, close enough to whisper. "Say, Cuz, how come you so interested in this detective?"

"I'm not interested, Uncle Bob. Just curious is all. You're the one brought it up."

"Bullshit. I stand here and tell you the next President of the United States has a bullet in his brain—and you go right back to reading your book. Then I tell you some honky cop stopped by—and you bout jump out your black hide. I'm holding on to my patience, Willie. What's going on?"

"Nothing, Uncle Bob."

"Don't lie to me, boy. Since when you know what color hair Detroit cops has got?"

"Since I saw one on the TV news the other night. Something about a murder during the riot. I thought maybe it was the same guy came out to talk to you."

There was a long silence, both of them trying to figure where this was going. Bob said, "Since you so curious, Cuz, he wanted to know if any of my tenants drives an older model car with a red-and-black interior and lots of chrome." Bob let that sink in good and deep before he went on. "He wanted a list of my tenants from last July."

"All your tenants? I mean, he know how many buildings you own?"

"He knows exactly how many buildings I own. He knows all kindsa shit. He just wanted to know about my tenants in the Larrow Arms. And he wanted to know who has a key to the roof."

"The roof? Why?"

"Cause he already talked to a widow lady lives alone on the second floor name of Mizz Armstrong. She told him she saw a shiny older-model car pull up under her window early in the morning last July 26th. That was during the riot. She saw two men get out—two black men, one fat, one tall and thin—then saw them come inside the building. Then she heard voices and nine gunshots coming from the roof. The cop didn't say so, but I'm guessing somebody died right about then, otherwise he wouldn't be asking so many questions. You hearing all this, Cuz?"

"Yeah."

"Did you drive Wesley home one night after curfew during the riot?"

"I guess . . . maybe . . . yeah, I did. Once."

"You got rocks in that nappy head a yours?"

"He was in trouble, Bob. He'd been beat up. Bad."

"Now here's the strange part. The last thing the cop asked me was whether any of my tenants in that building ever served in Vietnam."

This time the silence was so long and so deep that they could hear water rushing through pipes, could hear the building groan.

Finally Willie said, "So what you tell him, Uncle Bob?"

"Same thing I'd tell any cop—as little as possible."

"You didn't tell him bout my Buick?"

"No."

"Or bout Wes living at the Larrow?"

"No."

"Or bout him serving in Vietnam?"

"Hell no. But something tells me I haven't seen the last of that po-lice."

"Why's that?"

"Cause he's smart. He does his homework. And I could tell from his questions that he knows a lot more'n he's letting on. Now you listen to me, William Bledsoe. The more I think about this, the less I like it. If there's something you need to tell me—something I need to know—you better do it now. Fore that motherfucker comes back."

"There's nothing to tell, Uncle Bob. Honest. . . ."

"Suit yourself, but I'm going to tell you right now I don't like all these 'coincidences.' The car. Vietnam. Someone on the roof right after you and Wesley drove up—"

"That's all they are's coincidences."

"You be doing us both a big favor you tell me what you need to tell me right now so I know how to handle that cop. You know you can trust me, boy. I'm family. Now tell me if you and Wesley were up on—"

There was a roaring snort from the bottom bunk, then the voice of Edgar Hudson, thick with sleep: "Yallshuttafuckup."

Bob checked his watch. "I got to go. You think this over, Willie. And you think hard."

"There's nothing to think about, Uncle Bob."

"Don't feed me no more a your shit. I'm working the dinner shift tonight. We'll talk when I get back here this afternoon."

"I may be gone already. I'm working the lunch shift, then I'm off till Thursday."

"Then I'll call you at home. We going to talk."

13

AFTER BOB LEFT, WILLIE COULDN'T SLEEP. HIS MIND WAS jumping all over the place—from what his uncle had said about the detective, to Bobby Kennedy, to Blythe Murphy, back to the detective, back to Blythe Murphy. Sleep was out of the question, so he decided to go for a walk on the golf course, this time for real.

The grass was soaked from dew and the silvery jets of water shooting out of sprinklers. Willie left his shoes and socks under a bush and started walking across the miles of perfect grass. The sun hadn't come out of the trees yet, and the grass was squishy and cold on his bare feet.

As he walked, dodging the jets of water, he kept smelling his hands, smelling Blythe Murphy's perfume, their mingled sweat and sex. Her hair was brittle to the touch, unnatural, not quite human, but for that very reason even more mysterious and thrilling. Already the whole experience was beginning to seem like a dream, surreal now that it was over. But it was not a dream and it was not over and he knew it never would be.

He had spent his whole life being told that black people had to be above reproach, had to answer to a higher standard and be much better than white people if they ever hoped to be treated as an equal. Willie saw this in his Uncle Bob, the way he dressed and spoke and conducted himself. He saw it in his mother, her impossible standards, the way she insisted that her sons work harder, play harder, study harder and fight harder than other children, black and white, because she knew that nothing would ever be given to them and they would have to scrap like hell if they hoped to get a fraction of what they deserved. While the world urged Willie and his brother to make peace with mediocrity, their mother insisted that they aspire to excellence. Willie loved her for that.

Of course white women were off-limits. It was unthinkable that Beulah Bledsoe's boys could even want a white woman, for this was the very trap the white man wanted the black man to fall into, this was the final confirmation of the disdain that propped up the white man's shaky sense of superiority. To fall into the trap, Ma BeBe said, was to justify that disdain. Worse, it was to admit to a loathing of your own blackness. And that was the one thing she simply would not abide.

She used to tell her sons stories about working as a domestic for rich white people during her college years in Atlanta. Her employers were forever leaving cash and jewelry lying around the house. She understood why. They were baiting her. Tempting her. Testing her. Hoping she would steal so their stereotypes and their sense of superiority would remain intact. Ma BeBe took great delight in disappointing them.

And now Willie had done the very worst thing a black man could do. Yet as he walked across that rolling carpet of cold grass, he could sense something strange beginning to happen. He felt like a snake shedding its skin. He felt himself sloughing off the shame he'd been programmed to feel, and as it fell away he felt anger rising in his throat. He realized he was tired of being told what he was supposed to feel. How he was supposed to dress and act. Who he was supposed to follow. Who he was allowed to fuck. What had he fought for all those years? Why had he gotten his skull cracked, his lip split, his flesh burned? Why had he bled? So he would be free to live under a different set of rules?

But even as he tasted this anger, he understood it was a luxury he could not afford. He was a black man living in America. It was like living in a room without windows or doors, a room where the air is stale and unchanging. He knew there was no place in that room for an angry black man. Look what happened to Malcolm X. Better to keep your head down, go along, get by. When he was still in short pants he'd understood that the best a black person in the Deep South could hope for was a job teaching or preaching, maybe something with the railroad or the post office. His own parents were living proof of this fact. And now here he was up North, walking on a patch of pampered grass that existed for the white man's pleasure and the black man's continuing pain, working a menial job for The Man and despising himself for it, worrying himself sick about the police. Here he was, smelling the sex of a white woman on his skin—and, for the first time in his life, refusing to deny that he'd enjoyed his transgression. This refusal felt like the beginning of something immense. It felt like the beginning of a rebirth.

As he continued walking, he began to see that he was in an impossible predicament: His anger may have been a luxury he could not afford, yet it alone could set him free. His anger, more than anything in his Alabama box, more than anything he was likely to find in old newspapers and notebooks and photographs, was the key to writing his memoir. It was the key to everything.

He could see that there was a word for what he had to do if he ever hoped to be free. He had to *repudiate* the world that made him—his parents' world, the world of the movement, the world of the black striver—and then he had to learn to live by his own rules. That was the only path to true freedom.

He thought of the scene awaiting him back in the Quarters—the dice and the playing cards, the empty beer bottles and crushed cigarette butts of men who'd done what they had to do to make it through another night. As Willie had known for years, and as the author of *Black Like Me* discovered during his travels in the Deep South, those men understood that they had no options. They had to dull their senses with whatever was available and they had to laugh, had to laugh as hard as they knew how because if they ever stopped laughing they would start sobbing, and once they started sobbing they would be as good as dead. That would be the end of them, admitting how close they lived to despair. But at least those snoring men had never bought into the illusion that Willie once bought into and that his parents and his Uncle Bob still bought into—that education or religion or a change of scenery or political activism or the right president could possibly change the way their lives were destined to play out. There wasn't a romantic or an idealist among those sleeping men. Much as he loathed Hudson and Wiggins, Willie had to admit he admired their toughness and their fatalism. They reminded him of his Aunt Nezzie, the toughest and most fatalistic—the bravest—person he'd ever known. She knew for a fact that there would never be anything new under the sun, and that suited her just fine. She wouldn't dream of registering to vote or going to church, of admitting that some politician or some preacher or some new law might be her salvation. She had no desire to be saved. She was content to live by her own lights. Yes, Aunt Nezzie was the bravest person Willie had ever known.

Again he smelled his hands and thought of the lie he'd just told Blythe Murphy out on the parking lot. She was not his first white woman. Nancy Fegenbaum was his first white woman, his dark secret and, until this night, the source of a scalding shame.

Nancy Fegenbaum was a sophomore at Vassar, a stunning Jewish girl from Westchester County outside New York City, one of the volunteers who came south in droves from the best northern colleges for the Freedom Summer of 1964. Like most Snick veterans, Willie viewed these new arrivals as a bunch of anarchists, dopers and floaters.

He dismissed the occasional Negro among them as nothing more than a freedom-high nigger.

But Nancy was different. She truly believed they could change the world. She truly believed the races could, and should, live in harmony. She did menial jobs without complaint, and she didn't make fun of southern accents or boss people around the way so many of the northern students did. She was also a knockout with olive skin who wore her hair in long, thick henna-colored ringlets and believed a brassiere was an unnecessary encumbrance in the Mississippi heat. Willie couldn't take his eyes off her, and every time she caught him staring she gave him an asking look, followed by a smile. Never in his life had he gazed so brazenly at a white woman, and he found it both terrifying and thrilling. Thrilling because it was terrifying. Terrifying because it could get him killed.

They taught typing and American history together in one of the Freedom Schools in McComb, Mississippi. One day they got sent over to Alabama to post voter-registration drive flyers in and around Tuskegee. Such long-distance jobs usually fell to Willie because his Buick was one of the most dependable cars in the Sojourner Motor Fleet. After he and Nancy worked into the early evening posting the flyers, they decided it would be unwise to risk driving the 300 miles back to Mississippi in the dark. The three volunteers who'd disappeared while driving at night near Meridian were still missing. Willie suggested they spend the night in his apartment in Tuskegee, which was doubling as a safe house for Freedom Summer volunteers. There was no one staying there that night, and he offered to sleep on the sofa and let her have the bedroom.

Nancy was on him as soon as the door clicked shut. Willie didn't put up much of a fight, and neither of them did a whole lot of sleeping that night.

And neither of them said a word about it afterwards. In fact, Nancy hardly spoke to him at all the rest of the summer. He realized he'd performed his function and was no longer of any use to her. If he felt anger, it was at himself for allowing himself to be so casually used.

153

She'd flipped the tables and he never saw it coming. But his shame was real: he had taken the bait, he'd fallen into the very trap his mother had warned him about, the one the white man so badly wanted him to fall into. For reasons he never would have been able to imagine in the spring of 1964, he was glad when the volunteers packed up at the end of the summer and went back up north where they belonged. He had survived that bloody summer with nothing worse than a bruised ego and a guilty conscience.

Now, four long years after that night with Nancy Fegenbaum, he had finally overcome his guilt and his shame. He understood that this was a first step, a giant step, on the road to repudiating the world that made him. But even as he congratulated himself for taking this step, he could see that he had also stepped into yet another world of worry. Chick Murphy was not a man to fuck with. He was rich and powerful, he was white, and he had a temper and a gun. The thing that had been so thrilling to Willie just a few hours ago—the danger of being with such a man's wife—now looked like exactly what it was: stone craziness. Thrills, by nature, are fleeting things, but this one had not even survived the night. Willie had a terrifying vision of Blythe Murphy, in a drunken rage, screaming at Chick how much she adored Willie Bledsoe's black cock. . . .

He heard the chugging of a motor coming toward him. It was a member of the Oakland Hills grounds crew driving a cart full of rakes and tools across the golf course. It looked like one of those carts the traffic cops drove in Detroit. The sun was out of the trees now and the sky's blue was giving way to a harsh white glare. The coming day was going to be hot—not Alabama hot, but still hot and gummy. Willie turned back toward the clubhouse, keeping to the trees.

On the long walk back, he forced himself to quit thinking about Nancy Fegenbaum and the Murphys and start thinking about the bigger danger—the detective who'd visited his Uncle Bob. Willie took the visit as a sign. The cops knew a lot more than he thought they knew, and he had done almost nothing to cover his tracks. It was time to quit fucking around.

As soon as he got through the lunch shift today, he would get the Buick out of the garage and drive it to that Earl Scheib shop on Livernois and get a twenty-dollar paintjob. Then, on his next day off, he would drive to Murphy Buick and swap it for whatever the Surf offered. Just get rid of the damn thing.

After that he would have to sit tight and wait for his brother to call from Denver. He told himself that once he got rid of the Buick and found out what had happened to those last three guns, he would be in the clear.

Unless, of course, the cops were somehow able to prove that the unthinkable had happened that night on the roof of the Larrow Arms. That was still the one great unknown piece of this puzzle. That was still the thing that terrified him the most.

14

THE DAY AFTER HE TALKED TO BOB BREWER AND MADE THE pickup about the traffic stop, Doyle got sent out on a fatal stabbing at the Brewster projects. He didn't want to get distracted from the Helen Hull case—again—but fresh homicides always took precedence over old ones, so he followed Sgt. Harry Schroeder's orders and worked the Brewster case non-stop for a week, until he got a confession after grilling a scared teenager all night in the yellow room. After a few hours of sleep at home, Doyle walked into the squad room shortly before noon and went straight to the Bunn-O-Matic, yawning like an alligator.

"Whatsamatter?" Jimmy Robuck said, making a show of checking his watch. He had his white bucks propped on his desk and a big shit-eating grin on his face. "Couldn't sleep?"

"I was here all night working that Brewster stabbing. Got a confession a little after sunup."

"Congratulations. Whodunit?"

"Nobody you'd know. Fifteen-year-old kid with no priors named Cliff Robinson. A cousin of Smokey's, believe it or not."

"I believe it if you say it."

Doyle sat at his desk, sipping coffee. Jimmy was still beaming. Doyle said, "The fuck're you so happy about?"

"Come have a look."

Doyle walked over to Jimmy's desk, which was immaculate, as always. Only when he got close did Doyle see that there was something on the desk other than the telephone and the empty In/Out basket.

Nine pieces of shiny metal.

"Looky what I found," Jimmy said.

Doyle was staring at the pieces of metal like he thought they might jump up and fly out the window. "What is it?"

"Shell casings." Jimmy pointed to the three on his left. "These bad boys are thirty-aught-six, out of a Remington 700 with a heavy barrel."

"Where'd they come from?"

"Roof of the Larrow Arms. Same as the three in the middle— seven point six-two millimeter."

"How do you know all this shit?"

"Cause Sid Wolff told me so."

"You've already run them through ballistics?"

"Some people been workin while you been sleepin."

"Fuck you, Jimmy."

"And last but not least, over here on the right, we got us three thirty-cals out of a Winchester Model 70."

"Did you say thirty-caliber?"

"Is what I said."

"Jimmy, this is great!"

They had both read the Helen Hull autopsy report so many times they could recite it from memory, especially the faint ray of hope the medical examiner held out when she wrote that the fatal bullet was a .30-caliber and there was a possibility of comparison if the gun it was fired from was found.

"Now for the best part," Jimmy said. "According to Sid, all three of these types of ammo's got one thing in common. Care to guess what it is?"

"Goddammit, Jimmy, you know I don't know shit about guns."

Jimmy's smile stretched wider. "Sid says all three of these types of ammo's commonly used by military snipers in Vee-yet-nam."

"I'll be damned. How'd you get up on the roof?"

"The super let me up there. A brother name of—"

"Anthony Thompson."

Now it was Jimmy's turn to be impressed. "How you know that?"

"I went out and talked to the landlord last week, remember? He told me Anthony did some time, he didn't know what for. I'll check that out today. The landlord seemed to think he and Anthony are the only ones with keys to the top floor and the roof."

"Yes and no. There's only one key to the top floor in the building. Anthony leaves it on a nail in the mop closet downstairs, says everybody in the building knows about it case they want to get any of they things out of storage. Sort of an honor system. And the doors that let onto the roof have inside dead bolts, no key. So thee-retically anyone in the building can get out on the roof."

"Shit."

"It gets worse. Our man Anthony claims he spent the entire riot week at his cousin's crib on Burlingame, behind the Dexter Theater. Says they drank looted Johnnie Walker scotch like it was tap water, played cards, TV'ed it. Paid fifty cents a fifth for that top-shelf booze."

"His story check out?"

"Fraid so. Anthony's not going to be able to help us beyond what we already got from the roof. So how'd it go with the landlord?"

"Good question," Doyle said, yawning into his fist, sipping coffee. "He didn't give me all that much. Nice enough guy, but he's about as likely to help us as he is to join the Black Panthers, you catch my drift."

"I catch your drift. Man's all the way boor-zhwa-zee."

"Yeah. But when I asked him if any of his tenants had served in Vietnam, I know he lied."

"How you know?"

"Because it was written all over his face. I just know. I got some more good news. After I talked to him, while I was driving back down the Lodge, I remembered a traffic stop Jerry Czapski and I made last spring, my last night in a uniform—an older model car with lots of chrome and red seats, a lot like the one Charlotte Armstrong says she saw the night of the shooting. I looked up the run sheet and—you ready?"

"Course I'm ready."

"The driver's middle name was Brewer, same as the landlord's last name, and his driver's license had a Tuskegee, Alabama address. The landlord told me he grew up in a little town called Andalusia, halfway between Tuskegee and Mobile."

"You reckon the landlord and this Buick dude related somehow?"

"Don't know for sure, but I intend to find out."

"Where this Buick dude stay?"

"He gave Zap the Algiers Motel as his local address—"

"You mean the Desert Inn."

"Right. I'll swing by there this afternoon. I don't expect them to be able to give me anything, but I'll check it out anyway. Then I'll swing by the Tenth and have a chat with Czapski. I think I remember stopping a pink car, but I want to double-check it with Zap. At the very least I've got some more questions next time I go see the landlord."

Jimmy was nodding, taking it all in. "One other thing I forgot to mention. Sides the casings, there was some malt liquor cans on the roof. I got Anthony to padlock the door and told him not to let nobody up there. An evidence team's on the way over there now to dust the place, take pictures."

They could both feel it, the electrical charge that comes when a cold case suddenly gets a pulse. It was the kind of rush they lived for.

Jimmy got out a legal pad and they made a list of the fresh leads they needed to check out. They knew it was important to become very methodical now. Miss nothing. Play by the book. They knew that all of a sudden they had a chance.

As Doyle expected, the May 1967 guest log at the Desert Inn, formerly the Algiers Motel, yielded no guest named Bledsoe. Dives like that were why the name Smith was invented.

Next he checked out Anthony Thompson's criminal history, which was another disappointment. The super at the Larrow Arms was an undistinguished breed of bad-ass. His sheet contained nothing terribly sexy: a few drunk-and-disorderlies, aggravated assault, soliciting a prostitute, and six months at Jackson for breaking and entering. Not exactly the profile of a revolutionary Doyle was hoping for. Plus the guy had the air-tight Johnnie Walker alibi.

Doyle's next stop was his old stomping ground, the Tenth Precinct house on Livernois. He stood in front of the building in a warm, greasy drizzle and studied the modern, state-of-the-art piece of shit that went up during Jerome Cavanagh's first term as mayor. The walls were made of panels covered with gravel, like vertical slabs of somebody's driveway. Doyle was on hand the day the mayor cut the ribbon and proclaimed the building a fitting symbol of the city's progressive spirit, etc., etc., while every cop on the force grumbled that the money wasted on that building should have gone toward pay raises. If there hadn't been a pay freeze there might not have been an epidemic of "blue flu" on the eve of the riot, nearly a quarter of the police force out "sick" when the city could least afford it. But that was hindsight, and police work had taught Doyle there's no future in hindsight.

There were dozens of divots in the gravel facade of the precinct house, reminders that a bunch of drunk brothers had opened fire from the roof of the Earl Scheib shop across Livernois on the fourth day of the riot. Police stations and firefighters under siege by armed civilians. It had been a total breakdown, Doyle thought, a real civil war.

The staff sergeant behind the long counter today was an alcoholic tub of lard named Jimmy McCreedy, who'd spent the past quarter-century moving from one desk to another within the Detroit Police Department and was nearly ready to reap his pension and devote all of his time and energy to his Hibernian interests. Doyle could still remember standing in front of the J.L. Hudson department store on Woodward in a blizzard when he was ten years old, shivering, watching a pink-faced man in short green pants, a short-sleeved green shirt and a green bowler dance a jig in the middle of the street during the St. Patrick's Day parade. This leprechaun didn't even seem to notice that the snow was coming out of Canada in horizontal sheets and the temperature was in the single digits. That was Jimmy McCreedy for you, a man well acquainted with the wondrous power of 90-proof anti-freeze.

"Ladies and gentlemen!" boomed McCreedy's rich tenor now, a voice that made him a favorite in the handful of Detroit saloons where the singing of Irish ballads was still tolerated. "Come to us now, all the way from thirteen-hundred Beaubien Street in the heart of the Motor City—the fastest rising star in the history of Homicide, it's Francis Al—"

"Knock it off, Jimmy. How's tricks?"

He lowered his voice. "Fine, lad, just fine." The story was that when the snipers opened up on this building, Jimmy McCreedy was under the counter before anyone else was even aware they were under fire. "Might I offer you coffee, Frank? Or has our new line of work turned us into a tea drinker?"

"No thanks, Jimmy, I'm good." Doyle saw David Denekas, a Vice detective, shuffling through paperwork in the corner. Denekas had let his blond hair grow long, and he was wearing his shoulder holster over a paisley shirt, with bellbottom jeans and a pair of fancy white track shoes. Track shoes, for chrissakes. The better to chase down deviants? Denekas was one of the stars of Vice's cleanup squad, a true gung-ho street warrior. The cleanup guys spent the bulk of their time hassling pimps and their prostitutes and the prostitutes' johns, and they spent the rest of their time hassling homosexuals, who they called "browns." Despite his blue-collar jockstrap Jesuit upbringing, Doyle had never been able to work up the expected loathing of homosexuals. He believed that what people chose to do in the privacy of their own bedrooms was their own business. Besides, in this town there were bigger battles to fight.

"Who's the hippie with the gun?" Doyle said to Jimmy McCreedy. Denekas looked up and flashed Doyle the peace sign, then went back to his paperwork.

"Nice kicks, Dave," Doyle said.

"Thanks," Denekas said, admiring the shoes. "They're Adidas."

"What the fuck're Adidas?"

"Dave DeBusschere wears 'em!" he said, as though a certain brand of sneakers deserved to be bronzed simply because they were worn by the player-coach of the Detroit Pistons, a basketball team that always finished a couple dozen games out of first place and then got bounced out of the playoffs in the first round. "They're leather," Denekas added, admiring them some more.

Doyle still owned the last two pairs of canvas Chuck Taylor Converse All-Star high-tops he'd worn during his senior year at U. of D. High, white for home games, black for away games. Now they were making sneakers out of leather. When the brothers got hip to this, Doyle told himself, a pair of canvas Chucks will be about as prized as Aunt Jemima's head scarf.

"Is Zap working today?" Doyle said to Jimmy.

"He's in the back doing paperwork. You know how Zap loves his paperwork."

"Do I ever." Doyle went down the long corridor to the last room and found Jerry Czapski sitting at the battered Royal typewriter in the corner, chewing on a pencil and tapping out a report with his thumbs and stubby index fingers. The scary thing about Czapski was that he was more proficient with a typewriter than he was with the

.38-caliber Smith & Wesson strapped to his hip. Doyle still thought it was a miracle that Zap nailed that armed robber at Northland with a single shot.

"You take a speed-typing course?" Doyle said, sliding a chair up to the desk.

Czapski blinked, then broke into a big toothy smile. Doyle had forgotten how thick his lips were, how thick the flesh on his face was—how meaty the man was. He stuck out his right hand and gave Doyle a crusher handshake. "Hey pardsie, how they hangin?"

"Fine, Zap. What you working on?"

"Christ." He passed a hand over the bristles of his crewcut. "They're breaking my stones over that thing at Cobo—you know, that fucking Poor People's March? I got called in on it and I was there when the mounted guys charged the crowd, knocked a few people around. All we were trying to do was get a stalled car out of the way and now the NAACP and all the big niggers like Reverend Cleage are hollering police brutality."

"All the fun's gone, eh Zap?"

"You said it, brother. So what's up with you? Nice suit."

"Thanks, Zap. Coming from a clothes horse like you, that means a lot. I'll be sure to tell my tailor."

Czapski actually blushed, for even among members of the Detroit police force he was known as an atrocious dresser, partial to the white-belt-with-white-shoes combo known as the full Cleveland. Doyle took the photocopy of the run sheet out of his pocket and set it on top of Czapski's pile of paperwork.

"Take a look at this, Zap. Tell me if it rings any bells."

Czapski's lips moved as he read the run sheet. He was frowning, a bad sign. No light bulb blazed inside the thick skull. "Jeez," he said at last. "We jacked up so many smokes together back in the old days. . . ."

Yes we did, Doyle thought sadly. "Try to think, Zap. This one was different. Our last night together, we were heading south on Wildemere—you were driving, warm evening, lot of people out—and you said you didn't like the looks of a young black guy getting into a cherry old Buick with out-of-state plates. You were wondering where he got the money to pay for it. . . ."

"Ohhhhhh, sure," Czapski said, like a kid who'd just solved a difficult math problem. "Now I remember. Spade looked a lot younger'n he was. I figured him for a teenager but his license had him somewhere in his mid-twenties, as I recall."

"Anything else?"

"Yeah." He chuckled. "I remember when he reached for the glove box to get his registration, I gave him a little love tap on the side of his head with my flashlight. Told him not to pull out no gun on me. Just fuckin with him, you know."

"Yeah, Zap, I know. You remember what he looked like?"

"Like I say, young looking. Smooth skin, not too dark. Handsome enough kid. Looked like he coulda been a backup singer at Motown."

"You think you could pick him out at a show-up?"

"I dunno, Frank. It's been more than a year. And jigs all look alike to me."

"But you'd be willing to give it a shot?"

"Sure, if you asked me to. I can't make any promises, though."

"I understand, Zap."

"You want me to come downtown now?"

"No no, not just yet. I'll let you know if I need you. One last thing. You happen to remember what color the car was, the exterior?"

"Yeah, it had a two-tone paintjob—pink in the middle, with a black roof and black beneath that chrome strip that runs along the side of old Buicks. I remember asking the kid was he a pimp since he drove a car the color of pussy. Then I asked him was he a homasexual."

"He gave the Algiers as his local address. He say anything about having a roommate?"

"Not that I recall."

"Thanks, Zap." As Doyle stood up to leave, a young black uniformed officer walked into the room. Czapski looked up at him. "Jerome! Come over here and meet your predecessor. This is the legendary Frank Doyle. Frank, this is my new partner, Jerome Wright. He was an All-City guard at Cody. Averaged nineteen a game."

Jerome Wright gave Doyle a firm handshake, looked him in the eye. "Pleasure to meet you, detective. Heard a lot about you. You were All-City at U. of D., right?"

"A hundred years ago."

Jerome Wright smiled. The kid could have been a movie star. So the department's much-ballyhooed campaign to hire more black officers was finally paying off, and here was living proof. About time, Doyle thought. When the riot broke out the department was ninety percent white and one hundred percent blue-collar ass-kicker. Even the black cops, guys like Jimmy Robuck, made no apology for their allegiances or their methods. In fact, more than a few black suspects learned the hard way that they were better off taking their chances with polacks like Jerry Czapski and micks like Frank Doyle than with brothers like Jimmy Robuck. But the times demanded change—or the appearance of change—and so the department was beating the bushes for black recruits. Doyle said, "You're a lucky man, Jerome."

"I am, sir? How's that?"

"You're learning your craft at the knee of a true master. They don't make 'em like Zap anymore."

"No sir."

Doyle laughed all the way back to downtown. The irony was simply too beautiful: One of the worst racists on the force was now spending his working days trapped in a radio car with a member of the one race he despised above all the others. Let the punishment fit the crime. Doyle believed it was racist cops like Czapski, as much as any other single factor, that explained the fury of last summer's riot. The brothers were sick and tired of being called "boy" and "honey baby" and worse. They were tired of getting stopped for no reason, getting love taps from police flashlights, getting their justice served up in alley court. And now, as the department scrambled to recruit black officers, Jerry Czapski, of all people, had wound up riding with a black partner.

The world, Doyle thought, was truly a perfect place.

While talking to Caldwell Petty, the chief of police in Tuskegee, Alabama, Doyle imagined Rod Steiger sitting at a desk chain-smoking cigarettes and sending gouts of tobacco juice into a Maxwell House coffee can while the blades of a ceiling fan chopped the foggy air. Doyle wondered why so many Southerners had last names for first names. His second case during the riot was a yokel from east Tennessee named Wilson Lee Pryor who rode the Hillbilly Highway straight to a job on the line at Dodge Main and wound up getting shot six times on the roof of the Kentucky-Tennessee Apartments on Alexandrine because a half dozen National Guardsmen and cops, including Detective Frank Doyle, mistook him for a sniper. It turned out Wilson Lee Pryor had gone up on the roof of his building to watch for flying sparks from a nearby fire. But he was carrying a deer rifle for protection and now the poor dumb hick was dead.

"What can I do ya for, Detective?" came the gravelly voice of Caldwell Petty over the long-distance wire.

"I'm trying to run down some leads on a murder case," Doyle said. "You ever have any dealings with a young man named William Brewer Bledsoe?"

"Sho nuff have. He goes by Willie. This have something to do with that trouble yall had with yo Nigras last summer?"

"Looks that way."

"I figgered as much."

"How come?"

"Cause that boy ain't nothin but trouble."

"How do you mean, trouble?"

"Well, he come up here to go to school from some little piss-ant town down south a here, Troy or Opp. Can't rightly remember. Soon as he got here he started raisin sand—sat down at the lunch counter at the Sanitary Cafe, which was segregated at the time. That woulda been about nineteen and fifty-nine, maybe sixty, in there. Then he put some foolish sign on the lawn of the university's president. Can you imagine that? Some uppity little nigger accusing the president of Tuskegee Institute of being a Uncle Tom!"

"Amazing. Anything else?"

"Eventually he run off and joined that Student Nonviolence outfit. Tried to get ill-lit-rit Nigras to register to vote, such foolishness as that. I'm here to tell ya, Detective, we got some of the finest Nigras anywhere in the South right here in Tuskegee, Alabama, yessir. Folks get along here—or they did till uppity niggers like Willie Bledsoe come along."

"He ever get into any serious trouble?"

"Not here. I heard tell he was on that bus got fire-bombed outside Anniston. Too bad they didn't cook his ass. Happiest day of my life was when him and that worthless brother a his packed up and left for D-troit. They had a big send-off party night before they left."

"He has a brother?"

"Better believe it. Ornery sumbitch, name of Wes. He was with the Navy in Vee-yet-nam and something musta happened to him over there. That boy ain't right."

Doyle was scribbling in his notebook, trying to keep up. Again he said, "How do you mean?"

"Well, he just ain't right. Lazy as the day is long. Just pure-T worthless. All he ever done round here, so far's I can tell, was watch TV, drink beer and shoot guns."

"Guns?"

"Yeah. Way I heard it, him and his brother used to go out into the woods for a little target practice."

"What kind of guns they have?"

"Beats me."

"Any idea how many? Or where they got them?"

"Nosir."

"Weren't you curious?"

"Nosir. Most folks round here's got guns."

"Do you know where Wes is now?"

"Can't say as I do. All I know is that I haven't seen his black face in this town in over a year—and that suits me just fine. Wes Bledsoe's the kind that'll explode on you. Believe me, I seen it happen more'n once."

"How about Willie?"

"Ain't seen him neither. He could still be in D-troit for all I know. The folks at Tuskegee Institute—that's the Nigra college here in town—they could probably help you find his homeplace. Like I say, it's one a them little piss-ant towns down south somewheres."

Doyle wrote down the phone number for Tuskegee Institute, then thanked the chief and hung up.

Caldwell Petty's mention of guns reminded Doyle of the coroner's words about the fatal bullet—the possibility of comparison if the gun it was fired from was located. Doyle knew that the likelihood of finding that gun, almost a year after the murder, was slim to nil. Yet he was encouraged. The pieces were beginning to fit. Suddenly he had an angry young man and an unhinged Vietnam veteran. They were both able to put their hands on guns. And, best of all, they both knew how to use them.

Doyle crossed *Tuskegee Police* off the list on the yellow legal pad and added *U.S. Navy*. Then he reached for the telephone and placed a call to Tuskegee Institute. Five minutes later he was dialing another long-distance number, this one at the home of the Rev. Otis R. Bledsoe in the little piss-ant town of Andalusia, Alabama.

After going back to the kitchen three times to fetch a fresh beer, Doyle put four cans in a sack and took it out to the front porch and set it down next to the half-empty fifth of Jameson's. He didn't want to waste any more time walking back and forth to the kitchen. He wanted to finish getting drunk and telling his father about his day.

Where was I? Doyle said, re-lighting his cigar and cracking open a beer.

That Bledsoe woman, his father said. The one in Alabama.

Right. So it's obvious she isn't thrilled to hear from me.

How could you tell?

Because no black person in this country welcomes a call from the police. Who can blame them? There's only one kind of news it can be.

So what'd you say to her?

Small talk, at first. Asked her what she did for a living and she gave me a long speech about teaching history at Washington High School—which was not named after our slave-owning first president but after *Booker T.* Washington, I'll have you know—and how the school was much better before integration, when it was all black. She said as far as she's concerned, N.A.A.C.P. stands for the National Association for the Advancement of *Certain* People.

That's a good one, the old man said. Never heard that one before.

Me neither. Once I had her softened up, I started with the lies. I told her we were investigating a car-theft ring. Then after a lot of bullshit I got her to tell me that William Brewer Bledsoe is her son and that he drove his pink-and-black Buick to Detroit in the spring of last year with his brother Wes, who was a Navy SEAL in Vietnam.

I thought you already got all that stuff from the police chief.

Yeah, but I needed to confirm it. Then I got her to tell me that Bob Brewer is her brother, and that Willie works with him at Oakland Hills, which was news to me, and that her son Wes was living in brother Bob's Larrow Arms building last summer on the night Helen Hull died. Which was also news to me. Very good news.

You guys are sure the killer fired from that roof?

We're ninety-nine percent sure. Having a murder weapon would be nice. But. So I asked Mrs. Bledsoe where William bought his Buick and she said it was a gift from a friend of his brother's, a Navy buddy, a white guy who owed Wes some kind of favor. She said the buddy and his wife drove up to Willie's place in Tuskegee one day and just handed over the keys and title, free and clear. She said she'd never heard tell of such a thing—that white people in that part of the world aren't in the habit of giving cars to Negroes. I told her they aren't in the habit of doing it in this part of the world either.

Got that right.

She actually laughed. That's when I decided to go for broke— asked her if her sons owned any guns. The frost that came out of the receiver damn near froze my ear off. 'For your information,' she told me, 'my son William has been afraid of guns since he was a boy.' So I asked if she knew if Wes had brought any guns back from Vietnam. That did it. She told me, in case I didn't already know it, that men in the U.S. military are required to surrender their weapons when they're discharged from the service and that she raised her sons to obey the law and furthermore she resented the implication that one of her sons, a decorated war veteran, a hero, would even consider doing something so flagrantly illegal. She said she had to cut the call short. She had a meeting to attend. Which was even lamer than the bullshit I'd been feeding her.

Can you blame her?

Hell no. That's the whole point, Pop. I hate myself for what I'm about to do to that woman. She's obviously decent—articulate, edu-cated, hard-working. And I'm getting ready to stick it to her—or to her sons, which is the same thing. I felt the same way after I talked to her brother Bob.

Frank, quit beating yourself up. You were doing your job. Don't forget what happened to Helen Hull.

Yeah, but like you and Mom were always saying, two wrongs don't make a right. Lying to a decent woman like that is flat wrong.

Screw that. You made a promise to your mother and me—and to yourself. You promised to find Helen's killer if it's the last thing you do.

And I'm going to do it.

No matter what?

No matter what.

Good boy.

They were quiet for a long time, Doyle puffing his cigar, chasing whiskey with beer. When the beer was gone, Doyle put the cork back in the whiskey bottle and stood up. He said, I gotta run.

Run? It's almost midnight—and you're half in the bag.

Yeah, but there's somebody I need to talk to.

Well, be careful. This is no time get popped for drunk driving.

I'm not going far—and I'll be careful.

You better be. You still got a killer to catch.

15

THE DINNER RUSH AT OAKLAND HILLS THAT SATURDAY NIGHT was one for the ages. As soon as the busboys got a table cleared, a fresh party sat down, wave after wave. Willie worked in a daze, like a robot on bennies.

At the peak of the rush, while he was shoveling dirty dishes and glasses from his tray onto the dishwasher's conveyor, Willie felt a tap on his shoulder.

"Got some news for you, Cuz." It was Uncle Bob.

"Can it wait? I got four dirty tables to bus and Kowalski's been on my ass all night."

"Fuck Simon Legree. This is important. I stopped by this morning and had a chat with Mizz Armstrong—you know, the widow lady lives in the building where your brother use to stay? The one I told you talked to the po-lice?"

"Yeah? And? Make it quick."

"Turns out I was right about that detective."

"How so?"

"He's smart, all right. He didn't tell me everything he knew. I found out from Mizz Armstrong why he was so curious about an older model car with a red-and-black interior and lots of chrome."

"Why's that?"

"Cause she not only saw the car pull up under her window one night during the riot—she saw two men take a duffel bag out the trunk. That detective didn't say nothing to me about no duffel bag. Then Mizz Armstrong told me she saw the two men come into the building, heard them walk upstairs, then she heard voices coming from the roof. And gunshots. This is what she already told the po-lice, Cuz."

Willie didn't say anything.

Bob leaned in closer. "What was in that bag you took out the trunk?

Willie thought of his Aunt Nezzie. He knew he had to choose his next words with great care and remember them. "I didn't take nothing out the trunk, Uncle Bob, and that's God's honest truth." And indeed it was, technically.

"I sure as hell hope so. For your sake." Bob gave him a look that was hard to read—part accusation, part fear. As Willie turned to go, Bob said, "Your momma called me yesterday."

"How's Ma BeBe?"

"Not good. That cop called her too."

"In Alabama? Damn."

"Fed her some jive about investigating a car-theft ring—then asked her if you or Wes ever had any guns—"

Just then Dick Kowalski burst into the kitchen and barked at Willie to get back out on the floor and bus those dirty tables. The Murphy party was waiting.

Willie spent the rest of the night in a fog, replaying his conversation with his uncle over and over. At the end of the night, he made a point of bumping into Chick Murphy as he headed for the men's room. They made an appointment for Willie to visit the dealership on Monday morning.

As the Murphy party was leaving the dining room, Blythe Murphy, her eyelids at half-mast, slipped a piece of paper into Willie's jacket pocket. He went into the kitchen to read it in private. It was a phone number and the command CALL ME!!! As Willie tore the note into tiny pieces and let them float like confetti into the trash, he saw that his hands were trembling.

President Johnson declared Sunday a national day of mourning for Bobby Kennedy, and there was a minute of silence before the first pitch of that afternoon's game between the Tigers and the Cleveland Indians.

Standing in the centerfield bleachers, dressed in his T-shirt, denim overalls and brogans, Willie bowed his head along with Louis Dumars and Clyde Holland and more than 31,000 other fans. As the seconds ticked by, Willie heard the white man in front of him mutter to his wife, "Ain't this some shit. Martin Luther Coon gets killed and they postpone the season opener two whole fucking days. Bobby Kennedy gets killed and he gets one lousy minute of silence. You mind explaining that to me?"

His wife hissed, "Shut up, Roland."

"I mean, they arrested a white guy in London yesterday for killing King, didn't they? What more do these people want?"

She turned her head enough to see the three large black men standing behind her. "Shut up, Roland! You're gonna get us both killed!"

Though the game was a thing of beauty that featured crisp pitching, a pair of Norm Cash home runs, close plays at the plate, even a rhubarb that got the Tigers' testy manager, Mayo Smith, ejected, Willie couldn't concentrate on any of it. He lost track of who was batting, the ball-and-strike counts, the score. He didn't even hear much of the banter between Louis and Clyde, who were in unusually high spirits today. Willie was too busy retracing his steps, going all the way back to his first days in Detroit. He needed to remember everything and start lining up his lies, get himself ready for the inevitable.

". . . I ain't sayin she ain't a fox!" Louis Dumars was practically shouting. Willie realized his friends had been drinking two beers to his one and they were beginning to get right.

"Course she's a fox," Clyde said. "All my clients is foxes."

Willie finished his lukewarm beer and crushed the empty cup. He motioned for a beer vendor and bought a fresh round. "What're you two bellerin about?"

"A client a mine," Clyde said.

"What about her?"

"What about her? Where you been, Alabama?"

"Sorry . . . been watching the game."

Suddenly everyone was rising in unison. It was the bottom of the ninth inning, two outs. The Tigers were trailing the Indians, 4–3, but they had runners on first and second as Mickey Stanley stepped to the plate. He swung at the first pitch, and it was a full second before Willie heard the crack of the bat and picked up the ball, a little white bullet coming straight at him. His voice joined the rising roar.

The roar grew hoarser, wilder, louder as the ball kept coming. The Cleveland centerfielder, Jose Cardenal, was sprinting toward the wall but Willie could see that he would never catch up with the ball. The runners were white blurs wheeling around the bases and then the ball disappeared from Willie's field of vision and there was a moment when the roaring seemed to stop. After a long silence the ball sailed back toward the infield like a wounded bird. Mickey Stanley was already standing on second base. Two runs had scored and the Tigers had won their fourth game in a row, 5–4, winning it on their last at-bat, which was becoming this implausible team's implausible trademark.

Louis and Clyde were so elated by the Tigers' dramatic come-back—and by the half dozen beers they'd each consumed—that they insisted on taking Willie out for a celebratory nightcap. They had a place in mind up on Woodward. Clyde rolled back his Deuce's convertible top and got WJLB on the radio. Sprawled on the Buick's back seat, drinking in the music and the balmy afternoon, Willie watched the trees flash overhead and tried to forget his worries. They were on a street that looked vaguely familiar. At the next corner he checked the sign—they were on Dexter—and after a couple more blocks he saw it coming up on his right, the Dexter Bookstore. A big poster of Malcolm X filled the front window, but Willie didn't see Edgar Vaughan or any signs of life inside the store.

Edgar Vaughan was the Bledsoe brothers' second-to-last customer on their gun-selling spree when they first hit Detroit last spring. They did business in apartments, bars, stores, garages, barbershops and car lots, even in a couple of mosques and churches. Their customers wore berets, dashikis, smocks, box-back suits, greasy overalls, sharkskin, military camouflage and olive drab. They sold everything from books to burial insurance to used cars to Jesus. They ran numbers and they ran dope. They ranged from menacing to pathetic, from street toughs to dime-store Marxists, but they all had one thing in common: They all yearned to shoot white people, preferably cops.

Edgar Vaughan had led Wes and Willie into his cramped office at the back of the bookshop, where he served them coffee and half an hour's worth of quotations from Lenin and Chairman Mao and Malcolm X. Vaughan wore an Afro that had never been touched by a pick. He had a could-be-twenty, could-be-forty face, and when he ran out of rhetoric he asked Wes and Willie if they'd caught Rap Brown's speech at the Black Arts Conference. The brothers shook their heads. They'd been too busy selling guns.

"The cat was very right-on," Vaughan said. "Got up there on the stage and said, 'Motown, if you don't come around, we gonna burn you down!' Place went crazy. I'm tellin you, my brothers, this city's a tinderbox—and all it's waitin for's a match."

"A tinderbox," Wes said, shooting Willie an amused look. "And who got the match?"

"I believe you got the match right there, my brother." Vaughan motioned at the duffel bag on the floor between Wes's feet.

"Ahh, of course," Wes said, unzipping the bag and removing the pieces of a Winchester Model 70 rifle and laying them on the desk.

"That a sniper's rifle?" Vaughan said.

"Thas right. For brothers who don't like to be in the same zip code as the honky they fixin to shoot."

Willie watched Vaughan's eyes get big as dinner plates while Wes snapped the gun together with crisp, expert movements. Willie guessed Vaughan had never held anything more dangerous than a copy of Mao's little red book.

"You want a scope too?" Wes asked, laying the assembled rifle on the desk.

Vaughan was staring at the gun like it was a poisonous snake. "How much?"

"Six for the gun, two for the scope. Them's fire-sale prices."

"What kind of scope goes with it?"

"All I got left's a Unertl."

"It any good?"

"The best. Good up to a thousand yards. Had a tendency to fog up in the jungle in Nam, but it shouldn't give you no trouble if you plan to use it in D-troit."

"I plans to use it in D-troit."

"Then you all set. That'll be eight hundred."

Driving away from the bookstore after making the sale, Wes pounded the Buick's dashboard and roared, "Could you believe that nigger? All that shit about revolution and tinderboxes? I swear, they got more groups with more initials up here than a can a mother-fuckin Campbell's alphabet soup—RAM, DRUM, UHURU, all this Marxist back-to-Africa, Swahili shit."

"Yeah," Willie said, "they actually believe buyin a mess a guns is gonna get whitey off their backs."

"Fuck 'em. Long as they pays cash, I don't give a fuck what they believe."

Their next and last customer was a slack-jawed blue gum who went by the name Kindu and lived on Wildemere in a filthy hole with cats and brimming garbage cans and a dank diaper smell to it. The two incense sticks burning on the kitchen table weren't doing a thing about that smell. Or the cockroaches.

Kindu had served in the First Cav in Vietnam and he was wearing his uniform to prove it—combat boots, dog tags, and the yellow shoulder patch with the black diagonal bar and the black horse's head. At least he knew guns. He wanted an M-16 and was disappointed to learn that all Wes had left was a pair of AK-47s, clunky Russian guns which, Wes assured him, would do in a pinch. Wes and Kindu chatted about banana clips, hollow points, hand loads and a lot of other things that meant nothing to Willie. He was nervous as a kitten, afraid of getting busted during their very last sale, the way the world worked.

When they finally closed the deal, Wes decided to stick around and celebrate by sampling some of Kindu's Thai reefer and Bali Hai wine. It had taken just three days to unload that trunkload of guns—all but the three Wes had stashed between his mattresses at the Algiers Motel and planned to keep for his "personal use." He was flush, feeling good, ready to party. Willie begged off, said he was going to see Edwin Starr at the Twenty Grand that night and needed to swing by the Algiers and get cleaned up. In truth he just wanted to get far far away from that diaper smell and those guns and those two crazy niggers.

"Turn that up!" Louis suddenly cried.

Clyde had cut over to Woodward and they were passing between those two blocks of chiseled ice, the Public Library and the Institute of Arts, just as Otis Redding was bending into the whistling part on "Dock of the Bay." Suddenly Willie was whistling along with Otis and Louis and Clyde, whistling as hard as he knew how, whistling until Edgar Vaughan and Kindu finally left him in peace. He even managed to forget the close call when that white cop had pulled him over right after he left Kindu's apartment.

Clyde docked the Buick in front of a place called the Seven Seas. As he climbed out, Willie looked across the street and was surprised to see his very first home-away-from-home in the Motor City, the Algiers Motel, where his brother had nearly become a statistic. Only then did Willie notice the sign. The familiar neon palm tree was still there, but they'd changed the name. The Algiers Motel was now the Desert Inn. Willie laughed out loud at this, at the vanity of believing it was possible to erase a disgrace by changing its name.

"The fuck you laughin at?" Louis asked, following Willie's gaze across the street.

"That's where my brother and I stayed when we first got to town last spring."

"Why's that so funny?"

"They changed the name."

"I seen that. Place is a shit hole no matter what they call it. You wasn't staying there during the riot, was you?"

"No, I'd moved out by then. Me and my brother both."

"Lucky for you, son. Come on. Clyde wants to introduce you to somebody."

16

CECELIA CRONIN WAS STANDING IN HER BEDROOM DOORWAY
drinking her third cup of coffee when Doyle's eyes finally popped
open. It was past noon. From the way he looked around the room,
sort of panicky, she could tell he didn't know where he was.

She said, "Coffee? Aspirin? Gun?"

He turned his head slowly, surprised to see her standing there. He
said "Hi" in a small voice, like it hurt to talk.

"Can I get you anything?"

"Aspirin," he croaked. "Water."

She brought him a glass of ice water and three aspirins and
sat on the edge of the bed. Propped on one elbow, he swallowed
the aspirins and thanked her. "Whew," he said, handing her the

glass and returning his head gingerly to the pillow. "What ran over me?"

"Stroh's and John Jameson. I've never seen anything like it. You were fine one minute—telling me a hilarious story about a phone conversation you had with some redneck cop in Alabama—and the next minute two busboys were helping me pour you into my car."

"So you drove me here from the Riverboat?"

"I wasn't about to let you drive."

"And this is . . . your bedroom?"

"Correct."

"Jesus. I'm sorry. . . ."

"No need to apologize. You do a great southern accent. But there's something I gotta tell you, Detective Doyle."

He frowned.

"You snore like a chainsaw when you're drunk. I finally had to go sleep on the sofa." She laughed and brushed the hair off his forehead. His frown disappeared. "You poor thing. You think a Bloody Mary might help?"

"You got any Vernor's?"

Half an hour later Doyle was halfway through his second can of Vernor's ginger ale and his first cup of coffee, sitting at the glass-topped table in the dining nook with his back to the big blue sky. He had no interest in how pretty Windsor, Ontario, looked this morning.

After he got down a soft-boiled egg and two pieces of toast, Cecelia said, "You got plans for the day?"

"I was thinking I might swing by Detroit Receiving for a blood transfusion."

"I've got a better idea."

An hour later they were on a bench in the Garden Court at the Institute of Arts, gazing wordlessly at Diego Rivera's "Detroit Industry" frescoes. Frank was lying on his back, using Cecelia's left thigh as a pillow. He looked content lying there, like he might actually survive this day.

They were surrounded on all four sides by frescoes that depicted the entire cycle of human life in the industrial age, from the germination of a cell to the brutal act of turning minerals into machines. The cycle began with an infant (or was it a fetus?) cradled in the bulb of a plant, and there were female nudes holding fruit and sheaves of wheat, then airplanes and birds, boats and fish mushrooming into immense portraits of how man uses the natural world to feed his technology: animals whose blood is turned into serum for vaccines, minerals being heated and poured to make poison gas and V-8 engines, a world of blast furnaces and paint ovens and smokestacks, a roaring inferno where men stamp, hone, deburr, hammer and curse cars into being.

They studied the frescoes for a long time without speaking. It was Doyle who broke the silence. "You never told me—how'd your paper about the Cubists turn out?"

"Pretty well, actually."

"Did you mention Rivera?"

"Just briefly. The time he spent in Paris with Picasso and Juan Gris. Mainly I concentrated on Orozco and Siquieros. But I've got bigger news."

"Oh?"

"My thesis proposal just got accepted. I'm going to write about the Monuments Men, you know, the Roberts Commission, the guys who cataloged and returned artwork the Nazis looted during the war."

"There was a ton of stuff, wasn't there?"

"The Nazis looted so much art that they had to store it in caves and mines."

"How'd you get into that?"

"My thesis advisor was on the Roberts Commission before he came to teach at Wayne State. While he was doing some provenance research he learned that a Monet in this museum's permanent collection had been looted by the Nazis. He saw to it that it got returned to its rightful owners, a Jewish family in France. It was the first time an American museum's ever done that."

"Good for the D.I.A. That's very cool."

"I think so too. I've decided to go into provenance research after I get my degree. My advisor believes it's going to be the wave of the future."

They were quiet again, gazing at the frescoes, neither of them feeling pressure to make small talk. Again it was Doyle who broke the silence. "You know this whole thing's a lie, don't you?"

"What is?"

He waved at the frescoes. "Those beautiful earth tones. Those workers who look like dancers. All that noble toil. It's all bullshit!"

Several people turned in their direction.

"Down boy," Cecelia said, stroking his hair.

He lowered his voice. "In a real car plant all the men are thick and muscular and everything's black and white and gray, even the people. Especially the people. It was like we were being covered with metal shavings, turned from black men and white men into gray men. The only color I remember was orange. Usually the sparks were white, but every once in a while they were orange for some reason. I remember thinking those orange sparks were the most beautiful thing I'd ever seen. Probably because everything else was so ugly."

"You worked on the line?"

He told her about his brief career attaching leaf springs at Chevy Gear & Axle the summer after his junior year of high school. On his third day he saw a defective drop forge slice off a man's left hand cleanly at the wrist. The blood came out like water out of a garden hose. Fifteen minutes later, after a cursory inspection by some foremen, another man was running the forge. Doyle walked out of the place and never went back. Then he told Cecelia about how his father's forty-two-year career at the Rouge came to an abrupt end six weeks before his retirement—the meatloaf sandwich, the heart attack.

Doyle said, "Notice how everyone on these walls is looking down, everyone except the overseers and the foremen? That's the one thing

Rivera got right. My father wound up just like that, could barely lift his head enough to look you in the eye. The older he got, the more he shrank. I think he would've disappeared completely if he'd lived much longer."

"You come here a lot?"

"Every chance I get."

"I don't understand. If you hate these frescoes so much, if they make you so angry, why do you keep coming back? You some kind of masochist?"

"No, I come here for two reasons. Because I do think the frescoes are beautiful, and because I never want to forget what the Henry Fords of this world do to men like my father, the way they get rich by grinding human beings into dust. The prettiest art in the world can't hide that fact."

"I'm no head shrinker, but it sounds to me like you're as mad at Rivera as you are at Henry Ford."

He chuckled. "I never thought of it that way, but I guess I do blame Rivera. Henry was just doing what industrialists do—the same way fish swim and birds fly. I'm inclined to give the devil his due. The man was an anti-Semite and a crank, but he was also a genius and at least he was pure about being evil. But Rivera—what a fraud."

"Did you know he was all gung-ho for the Mexican revolution— but he was nowhere near Mexico while it was happening. He was in Paris."

"I didn't know that, but I'm not surprised."

"Know how much he got paid for this job?"

"Five grand?"

"Try twenty. A small fortune in 1932."

"Where'd the money come from?"

"Edsel Ford's bottomless pockets." She pointed at a little man in a suit and tie in the bottom right corner of the large mural on the south wall. "That's Edsel, Henry's son. When the murals were unveiled to the public in '33, a lot of people in Detroit thought they should be white-washed—they thought the nudes were pornographic and the vaccination panels were sacrilegious. But old Edsel stood his ground, and the murals survived. And look at that small panel just below Edsel. It shows Rouge workers getting paid from the company's armored truck and crossing the Miller Road overpass to the employee parking lots. That's the famous overpass where Walter Reuther and his union organizers wound up getting stomped by Harry Bennett's goons in '38."

"The Battle of the Overpass. My father was working there when it happened. He said the union guys had it coming. He actually bought the company line that the organizers were a bunch of Jews and Commies. He thought Harry Bennett was a great man, and of course he thought old Henry walked on water."

"Who turned you on to this place?"

"My mother brought my brother and me here every chance she got. She loved it all—the medieval armor, the Morris Louis paintings, these frescoes."

"Was your mother an artist?"

"No, she was a housewife with a high school education who loved to cook and loved beautiful things. But she wasn't a snob. Much as she loved Rivera, she worshiped Frank Sinatra. Her favorite thing in the world was cooking while listening to Old Blue Eyes. Her name was Dolores—her maiden name was Carbucci—and when Sinatra would sing *I was made to serenade Dolores, serenade her chorus after chorus*, my mother would squeal, 'Listen, Frankie, he's singing about me!'" Doyle smiled at the memory. "You want to hear a little secret?"

"Absolutely."

"You may not believe this, but my mother actually named me after Sinatra. My full name's Francis Albert, same as his."

"Did your father come here a lot too?"

"Yeah, he used to spend hours in here on Saturday afternoons, just staring at these walls. He said the frescoes made him feel like what he did during the week was worthwhile, gave his work dignity. The poor deluded bastard. He actually bought the bill of goods Ford and Rivera were selling."

"Well, at least these frescoes made his life more bearable. That's something." Like father, like son, she was thinking.

"Yeah, I suppose so. Whatever gets you through the day."

They lapsed back into silence. After a while she said, "First Chopin, now Diego Rivera and Frank Sinatra. What's the next surprise, Francis Albert Doyle?"

"Why shouldn't I know a few things about music and art? Like I said before, I hate all the assumptions people make about each other—cops can't love art, artists can't commit crimes, black guys can't be brain surgeons, white guys can't play basketball."

"Can you?"

"Can I what?"

"Play basketball?"

"Once upon a time. I led the city in rebounding my junior year."

"What about your senior year?"

"I blew out my left knee during the Catholic Central game—along with my shot at a scholarship to Michigan. I can predict rain now better than the weatherman on Channel 7."

"Anybody can do that."

They laughed. Then she tugged him to his feet and said, "Come on, let's go outside and get some fresh air."

They sat on the museum's white marble steps and looked across Woodward at the Public Library, its mass and elegance, another monumental building that had always made Doyle proud to be a Detroiter. He put his arm around her shoulder and they watched the traffic flowing up and down Woodward, watched the sun sink toward the library. There was no need to talk.

A big red convertible sailed past, three black guys in it with the radio blasting, sending music trailing in its wake like smoke: *Sittin here restin my bones—and this loneliness won't leave me alone . . .*

"Looks like fun," Doyle said.

"What looks like fun?"

"Riding around on a sunny afternoon in a convertible listening to Otis Redding."

"I'm having fun sitting here listening to you."

"Yeah, same here. This is nice."

"I loved hearing your stories about your mother and father coming here, and your job at Chevy Gear & Axle, and how your father died. I wish you'd been open like that last night."

"Last night?"

"When you started to tell me about that lady in Alabama, on the way to my place. Beulah something."

"Jesus Christ. I told you about Beulah Bledsoe?"

"You started to—you said she was making you hate yourself. When I asked why, you clammed up. It reminded me of that night when we were at the Drome and you saw that guy from work, that detective, in the men's room. Boy, when you shut down you really shut down. You let me in so close and then, I don't know, you just slam the door in my face. And then all of a sudden you're so far away. Detached, like. I gotta tell you, it's awful."

"Detachment's what keeps homicide cops alive. What am I supposed to do? Come in at three in the morning and tell you how pathetic those two stiffs looked in that lake of blood outside the Driftwood Lounge? No, it's better to keep the two worlds separate. My partner's always telling me there's no way around it and there never will be."

"You believe him?"

"I'm afraid I do."

She knew it was unwise, but she said, "So who's this Beulah Bledsoe?"

"You don't want to know."

"Yes, I do."

"Well I don't want to talk about her."

"Why not? You sure wanted to talk about her last night."

"That was John Jameson talking."

"In vino veritas."

"I've never believed that shit."

"I've always believed it."

"Well, I can't tell you about Beulah Bledsoe."

"How come?"

"Because she's part of an ongoing investigation. I'm not allowed to talk about her. I'm sorry, but that's just the way it works."

It sounded like a canned defense, but she didn't press him. "I'm sorry, Frank. I shouldn't pry. . . ."

"You don't got to apologize. I should apologize for getting drunk and running my mouth. What a lightweight. I appreciate your interest, Cecelia, I really do. It's just that I can't talk about cases I'm working on."

"I understand."

"Believe me, I'd love nothing better than to be able to talk to you about some of the things I see every day." Saying the words made him realize how much he valued his late-night talks with his father. He couldn't imagine life without them.

She rested her head on his shoulder and they went back to watching the traffic. When the sun came to rest on the roof of the library, she said, "I promise I won't ask you about work anymore. But if you ever need to talk about it, you just go ahead and talk." Then she took his chin between her thumb and forefinger and kissed him, her tongue skating along his lips. The world went away for both of them then, and by the time it came back the sun had disappeared behind the library and the museum was closed and they were all alone on the cooling white marble steps.

They made love in her bed, beginning in the soft, washed-out light of dusk and continuing as the moon came up out of the river and filled the room with hard white light and wine-colored shadows. His tongue was on fire. It traveled over every inch of her, along the creases behind her ears, over the bumps of her vertebrae, across the hot patches behind her knees, up between her legs. Sweat and frenzy followed by cooling and calm, then building right back up, again and again.

She awoke at dawn with her jaw welded to the crook of her elbow. It was like emerging from the deepest sea. There was a note on the other pillow: *Had to go to work. Thanks for THE most wonderful day—and night. I'll call later.*

She felt goose bumps race across her skin, then she was diving back into that deep, deep sea.

17

WILLIE WAS BRIEFLY BLINDED WHEN HE STEPPED FROM THE SUNSHINE into the chilled gloom of the Seven Seas. He put a hand on Louis's shoulder and followed him through the smoke and noise to the bar.

She was sitting on a barstool in a blue dress that looked like it was spray-painted on her. Clyde had an arm around her bare shoulders, and every man in the place was checking her out. The women were too, but in a different kind of way.

"Alabama!" Clyde cried. "Come on over here and say hello to Octavia Jackson." He turned to the woman. "Shug, you know Du. And this here's Willie Bledsoe from Alabama, cat I been telling you bout, the big civil rights hero. He warrior stock." Clyde turned toward Willie. "Octavia works for Mr. Berry Gordy."

Willie was flustered, as much by Clyde's introduction as by the woman. She had enormous almond eyes that looked vaguely Asian and skin the color of coffee with a lot of cream. Her hair was shiny and straight, what he called blow hair because the wind could blow right through it. It brushed her shoulders, and the curtain of bangs was chopped at her eyebrows. He couldn't say for sure if she was black or Hispanic or Asian or some exotic hybrid. She was drinking orange juice through a straw. Her lips were thin and bright red.

"Pleasure to meet you, Octavia," Willie said, shaking her hand, her warm and soft hand. His face was burning. He could see that she was laughing softly at his discomfort, with no malice, just a gentle laugh from a woman who was at home in her body, at home in this noisy room, at home in the presence of all these admiring men and envious women.

"Pleasure's mine," she said, "meeting a man who do what you do."

"What I do?" He looked for help to Clyde, who was beaming like a proud daddy seeing his son off to the senior prom with the prettiest girl in the class. Willie said, "What's this noise about warrior stock, Clyde?"

"Don't gotta be modest, Alabama. I know all about the shit you done. That bus you was on got fire-bombed. That day you got your mouth busted open at the Montgomery bus station by that cracker hit you with a Co-Cola box."

"How'd you hear about that?"

"Read about it in the Michigan *Chronicle* while I was doing research for a case I'm preparing. They had a picture of you in Montgomery, bloodier'n a stuck pig, next to that white boy got his teeth knocked out."

"You just gettin off work, Willie?" Octavia said. All eyes swung back to her. She was slightly buck-toothed, and Willie found this imperfection even more attractive than her obvious assets.

"Work? No, we were at the ball—"

"But them clothes. Looks like you been fixin cars. Or choppin cotton."

"Oh!" He looked down at his overalls and brogans. "This is—these are—what we use to wear in Mississippi. . . ."

She patted the empty barstool next to hers. "Sit down and tell me all bout Mississippi. I ain't never been to Mississippi."

Louis and Clyde took this as their cue and drifted to the back of the place to shoot a rack of pool. After ordering a beer for himself and a fresh orange juice for Octavia, Willie said, "So what do you do at Motown? You a singer?"

"Lord no!" She laughed, like the idea was ridiculous. "I'm just a lowly receptionist. Don't try to change the subject. Tell me bout them clothes."

He explained the evolution of the Snick uniform. She had never heard of Snick, she confessed, but she had a way of asking questions that set him at ease, made him open up. He found himself telling her about the Freedom Rides, all those bus stations in Rock Hill, Atlanta, Birmingham, Montgomery, Jackson. What it was like to be trapped inside a burning bus. What it was like to live in a cage at Parchman Farm.

A bunch of brothers at the far end of the bar started singing along with the new James Brown song on the jukebox: *"Say it loud—I'M BLACK AND I'M PROUD!"*

Willie didn't know what to say next. He had never told these stories to anyone but his mother and Aunt Nezzie. Other than Blythe Murphy, whose motives proved to be shamelessly transparent, Octavia was the first person in Detroit who'd shown the slightest interest in what he'd been through down South. Everyone up here was too busy making it to care what had happened in Jim Crow country. Everyone except this woman with the unblinking almond eyes.

Willie's eagerness to talk made him wonder if he'd been waiting to find a stranger, the right stranger, to tell his stories to, someone who would simply listen without pegging him for a hero or a fool. Maybe, without even realizing he was looking, he had found his perfect stranger. Or maybe it was simpler than that. Since he didn't have a snowball's chance with such a fine woman, maybe he was thinking he might as well lay it all on her.

She said, "Y'all were some bus-ridin fools, weren't you?"

"Yeah, we were. We really were."

"So why'd you leave home and come all the way up here?"

"Work, like everybody else," he began, but instantly felt dissatisfied with the tired lie. "But there's more to it than that."

"Like what?" she said, sipping orange juice through the straw.

He couldn't afford to tell her about the guns or the riot—not yet—but he could tell her a lesser truth. "My mother keeps pushing me to write down the things I went through. She's a history teacher, see, and she believes every generation has to pass on the lessons it learns. She says future generations gonna need to know what it was like to fight Jim Crow, and the people with first-hand experience, people like me, are the ones who need to do the telling. That's why I still wear these clothes sometimes. They help me remember things."

"You think your momma's right about that, about passin on lessons?"

"Yeah, I do."

"Sounds like you two pretty close."

"A lot closer'n me and my father. My mother's so damn smart—but she's not one of those educated Negroes who makes a-gain rhyme with rain, if you know what I mean."

She giggled, a blaze of teeth. "I know zactly what you mean. My daddy, he use to sell insurance, he says a-gain. And instead of e-*leet* he says *ee*-lite. So you writin down what you been through?"

He took a deep breath. "I started to write it down, but. . . ."

Gently, almost whispering, she said, "But what? You can tell me."

"I'm not all the way sure. I couldn't seem to get it together in Alabama, so I came up here thinking the change of scenery would help. But it didn't. Then the riot happened and everything changed."

"The riot didn't change nothin you ax me."

"Oh yes it did. It changed plenty."

"Like what? Name one thing."

He looked away. This was as far as he was willing—as far as he dared—to go. Octavia patted his hand. "Thas okay, baby." He could tell he'd disappointed her, and he desperately wanted to repair the damage. But before he could think of anything to say, she stood up. "Don't go nowhere. I need to freshen up real quick. Be right back."

Like everyone in the place he watched her walk to the back of the room, her high heels clicking like castanets on the tile floor. Her blue dress was packed just right, and the way she moved announced that she knew that every eye in the place was all over her and she didn't mind one bit.

Y'all were some bus-ridin fools, weren't you?

Her words made him realize something that was so obvious he'd never stopped to consider it before—just how big a part buses had played in his journey. Buses could be the thread that tied his book together. The Montgomery bus boycott was the dawn of his realization that there was a momentous struggle taking shape just beyond the fringes of his tiny world. Then there was that bus ride to Nashville to help with the sit-ins. Then the bus ride to Raleigh, North Carolina, for the first meeting of Snick. The Freedom Rides. The burning bus outside Anniston. That grim bus ride back from the 1964 Democratic convention in Atlantic City. And he was still riding the bus because he was afraid to let his Buick be seen on the streets of Detroit. I'll probably ride a bus to my own funeral, he thought with a mirthless chuckle.

"What's so funny, Alabama?"

Clyde had glided up with a pool stick in one hand and an empty beer glass in the other. He motioned for the bartender to give them both a refill.

"Nothing, Clyde. Just thinking bout something Octavia said."

"You quicker'n I thought, homes. She just whispered on my ear you the most interestin cat she met in a blue moon."

"She didn't say that."

"She sho nuff did. What kinda lies you been tellin her?"

"Oh, just some of the stuff we did down South."

"Well keep it up. It's workin." He took his beer and went back to the pool table.

Watching the bubbles rise in his beer glass, Willie saw the ending of his book. It was perfect—that grim Greyhound bus ride from Atlantic City back to Montgomery after the 1964 Democratic convention. They'd registered 17,000 black voters in Mississippi that summer, and the Mississippi Freedom Democratic Party sent sixty-eight delegates to Atlantic City, determined to have them seated in place of the regular party's all-white state delegation. But Lyndon Johnson, that great friend of the Negro, offered the Freedom Party two measly seats for fear of alienating his fellow white Southerners and losing the White House. After Johnson's brutal arm-twisting carried the day, Willie rode home in that tomb-like bus realizing he was finished. They had jumped through all of Mr. Charlie's hoops and they came away with two delegates. It had taken Willie four years of playing by the rules to realize the game was rigged, always had been, always would be. In Montgomery he bought a ticket to Tuskegee, and when he got home he closed his door and sat down to write his story. For a while it worked, and then it didn't. And so he came to Detroit.

"You ready?"

Octavia had touched up her lipstick. When she smiled, the lips disappeared and those buck teeth reappeared. She motioned toward the exit. "Come on, let's go."

"Where we going?"

"For a drive. I love Sunday drives."

He left his untouched beer on the bar and said goodbye to Louis and Clyde and found himself following her out of the Seven Seas, every leering, jealous eyeball nailed to them, everyone wondering how a yokel like that managed to snag such a sweet piece of tail. Willie could practically hear the men groaning and the women sighing with relief.

The sun was low in the sky but painfully bright after the bar's dim interior. Squinting, Willie watched Octavia sashay toward the cars parked at the curb. Passing drivers slowed to get a look. One honked his horn.

Her car was an immaculate white Austin-Healey convertible with wire wheels, its top rolled back. The dashboard was made of burnished wood. When he hurried to open the driver's door, she blinked at him. "Why, thank you, Willie. Ain't you the gentleman."

Her surprise surprised him. Didn't other men treat her like a lady? He watched her swing her legs deftly under the wooden steering wheel, watched her shimmy her hips till she was settled into the snug bucket seat. When she kicked off her shoes so she could work the pedals, Willie flashed on that car ride with barefoot Blythe Murphy.

"Where to?" she said, blipping the engine as he slipped into the passenger seat. It felt like his ass was three inches from the pavement, yet he could stretch his long legs straight out. Amazing how much room there was in such a tiny car.

"It's your town," he said.

She headed out Woodward, weaving between cars, even taking on some of the gear heads who pulled alongside them at red lights, revving the engines of their muscle cars, challenging her to drag race. She beat them all. It was obvious she loved the attention.

She turned left on McNichols, 6 Mile. They passed near Uncle Bob's new house, passed the University of Detroit. Willie found himself succumbing to her laughter and the engine's purr, to the way the world whipped past faster and faster as they sliced through the hot afternoon. Soon they crossed the Lodge Freeway and the Rouge River and were leaving the city, entering Redford Township and Livonia, leafy suburbs Willie had never heard of. Amazing. You blinked your eyes and Detroit became a gritty memory.

When they were free of the city Octavia reached across and popped open the glove box, revealing an eight-track player. She pushed in the tape that was in the slot. Otis Redding was singing again: *You got to, you got to, try a little tendernesssssss* . . .

They rode almost all the way to Ann Arbor, not saying much, listening to Otis, then Smokey and the Miracles, Al Green, Curtis Mayfield, Aretha. Willie felt no need for talk. He was content to be in motion, going nowhere just for the sake of going, and going there with her.

When the sun touched the treetops Octavia down-shifted and turned onto the Ann Arbor Trail, which ran along a chain of lakes and ponds and carried them away from the sunset, back toward the city. As soon as they passed the Detroit City Limits sign, Octavia lit a cigarette and dragged on it fiercely. She said, "I don't know how much Clyde's tole you bout me."

"Not much. He said you were a client of his."

"Yeah, he helped me out of a jam a couple years back."

He waited, hoping to hear more about Clyde and the jam. When she didn't offer anything, he said, "So what's it like working at Motown?"

"I hate it. Company's run by white men now—bunch a slave drivers." She took another deep drag on the cigarette. "I shouldn't bad-mouth all the white men work there. Joe Messina, he white, eye-talian, plays guitar and just as sweet as he could be. Always buying me presents, telling me how nice I look."

"Which band's he with?"

"The house band. They call theirselves the Funk Brothers, but nobody ever heard of 'em."

"Why not?"

"Cause Berry won't put they names on any records. I'm tellin you, place is run just like a plantation. They even hired a spy to keep tabs on the musicians after hours, make sure they ain't breakin they exclusive contracts. Don't do no good. I know for a fact the Vandellas is singin backup on the new John Lee Hooker record." Twin tusks of smoke shot from her nostrils. "There's this brother hangs around the studio, he ain't like the others. He don't hit on me or try to get in on the recording sessions. He just likes to hang out and talk. He teaches African history at Cass Tech and he tells me about people I never even heard of—Moise Tshombe, Kwame Nkruma—says every black person in America has a responsibility to know what's going on in Africa. Shit, I don't know what's going on in D-troit half the time. I don't even read the newspaper. It's shameful to be so ignorant. I've never traveled farther than Chicago, and now on account of Daddy it doesn't look like I'll be able to go anywhere for a while."

"What's up with your daddy?"

"He's got the sugar, and it's gonna kill him. I try to look in on him every day. Sometimes when I meet a brother like you who's gone places and done things, been to college—"

"I didn't even finish a year of college."

"Well, I didn't even finish high school. But that's not the point. Point is you had a dream and you put your body on the line. You tried to change the world."

"I didn't change shit, Octavia."

"But you tried."

"Trying don't mean a thing."

"Yes it does! Can't you see that? Tryin's all there is—and I ain't never tried nothin."

It was near dark now. They were heading south on Woodward and Willie's euphoria was gone. Listening to her lament reminded him of something Aunt Nezzie had told him: The best listeners are people with the greatest ache to unload their own tales.

Octavia took a right onto Boston Boulevard and slowed down as they passed the biggest houses Willie had seen inside the city limits of Detroit. The biggest one on the block was lit up, and they could hear music pouring out of the open windows—live music, jazz. Elegantly dressed people were milling beneath a blazing chandelier, a mixed crowd, blacks, whites, even a few Asians.

"That's my boss's crib," Octavia said, slowing to a crawl.

"No lie? That's where Berry Gordy stays?" He turned to get a better look. A woman's bawdy laughter rolled across the lawn, then the throaty whisper of a saxophone, drums stroked by brushes.

Octavia pulled over to the curb between two mammoth Cadillacs and cut the engine. They both stared at the house. "I went to the company Christmas party here last year," she said. "Y'ain't never seen so much marble and gold in all your life."

The awe in her voice disappointed him. It reminded him of his wide-eyed brother telling him, during the long drive from Alabama to Detroit, that the Temptations' lead singer had a limo upholstered with mink. Flashy displays of wealth had never impressed Willie.

"There's a tunnel that runs to a movie theater behind the house," Octavia went on. "And you'll never guess what's on the wall in the living room."

"I hate to think. Gold records?"

"No, a portrait of Berry—dressed up like Napoleon."

A Negro Napoleon! It was so sick Willie had to laugh.

"I'm surprised Berry's even in town," she said.

"What do you mean?"

"He spends most of his time out in Vegas and L.A."

"Doing what?"

"Gamblin, playin golf, tryin to figure out a way to break into the movies. All he cares about anymore's makin Diana Ross into a movie star. He lets his white slave drivers run the company day-to-day."

This was all news to Willie. The few things he'd read about Motown, mostly in magazines like *Jet* and *Ebony*, made the company out to be one big happy prosperous black family.

"The initials H-D-H mean anything to you?" Octavia said as the saxophonist in the house broke into a wailing solo. People were whooping, urging him on.

"Sorry."

"How bout Holland-Dozier-Holland?"

At last they were getting back to Clyde. "Is that the name of Clyde's law firm?"

She laughed, shaking her head. "I forget you from down South. You still got a lot to learn."

Coming from her, the put-down carried a frightful sting. It was one thing for Clyde Holland to cluck his tongue, as he'd done on Opening Day at Tiger Stadium, and let Willie know that his busboy job branded him a hopeless chump. But it was something else for this woman to tell him he still had a lot to learn. He could feel his hurt shading instantly toward anger. "So what's Holland-Dozier-Holland?"

"You heard of the Four Tops? Or the Supremes?"

"Of course." God *damn*.

"Eddie Holland, Lamont Dozier and Brian Holland's the team wrote most of they hits—'Bernadette,' 'Standing in the Shadows of Love,' 'Can't Hurry Love,' 'I Hear a Symphony'—hundreds a songs."

Now Willie was remembering how Louis Dumars had introduced Clyde on Opening Day—as the famous barrister with the even more famous brothers. "So Eddie and Brian are Clyde's brothers?"

"Now you catchin on. Thas how I got my job, through Clyde. But he's more than just they brother. He they lawyer too. Motown just sued H-D-H for four million dollars."

"Why?"

"Claim they breached they contract cause they haven't written no songs since last year. Can you imagine that? After all the money they done made for the company? Now Clyde's fixin to counter-sue the company for twenty-two million. And Eddie and Brian's gonna start they own record label, gonna call it Hot Wax."

There it was again, Willie thought, the oldest story in the book: black people sticking each other instead of sticking together and fighting the actual enemy. So much for the big happy Motown family.

A car pulled up alongside the Austin-Healey. A radio crackled and a man's voice said, "You comin, goin, or just gawkin?"

Octavia and Willie looked to their left. It was a blue-and-white Detroit police car. The cop behind the wheel was black; the white cop in the passenger seat was wearing a big phony smile. He had bad teeth and bad skin.

Then it hit Willie like a fist: it was the same cop who'd stopped him right after he and Wes unloaded the last of the guns on that Vietnam vet, Kindu.

Within seconds of pulling away from Kindu's apartment, Willie had seen the red light in his rearview mirror. His first feeling was relief—at least the Buick's trunk was empty. But even as he pulled over to the curb, his relief melted. What if the cops had seen him come out of Kindu's apartment building? Wes was still in there with a big bag of reefer, all that cash, and those AK-47s.

In his Buick's sideview mirror Willie had watched the cop approaching. Big white sonofabitch with a beer gut and a rolling swagger, thumbs hooked on his belt, eyes moving like ball bearings from the car to the street and back to the car. Willie had his driver's license out before the cop's face filled the window.

"License and registration," the cop had said. His fleshy lips were parted in a smile that carried no warmth. His teeth were yellow. He was so close Willie could smell him—coffee and greasy food on his breath, hair tonic, gun oil. It was a mechanical smell, not even human.

While the cop studied the license, Willie noticed he was carrying a long black flashlight even though there was plenty of daylight left. In the rearview mirror he could see that the cop's partner was still in the squad car, a good sign. The cop bent back down, eyes scouring the interior of the car. "You realize you failed to make a complete stop at the corner of Wildemere and Tuxedo, Mr. Bledsoe?"

"Nosir, I didn't realize that. I believe I came to a complete—"

"You calling me a liar, boy?"

Here we go, Willie thought, slowly placing both hands on the steering wheel. He heard a dog bark, a child's laughter, and again he smelled the cop, that oily machine smell. Been in the Promised Land less than a week, he told himself, and here it was again—already, still, forever—the bowel-cramping terror he thought he'd left behind when he left the South. He almost wanted to laugh at his own stupidity.

"Where's that registration?"

Willie removed his right hand from the steering wheel and reached slowly for the glove box. Just before his thumb pressed the button, his left ear caught fire and stars jumped off the windshield. Stunned, his head ringing, he looked to his left. The cop was grinning. He'd whacked the side of Willie's head with the flashlight.

"Don't go pulling no gun on me now, honey," he said, lips stretching to reveal those yellow teeth.

"Nosir . . ." Willie opened the glove box and gave him the registration. While the cop studied it, Willie kept his left hand on the steering wheel, stretched his right arm across the back of the seat, in plain view. He was not going to rub the spot where the flashlight hit, give this pig any satisfaction. He saw that people had come out on their porches to watch the show. Most of them looked bored, a few looked angry. Someone shouted, "What the fuck he do wrong? Leave him be!"

The cop ignored this and studied the registration even longer than he'd studied the license. "Tuskegee, Alabama, eh? You sure are a long ways from home."

"Yessir." The ringing in his left ear was so bad it was hard to hear him.

"What brings you to Detroit?"

"I'm here . . ." And then the black man's oldest reflex took over, that ageless survival instinct, the automatic gift to tell the white man the lie he wants to hear. "I'm here for a job interview, sir."

"Where at?" He was still studying the registration. His lips were moving.

"At . . . General Motors."

"Doing what?"

"They've got an opening in the Mail Room."

The peckerwood nodded at this, and Willie applauded himself for coming up with such a perfect lie, a lie this cop would love because it fit so neatly into his view of the world: black people were put on the planet to work in the Mail Room and the kitchen, to sing and dance, to cut the grass and polish the brass.

The cop started copying the information from the driver's license into a notebook. Willie assumed he was writing a ticket, but the cop handed back the license and registration, no ticket, and gave the Buick a long, admiring look. "Where'd you pick up a fine ride like this, boy?"

"In Alabama, sir. Restored it myself." He realized it was the second time he'd told this lie. No sense stopping now. "Picked it up in a junkyard for twenty-five doll—"

"What're you doing in this neighborhood?" He was still admiring the car. Willie realized he was seeing jealousy on the cop's face.

"I was on my way back from my job interview, sir."

"Back to where?"

"My hotel."

"Which one?"

"The Algiers, over on Woodward."

"The *Algiers*?" The cop gave out a single snort of laughter. "Buncha pimps and dope dealers and queers over there. You a homasexual, honey?"

"Nosir."

"You like smokin dicks?"

"Nosir."

"You a pimp? Only pimps drive cars painted like pussy."

"Nosir, I'm not a pimp."

"Well, you'll fit right in at the Algiers anyway. What you got in the trunk?"

"Nothing, sir." The ringing was dying, but now the side of Willie's head was beginning to throb. He could see in the rearview mirror that the other cop, another white guy, was out of the squad car now, hands folded on its roof. "I'd be happy to open the trunk for you—"

"What were you doing in that apartment building three blocks back?"

Willie managed to sound calm. "I was . . . looking for an apartment, sir. A permanent place to live. They have a vacancy on the third floor."

"You buy any dope while you was in there?"

"Nosir, I don't do drugs."

"Don't lie to me, boy!"

This was obviously for the benefit of the people who were now crowding the nearby porches. A few had spilled down to the sidewalk, children mostly. So this was a Motown spectator sport. The cop studied his audience, nice and slow, not in any hurry. He was enjoying himself. Willie felt ashamed for allowing this fat white cop to humiliate him in front of these people.

The cop said, "All right, boy, I'm going to do you a big favor and give you a warning this time. But don't go running any more stop signs."

"Nosir."

"And don't go giving your money to those dope dealers and hookers at the Algiers, you hear me?" He was smiling again, pleased with his wit.

"Yessir, I hear you."

The smile vanished. "Now gitcher ugly black ass outta my sight."

By the time he got back to the Algiers Motel, Willie had come to the realization that he was capable of killing that fat white cop. He *wanted* to kill him. He also realized this was precisely what The Man wanted him to want. He drives you to murder so he can turn around and kill you dead for allowing yourself to be driven.

Now he heard Octavia saying to the cop, "We was just leavin, officer." She was giving him a big phony smile of her own. "I work for Mr. Gordy."

"'That a fact," the white cop said. He leaned forward to get a better look at the passenger inside the sports car. Willie stared straight ahead. His heart was going like a jackhammer. The white cop said, "And what all do you do for Mr. Gordy?"

"Answer the phones. Type. Lick envelopes."

"I bet that ain't all you lick."

The black cop said something sharp to his partner. Willie was still staring straight ahead. His heart was going so fast it actually hurt.

Octavia bristled. "What the hell is *that* suppose to—"

"He didn't mean nothin, ma'am," the black cop said. "If you're leavin, you should go ahead and leave. Right now."

Willie exhaled as Octavia fired the engine and dropped the car into gear and eased away from the curb. He kept looking over his shoulder until he was satisfied the cops weren't following. He told Octavia to take a left on Hamilton, the quickest way to his apartment.

"That motherfucker," she muttered, lighting another cigarette. "That fee-simple honky motherfucker. . . ."

They didn't speak as they passed over the Lodge Freeway, then took a right on Pallister. Willie watched the Larrow Arms slide by, wondered which window belonged to Mizz Armstrong. When Octavia pulled up in front of his place, she left the engine running and glanced up at the building. "So this where you stay?"

"This is it."

"Ain't much to look at."

"No, but it's clean. And cheap."

"What happened to that burnt-up place next door?"

"The riot happened."

"Damn, you was right in the middle of it, wasn't you?"

"You got no idea." Now that, he thought, reaching for the door handle, is the truest thing I've said all day.

She touched his knee. "You okay, Willie?"

"I'm fine as wine. Why?"

"You acted like you seen a ghost when them po-lice pulled up."

"Something like that."

"What is it?"

"I know that white cop."

"Where from?"

"Some other time," he said, even though he had already decided there wasn't going to be another time.

"You in some kinda trouble with the po-lice?"

"A hick like me?" He tried to laugh as he climbed out of the car. He was angry at himself for having such thin skin, but he couldn't help it. He was fed up with being talked down to by all these smug northern niggers who hadn't seen a fraction of the things he'd seen. They were the ones who still had a lot to learn, and in that moment he made a vow that he would teach them.

"Thanks for lettin me run my mouth, Willie. I really needed that. Maybe we'll go for a ride again next Sunday."

"May be."

"And next time you do the talkin."

"Sounds good."

"You think you might call me sometime? I'd love to hear more a your stories bout Mississippi."

"Sure."

She was smiling again as she wrote her phone number on a matchbook. "You promise you'll call?"

"I promise."

"I'm usually home by nine in the evening, but don't call too late. I go to bed early. They work us like dogs." She handed him the matchbook and dropped the car into gear. It squealed away from the curb, leaving behind nothing but a smudge of burnt rubber and a long blue ribbon of smoke.

He didn't even wave goodbye because just then he saw a blue-and-white making the turn onto Pallister by the Larrow Arms. The last thing he wanted to do was let that honky cop find out where he stayed.

It would never end, he thought as he hurried up the front steps and let himself into the building. At least his Buick had a fresh coat of Earl Scheib's finest black paint and tomorrow, if all went well at Murphy's, it would disappear once and for all.

He hugged the wall in the foyer while the cop car eased past. His heart was going like a jackhammer again, and it didn't stop even after the cop car made a left onto Poe and disappeared.

PART THREE

WORLD CHAMPIONS

18

MONDAY MORNING AND CHICK MURPHY WAS IN HIS MURDEROUS mood. Blythe had tied on one of her fifty-megaton loads after the Tigers' game Saturday night, insisting they stop at the club for dinner, then ordering unnecessary nightcaps, getting loud and sloppy, flirting with the help, even with some of the colored guys, for chrissakes. Then she refused to get out of the car when they got home. It was way past midnight when Chick finally wrestled her into bed.

She still hadn't emerged from her bedroom by noon on Sunday so he went back to Oakland Hills to hit some golf balls and take a swim. After lunch he wound up playing gin rummy in the men's grill with a bunch of young huns from the G.M. Tech Center. They called themselves "stylists" but he thought they were a bunch of eggheads because they spoke a language he barely understood, sprinkled with big words like "co-efficient of drag." They were all college boys—art students, at that—which meant they had no idea what it was like to stand out there at the corner of 9 Mile and Mack in all natures of Michigan weather, in sheets of snow and razor-toothed spring rains, under the egg-yolk August sun that turned the outdoors into a steam bath and, despite that weather, to stand out there under the snapping pennants and plaster a thousand-watt smile on your face and tell lies until you sold a fucking car, preferably a plush new fully loaded Buick, to some poor sap who could no more afford it than he could afford a trip to the moon. That was where G.M.A.C. came in—Alfred Sloan's genius idea that you could amp up sales and profits by lending money to your customers and then charging them a grand-larceny interest rate. Most of those art school boys from the Tech Center didn't even know what G.M.A.C. stood for—that to the bluesuits on West Grand Boulevard the initials meant General Motors Acceptance Corporation, while to trench warriors like Chick Murphy they meant Give Me A Chance.

His joyless Sunday at the club ended late in the afternoon when someone in the men's grill switched the TV from the PGA golf tournament to the Olympics in Mexico City. When the American national anthem started playing, Chick looked up from his cards and saw three men on the awards stand with medals draped around their necks. Suddenly two of the men, Americans, both Negroes, bowed their heads and raised their gloved fists in the black-power salute. Chick said, "What the fuck . . ." and felt himself rising from his chair, felt his right hand groping for the nearest object, which was an empty Michelob bottle. Chick Murphy, a former Marine, had lost his left pinkie to frostbite during the savage fighting at Chosin Reservoir in Korea, and he loved his country. Without thinking, he hurled the beer bottle at the TV screen. There was an explosion, a shower of glass, smoke. Then he was storming out of the room to applause and laughter and howling. The black waiters and busboys lounging by the door got the hell out of his way.

So by the time he walked out his front door on Monday morning he was locked into his murderous mood. It got worse when he noticed a pair of Blythe's high heels under a rose bush by the driveway. Rain had ruined them, a pair of sixty-fucking-dollar burgundy suede pumps from Saks. Why had she left a pair of expensive shoes out in the rain?

The only thing that lifted Chick's spirits on that gummy Monday morning was the sound of his radio spot coming out of the Electra's dashboard as he cut across the northern suburbs toward the dealership:

> *Stay on the right track*
> *To 9 Mile and Mack.*
> *A Chick Murphy Buick's gonna*
> *Make your money back.*
> *Ole Chick Murphy's got some buyers*
> BUYERS!
> *Who come from many miles a-waaaaaaay.*
> *You'll save yourself a lot of dollars*
> DOLLARS!
> *By driving out his way to-daaaaaaay!*

Hearing that radio spot never failed to give Chick a boost. He considered it a work of genius. He wrote the lyrics himself on an Oakland Hills cocktail napkin late one Sunday night after a Lions football game and half a dozen brain dimmers. Edgar Hudson, the waiter with the bottomless baritone and the quick laugh, had helped with the tune. The guy had a great singing voice. The jingle was catchy and unforgettable, destined to stay with you like a gold-digging wife. Chick had a hunch it had sold more Buicks than all the lies he'd ever told at the corner of 9 Mile and Mack.

As he pulled onto the lot now, his commercial gave way to the familiar voice of J.P. McCarthy, who was talking with Mickey Stanley about the double Stanley hit in the bottom of the ninth yesterday that brought the Tigers from behind—again—to beat the Indians. This good news did nothing to dispel Chick's mood. It was his very best car-selling mood, a blend of cold rage and false bravado that told him the world owed it to him to buy a truckload of Buicks. He once sold thirteen cars in a single day while in his murderous mood. Those customers didn't have a prayer.

In his paneled office, surrounded by all the celebrity golf photos and model cars and autographed baseballs, Chick studied the second-quarter sales figures. He realized one reason sales had fallen off in '68 was that the riot buyers had dried up. These were the city dwellers, usually black guys, who showed up at the dealership last summer and fall wearing sherbet-colored slacks and pointy alligator loafers, their pockets full of cash from all the fur coats and guns and booze and jewelry they'd looted during the riot and then fenced for a tenth of its value. They came in waves, in battered cars, in taxis, on buses, just poured out Mack through Grosse Pointe, all the way out here to St. Clair Shores because the word was out on the street that Murphy's made the best price on a Buick. And every last one of them absolutely had to have a new Deuce and a Quarter. Much as Chick hated to see these flashy assholes turn his hometown into a gigantic ashtray, he was a businessman and he knew better than to look a gift horse in the mouth. Sadly, he now realized, all that riot money was gone. The only thing Murphy Buick had to show for it was banner third and fourth quarters in 1967—followed by a sharp drop-off in the first and second quarters of '68.

Time to change that. Chick shoved the sales reports into a desk drawer and popped a Certs breath mint. He loved the Certs jingle—*Two . . . two . . . two mints in one!*—and when he strode out onto the lot he knew instantly it was going to be a good day for selling cars. The sun was out, making the '68s look a littler newer and the used cars a little less old. It was humid but not too hot, a kiss of breeze coming off Lake St. Clair and stirring the pennants. Lately he'd noticed that more and more of the people wandering around the lot peering into windows were eager to talk about the Tigers. It was the kind of small talk every salesman loves, a superb lubricant. The team's inspired play was lifting the city's shaken spirits, bringing people together again and, best of all, making them less reluctant to part with their money.

Within minutes Chick was pounding on an old black couple from Highland Park, trying to get them to open their eyes and see why the four-door '65 LeSabre with only 32,000 "original" miles on the odometer was an irresistible deal even though the body had a little rust and there was a hairline crack in the windshield. (Chick didn't bother to mention the hairline crack in the engine block.) That rust had them worried. Just as Chick was about to throw in a cosmetic paintjob to nail down the deal, his eye caught a flash of black and silver easing onto the lot from 9 Mile. He kept talking, but his eyes stayed on the black car, an immaculate '54 Buick Century. "If you're so worried about a little rust," he told the black couple, "then I'll paint the car for free. What do you say to that?" They were mulling it over as Willie Bledsoe unfurled himself from the driver's seat of the black '54 Century. He was wearing sunglasses, sharp clothes. A man who'd come here to deal.

As expected, the offer of the "free" paintjob clinched the sale, and Chick sent the old couple off to the finance office to get their pockets hoovered. He'd forgotten all about them by the time he turned on the smile and walked up to Willie Bledsoe with his right hand out.

"You finally made it!" he cried, pumping Willie's hand.

"Yessir. Finally."

Chick looked at his car. "Where'd you pick up the hearse?"

Willie chuckled. "It was a gift, actually. From a friend of my brother's."

It had a cheap paintjob on it, but there were no dents or visible rust, the chrome sparkled like new, and the red-and-black interior was perfect. Cars didn't hold up this well in Michigan. This one would fetch a pretty dollar. "Looks like you've been taking pretty good care of her, Willie," Chick said.

"Oh, yes sir. Car spent its whole life in Alabama—till I drove it up here last spring. I kept it in a garage all last winter. Isn't a speck of rust on it."

"How many miles she got on her?"

"Not even twenty-five thousand—all original."

Right, Chick thought, and I was born last Tuesday. His suspicions were confirmed when he walked around behind the car and saw the chrome nameplate of the original dealer bolted to the trunk lid—*Tucker Buick, Levittown, Long Island*—which meant this was originally a New York car and Willie had already told at least one major lie and therefore it was open season. Chick slid behind the steering wheel. The odometer read 24,767, and he wondered if that meant 124,767 or something else. It didn't matter. What mattered was that he wouldn't even have to run the car through the Fountain of Youth—the windowless room at the back of the lot where the boys rolled back odometers, changed the oil, gave used cars a cheap paintjob and a fresh set of shoes. The interior had that moldy smell common to old cars, a smell Chick had loved since he was a boy. "Why you want to give up a classic like this, Willie?" he said, climbing out of the car. "She's a beaut."

"Ever since that day my Uncle Bob took me for a ride in the Deuce and a Quarter you sold him, I knew I had to have me one."

"So you got your eye on a Deuce?"

"Yessir. A used convertible, if you've got one."

"As a matter of fact I just got a ragtop in Friday. It's a repo, practically fresh off the assembly line. Let's go have a look."

Fifteen minutes later Chick was sitting in the passenger seat of a '67 Deuce convertible, its top rolled back, its pale blue skin gleaming in the morning sunshine. Willie was driving, his left elbow resting on the driver's door, his right wrist on top of the steering wheel. He looked right at home.

They were sailing out Jefferson, the lake glistening like Turtle Waxed sheet metal off to their right as Willie described how Jose Cardenal had tried to outrun Mickey Stanley's drive to deep center in the ninth inning yesterday but couldn't catch up with it. Chick pretended to listen as he lit a cigarette. There was something he wanted to get off his chest before they got down to business. When Willie got through with the play-by-play, Chick said, "Listen, Willie, I want to apologize for Saturday night."

"Apologize, Mr. Murphy? For what?"

"For my wife. You saw her. She was drunker'n a boiled owl."

"No need to apologize, Mr. Murphy. We all have a little too much now and then."

"I swear to Christ, she gets a load on and you can't even talk to her." The cigarette tasted terrible and he tossed it toward the lake. "Tell me something. You ever see her flirt with anybody at the club, members or guys on the staff?"

The answer came back so fast Chick knew he was lying. He almost sounded scared. "Flirt? You mean, like, come on to? I . . . Mr. Murphy, I . . . wouldn't know a thing about any of that."

"Ah, let's drop it. Sorry I said anything. So tell me, you like the blue color?"

Chick could tell he was relieved by the change of subject. Willie's lie, the fear in his voice, his obvious relief—it convinced Chick that there was something to his suspicions about Blythe. He'd heard whispers that Dick Kowalski got run out of the Flint Golf Club for sporting with a member's wife before he washed up at Oakland Hills. Chick made a note to keep an eye on that Polack weasel.

Willie said, "The color's fine."

That sounded a little lukewarm, like he was still wrestling with this, the most crucial question in the average car buyer's mind. Chick said, "The factory calls it 'Bahama blue'—whatever the fuck that means."

"Means driving the car's supposed to feel like a Caribbean vacation. Which it does. I look at this car and I see a tropical sky on a sunny day."

That sounded a lot more promising. "You look like you were born sitting there, Willie. It's a great fit."

"I really like these white seats and red carpet. And I love the way it drives. Practically steers itself."

Chick knew then that the car was sold, so he asked Willie if he'd given any more thought to coming to work at the dealership.

"Tell you the truth, Mr. Murphy, I don't really know much about cars."

"I'll teach you. The main thing's how you deal with people. Selling cars to people is all about the people, not the cars."

"I might be doing some traveling soon."

"Ahh, must be nice."

"What must be nice?"

"To be young and single, not a care in the world."

"I wouldn't know about that."

Chick noticed he didn't smile when he said it. They rode in silence for a while. Chick knew what Willie was thinking. He was wondering how much money he would need to cover the difference between the value of his trade-in and the price of this Deuce. To get the ball rolling Chick said, "How much you think your Century's worth, Willie?"

"Gee, Mr. Murphy, how much you think—"

"You ever heard of G.M.A.C.?"

"G.M.A. what?"

"It's how us General Motors dealers finance car sales. You understand how that works, don't you?"

"Not really. Like I said, that Buick of mine was a gift. It's the only car I've ever owned, so I don't really understand fi—"

"Ah, screw it. I'll swap you straight up. That sound like a deal?"

It damn sure did, and by the time Willie brought the Deuce to a stop outside the showroom, the trade was complete. Chick's largess was explained by two things: his genuine fondness for Willie, and the fact that the ragtop had had its frame bent when it got rear-ended by a gravel truck in Inkster. The boys in the Fountain of Youth worked on it for a solid week, and they were able to fix the bumper and trunk lid good as new, but they said the frame would never be straight. Chick wanted to get the thing off the lot. He figured he could get at least a grand for Willie's '54 Century from one of the downriver motorheads who dropped by all the time looking for something to soup up. Maybe even twelve hundred. It would be a loss, but getting rid of that damaged Deuce was worth it.

"A pleasure doing business with you," Chick told Willie when he emerged from the sales office with his paperwork in hand. "Drive carefully now—and give some more thought to that job we talked about."

"I will. Thanks for everything, Mr. Murphy." Willie shook the offered hand and guided the Bahama-blue Deuce and a Quarter south toward the city, joining the legion of satisfied customers who'd stayed on the right track to 9 Mile and Mack and didn't even realize they'd gotten bushwhacked by Chick Murphy's murderous mood.

19

DOYLE AND JIMMY ROBUCK TOOK A RARE TUESDAY AFTERNOON off to watch the Tigers play the Yankees on Bat Day. It was one of the scariest things the detectives had ever seen—51,000 Detroiters buzzed on fire-brewed Stroh's and armed with giveaway Louisville Sluggers. Miraculously, no one's brains got bashed in. The Tigers lost that day but then won ten of their next eleven, putting the rest of the American League in their rearview mirror.

Doyle and Jimmy barely noticed. A heat wave in late June did what heat waves have always done in Detroit—it inspired a burst of violence that sent a dozen citizens to the morgue and sent every homicide detective into maximum overdrive. To make matters worse, as July wore on and the Tigers kept tearing up the American League, there was talk on the street that Armageddon II was going to erupt on the 23rd, the first anniversary of the outbreak of the riot. Word was that some of the Motor City's better-equipped bad-asses were declaring July 23 open season on anyone with white skin, especially if he or she happened to be employed by the Detroit Police Department.

Nerves, understandably, were fraying at 1300 Beaubien, and the Helen Hull investigation went back onto the back burner. But then on the eve of Armageddon II, Doyle and Jimmy worked all night to get a signed confession from a shitball named Rayfield Gaudet in the Jeffries Homes shooting during the summer's first heat wave. It was their last open case. The next morning, after a two-hour nap on the sofa in Sgt. Schroeder's office, Doyle pulled the Helen Hull file back out. An hour later, as he was reviewing his notes from his conversations with Caldwell Petty and Beulah Bledsoe, his telephone rang.

"Homicide, Doyle."

"Got some great news, Frankie!" came Henry Hull's familiar squawk.

"Glad to hear it, Mr. Hull," Doyle said. He needed to sleep for a week.

"Did you happen to see the eleven o'clock news last night?"

"No sir, I was busy."

Henry told him what he'd missed. Detroit police, acting on an anonymous tip, had raided a warehouse on Riopelle and seized a small arsenal of rifles, handguns, ammunition, even a few boxes of hand grenades. This was indeed good news. The raid surely had put a large dent in the bad guys' plans for Armageddon II. A lot of Detroiters, black and white, in and out of uniform, could breathe easier this morning.

"That's terrific, Mr. Hull."

"Hold on, I haven't even gotten to the good part yet. While I was watching the news I recognized one of the officers involved in the raid. It was Charlie Dixon."

The uniform who was in the crime scene photo the night Helen Hull died. "I thought Charlie was assigned to the Third Precinct," Doyle said. "What's he doing raiding a warehouse down on Riopelle?"

Riopelle dead-ended into the Detroit River a few hundred yards from where Doyle was sitting. It was where bootleggers used to unload their boatloads of Canadian whiskey during Prohibition, and it was nearly four miles south of the Harlan House Motel.

"I wondered what Charlie was doing on Riopelle myself," Henry said, "so I picked up the phone and called him first thing this morning. Come to find out he's been reassigned to the First Precinct. He just happened to be the guy who picked up the phone when the tip came in about the warehouse full of guns. That's how he got his face on TV."

"Go on."

"He didn't have much time to talk, but I did get him to tell me a little about the stuff they seized. And guess what. There were some .30-caliber rifles with scopes on them. He said it's going to take a while to catalog everything, there's so much of it. How do you like them apples, Frankie?"

Doyle liked them just fine, but he didn't let on. He thanked Henry for the information and promised to be in touch. Then he scribbled a note for Jimmy to call Charlie Dixon and check the seized weapons for a possible match with the bullet that killed Helen Hull.

Feeling proud of himself—this could be the break they'd been dreaming of, and he was acting like it was just another routine lead—Doyle rode the elevator down to the stinking basement garage. All the prowl cars were signed out, so he climbed into his Bonneville and headed north.

In the front lobby of the Oakland Hills clubhouse Dick Kowalski greeted Doyle like a long-lost brother. He led the way into his office, pushed a pile of papers off a green leather chair and motioned for Doyle to have a seat. He went to a metal urn in the corner and filled two mugs with molten tar. The guy drinks this swill by the gallon, Doyle thought, just like a cop. Kowalski looked even wearier than before, the sockets of his eyes a little ashier, the slump of his shoulders a bit more pronounced. He swung his wingtips onto the desk. There was a hole in the sole of his right shoe. It looked to Doyle like babysitting rich white people and keeping tabs on their black retainers was a lot of work.

"So," Kowalski said, "what can I do for you today? You need to talk to Bob Brewer again?"

"Actually, I'm looking for his nephew."

"Willie? Don't tell me he's in trouble."

"I'm not sure yet."

"He's one of the best I've got—him and his uncle both. Well-spoken, courteous, always shows up on time and works hard. I don't even think he plays cards or shoots dice with the other guys."

"You said on the phone he's working tonight?"

"Yeah." Kowalski craned his neck to read a schedule taped to the wall behind him. "He's due in at four to set up for a private party for—oh, shit."

"What's wrong?"

"The party's being thrown by Chick Murphy, world's biggest Buick dealer and second biggest blowhard. Word around the clubhouse is he thinks I'm screwing his wife."

"Are you?"

Kowalski laughed. "That old lush? I wouldn't fuck her with some-body else's dick."

"Why don't you tell that to this big Buick dealer?"

"You don't know Chick Murphy. I'm just keeping my head down. So. Willie's due in at four, which means he'll be showing up any minute. He's always early. Like I say—"

"He still driving that big old pink-and-black Buick?"

"I'll tell you something. Just between you and I, Detective—"

"Frank."

"—between you and I, Frank, I make a point of not knowing what my employees drive or how they got hold of the keys. To be honest with you, I don't know how busboys and waiters and bartenders can afford to drive some of the cars parked out on our employee lot, and I don't ask. The less I know, the better. I'm sure you understand."

"Sure." What Doyle understood was that bartenders drive what they steal. "You happen to have a picture of Willie handy?"

"I should." Without removing his wingtips from the desk, Kowalski dug in a drawer and produced a job application with a black-and-white photograph stapled to it. Doyle took one look at Willie Bledsoe's face and immediately thought of Jerry Czapski's description of the driver of the cherry Buick they'd pulled over at the corner of Wildemere and Tuxedo back in the spring of '67: smooth skin, not too dark, handsome enough kid. The young man staring at the camera fit the description. Solid jaw, trim Afro, full lips that curled up at the corners in a permanent smile. Doyle couldn't read that smile. Was it cockiness? Only after studying the picture for a full minute did Doyle notice the most obvious thing of all: the flaw: the scar that ran through the upper lip, near the left corner of the mouth. It was the result of a badly botched sewing job, and he tried to guess what could have caused such a nasty wound. A windshield? A knife? A nightstick? This, he told himself, was a worthy adversary. He said, "Good-looking kid."

"And smart too," Kowalski said, checking his watch. "It's almost three-thirty. He'll be showing up any minute if you want to talk to him."

"No, I think I'd rather just hang around in the parking lot for a while if you don't mind."

"Be my guest. The employees park in the far lot, up by Maple Road."

"And one small favor, Dick. Don't let anyone know I stopped by."

"Sure thing."

Ten minutes later Doyle was sitting at the wheel of his Pontiac reading the tea leaves of the Tigers' box score in the *Free Press*. He looked up as an enormous sky-blue convertible turned off Maple and eased into the employee lot. When Willie Bledsoe climbed out, Doyle put his newspaper down. What the hell happened to the pink-and-black Buick?

Willie was lean, well over six feet tall, and he was wearing a charcoal-gray sport shirt and light gray slacks, creases like razors, hip but not flashy. His black loafers gleamed. His tortoise-shell sunglasses had little gold screws at the corners. If bartenders drive what they steal, Doyle thought, then maybe busboys drive—and wear—what they steal. Over his shoulder Willie carried a white jacket and a pair of tuxedo pants in a dry-cleaning bag. The man looked as sweet as Marvin Gaye, way too cool to be working for The Man out here in the burbs.

Doyle watched him glide across the parking lot. He had a fluid walk, smooth and rhythmic. He moved to music only he could hear. Doyle watched him until he disappeared into the service entrance in the clubhouse basement.

When he was gone, Doyle walked over to the blue convertible and squatted behind the back bumper. The Society of Automotive Engineers serial number on the taillight contained the numeral 67, which meant this Electra 225 was a 1967 model, just a year old. The dealership's decal was on the trunk lid: *Murphy Buick—Stay on the Right Track to 9 Mile and Mack!* Chick Murphy, the suspicious car dealer with a wandering lush for a wife.

Driving east toward St. Clair Shores, Doyle had a warm feeling. If Willie Bledsoe had swapped his '54 Buick for the blue convertible, it was a sure sign he was trying to get rid of incriminating evidence. Doyle liked having an adversary who took precautions. And he absolutely loved the moment when he first laid eyes on a suspect, when an abstraction became flesh and it was suddenly possible to imagine sitting across the Formica table from another human being in the yellow room, going through the familiar dance, the dance Doyle loved so much because he did it so well.

Chain-smoking, rattling breath mints across his teeth and talking like a machine gun, Chick Murphy couldn't seem to get it through his skull that Doyle had not come here to buy a car but to gather information in a criminal investigation. Murphy was on some kind of automatic pilot, like a wind-up doll. Doyle noticed his left pinkie was missing and his knuckles were laced with scar tissue and there were little gaps in his yellow eyebrows. The man had punched and he'd been punched, Doyle thought. No wonder Dick Kowalski was afraid of the guy.

"Whaddaya say we take her for a quick spin up the lake?" Chick Murphy said, spanking the hood of a yellow Electra 225 with a white vinyl top.

"Some other time," Doyle said. "I'd rather have a look at the paperwork on the car Willie Bledsoe traded in."

Chick Murphy led the way inside to the finance office. His fingertips drummed the desktop while Doyle went over the papers on the 1954 Buick Century that had been sold last week to a man named Ernest Roquemore from Wyandotte. There was a new state law that required car dealers to list the odometer reading on every used car they offered for sale, and the '54 Buick's mileage caught Doyle's eye. "A fourteen-year-old car with less than twenty-five thousand miles on it? You believe that?"

"If that's what's on the odometer, that's what I put on the paperwork," Chick Murphy said. "It's the law."

"The paperwork doesn't say anything about how he acquired the car."

"No, but the title was in his name. That's all I care about. He did tell me the car was a gift, or somesuch shit."

Doyle remembered his conversation with Beulah Bledsoe. Her saying the car was a gift to Willie from some Navy buddy of his brother's. Still studying the paperwork, he said, "The car was black? *Solid* black?"

"Blacker'n the ace of spades. I gave him some shit about driving around in a hearse. It had a cheap paintjob on it."

"Did he paint it?"

"Don't know. Didn't ask."

"So do you think he turned the odometer back?"

"I did at first. Not anymore."

"Why not?"

"Because my mechanics did a compression check—and they tell me the mileage is real. I was a little pissed at myself for doubting the kid. I'm convinced he doesn't have a dishonest bone in his body."

"You sure about that?"

"Look, Detective, you learn to size people up pretty fast in this business. I can tell you most people's life story five minutes after I meet them."

"Tell me mine."

"I'd say you're single, played sports, never been to college, and you work too hard, drink a little more than you need to. Probably went to Catholic schools. That suit—you're obviously a clothes horse. And I'm guessing you're a skirt chaser."

"Not bad." In fact, he was right on all counts except one. Doyle didn't have time to chase skirts anymore. He made a mental note to call Cecelia, let her know he was still alive.

"Look," Chick Murphy said, "I'm sure about Willie Bledsoe the same way I'm sure that Deuce I showed you is white over yellow with a vinyl top. He's not the type to turn back an odometer. Or gamble. Or steal. Or screw another guy's wife."

The guy called the car a Deuce. Simply talking about a black man made him talk like a black man. Well, Doyle thought, everyone makes errors of judgment, even street-smart Buick dealers. "So, Mr. Murphy, if you don't think Bledsoe has it in him to turn back an odometer or screw another guy's wife, then I guess it's safe to assume you don't think he has it in him to commit murder."

Chick Murphy actually looked angry. *"Murder?* Fuck no. What is it with you city cops? You think every black guy's automatically a murderer?"

"No, I don't think any such thing. I'm just running down leads. Doing my job."

"I understand, but for whatever it's worth I really think you've got the wrong guy if you think Willie Bledsoe's involved in some murder. He's just about the most decent colored guy I ever met."

After a secretary photocopied the paperwork for Doyle, he thanked Chick Murphy and left, promising to come back soon to test-drive that yellow-and-white Deuce.

Doyle took Jefferson back into the city, the scenic route. The smooth silver lake was on his left, salted with sailboats, and off to his right, roosting behind their three-acre lawns, were the palaces of the Motor City's tycoons. It never ceased to amaze Doyle that you could throw a stone from this stretch of Grosse Pointe and hit Detroit's rotting East Side—or vice-versa—yet the two places might as well have been in different hemispheres. No wonder every rich suburbanite's teeth were on edge. If Armageddon II arrives, the black mob will have to travel just a few short blocks before the fun begins.

Wyandotte was way the hell downriver, so Doyle got on the Fisher Freeway where it started, just west of downtown. He obeyed the speed limit, which meant cars blew past the Bonneville like it was up on cinderblocks. Doyle didn't mind. He had plenty to think about. He kept seeing Willie Bledsoe gliding across the Oakland Hills parking lot, kept hearing Chick Murphy saying *He's just about the most decent colored guy I ever met*, kept hearing Dick Kowalski saying *He's one of the best I've got*.

What if they were right? Weren't all the signs pointing to a Vietnam vet as the shooter? But Doyle reminded himself of another of Jimmy Robuck's commandments: You work with what you've got. And all they had right now was Willie Bledsoe, who might lead them to Wes Bledsoe, who might be the shooter and who, if he was not, might lead them to the shooter. Or not.

Doyle was rescued from these gloomy thoughts by the sight of Ford's River Rouge complex looming on his right. The six slender silver stacks were belching smoke at the heavens, and Doyle could see a freighter off-loading iron ore, sending up an orange cloud that drifted off to the south like fallout. It was a blasted world—rusty silos, mountain ranges of coal and slag, spurts of fire, conveyor belts and railroad tracks, all of it coated with ash and bisected by a river as green as a lizard. The sight could not have been any more personal to Doyle—this was the monster that killed his father—and yet it was so vast and so faceless, so inhuman, that it had always been an abstraction to him. It filled him with conflicting emotions he could not begin to untangle—awe, terror, rage and a kind of perverse civic pride. This place was the essence of Detroit, what the city stood for and what it did, and as much as Doyle loathed it he could not deny that he felt humbled and amazed every time he saw it.

To settle his nerves and his growling stomach, he stopped at a place called Riverside Coney Island in Wyandotte and ordered a tall Vernor's ginger ale and two Coneys all the way. Doyle was a gourmet but not a food snob, and he understood that there were times when nothing could beat a Detroit Coney. The hot dogs under their piles of chili and chopped onions, the sharp mustard, the bittersweet bite of the Vernor's—like magic, it brought him back to himself. His earlier doubts were gone. Pursuing the lead on Willie Bledsoe's old car was the right thing—the only thing—to do.

Restored, he went looking for the address on Arch Street. At first he thought the place was a junkyard. The tall cyclone fence was topped with razor wire and plastered with signs advising you to KEEP OUT and NEVER MIND THE DOG, BEWARE OF OWNER. In case those messages didn't sink in, there was another sign that proclaimed the premises were PROTECTED BY SMITH & WESSON.

Doyle saw no evidence of dogs or guns when he pushed through the gate into a cluttered wasteland of cars in various stages of amputation. He assumed they were victims of late-night wrecks and explosions—some were missing doors, others were missing fenders and bumpers and wheels—but then he realized these cars were not wrecks. They were some mad customizer's raw materials, cars that were being scavenged, chopped and channeled, transformed into things only a man with gasoline in his veins could possibly dream up. Doyle didn't know a solenoid from a socket wrench, but he'd always admired the way Detroit's legion of motorheads were forever tearing cars and engines apart, souping them up, then putting them back together and taking them drag racing out on Woodward.

Doyle was careful not to step in any puddles of motor oil or anti-freeze with his new Italian loafers as he approached a man draped over the front fender of a canary-yellow Ford two-seater coupe, something from the Thirties, a moonshiner's chariot. A transistor radio on the car's roof was tuned to a country/western station, and a woman with a brassy twang was bemoaning one of life's eternal verities: *"Sometimes it's hard to be a woman . . . giving all your love to just one man . . ."*

The man draped over the Ford's fender was wearing a T-shirt and Levis. The T-shirt had ridden up and the Levis had ridden down enough to give Doyle a superb view of the top half of his gefilte-fish ass cheeks. Good to be downriver again, back among the butt-crack crowd. Doyle coughed into his fist to announce his presence.

The man who emerged from under the hood of the Ford had shiny black hair combed straight back and a pair of bushy gun-nut sideburns. His skin, pitted with acne scars, was the color of a sidewalk, and his arms were paved with muddy blue tattoos. Doyle showed him his shield and said he was looking for Ernest Roquemore.

"You got him," the man said, smiling. He had gorgeous teeth. He held out his right hand, then looked at it and withdrew it. It was as black and oily as his hair. He started rubbing his hands with a clean red shop rag.

Doyle said, "I understand you just bought an old Buick from Chick Murphy up in St. Clair Shores."

"Sure did. Wanna have a look?"

Doyle said he did. He followed the guy along a path that zig-zagged through dismantled engine blocks and transmissions and axles. There was a strange tidiness to all this disruption. A freight train was rumbling past the yard's back fence, loaded with shiny Ford Torinos still wet from the womb at the Rouge. The men entered a garage, a windowless cave lit by fluorescent tube lights.

And there it was.

The bumpers and the chrome had been removed and the paint had already been stripped off all the way down to the sheet metal—except on the right front fender, which was black. The engine was gone.

"You getting ready to paint it?" Doyle said.

"Candy-apple red, metal-flake. Gonna have flames coming out of the front wheel wells." He gazed fondly at the car, which looked as naked as a plucked chicken to Doyle but no doubt like a blank canvas to Ernest Roquemore. "Gonna drop the roof four inches," he went on, "then slip in a Hemi and a Chrysler drive train. Glass packs, Hurst shifter, positraction, the whole nine yards. She's gonna scream, believe me."

Doyle walked close to the fender that still had paint on it. He could see, to his delight, that there was a coat of pink paint between the black outer coat and the sheet metal. "Looks like the guy who owned it before you had it painted."

"Yeah, that's something I don't get."

"What is?"

"Well, Mr. Murphy told me the guy who traded it in was colored. I never heard tell of a nigger covering up a pink paintjob with a black one. Usually they go the other way." Ernest Roquemore grinned at his little insight. A greaser who thought he had things figured out. "And I coulda puked when I seen that paintjob."

"You mean the color?"

"No, I mean the paintjob. Looked like he done it himself when he was drunk."

"How could you tell?"

"Cause it looked like shit—orange peel, drip marks, holidays, you name it. Didn't even tape off the chrome right. Typical nigger thing to do, fuck up a cherry ride with a twenty-dollar paintjob. Guess he was trying to tell the world he's black and he's proud, or somesuch shit."

When Doyle leaned close to the driver's door, his delight doubled. The seats were pleated red vinyl halfway down, then black fabric shot through with silver glints. He thought of that traffic stop when he'd seen Willie Bledsoe's long brown arm resting on red vinyl. On *this* red vinyl. He thought of Charlotte Armstrong seeing a shiny old car with red and black seats pull up beneath her window on the morning of July 26, 1967. *This* shiny old car.

There was no doubt in Doyle's mind that he was looking at the car that transported the gun that fired the bullet that killed Helen Hull. If that gun had been seized in the Riopelle raid . . . Doyle forced himself to snuff the thought and the tingling sensation that came with it. He said, "Interior looks good."

"Yeah, I'll say that much for the nigger. He had the good sense to leave the interior alone. And he babied her. Everything was original—except that fucked-up paintjob."

"How many miles it have on it?"

"That's the most amazing thing of all. The paperwork said twenty-four thousand and change, so of course I figured the odometer'd been turned back. But when I did a compression check, the engine was like brand new."

"Chick Murphy told me the same thing. Anything in the trunk when you bought it?"

"Just a bumper jack, a spare tire and some oil stains."

Gun oil stains, Doyle thought, burping a toxic little cloud of chili and onions. He asked Ernest Roquemore not to touch the car until an evidence team came down to go over it. Roquemore happily complied, said he needed to get that yellow Ford coupe back on the street anyway.

As Doyle let himself out through the gate, Roquemore was already draped back over the front fender of the yellow Ford. He was cursing. The top halves of his ass cheeks glowed proudly in the summer sun as a different woman's voice came out of the radio: *"My momma socked it to the Harper Valley Pee Tee Ayyyyyyy. . . ."*

Ah, downriver.

There were only three people in the squad room when Doyle got back from Wyandotte. Walt Kanka was in the far corner watching

TV, and Jimmy Robuck and Sid Wolff were at Jimmy's desk playing checkers, which was strictly no-contest. By the time he was old enough to drop out of high school, Jimmy was the undisputed checkers champ of Paradise Valley, the throbbing heart of Detroit's black East Side, able to whip all the barbershop hangers-on and street-corner hustlers. He was also skilled at carrying bags of money, running numbers, rolling drunks and hot-wiring cars. Eventually he graduated to strong-arm robbery and dope dealing, even ran a short string of girls out of the Gotham Hotel, a promising and diversified career that got cut short by a two-year stretch at Ionia on a weapons charge. Upon his release Jimmy decided that since he was going to carry a gun for the rest of his life he might as well have a badge to go with it, and so he enrolled in the police academy and became a legendary East Side uniform, in touch with the streets like no one else because he'd spent his first twenty years working those streets. He knew every blind pig, chop shop and five-dollar whorehouse, and he forgot nothing—no face, no name, no bad debt or grudge. And he wasn't afraid to fight. Doyle had never seen anyone beat Jimmy Robuck at checkers or anything else.

That didn't appear likely to change soon. Sid Wolff had his chin cupped in both hands. His face sagged like a melting candle. It was obvious he didn't like what he was seeing on the checkerboard. Then again, Sid Wolff rarely liked what he saw, on a checkerboard or anywhere else.

Walt Kanka, his feet on a desk, was watching Walter Cronkite on the black-and-white Motorola with aluminum foil wrapped around its rabbit ears. On the screen Doyle could see a wall of helmeted cops wading into a crowd, nightsticks whirling.

"What's that, Walt?" Doyle called across the room.

"Chicago, the Democratic convention," he said without taking his eyes off the screen. "Would you look at those filthy sonsabitches! They never take baths and they think everybody should be effin each other all the time. Hit 'em harder! That's it, stomp those long-haired pricks!"

Jimmy was looking at his watch, but Doyle beat him to the punch. "Don't start, Jimmy. I just put sixty-six miles on that old Bonneville. You get my note?"

"Oh yeah. I got you note."

"Where you been, Frank?" Sid said. "Scoping out the co-eds in Ann Arbor?"

"No, I went out to Birmingham. Got a good look at Helen Hull's killer."

Jimmy yawned. "It's still your move, Sid."

"Fuck you. I know whose move it is."

"Where else you been?" Jimmy asked Doyle.

"Went to St. Clair Shores to talk to a car dealer. Then down to Wyandotte."

"What's in Wyandotte?"

"Our man Willie Bledsoe's old Buick—the one that carried the guns to the Larrow Arms. I got there just in time, too. The new owner'd already stripped off almost all the paint. Turns out Bledsoe painted the car solid black just before he traded it in."

"So what?"

"So doesn't that tell you something?"

"Tells me the man likes black cars. So do I." Nobody played devil's advocate better than Jimmy Robuck. It drove Doyle up the wall sometimes, but they both knew it had to be done. Kept a cop honest. "Is painting you car black a crime now?"

"No, Jimmy, painting your car black's not a crime now. But why does a guy get a cheap paintjob on a mint-condition classic car just before he trades it in—unless he's trying to hide something? For that matter, why does he trade it in in the first place?"

"People trade up every day in this man's town. That ain't no crime neither."

"The seats are still red and black, though, just like Charlotte Armstrong remembers them. And there's oil stains in the trunk. May be gun oil. An evidence team's on the way to Wyandotte to tear the car apart."

"Terrific." Jimmy turned to Sid. "It's still your—"

"Fuck *off!*"

"—but while you been out scopin circumstantial shit, Frank, we been doin some real legwork. Ain't that right, Sid?"

Sid Wolff groaned and pushed a checker forward one square. "That's right, you prick."

Jimmy performed a triple jump and added Sid's captured pieces to the tidy stack beside the board.

"What'd you guys find out?" Doyle said, walking up to Jimmy's desk and noticing the tomatoes for the first time. There were four plump beefsteaks lined up beside the empty In/Out basket. Doyle picked one up and smelled it. "Where'd you get these?"

"Grew 'em. They for you. A little thank-you note for turnin me on to the joys of gettin my hands dirty."

"Thanks, Jimmy. They're beautiful."

"Thank you, Frank. Flo's makin ratatouille as we speak." It was the French dish Frank served the first time he had Flo and Jimmy over to his place. Most delicious food Jimmy ever ate. Doyle said he made it from scratch with things he grew in his back yard and on his kitchen windowsill—all the vegetables, even the garlic, basil, thyme and parsley. That was the night Jimmy decided to take up gardening. It made sense. When he and Flo got urban-renewed out of Paradise Valley—the planners flattened the whole neighborhood to make way for the Chrysler Freeway, a slap in the face to every black person in the city—the Robucks bought a place in Conant Gardens, out near 7 Mile. Every house had a deep back yard designed to accommodate a garden. After that ratatouille feast at Frank's, Jimmy decided to plant a garden of his own. These four beefsteaks were the first things he'd harvested, and he hadn't felt so proud since his youngest girl's college graduation. He turned to Sid. "Your move again."

"You say another fucking word and I'm gonna come across this desk and ring your neck, you ruthless black bastard."

After putting the tomatoes on his desk, Doyle said, "So what'd you guys find out?"

"Tell him what we found out, Sid."

"We matched the thirty-cal bullet that came out of Helen Hull with one of the guns from the Riopelle raid."

Doyle couldn't speak at first. Then he was babbling. "Jimmy!—Sid!—that's the best fucking!—that's!—we've!—*this is the one we been waiting for!*"

"Calm down," Jimmy said. "Turns out they were half a dozen Winchester Model 70 target rifles in that warehouse. One of 'em had a very nice Starlight scope on it. Infra-red. The kind preferred by snipers in Namland after the sun goes down. That was the one the slug matched."

"God damn, Jimmy! We got our murder weapon!"

Between Doyle's delight and Sid's misery, Jimmy was having himself a time. "Man, you wouldn't believe some a the shit come out that warehouse. Am I right, Sid?"

"You're always right, Jimmy. Your ass is the blackest."

"Automatics, assault rifles, M-1s and M-14s, Remington M-700s, grenades, claymore mines, thousands a rounds a ammo. Man, them niggers was fixin to make some *noise*. No wonder Mr. Viet Cong's kickin so much ass—the shit that's suppose to be killin him's on the wrong side a the Pacific Ocean."

Jimmy could see that Doyle wasn't thinking about Vietnam. He was thinking about the gun. He'd spent the day chasing his tail all over metropolitan Detroit and had come up with nothing they could use in court—while Jimmy walked up one flight of stairs and came back down with the single most crucial piece of the whole puzzle. Now Doyle said what Jimmy expected him to say: "You able to get any prints off the gun?"

"Got a few decent latents," Sid said. "Nothing we've been able to match so far. Records is still running the prints, said it might take 'em a couple days."

"They make any arrests when they raided the warehouse?" Doyle said.

"Just one," Jimmy said, standing up and stretching. "Gentleman name of Alvin Hairston. Apparently it was his job to make sure nobody broke into the armory. I'm afraid he's not the talkative type."

"Alvin Hairston," Doyle said. "Why's that name familiar?"

"Probably cause he's a wild-eyed nigger likes to see his name in the newspaper. He come here from New York a couple years back with that group called itself the Northern Student Movement. All they are's unemployed niggers. He set up a bunch a Black Power rallies, called Detroit 'Upper Mississippi,' shit like that."

"Right. You find Alvin's prints on any of the guns?"

"Not a one," Sid said. "I don't even think he knows how to use the damn things. Kid looks like a fag you ask me."

"Where is he?"

"Got him housed on the seventh floor," Jimmy said. "He pulled Judge Columbo at his hearing. I do believe Hizzoner's still pissed off about last summer. Hank the Deuce couldn'ta covered Alvin's bail."

"He ask for a lawyer?"

"Nah, he ain't that smart. He's asleep."

"I give up," Sid said, brushing the pieces off the checkerboard and standing up. He reached for his sportcoat, a nice plaid polyester number. "Can I buy you boys a drink?"

"You certainly may," Jimmy said. "To the victor go the spoils—and the Chivas Regal."

"But Jimmy," Doyle said, "what about Alvin?"

"What about him? He ain't goin nowhere. Come on, let's go have a few pops, celebrate a little. Sid's buyin. We can start beatin on Alvin in the mornin."

It was Frank's turn to make the call on where they went, so Sid and Jimmy followed his ratty old Bonneville out East Jefferson to the Riverboat. Jimmy had only been in the place a couple of times. It had brass rails and a lot of mirrors and a nice view across the river, a mixed-race clientele of salesmen and car guys and secretaries. More of a pickup place than a cop kind of place. Jimmy figured Frank had a reason for bringing them there.

He saw the reason standing behind the bar, flipping cardboard coasters like a blackjack dealer. She was tall with some serious curves, and she was looking at Doyle in a way that made it hard to tell if she wanted to kiss him or slap him.

"Well hello there, stranger," she said with a crooked smile.

"Hello, Cecelia," Doyle said. "Brought you two of the worst reprobates in the city. This is my partner, Jimmy Robuck. And this is Sid Wolff, from ballistics. Cecelia Cronin, gentlemen. She's in grad school at Wayne State."

They shook her hand and said their hellos. Then she was back on Doyle, still smiling but a little sharper now. "Your phone broken?"

"Um, no . . . listen, Cecelia, I've been meaning . . . we been busier'n hell for—"

"The past *three weeks*?"

Jimmy took pity on him. "He ain't lyin, Cecelia. They been workin us like dogs the past month. It's been Murder City out there. Ain't that right, Sid?"

"That's right, Jimmy. Murder City."

"So what'll it be, gentlemen?" she said, still looking at Frank, her smile not quite so crooked.

"Chivas on the rocks," Jimmy said. "Better make it a double."

"I'll have a Stroh's," Doyle said.

"Just a Coke for me, thanks," Sid said.

They were sitting at the curved part of the U-shaped bar and they all watched her walk to the far end to fix the drinks. Her green skirt was cut tight and didn't try too hard to hide her legs.

"That," Jimmy said, "is some serious boo-tay."

"Since when you start effin college girls, Frank?" Sid said.

"Fuck the both of you," Doyle said. "She's in grad school. She's a year older than me."

"If I ever forgot to call Flo for three weeks like that . . ." Jimmy shook his head. He didn't even want to think about it.

"You and Flo've been married for twenty-five years, Jimmy. I've been out with Cecelia twice."

"Still and all. . . ."

"Legs like that," Sid said, "I'll bet she's a real tiger in the sack, eh Frank?"

Doyle told them to fuck off again but Jimmy could tell that for once he wasn't bothered by the teasing. When the drinks came they talked a little shop, they talked about the Tigers, they talked about their gardens. Doyle wasn't all the way there. He had one eye on Cecelia as she moved back and forth behind the bar, but Jimmy knew him well enough to know that mostly he was thinking about the good news they'd gotten today and how he was going to play it with Alvin Hairston in the morning.

After their second round, Jimmy said he had to be getting home, had a date with a pot of ratatouille. When Sid asked for the check, Frank said he was going to stay and have one for the road. Jimmy reminded him to go easy. They had a big day tomorrow.

Just before he and Sid left the room, Jimmy turned to wave goodbye. Cecelia had her elbows on the bar, her face inches from Doyle's. There wasn't anything crooked about her smile now. Jimmy had a hunch his partner was going to show up late for work tomorrow morning. If he showed up at all.

Didn't matter one way or the other to Jimmy. Like he'd said, Alvin Hairston wasn't goin nowhere.

20

AFTER HE TRADED HIS '54 BUICK FOR THE DEUCE AND A QUARTER, Willie made a point of swinging by Murphy Buick at least once every day. He wouldn't be able to quit worrying until the old Century disappeared. Every day, to his horror, it was right there in the front row on the Mack Avenue side of the lot, the chrome teeth of its front bumper winking in the sunshine, a pink helium balloon bobbing from its antenna, and *CHERRY '54!!!* written in big red block letters on its wraparound windshield. The car sat there for an agonizing week, just begging the cops to come in and ask all the wrong kinds of questions.

And then one day—just like that—it was gone. Vanished. Willie couldn't believe his eyes at first. He made three laps around the lot to make sure they hadn't moved the car. It was definitely gone. A fifty-pound sack of sand was lifted from Willie's back.

At Oakland Hills that night he worked a private cocktail party attended by Chick Murphy and a couple dozen other drunk and boisterous Buick dealers. As the party was breaking up, Willie took an empty glass from Chick Murphy and managed to sound casual as he asked what had become of his old Buick.

"Sold that crate this morning," Chick Murphy said. "Kid from downriver practically stole it from me, says he's going to turn it into a hot rod."

The very next day Uncle Bob dropped by Willie's apartment for their long-overdue heart-to-heart talk. It took some doing, but Willie managed to convince his uncle that he and Wes had had nothing to do with any shooting from the rooftop of the Larrow Arms; they hadn't even heard any gunshots. Willie said he'd driven Wes home that night and patched him up because Wes had gotten a vicious beating from the cops who broke up the craps game and shot those people at the Algiers Motel. This finally placated his uncle. Can't fault a man for looking after family in a crisis. It hurt Willie to dupe a man as decent as Uncle Bob, but he didn't see that he had any choice.

After his uncle left, Willie spent the rest of the afternoon on his porch admiring the shiny blue ragtop parked at the curb. Seeing his new Deuce in plain view out on Pallister and knowing that his old Buick was gone gave Willie the giddy feeling that he'd slipped the noose. He knew he wasn't in the clear yet, but he quit waiting for his brother to call from Denver. No detective revisited his uncle or telephoned his mother. Alphonso Johnson's legal woes became old news, and there was no new news about investigations or arrests related to the riot. Willie even managed to convince himself that during the test drive in the Deuce he'd done a good job of deflecting Chick Murphy's suspicions about Blythe flirting with the guys at Oakland Hills. It helped that the weather had turned hot and the city was gripped by a strange malady known as pennant fever. All anyone could talk about was the Tigers. As long as they kept winning, Willie felt safe.

A new sense of ease possessed him. While he was smart enough to be distrustful of it, he was also desperate enough to be grateful for it. It helped that he'd missed the news about the raid on the Riopelle warehouse.

After working the dinner shift at Oakland Hills several nights later, he was sitting at home listening to some Thelonious Monk and talking to Octavia on the telephone. They talked almost every night now, and he found it strangely soothing to listen to her gossipy monologs about life inside the Motown studios. It was a welcome escape, like watching a soap opera on TV. As the conversation was winding down that night, he was idly thumbing through his files when the picture of him with Bob Moses at the Farce on Washington fell out of a folder and landed face-down on the floor. Only then did he realize there was writing on the back. It said: *Two soulful brothers, Bob M. and Willie B., at the March on Washington, August 1963. With love and respect, D.N.*

For days the initials tormented Willie. The harder he tried to place them, the dimmer they seemed to grow. His torment was made worse by his hunch that the identity of D.N. might be the key that would finally unlock the door. He kept returning dutifully to the microfilm room at the library, but nothing jogged his memory. He began to feel panicky. Had his brief run of good luck already dried up?

He kept scrolling through newspaper microfilm and reading back issues of magazines, hoping something would reveal the identity of D.N. Finally he came to the edition of the Michigan *Chronicle* that carried the front-page picture Clyde had mentioned at the Seven Seas. Snapped moments after the Freedom Riders were attacked outside the Montgomery bus station, it showed Willie in the middle of the frame, looking dazed, blood pouring out of his mouth. On the right was a tall lanky white guy named Jim Zwerg, who was reaching into his own bloody mouth for loosened teeth. On the left, looking strangely composed, was John Lewis, his shirt spattered with blood. The accompanying article appeared under the by-line of *Moses Newsome, Special to the Chronicle*. The same writer from Baltimore who had been interviewing Willie when the fire-bomb came through the Greyhound's rear window outside Anniston. Willie knew he was getting close.

Two days later the front page of the May 24, 1961, *New York Times* swam onto his microfilm screen at the library. There was a picture of Jim Farmer, Ralph Abernathy, Martin Luther King Jr., and John Lewis at a press conference in Montgomery, announcing after three days of fierce debate that the Freedom Riders would continue from Montgomery into Mississippi and from there on to their original destination, New Orleans. Though Willie was certain he had never seen the picture before, it looked familiar. It was spooky, like déjà vu before the fact. He kept staring until it hit him: He had been standing next to the man who took the picture. He had seen the picture before it was a picture. Now Willie remembered the photographer—a big sweaty white guy named Larry something who worked for the Associated Press and wore a pistol on his hip to discourage people from messing with him or his cameras.

The most arresting detail in the photograph was the bandage on John Lewis's head, which covered the gash where he'd had his skull cracked during the melee at the bus station. The sight of that bandage was enough to make Willie's lip throb. He kept studying the four Negroes sitting at the table full of microphones. Jim Farmer was at the top of the frame. The head of a New York group called CORE, Farmer had come up with the idea of the Freedom Rides as a way of testing new desegregation laws on interstate bus routes in the Deep South. He was on one of the buses that left Washington, D.C., on May 4. He rode as far as Atlanta but had to return to Washington for his father's funeral. When the story started making national headlines—that is, when buses and riders started getting photogenically attacked—Farmer had flown from Washington to Montgomery, eager be part of the blossoming coverage. Willie and his fellow riders distrusted Farmer instinctively. To them he looked like an overfed businessman who'd gotten off a plane at the wrong airport.

Next to Farmer sat solid, decent Abernathy, who, as always, looked like he was melting from the glare of all this unwelcome publicity.

Next to Abernathy sat King, who had flown in from Atlanta for the mass meeting at Abernathy's church the night after the riot at the bus station. To King's left sat John Lewis, the only Freedom Rider in the picture, the only one of the four who had put his body on the line.

Willie's eye went back to King's face, that smooth patrician face, so at home in front of all those cameras and microphones. Then Willie heard that voice again, that satiny voice. This time it said, *Where is your body, Dr. King?*

And when he heard that voice, he knew what D.N. stood for. Of course: Diane Nash.

She was part of Snick's Nashville contingent, a student at Fisk University, a light-skinned, green-eyed beauty who Willie had first met back in 1960 when he dropped out of Tuskegee and went to Nashville to learn the art of nonviolent protest and help with the downtown sit-ins. The woman had an aura about her. Once, during the lunch-counter sit-ins, she'd walked up to the mayor of Nashville and asked him point-blank: "Do *you* feel it's wrong to discriminate against a person solely on the basis of their race or color?" The mayor, flummoxed, allowed that, yes, as a matter of fact he did feel it was wrong. His admission made national news. Action didn't get any more direct than that. Later, Diane got thrown in jail when she was pregnant. Like everyone in Snick, Willie revered her.

Now he remembered that it was Diane, resourceful and determined Diane, who'd persuaded a reluctant black taxi driver to take Willie and John Lewis and Jim Zwerg to a house on the outskirts of Montgomery an hour after the attack at the bus station. No doctor in town, black or white, would patch up the three battered Freedom Riders. Too dangerous, they said. Not worth it. Diane, who knew the streets of Montgomery cold, directed the cab driver to a house at the dead end of a leafy, middle-class block. A black woman in her bathrobe let them in through the back door. She eyed their bloody clothes and the bloody towels they were pressing to their wounds, none too happy about it, but she went upstairs to wake her husband. He shuffled into the kitchen in his bathrobe, squinting and yawning. While he was sewing Willie's split lip at the kitchen table, they could all hear Diane in the living room shouting at Jim Farmer on the telephone: "We can't let them stop us with violence! If we do, the movement is dead! You hear me? *Dead!*" Not until they were back in the taxi did Diane tell Willie that the man who'd sewn up his lip was a veterinarian.

Three nights later, after the big press conference, they all gathered at the home of a Montgomery pharmacist to decide exactly what came next. Willie could see the house again: green clapboards with paint so fresh it looked wet; a broad front porch with rocking chairs and potted geraniums; and inside, gleaming floorboards. He could see the couple that greeted everyone at the front door: the prim little pharmacist with his bow tie and rimless spectacles, his big wife in her flowery dress and the enormous please-don't-sit-in-front-of-me hat she surely wore to church every Sunday. Yes, Willie remembered thinking, these were church people. King's people.

Everyone crowded into the living room. There was a certificate from the NAACP and a diploma from Meharry above the mantelpiece. For once there were no photographers or reporters on hand. The air in that room was thick with humidity and distrust. An ax seemed to be cleaving the air, splitting it between young and old, between the vulnerable and the protected, between the warriors and the generals. The former stood along the walls and sat on the floor; the latter helped themselves to the plush sofas and chairs.

The pharmacist's wife circulated with trays of cold lemonade. "Made it from scratch myself," she said proudly, though Willie, for one, didn't believe it. The generals all snatched at the sweating glasses and drank lustily in the unseasonable heat. The young people shunned the offering, a small act of solidarity in the face of what lay ahead, both on that night and in the coming days.

Willie sat in a corner. To his right was a white girl named Joan. Her stringy hair was the color of mud and her T-shirt said JUST A CRACKER FROM GEORGIA. Hard to believe anything could coax a smile out of him at a time like that—his mouth was hurting like hell, his head was hurting, everything was hurting—but Joan's T-shirt actually made Willie smile. She smiled back.

To her right sat beautiful Diane Nash. She was fidgeting, wound up, obviously spoiling for a fight.

Farmer went first. He called the Freedom Rides "my show" and vowed they would continue with fresh CORE volunteers currently on the way from New Orleans. This was greeted with angry shouts, accusations, vows that no one could tell the riders to get off the buses. Abernathy restored the peace.

That was pretty bad, but they were willing to let it slide because they were more interested in King—and if he planned to board the buses with them in the morning.

That was when Diane Nash stood up. Gripping her Bible, as usual, she delivered a short speech and then said to King, "Where is your body, Dr. King?" They'd all heard the question a thousand times, but this time it took the air out of the room. King looked like he'd stopped breathing. "Where is your body, Dr. King?" Diane repeated, louder.

All of King's flunkies came to his defense, saying he was needed for fund-raising speeches and high-level negotiations with Attorney General Robert Kennedy, important missions that couldn't be accomplished from a bus seat or a jail cell. That got everyone riled up again, and again it was Abernathy who called for quiet. Finally Diane did what she had done to the mayor of Nashville. She asked King point-blank: "Are you getting on the bus with us in the morning or not, Dr. King? Yes or no?"

Again King's flunkies rose up, saying he was still on probation for a 1960 traffic arrest in Georgia, and any new arrest would land him in jail for six months.

When Willie heard that, he felt himself getting up off the floor, heard himself saying through swollen lips, "I'm on probation—and I'm going."

"Me too," said Joan, the cracker from Georgia.

"Me too," said someone across the room.

Willie said, "What's the big deal with going to jail, Dr. King? Most of us have been to jail. Are you afraid of going to jail?"

And then he saw it—a sudden crack in the famed King composure. King looked at Willie, saw the stitches in his lip, then looked away. His tongue darted. He huffed. He knew he was cornered. Finally he said, "I think . . . I think I should choose the time and place of my Golgotha."

My Golgotha!

There was stunned silence and then Diane Nash hissed, "Would you listen to that? Man thinks he's de Lawd hisself!"

And that, Willie saw now, seven long years after the fact, was the moment when the trap door sprang open beneath him. That was the moment when he began to fall because he saw, for the first time, the wrongness of his belief that the world—that people, black or white—could be made to change for the better. Martin Luther King was just another garden-variety demagogue who thought he was de Lawd hisself. And that was how Willie had thought of King ever since that night at the pharmacist's house, as a self-anointed deity getting ready to go back to Atlanta to take care of more important business while the Freedom Riders got ready to journey into the lion's mouth. That night in Montgomery was the beginning of the end for Willie, and he owned it at last.

He rewound the reel of microfilm, shut down the machine, and left the library in a daze. The next morning he started writing his memoir. It felt good, but it was painful too. Disillusionment always is. The most painful thing about his disillusionment was its irony, the fact that it sprang not from the expected source—the racism of the white man—for that was a given, something almost comforting because it gave shape and substance to the black man's rage, was as reliable and implacable as the passing of the seasons. No, his disillusionment was painful because it sprang not from the venality of any particular race, but from the greater venality of being human, trapped inside a sack of skin that happened to be black, trapped inside history, trapped by his own imperfect past and by the ambitions and egos and smallness of men he wanted to revere but could not.

His life was simple now. He had a job to do, a story to tell. Now that he knew the framework of that story—the beginning, the middle, the beginning of the end, and the end—he could start telling the truth about men like Jim Farmer and Martin Luther King and Willie Bledsoe. The truth about his first white woman—and his second white woman. Even the truth about carrying the guns from Alabama to Detroit.

Of course he still wanted to know what happened to the last three guns. He was pretty sure one of them was a murder weapon. But which one? Now that his '54 Buick had vanished, the answer to that question was the only thing that could undo him—and then only if the cops were able to come up with the answer and prove it in court. For the first time, Willie was beginning to like his chances.

21

It turned out to be a smart move on Jimmy Robuck's part to let Alvin Hairston stew in his cell overnight before beginning the interrogation. For on that very night, while Jimmy and Flo were at home eating ratatouille, while Doyle and Cecelia were talking late at his house over a bottle of Chianti and plates of ravioli in *puttanesca* sauce, a man who was obviously not a newspaper subscriber or faithful viewer of the eleven o'clock news dropped by the Riopelle warehouse to check on Alvin and the Armageddon II arsenal. His name was Kenneth Smith. He was arrested by the detectives staking out the place, and he, like Alvin Hairston, spent the night alone in a seventh-floor cell at 1300 Beaubien, wondering what the morning would bring.

Though he had a mild hangover from the wine and lack of sleep, Doyle showed up for work before Jimmy. It was all he could do not to take Alvin Hairston into the yellow room by himself, but he knew that would be a mistake. So he drank coffee and read about the Tigers in the *Free Press* and tried to ignore the clock.

Jimmy finally showed a little after nine, raving about Flo's ratatouille. Doyle wasn't about to tell him that Cecelia had raved about his ravioli and *puttanesca* sauce—or that she was charmed by the buckets scattered around his bedroom floor to catch the rainwater that came through the Swiss-cheese roof.

Doyle and Jimmy took turns working on Alvin Hairston. First, Doyle got him to initial and sign the Miranda warning while he distracted him with some ice-breaking small talk and assurances that the paperwork was just a formality. It was a technique Doyle had developed shortly after joining the squad, and it worked so well it had become standard department procedure. It was every cop's wet dream: The perps did the paperwork, and the paperwork guaranteed that the cases against them wouldn't get thrown out of court. Kiss my ass, Earl Warren.

But after three hours Alvin Hairston hadn't given up a thing, and the detectives adjourned to the hallway for a conference. While Alvin had not yet insisted on seeing a lawyer, he had refused to go for any of their bait. When Jimmy showed him a picture of the .30-caliber Winchester rifle that had just been positively identified as the weapon in a riot-related murder and pointed out that his fingerprints were on it, Alvin shrugged and said he'd handled several of the guns in the warehouse but had never fired a single one. He said he was in Cleveland during the riot attending his mother's funeral. He even volunteered the name of the funeral home.

Out in the hallway Jimmy said, "Let's look at the situation straight on, Frank. We don't got shit on the nigger and he knows it. I just called the funeral home in Cleveland and his alibi checks out. I say we ship his ass back upstairs and let him go to trial on the weapons charge and get on with our lives."

"I've got a better idea," Doyle said.

"I'm listening."

"We both know Alvin didn't pull the trigger, but he knows more than he's letting on. I'm sure of it."

"Such as?"

"Such as where that gun came from. I know he knows."

Jimmy, the great respecter of gut instincts, said, "So what's your idea?"

"You go get Kenneth Smith and walk him by in the hall real nice and slow. No handcuffs. I'm going to go back in with Alvin and leave the door open."

"Not the oldest play in the book, Frank? You really think Alvin's that stupid?"

"I know he is."

Fifteen minutes later, Doyle watched Alvin Hairston's eyes widen at the sight of his fellow revolutionary, Kenneth Smith, being led down the hallway by the big black detective.

"Oh, I forgot to tell you," Doyle said, glancing over his shoulder. "We picked up your buddy Kenneth at the warehouse last night. Guess he hadn't heard about the raid. Man, Kenneth's a pussy."

"What you mean?" Alvin sat up straight.

"What I mean, Alvin, is that Kenneth rolled over in five minutes flat."

"Rolled over?"

"Yeah, Kenneth's on his way home."

"Home? I don't take your meaning. I thought you just got through tellin me you picked him up at the warehouse."

"We did. But it's not exactly a capital offense to walk into an empty warehouse, is it? I got to tell you, though, Kenneth's not the smartest guy I ever met."

"No, he a dumb motherfucka."

"Yes, Alvin, he's a dumb motherfucker, all right. He's so dumb, in fact, that he actually believed we've got enough evidence to pin a piece of that riot murder on him—accessory before and after the fact.

But the reason he's going home now is because he was smart enough to cut a deal and sign a statement for us."

"A statement?"

"That's right."

"What it say?"

"It says you pulled the trigger, Alvin. We're talking Murder One here, my friend. Do you know what the punishment is for Murder One in the state of Michi—"

"*You a lyin motherfucka!*" Alvin shouted toward the hallway, springing to his feet.

Doyle had to bite a knuckle to keep from laughing. He'd guessed right about Alvin's intelligence. Doyle said, "Sit the fuck down." Alvin sat down. Doyle walked over and closed the door and returned to his chair. "Maybe Kenneth is a lying motherfucker, for all I know. But we've got his name on a signed statement, we've got your fingerprints on a murder weapon, and I know a guy in the District Attorney's office who's an old pro at getting all-white juries. Now let's you and me do the math here, Alvin. We've got a dead woman—a dead white woman—who was shot during the riot. We've got a defendant—a black defendant, namely you—who's been identified as the shooter by an eyewitness. Your fingerprints are on the murder weapon and, to make matters worse, you were caught red-handed in a warehouse full of guns and you're a known troublemaker who thinks it's time to get rid of the white race. You with me so far, Alvin?"

Silence. But Alvin was chewing his lip, so Doyle pressed on.

"What do you think that all-white jury's gonna do when it comes time to reach a verdict in this case, Alvin? You think they're gonna believe you? And I don't want to hear any more shit about your momma's funeral."

"I ain't killed nobody."

"You know something, Alvin? I want to believe you. I really do. But the only way you're going to convince me is if you start talking— right now—about where those guns came from and who was planning to use them. And when. And where. I need names, Alvin, and

I need them right now. It's your ass or theirs. You don't deserve to go down with these people, and they *are* going down. It's your call." Doyle stood up. "I'm gonna go smoke a cigarette. I'll be back in ten minutes, Alvin, and when I come back in here I want names."

Jimmy was standing in the hallway gazing at Alvin through the one-way mirror. "Man, Frank, that was good."

"You think?"

"No, I know. He yours. Since when you start smokin cigarettes?"

Doyle laughed. "Let's get a cup of coffee."

When they got back to the one-way mirror, Kenneth had his forehead on the table. Doyle said to Jimmy, "You got that picture of Wes Bledsoe?"

"Got it right here," he said, motioning to the folder under his arm. "U.S. Navy sent it over yesterday."

"You got some other mugs to go with it?"

"Three."

"Two'll do. No sense confusing the man."

Jimmy handed over two mugshots and the photocopy of the U.S. Navy's official discharge picture of Seaman W. B. Bledsoe. Doyle shuffled them and took them into the yellow room. Alvin actually flinched when he heard the door open. Jimmy was right, Doyle thought, we've got Alvin. Doyle laid the photos face-down on the table and sat down.

Alvin's eyes danced around the yellow walls for a while and finally came to rest on Doyle's. Then Alvin looked down at his hands. "I ain't killed nobody."

"You already told me that. Tell me something new."

"Alls I can tell you—let me get somethin straight, first."

Doyle waited.

"That jive piece a paper Kenneth signed—you gonna tear it up I give you what you want?"

"That all depends."

"What it depend on?"

"On whether or not your story checks out."

"It'll check out cause it's the truth."

"Then we got a deal."

"I give you a name and you tear up that piece a paper?"

"No, Alvin, you give me names—plural—and I tear up that piece of paper." That piece of paper that didn't exist. "Provided your story about your momma's funeral checks out."

"I only got three names. And that's God's honest truth."

Doyle asked himself what Jimmy would do under the circumstances. He would say follow your gut. Doyle's gut told him that Alvin believed he was cornered and he was too scared and too stupid to lie his way out of the corner, so this was the best they were going to get. Way better than they had any right to hope for. "Okay then," Doyle said. "You give me those names and we got us a deal."

"You tear up the paper."

"That's right."

Alvin sighed. "The onliest people I ever saw in that warehouse was Kenneth and a brother name Yusef. That's his Muslim name and I swear to God I don't know his real name."

Doyle waited.

"You got to realize I only been in that warehouse two, three times—"

"I'm waiting for another name, Alvin, not another story."

"—I'm comin up on that. Yeah, I was there one day Yusef brought some guns, including that one in the picture you showed me. I put 'em on the racks, which is why my fingerprints is on 'em—"

Doyle held his breath.

"—we talkin three guns here. The guy who brought 'em in use to be in the Navy. He was suppose to be some big bad-ass, cording to Yusef, but he fat now. I think he were half-drunk too. Or high, one."

Doyle was still holding his breath. "The name, Alvin."

"Yusef called him by Wes."

Doyle exhaled. "Any last name?"

"Jus Wes."

"Was anybody with him?"

"No. He were alone."

Doyle turned the pictures over and lined them up for Alvin to see. "Now I want you to take your time, Alvin, and look at these three pictures. Tell me if you see Wes."

Alvin didn't hesitate. He tapped a finger on the picture of Seaman W. B. Bledsoe. "That's the motherfucka right there."

"You sure about that?"

"Stone positive."

Jimmy gave Doyle high fives and a bear hug out in the hallway. While Jimmy took Alvin back to his cell, Doyle went to the squad room and placed a call to the F.B.I. in Washington. It was time to find Wes Bledsoe.

An hour later Doyle called his home phone on the off chance that Cecelia was still sleeping off the red wine and the after-dinner calisthenics. She picked up after the fifth ring. "I wake you up?" Doyle said.

"God no, it's past noon. I made coffee and ate some toast. I've been . . . I hope you don't mind. . . ."

"What?"

"I've been weeding your garden. I used to love gardening but I haven't done it since Ronnie and I moved into the high-rise. I'd forgotten how . . . therapeutic it is. I hope you don't mind."

"Be my guest. If you want to take a crack at that jungle in front of the house, the mower's in the garage."

She laughed. "Don't press your luck. So how'd it go with that interrogation?"

"Better than good. Perfect. Unbelievable."

"So you've got your murder suspect?"

"We've got the name of the man who sold the murder weapon. Just about the same thing."

"You've already arrested him?"

"No, but we know who he is. Now we just have to find him. The F.B.I.'s helping us."

"You sound happy."

"No, I'm on cloud nine." He paused. "You planning on hanging around the house for a while?"

"I'm going to finish this weeding. I'm not even halfway done. Why?"

"Because I'm in the mood to celebrate, take the rest of the day off. I've got a nice bottle of French champagne in the fridge and I thought—"

"I'll be right here."

And she was. Her Mustang was still parked in front of the house and from the kitchen window Doyle could see her in the garden, dressed in gloves and a pair of his boxer shorts and a faded U. of D. T-shirt. She was down on her knees in the dirt, humming to herself. Her hair was piled up crazily, held together with a pencil, and when she shooed a fly Doyle could see she had a smudge of mud on the tip of her nose. He tapped on the window and she looked toward the house, a smile spreading on her face as she came out of the garden, up the back steps, into his waiting arms. They kissed. Then she followed him upstairs to the big room with the buckets half-full of rainwater scattered around the king-size bed.

22

WILLIE HAD THE WEEKEND OFF, AND AFTER WORKING ON HIS book all day Saturday he decided to take Octavia out for a Sunday drive in the country. He'd earned a day of rest. He rose early, washed the Deuce, then fixed a simple breakfast and ate it at the kitchen table while reading about the Tigers' 12-1 victory over the woeful White Sox.

Half an hour later he was watching Octavia slide onto his convertible's front seat. She'd worn her hair up, wrapped in a scarf made of colorful African cloth, and her skin glowed against the white upholstery. She was wearing a long loose creamy linen dress and sandals, gold hoop earrings, very little makeup. Her toenails were painted copper. Willie had trouble keeping his eyes on the road.

He took Jefferson, the same route he'd taken when he took the car for a test drive with Chick Murphy. The lake was even shinier this morning, the air tropical humid, the kind of heat Willie liked. On the north shore of Anchor Bay they passed through towns with nautical names—Anchorville and Fairhaven and Pearl Beach—and they saw men sitting on overturned buckets fishing in a canal, the same way Aunt Nezzie taught Willie to fish in the teeming roadside creeks and bayous. The memory reminded him that the similarities between Alabama and Michigan were not all bad.

As they were leaving Pearl Beach, Octavia reached for the radio. "You got JLB on any a these buttons?"

"Second one from the right." She turned on the radio and pressed the button and the day filled with the Temptations' familiar voices: *Like a snowball rollin down the side of a snow-covered hill, it's grrrr-owin . . . Like the size of the fish that the man claims broke his reel, it's grrrr-owin . . .*

"Oooh, I love me some David Ruffin," she said, turning up the volume.

David Ruffin, the singer whose limousine was upholstered with mink. For the first time in weeks Willie thought of his brother. He wondered if Wes ever made it to Denver—or if he was still alive.

"You never axed me how someone works as a receptionist managed to afford that Austin-Healey," Octavia said. "That's usually the first thing men ax me."

There it was again, the subtle put-down, that northern smugness that had so infuriated Willie the day Octavia took him for a ride in her Austin-Healey. He realized the work he had done on his book so far was fueled by anger—by a desire to show people like Octavia that they were the ones who had a lot to learn and that he, a man who had walked through fire, was the one to teach them. In the past he would have been distrustful of such anger as a sign of an overblown ego. But now he welcomed it. His mission, as he'd known for many weeks, was to repudiate the world that made him. Anger would be a useful tool—as long as he didn't use it recklessly. He took a deep breath and said, "Tell me, Octavia, how'd you manage to afford that fine ride?"

"David gave it to me. Walked up to the switchboard one day and handed me a set a keys and told me to go look what's out in the parking lot. Ain't that somethin? A free car!"

He wanted to tell her she wasn't the only person in the world who ever got a car for free, but he let it go. Trying to one-up her seemed like a puny thing to do.

He parked in the shade beside a restaurant called Roberta's near Algonac that Erkie had recommended, a sun-bleached shack roosting on a pier that jutted out into the St. Clair River. He could see freighters riding low in the silver water, enormous boats named Medusa and Blue Star and Edsel Ford.

Willie ordered smoked chubs and cole slaw; Octavia asked for broasted chicken and onion rings. She explained that her mother had taught her never to order the fish in a dive. Willie's Aunt Nezzie had taught him that the best fish was always found in places like this, where the paper place mats were decorated with seahorses and the menu was a chalkboard on the wall and the waitresses were all fat.

Their waitress had a big round pink face and she brought a pitcher of beer while they waited for their food. They drank and looked out across the river at the flatlands of Ontario, a soothing breeze skating at them across the water. Someone in the kitchen was listening to the Tigers game on a scratchy transistor radio and when the door swung open Willie heard the familiar voice of Ernie Harwell: *"It's deep . . . it might be . . . it's a* HOME RUN *for Willie Horton!"*

He decided the time wasn't going to get any more right. "Got some good news," he said. "I got started writing my book."

She touched his hand. "Willie, that's wonderful! What happened?"

He looked across the water and realized it would be impossible to tell her the whole truth, so he did the next best thing and told her about remembering the confrontation in the pharmacist's house in Montgomery. Once he got started writing, he told her, fresh information started finding him. There was a story just yesterday in the *Free Press* that he'd clipped and put in his wallet. He took the clipping out and smoothed it on the table. "Check this out. This is a review

257

of a documentary called 'Revolution.'" He read the opening aloud to her: "'There are so many American scenes—S.N.C.C. and the Haight-Ashbury in particular—that have gone over-reported and under-recorded, to vanish without any real trace in the novel or on film, of how they were. Day-to-day coverage in the press or on television couldn't do it, and now these scenes are gone, dispersed, or so much changed they do not matter anymore. . . . '"

He returned the clipping to his wallet. "I especially like the part about how Snick was over-reported and under-recorded. It's *so* true. There damn sure wasn't any shortage of reporters following us around—but none of them told it like it was. How could they? Most of them were white and even the black ones were just doing a job, not risking their lives for a cause like we were."

"So," Octavia said, "once you remembered that meeting at the pharmacist's house, you was able to start writing?"

"Yeah. I started the next day."

"Just like that?"

"Just like that. Been writing every morning before I go to work. Sometimes I write more when I get home at night. Sometimes I write all night."

Octavia squeezed his hand. "I'm so glad for you, Willie."

"Yeah, me too. You got no idea how glad I am."

Their food came. It was delicious, as Erkie had promised, and Willie ate with gusto, cleaned his plate and then helped Octavia finish her chicken. Afterwards they sat there gazing at the boats on the shimmering water. The kitchen door swung open with a roar. Al Kaline had just hit a triple with the bases loaded. Octavia lit a cigarette, picked at a fingernail, cleared her throat. "Say, Willie?"

"Yeah?"

"You remember me telling you that Clyde helped me out of a jam?"

"Yeah."

"Reason I needed his help was cause I got picked up on Kercheval back in '66—you know, when we had that near-riot?"

"I hadn't moved here yet but, yeah, I've heard about it. What happened?"

"Friend a mine, this artist cat name Glanton Dowdell, he picked me up one night to visit some friends a his on the East Side. You may of heard of Glanton—he painted those murals in Reverend Cleage's church. So we're ridin up Kercheval when all of a sudden people's throwin rocks at our car, and we see a po-lice car on fire. Next thing you know, one a them cars packed with cops, you know, a, a—"

"Big Four."

"Right, a Big Four pulls up in front of us and just stops. Glanton has to slam on the brakes, and then there's cops all around us, pointin rifles, yellin nigger this and nigger that and everybody out the car. They lie us down on the street like dogs, then they break open the trunk and start whistlin and laughin. Turns out Glanton's buddies was some kind a militants and that trunk was full a guns and ammunition."

"What'd the cops do?"

"They handcuffed us, slapped us around some, called us a lot of salty names. I was scared half to death. I tried to tell em I didn't know nothin bout no guns but they told me to shut up." She was biting her lip, and Willie could see she was trying not to cry. "They took us downtown, threw me in a cage with a bunch a addicts and drunks and flat-back hookers, some filthy womens, and I tried to tell the po-lice I had a job at Motown records but they just laughed and told me to shut up, wouldn't even let me make a phone call."

She lit a fresh cigarette and blew a huge cloud of smoke. Her voice had started getting shrill. "It was the awfullest night a my life. So degrading. The hookers was all talkin bout how much they charge for a straight lay versus round-the-world, how they pimps beat em with coat hangers—but always on they back so they can still work." Another cloud of smoke. "I still have nightmares." A bigger cloud of smoke. "You got no idea how awful the po-lice is in this town. . . ."

He was looking across the water. Octavia kept talking but he no longer heard a word she said. He didn't doubt that her night in jail was hell, but he could not let this slide. This was his first opportunity

259

to assert himself, which was the only way he would ever be able to repudiate his past and make his voice heard. He needed to finish the job he'd begun during that long walk on the Oakland Hills golf course. He needed to finish shedding the skin of the dutiful son, the compliant kid brother, the faceless foot soldier, the meek listener—it was the only way to become the man he meant to become, shorn of all illusions and causes and messiahs, rid of the world that made him, healthy and breathing free in that sick and suffocating place known as America.

". . . oh, Willie, you got no idea what lockup's like in—"

"You're wrong, Octavia."

She froze, the cigarette an inch from her lips. Her face crinkled. "Say what?"

"I said you're wrong if you think I got no idea what lockup's like."

She took a drag on the cigarette. "I'm sorry, Willie, I'm just depress. I know you been thrown in plenty a jails down South."

"I'm not talking about down South."

"You ain't?"

"I'm talking about Detroit."

"You been in jail in D-troit?"

"I damn sure have."

"When?"

He didn't hesitate. "It was a Saturday night last summer and it was so hot I knew I wouldn't be able to sleep, so I took a near cold bath and dragged my mattress out onto the porch, hoping to catch a breeze."

She reached for a fresh cigarette without taking her eyes off him. He noticed that her eyes were bigger than before. Good.

"Even on the porch I couldn't sleep," he went on. "Sometime way past midnight my brother knocked on my door, said there was a party at a blind pig down on Twelfth Street for a guy who'd just gotten home from Vietnam. I told him I wasn't in a party mood. He gave me the address in case I changed my mind, then told me he was going to the Algiers later cause they have a rolling craps game on Saturday night that sometimes runs for days."

"You mean the Algiers Motel?" Octavia said.

"Yeah. So I try to go back to sleep but it's too hot and too noisy, sirens off in the distance. I musta dozed off eventually cause the telephone woke me up sometime after sunrise. It was Walter Mitchell, an old buddy from college, wanting to know what was going down with the riot. I said, 'What riot?' There he was, hundreds of miles away in D.C., filling me in on what was happening a few blocks from where I was sitting. Walter told me he'd just gotten back from photographing the riot in Newark, and his editors at *Ebony* wanted him to get on the next plane to Detroit. I agreed to pick him up at the airport."

"Now this is Sunday morning?"

"Right. Soon as Walter gets off the plane he asks me to drive him to the Sheraton Cadillac Hotel so he can drop off his suitcase and pick up his press credentials. We got stopped at half a dozen police checkpoints on our way into the city. The farther we drove, the scarier it got—police cars and fire trucks with their sirens going, this huge black cloud drifting toward downtown. We saw dozens of buildings on fire, saw a man throw a cinderblock through a plate-glass window at an A&P supermarket and people poured into the store. People were cheering them on, like it was a game or something."

Octavia touched his arm. "Keep your voice down," she said. Willie's eyes swept the restaurant. There were only three other customers in the place—a black couple in church clothes attacking a pile of clams, and a white guy two tables away in an ugly Hawaiian shirt drinking a pitcher of beer and reading a newspaper.

Willie lowered his voice. "When we got to the hotel Walter started making calls to police headquarters and a bunch of TV and radio stations. Like a foreign correspondent arriving in some war-torn capital, cool as could be. Someone told him the action was on the West Side, so we hopped in my car and followed a fire truck out Grand River to a burning warehouse. It was horrible but beautiful too—flames shooting through the roof of the building, hundreds of feet into the air. There were gunshots and I saw Walter crouching behind a yellow Cadillac snapping pictures of the firemen as they scrambled back to their truck. Then the windshield of the Cadillac exploded and Walter crawled back to my car on his belly. There were pieces of glass stuck in his hair. He wanted to go, but I told him to look across the street. The flames from the warehouse had jumped to the roof of a little two-story house next door. Women and children were running out of the building carrying the most pitiful shit you ever saw—lamps, hats, dolls—while two men stood in the yard and sprayed the building with a garden hose. A *garden* hose. Walter got pictures of them. Some of the best pictures he took."

The plump waitress appeared at Willie's elbow. "Anything else here?"

"Just the check, please, ma'am."

When the waitress was gone, he said, "It was getting dark, so we headed back to my crib. Now there were National Guard at the checkpoints, and some of them were so jittery I could see their rifles shaking. But the scariest thing was the carloads of white men cruising around with shotgun and rifle barrels sticking out of their windows. I thought I was back in Mississippi."

"Wasn't you scared?"

"Hell yes I was scared. When we got back to my place Walter called his boss in Washington, Thomas Henderson, told him we'd go back out after curfew was lifted at sunrise. The noise outside went on all night—gunfire, screams, sirens, laughter, breaking glass."

"You think to keep your lights off?"

He ignored the question. "In the morning I drove Walter downtown to police headquarters for a press conference. The city looked like it'd been bombed, fires still smoldering, glass and rubble everywhere. All I could think was that the race war had finally started."

"Was you glad like I was?"

"No, I was just numb. Walter spent the day taking pictures—families sitting on their furniture in front of their burnt-out houses, a looter walking down the middle of the street hauling a bass fiddle, some wild stuff. It was starting to get dark when a fire truck passed us on Lawton and Walter told me to follow it, said he wanted to talk to some firemen. I followed it to the fire station at the corner of Lawton and Warren and I stayed in the car while Walter went off to do some interviews. I saw a tank at the end of the street. When a ladder truck pulled out of the firehouse, Walter hopped back in the car and told me to follow it. That's when I heard someone shout, 'Halt! You in the pink car! Halt!'

"I stopped the car. A Guardsman walked up and I handed him my license and Walter's press credentials. He told us to get out the car. Then he told us to put our hands on the hood and spread our feet. A state trooper walked up and said, 'They're okay, they're press,' but the Guardsman said, 'I don't give a fuck who the niggers are.' He patted us down for weapons, then he jabbed me in the shoulder blades with the butt of his rifle and told us to move. I realized he was pushing us toward two lines of firemen. One of them spit in my face and suddenly they were all spitting, kicking us, punching. I ran with my head down, trying to fend off the blows, trying to reach the station house without falling because I was afraid that if I fell down they'd stomp me to death."

"But I don't understand," Octavia said. "You had ID and you weren't doin nothin wrong."

Willie smiled. It was working. "We were put in a small detention room," he went on, "and we could hear the Guardsmen taunting and beating other guys outside, screaming things like 'Castrate that coon!' and 'Beg, nigger, beg!' Every time a Guardsman walked by the room Walter started yelling about his press credentials, but the men told him to shut up or they'd beat him some more."

"You didn't complain?"

"No, I knew from experience we were past the point where complaining or pleading would do any good. After a while we were all led outside into a paddy wagon. I noticed my Buick was still parked at the curb where I'd left it. On the way downtown some of the men moaned about their injuries, others bragged about the sniping they'd done, the stores they'd looted. When the paddy wagon finally stopped we were led into a large building. I realized it was the back of police

headquarters, the building where Walter had attended the press conference. Inside we were photographed, fingerprinted and told to sign a card
that said Curfew Violation. Walter and I both refused. We demanded to
make a phone call and see a lawyer but the cop with the camera laughed,
and we were led downstairs and turned loose in a huge garage. The floor
was greasy and there was a single spigot and a rain drain in the corner—
our latrine. I found a dry patch of concrete and fell asleep."

"You was able to sleep in a place like that?"

"I was exhausted and sore. Besides, I've seen worse." Her eyes
widened, and he felt another trill of satisfaction. "When I woke up
there was sunshine coming through the caged windows. My back and
ribs hurt and I had a wicked headache. Walter came out of nowhere
and handed me a bologna sandwich and a cup of water. The sandwich
tasted like cardboard and it hurt to chew, but I ate the whole thing
and drank all the water. A lot more prisoners had arrived while I was
asleep, and the heat and the smell were enough to knock you down.
Everyone had been beaten. One guy'd been beaten so bad his left
eyeball had popped out of its socket and was dangling by a thread on
his cheek. Another guy was having convulsions, twitching on that
greasy floor, foaming at the mouth."

"Where was Walter's boss the whole time?"

"I'm coming to that. I started to doze off again. The last thing I
heard was a woman with her left eye swollen shut saying, 'I ain't looted
no store or fired no gun—and the motherfuckers picked me up and
done *this* to me. I tell you one damn thing, though, when I get out
this hole The Man is gonna pay.'

"Walter woke me up. He said they'd called our names. His boss
had arrived from D.C.—"

"Bout damn time."

"—and they led us upstairs. This dapper dude with a moustache,
made me think of Cab Calloway, he's talking low with a plainclothes
cop. They're nodding their heads, obviously working something out.
When they're finished, the guy with the moustache introduces himself
as Thomas Henderson, the editor of *Ebony* magazine. He told us to

sign the release forms, then he led us out of the building through the front door. The street was much cooler than the garage. God, that air tasted fine! Thomas Henderson had a rental car and he drove us to the Sheraton Cadillac. In Walter's room I took the longest hottest shower of my life. I couldn't help but remember all those southern towns where I'd walked out of jails and how good that first hot shower felt, how good that first hamburger tasted. When I got out of the shower, Walter was packing and the phone was ringing. Thomas Henderson answered it. 'It's for you,' he told Walter. 'Make it quick. We can't miss that plane.'

"Walter took the phone. He didn't say much. When he hung up he said, 'I can't believe this shit.' I asked him who it was. He said it was the mayor of Detroit calling to apologize personally for what had happened to us. We all just looked at each other, not believing anything anymore."

"Keep your voice down," Octavia said again.

"Then Thomas Henderson drove us back to the firehouse. My Buick was still there, not a scratch on it. Walter's camera bag was still on the floor, right where he'd left it. I was afraid to drive home alone, afraid of the checkpoints, so Thomas Henderson and Walter agreed to follow me. Soon as we got to my building, they split for the airport. The building next-door to mine had burned while I was in jail. It was still smoking."

There was a long silence. When it became apparent he had finished telling his story, Octavia said, "That's it?"

"That's it—my humble experience in a Detroit lock-up."

"Wasn't you mad?"

"Mad doesn't begin to get it."

"So what'd you *do*?"

It hit Willie then that his story had not had the intended effect. It had not put her in her place. She wanted to know how he went about exacting his revenge—for it was a given, in her eyes, that any black man who took such treatment lying down was less than a man. But answering Octavia's question was something he simply could not do yet, even if he'd wanted to. He was still missing that one crucial piece of information: what happened, exactly, on the roof of the Larrow Arms.

She couldn't believe he was finished. "You mean to tell me you didn't do *nothin*?"

"Oh, I did something. But that's another story for another time." He grabbed the check and stood up. He could see his brother standing in the doorway of his apartment, all that blood. He could see Detroit burning down below the edge of the roof. He blinked the memories away and stepped to the cash register.

As they rode back to the city Octavia sang along with the songs Ernie D was playing on the radio, raised her hands above the windshield and let the breeze dance through her fingers. She had already forgotten Willie's story, and he was glad for that.

Ernie D was saying, "It's your ace from inner-space with the swinginest show on the ray-dee-oh. Don't go way cuz I'll be right back, Jack, with another stack of shellac for you and doll-face too. . . ."

Octavia laughed. "You hear that? Man just called me doll-face."

The familiar Q&A came out of the radio's speaker:

> *What's the word?*
> *Thunnnnnn-der-bird!*
> *What's the price?*
> *Forty-four twice!*
> *What's the reason?*
> *The grapes are in season!*
> *Who drinks it most?*
> *Us city folks!*
> *That's right, Thunderbird is a delightfully fruity fortified wine. . . .*

Willie snapped off the radio. He wasn't in the mood for this happy-go-lucky darkie routine. The day had been an emotional roller-coaster ride, beginning with his high spirits at breakfast, rising with the drive out of town, peaking when he told Octavia about starting his book, then plunging after he finished telling her about the riot and heard disappointment instead of awe in her voice. He felt cheap and foolish. He needed to shut up and get back to work. The world was full of people who talked away their books.

When he pulled up in front of Octavia's building he left the engine running and turned to say goodbye. Before he could speak she had her arms around his neck and she was kissing him. When their teeth clicked together, she giggled. They kissed for a long time there in the open car under the high sun-washed trees.

Finally she pulled away and said, "You wanna come in?"

"I don't think so, baby."

"You sure?" She cocked her head and smiled. Making it easy for him to reconsider.

"Yeah, I'm sure. I just remembered something and . . . I need to go write it down."

She reached for the door handle. Her next words sounded more sad than angry. "I'm beginning to think you and me ain't never gonna get it together."

He had begun to think the same thing. The woman had so much going for her—that body for starters, but also an unfed hunger to know things, to travel, to break out of her small world. He found her hunger attractive, sexy even, and yet he could see that it was unlikely she would ever feed it. There was a gulf between them. He needed to get far away from this place, the only place she had ever known and was ever likely to know. She had a dying daddy to look after, a berth at Motown, a frisky sports car, a nice crib, family and friends all over town—no wonder she was unable to imagine living anywhere but Detroit. But Willie couldn't allow himself to get tied down here. It would be suicide, spiritual and physical suicide. But instead of saying these things to her now, he said something that was as bland as it was true. "Come on, baby, there's no way of knowing how things're gonna play out. This book's important to me."

She got out of the car then and closed the door, gave him a sad smile before she turned to go. Watching her walk up the sidewalk to her apartment building, he thought back to the day they'd first met, when he'd watched her walk to the restroom in the Seven Seas. That day seemed like half a lifetime ago. She waved to him now from her doorway and blew him a kiss before disappearing into the building.

Willie's phone was ringing when he opened the door to his apartment. He picked up the receiver and found himself listening to the very loud voice of a very drunk man. "Where you been, bruh?" Wes bellowed. "Been tryin to reach you all damn day long."

"I been out. What up?"

"Just wanted to let you know I's goin back."

"Back where?"

"Southeast Asia. Gonna take the money and run."

"Why you going back there?"

"Cause it's gonna take me away from this town. From this whole messed-up country."

"Did you re-up?"

"Fuck no. Gonna open a restaurant over there with an old Navy buddy. In Saigon, or maybe Bangkok."

"Where are you now?"

"Oakland."

"California? Ma said you were on your way to Denver."

"Got to keep movin, man, keep the pigs guessin."

"How long you been in Oakland?"

"Bout a week."

Willie decided to come right out with it. "Wes, there's something I need to know."

"Anything for my baby bro."

"You remember those three guns from the roof of your building, that night during the riot?"

"Fuck yeah, I remember."

"You know where they are?"

"Not exactly."

"What's that mean?"

"Means I sold 'em."

"To who?"

"Some black Muslim fool name of Yusef."

"All three of 'em?"

"Yup. Made the sale in a warehouse down by the river. Package deal."

"When was this?"

"Just before I left D-troit, a month or so ago. Why you axin all these questions?"

"Just curious. Want to make sure those guns don't come back to bite us."

"Don't worry. They long gone."

"So what're you doing in Oakland?"

"Just brokered a big shipment a guns to the Panthers. Matter of fact, I'm at Panther headquarters right now. I'm callin on their nickel."

Willie's stomach did a flip. "You're calling me from *Panther headquarters?*"

"Thas right," Wes said, failing to hear the horror in his brother's voice. "Just took an order for a mess a M-1s from this brother name Geronimo—"

"Get off this line right now!" Willie shouted. "Call me collect from a pay phone!" He slammed down the receiver.

Ten minutes later his phone rang again and Willie told the operator he would accept a collect call. Then he said to his brother, "You got to be the dumbest nigger in the cotton patch. It ever occur to you the phones in Panther headquarters might be tapped? *Je-sus!*"

"Don't worry, my boat leaves in an hour. Once I'm gone they never gonna find me."

"That's nice for you. How about me?"

"Man, you worry too much. Ain't nothin gonna happen to you." There was a long staticky silence. Then came the question

Willie had been expecting all along. "How you fixed for bread, bro?"

The partial answer was that he was finally building the nest egg that would finance his exit from Detroit, hopefully in the fall; the complete answer was that he wanted no part of the money Wes was about to offer. He'd gotten nigger-rich off gun money once before, and he knew all about the grief that came with it. "I'm fine," he said.

"You sure? I could wire you a couple hun—"

"Keep it. You're gonna need it worse than I am."

"Suit yourself. But just as soon as you's able, you run away from *that* town. Ain't nothin there for neither one of us but trouble. You hear me?"

"I hear you. Believe me, I'm working on it. And don't you go anywhere near that Panther house. The F.B.I.'s probably on their way to kick the door down right now."

Wes, fool that he was, laughed off the warning. After Willie hung up the phone he opened the shades in the living room just as a rusty green Pontiac was pulling away from the curb across the street from his Deuce. Willie realized he'd seen that car before—parked down the block on Pallister, parked outside Octavia's apartment, parked in the visitors' lot at the Public Library. Did Chick Murphy have a private eye on his tail?

As the car pulled away, Willie caught a glimpse of the driver. He had his left elbow out the window and he was wearing a Hawaiian shirt. It was the white guy from the fish shack, sitting two tables away, drinking beer and pretending to read the newspaper. And, Willie realized with a flash of terror, hearing every word that came out of my big mouth.

23

JIMMY HAD DROPPED ANCHOR IN A LITTLE COVE JUST UPRIVER from the Belle Isle Bridge, out of the way of the boat traffic. It was his favorite spot on the river. From here you could see the bridge's graceful arches and its string of lights bouncing off the water. It was how he imagined Europe looked, places like Paris and Prague. It was a steamy night with a fat yellow moon, a good night to be out on the water, catch the breeze. While Jimmy fished a couple of fresh beers out of the cooler, Doyle re-lit his cigar.

"What you call that sauce again?" Jimmy said, handing a beer to Doyle. Earlier that evening Jimmy had nosed his Chris-Craft up the canals that thread through the Jeff-Chalmers neighborhood. He'd tied up at the end of Klenk Street, then walked the two short blocks to Doyle's front door. He could smell the food from half a block away.

"It's called *puttanesca* sauce," Doyle said. "Comes from the Italian word for whore, *putta*, cause it's so easy to make hookers can whip up a batch between tricks. My mother taught me to make it when I was still in grade school. Like I said, anybody can make it."

"Might be easy to make, but it damn sure tastes good. And all these years I thought I hated anchovies and capers. And that wine."

"Yeah, that was nice and chewy. A '54 Barolo."

"That Spanish shit?"

"No, it's Italian."

"And that dessert? Tara . . . tara . . ."

"Tiramisu."

"Man, you got to teach me to cook."

"Any time, Jimmy, any time. Anybody who can read a recipe can learn how to cook."

"Yeah, but you got the touch."

They were quiet for a while, just watching the river and the bridge lights and the moon, Doyle puffing on his cigar. Jimmy could tell Doyle didn't want to talk about food anymore. He wanted to keep talking about what they'd talked about all through dinner—what to do with the stuff he'd learned on Sunday afternoon at Roberta's fish shack in Algonac.

One of the first things Jimmy had taught Doyle was that a good homicide police doesn't have a whole lot of use for motive. "Give me the how, the where, and the when," Jimmy liked to say, "and nine times out of ten I'll give you the who." *Why* a person killed another person was usually beside the point. A luxury. Something a competent detective could live without.

But that didn't mean you should run away from a motive if one hopped onto your lap. After he spent that Sunday afternoon eavesdropping on Willie Bledsoe, Doyle went to the records cage and combed through arrest reports from the second day of the riot, Monday, July 24, 1967, and learned that William B. Bledsoe and Walter Mitchell of *Ebony* magazine had been jailed for curfew violation and resisting arrest, then released into the custody of Thomas Henderson after spending twenty-three hours in the rat hole garage at 1300 Beaubien Street. All charges against them were dropped. Through his brother's contacts, Doyle even got confirmation that Mayor Jerome Cavanagh had placed a phone call to the Sheraton Cadillac Hotel to apologize personally to Walter Mitchell and all the readers of *Ebony* magazine. Crafty old Cavanagh, always hip to how his act was playing with the colored crowd. Not that it mattered anymore. The riot had finished Jerry Cavanagh just as sure as it had finished the city of Detroit.

So suddenly they had a nice tidy motive in the murder of Helen Hull, the oldest one in the book: revenge. But instead of making Doyle's life simpler, this had complicated things. All through dinner he'd talked about the questions that were eating at him. Who could blame a young black man—who could blame any man?—for going off the deep end after getting thrown in jail for no reason, beaten, terrorized and humiliated by a pack of vengeful firemen and cops? Jimmy had reminded him that none of it justified the killing of an innocent woman—or anyone else. Frank agreed, but he said he had to ask the questions Willie Bledsoe had surely asked himself after his nightmare in the basement garage came to an end. Who were the true criminals here? And did they really believe that their acts of brutality would not—should not—be answered with equal brutality? Even as he asked himself these questions, though, Doyle said he could hear the answer coming back from Jerry Czapski and Jimmy McCreedy and Walt Kanka and the other ninety percent of the force that was white: "Oh, sure. Cops were the bad guys during the riot. Cops burned down half the city. Cops shot up precinct houses and fire-bombed stores and hauled away as much free shit as they could carry. Tell me all about it."

Jimmy had said to Doyle at the dinner table, "Ain't just the white guys on the force feel that way. I do too. The thing you gotta realize, Frank, is that this country ain't nothin but a great big motherfuckin tease, especially for the black man. Civil rights—shit—makin it a law don't make it so. What The Man gives with one hand, he takes back with the other. You watch 'Star Trek,' don't you?"

The question surprised Doyle. "Sometimes," he said. "Not religiously."

"But you seen Lieutenant Uhura, the 'communications director' on Starship Enterprise. See, this is zactly what I'm talkin bout. The Man makes a prime-time TV show bout what the future's gonna look like, he puts an attractive black character on it—then he makes sure she ain't nothin but a glorified switchboard operator."

Doyle thought Jimmy sounded like Vicki Jones. She was always bitching about the fact that there were plenty of black janitors and secretaries but hardly any black executives at Ford's Glass House, where she worked in data entry. Or else she was bitching about having to wait longer than white people to get help from a clerk in a store. Or, even worse, about having some white customer assume she was a clerk simply because she was black. Doyle thought she was being paranoid and her tirades wore thin—until the day they were shopping in the women's shoe department at Hudson's and an old white lady walked up to Vicki and said, "Miss, do you have these pumps in a seven and a half?"

"So," Doyle had said to Jimmy at the dinner table, "what The Man gives with one hand, he takes back with the other, . . ."

"Right. But that don't justify nothin. *Nothin*, you hear me? It don't give a man the right to kill or burn or loot. Look, the way I come up I should be in prison right now, or dead. Reason I ain't is cause I made a decision. I decided they's a right way and a wrong way and they ain't no future in the wrong way. So I married a good woman, worked for a livin, paid my taxes, put my girls through college, all that noble shit. If I can do it, anybody can do it. Just like makin *puttanesca* sauce."

Doyle had smiled at Jimmy's little sermon, but he said he couldn't shake the belief that it was racist cops like Jerry Czapski who fueled the black rage that fueled the fury of the riot . . . and that the riot's fury demanded an equally furious response from the law . . . and that the law's response redoubled the rioters' fury. . . . Round and round and round it went. There were no winners, as Doyle saw it, only losers. Jimmy agreed there was truth in what he was saying, but as they were spooning down the tiramisu, Jimmy had reminded him that assigning blame and meting out justice was somebody else's job. Their job was to find killers. Period.

"You know, it's funny," Doyle said now, blowing cigar smoke toward the moon. "I've never wanted anything as bad as I want to nail Helen Hull's killer—and now that we're ready to sweat a suspect, I'm not even sure I want to do it anymore."

"You wanna let the motherfucker walk?"

"Of course not."

"Don't matter what we want or don't want, Frank. We got a job to do and we gonna do it."

"I know that, Jimmy. Of course I'll do what I gotta do. It's just that I never imagined this stuff could get so, I don't know, so complicated."

"Ain't complicated less you make it complicated."

"But it *is* complicated. Shit, I'm a white man sitting here trying to tell you that a black man might have been justified in killing a white woman, and you're a black man sitting here telling me that this black man—that no man—is ever justified in killing anyone. We're both right and we're both wrong. That's complicated, you ask me."

"Maybe so, but I still go back to what I said earlier. Do yourself a favor and keep it simple. Our job's to find killers. Let other people worry about all that justice shit."

They were quiet again. Watching the bridge lights play on the water, Jimmy decided he needed to get the boat out more often. This was even more relaxing than working in the garden.

"There's something else been bothering me," Doyle said. Jimmy waited. Then he waited some more. Finally Doyle continued, "You remember my second case during the riot, that firefight I stumbled into on my way home, that hick from Tennessee on the roof—"

"Wilson Lee Pryor, sure."

"There's something I never told you or anyone else. I fired two shots at him on that rooftop."

"So?"

"So one of the six bullets that hit him was a .38-caliber—from a department-issue gun. Maybe mine."

"And maybe not. I read that report a hundred times. Look, that man died six ways from Sunday—and rightly so. He refused an order to put down his rifle. A bullet went through the windshield a your Pontiac during the firefight, I recall correctly."

"That bullet was a nine millimeter, which means it was fired by a Guardsman. Pryor never fired a shot. He was on that roof trying to make sure his building didn't catch on fire."

"And he was carrying a rifle and he refused to put it down, so people made the reasonable assumption he was a sniper. Case closed. Where you goin with this, Frank?"

"Back to how complicated this is. There's a chance I got away with killing a man, and it's been bothering me ever since."

"Look, even if you did fire the fatal shot—which is unlikely, I seen you on the pistol range—you'd be justified. You was in a firefight. Your vehicle got hit. You were acting in self-defense—along with a dozen other po-lice and Guardsmen who did zactly what you did. What I'da done. Shit, Frank, you think too much. Like I just said, this stuff ain't complicated less you make it complicated. Do yourself a favor and let it go."

Jimmy got a beer out of the cooler and drank half of it in silence. Then he said, "Since we gettin all confessional tonight, I got somethin I ain't never tole you or nobody else." Now it was Doyle who waited while Jimmy finished his beer and went back to the cooler. "You want one?"

"I'm good," Doyle said.

Jimmy sat back down. "I got into the ponies at Hazel Park big-time back in the day. Lost so much money I couldn't make the car payments, the mortgage payments. We was in danger of losin the house."

"The house in Conant Gardens?"

"No, this was back on Brush, when I was still in a uniform. I was so desperate—I'm almost shamed to admit it—I stole some dope out the evidence room and sold it to a street dealer I knew. I never even tole Flo. Almost got busted too—and it scared me so damn bad I been clean as a whistle ever since. There. I ain't proud of it, but now you know. You ain't the only cop in this town with a secret."

Doyle finished his beer and his cigar without saying a word. When he flipped his cigar butt into the river—*pssssssst!*—Jimmy said, "So. When you want to snag Bledsoe?"

"The sooner the better, I guess."

"Tomorrow?"

"Might as well. We should probably run everything by Sarge one more time."

"Definitely. You want me to come with you to pick him up?"

"Yeah, absolutely."

"Gimme a rough time."

"Well, he's working the lunch shift at Oakland Hills tomorrow, so he'll probably show up at home around five and chain himself to his typewriter for the rest of the day. Let's say five-thirty?"

"Sounds good. What's he doin on the typewriter?"

"Writing a book about his time in the civil rights movement."

"I might like to read that. Too bad he gonna have to finish writin it in prison."

24

THE NEXT DAY, DOYLE AND JIMMY ATE A LONG LUNCH IN GREEKTOWN with Sgt. Schroeder, going over everything they had on Bledsoe, making sure it was the right time to bring him in. Bring a suspect in too soon and you might get burned; wait too long and he might disappear. When the baklava was gone and the coffee cups were empty, Sgt. Schroeder stood up from the table and said, "Bust him good, gentlemen. Break him in two."

The detectives checked out a Plymouth and headed for the corner of Pallister and Poe, Jimmy at the wheel. Doyle didn't say a word the whole way but Jimmy knew what was going on in his head. He was walking through how he was going to play it in the yellow room. He was like an athlete before a big game, getting his game face on.

When they pulled up in front of Bledsoe's building, Jimmy shut off the engine but didn't reach for the door handle. He lit a Newport and studied the building next to Bledsoe's, a three-story brick with no roof, no windows, blackened walls.

"That a riot fire?" he said.

"It happened during the riot," Doyle said, "but it wasn't your typical Molotov cocktail arson."

"What kind was it?"

"The pre-meditated kind. They just arrested the landlord. He lit—or paid someone to light—a pile of oily rags in the basement. Figured since half the neighborhood was on fire, nobody'd look too close and he'd pick up a nice fat insurance check."

Jimmy blew a smoke ring out the window. "Jewish lightning."

"Irish, in this case. Landlord's a guy named Sean Devine. He and my brother played football together at U. of D. Guy's worth a couple mill, lives in Bloomfield Hills, and he pulls a stunt like that. A little girl died in that fire."

"Man, this fuckin city. . . ."

Just then a sky-blue car blazed out of the driveway between Bledsoe's building and Sean Devine's botched insurance scam. It was a shiny convertible with its top rolled back, a young black dude at the wheel. It went east on Pallister, toward the Lodge.

"That our man?" Jimmy said.

"That's him. Funny, he usually parks out front."

"I thought you said he wouldn't get home from work till five. It's ten till."

"Guess he got off early. Let's go."

Jimmy nodded. "I could use a little OT."

They followed the Buick north out Woodward. Jimmy was thinking, again, that once the Helen Hull case went down he might go ahead and hang it up, retire. Frank didn't need him anymore. Being out on the water last night was so nice. He could use more of that, more time working in the garden and learning how to cook. And at night there would always be checkers and double-deck pinochle at the Masonic Lodge.

The Buick turned left on Tuxedo and stopped in front of a tidy brick apartment building. Jimmy pulled over half a block away. They watched Willie Bledsoe hop out of the convertible and jog toward the apartment building. He was wearing a gray shirt with a diamond print on it, sharply creased slacks, expensive-looking loafers.

"Brother knows how to dress," Jimmy said.

"Yes and no," Frank said. "Some days he dresses like a farmer."

"How you mean?"

"Sometimes when he goes to the library or sits on his porch, he wears overalls and these big clunky work shoes."

"Man wears brogans? What's that all about?"

"Beats me."

"Why don't you ask him?"

"I'm planning to."

Before Bledsoe reached the building, a girl came out. She was wearing a pink summer dress and matching head band, and she was carrying a white sweater. She gave Bledsoe a big kiss right there on the sidewalk for the whole world to see, then she let him hold the car door open for her. There was a flash of bronze thigh as she slipped onto the front seat.

"Ooooooo-we," Jimmy said, letting out a low whistle. "She the one from the fish shack?"

"Yep."

"You didn't say nothin bout that body. Who is she?"

"Name's Octavia Jackson."

"She a pro?"

"A professional receptionist. She answers the phones at Hitsville, U.S.A."

"They look pretty chummy. Our man screwin her?"

"Don't think so. They've been out a few times, but they've never spent the night together far as I can tell. A little tonsil hockey's all I've seen."

"He a homasexual?"

"Doubtful. Believe it or not, Jimmy, some guys like to take their time."

"And some guys got rocks in they head. I'd be on that like white on Uncle Ben's rice."

"I'm gonna tell Flo you said that."

"You do, I'll cut your tongue out. Then I'll shoot you."

They were laughing when Jimmy dropped the Plymouth into gear and followed the Buick back down Woodward toward downtown. They followed it all the way to Plum Street, to a house with a fucked-up paintjob where a barefoot longhair was standing in the front yard holding a Day-Glo sign that said *Stadium Parking $2*. The hippie could barely stand up, he was so stoned.

Jimmy parked down the block in front of a fire hydrant and cut the engine. "Looks like our lovebirds goin to watch Denny McLain make history with his thirtieth win of the season," he said. "I read in the *Freep* today that McLain drinks three Pepsis every morning with breakfast."

"Yeah, I saw that too," Doyle said.

"A wonder the man's still got any teeth in his head. You wanna snag Bledsoe now?"

"I've got a better idea. You got time to take in a ballgame?"

"Like I said, I could use a little OT."

"First beer's on me."

"What're we waitin for?"

"We're waiting for our man to pay the dipshit parking attendant so we can follow him to the ballpark. It's bound to be a sellout. We wouldn't want to lose him in the crowd now, would we?"

"No we would not," Jimmy said, getting out of the car and lighting another Newport. He could hear noise pouring out of an upper-story window of the hippie house, loud electric guitars, some guy screaming, *"Kick out the jams, motherfuckers!"* Man, the shit white people call music.

They followed Bledsoe and the girl up to the bleachers and sat a dozen rows behind them. Bledsoe slapped hands with two guys sitting on the row in front of him. Jimmy recognized one of them—Clyde Holland, the slickest criminal lawyer in town. Clyde and Jimmy used to run numbers together with Berry Gordy out of a barbecue joint on Hastings called C.T.'s. All three of them wound up going legit, doing all right by themselves. What, Jimmy wondered, were the odds of that?

Denny McLain didn't have his best stuff that night, but Jimmy and Doyle got all the way into the game, almost forgot why they were there. McLain gave up two home runs to Oakland's showboat rookie, Reggie Jackson, and Mayo Smith lifted him for a pinch hitter in the bottom of the ninth with the Tigers trailing, 4-3.

Al Kaline, the pinch hitter, drew a walk. Mickey Stanley singled him to third. The next batter hit a ground ball, and Kaline broke for the plate. A good throw would have nailed him easy, but the ball sailed over the catcher's head to the screen. Kaline scored the tying run and Stanley went to second. Willie Horton drove the next pitch over the left fielder's head, scoring Stanley with the winning run as Denny McLain—a 30-game-winner—sprinted out of the dugout and his teammates hoisted him on their shoulders.

Doyle wanted to make his move right then but Jimmy pointed out Clyde Holland, said if Clyde saw them collaring Bledsoe he'd damn sure come downtown and make sure Bledsoe kept his mouth shut and didn't give up a thing. Doyle's eagerness reminded Jimmy just how much the kid still had to learn. Maybe he should put off retirement a little longer.

So they followed at a distance as Clyde and his buddy walked down the switchbacks with Bledsoe and the girl. The group finally broke up out on Trumbull, and the detectives followed Bledsoe and the girl back to Plum Street. They held hands the whole way. Too bad if tonight was going to be their first time, Jimmy was thinking, as Doyle called out, "Mr. Bledsoe!"

"Gentlemen?" Bledsoe said, turning, not yet realizing the two men were police.

They showed him their shields and half of his cockiness disappeared.

"We'd like to ask you a few questions, Mr. Bledsoe," Doyle said. "Would you mind coming with us?"

"Right now? But—"

"Right now."

"Where we going?"

"Downtown."

"What for, exactly?"

"We'll tell you when we get there," Jimmy said.

Bledsoe was looking at Doyle, looking him in the eye like they were old buddies who hadn't seen each other in a long time. "What took you so long?" Bledsoe said.

"Sir?"

"What took you so long? All the places you been following me, all the hours you spent camped outside my apartment—and hers—in that old Pontiac of yours. Why didn't you just knock on my door and save everyone a lot of trouble?"

The girl said, "Will someone please tell me what the *hell's* goin on here?"

"Please come with us, Mr. Bledsoe," Jimmy said, stepping closer.

"My pleasure." A chubby woman had come out of the hippie house and was standing on the front porch, taking in the scene. Bledsoe called to her, "Hey, Sunshine, can my friend use your phone to call a cab?"

"Sure, Willie."

Bledsoe took a $20 bill out of his wallet and gave it to the bewildered girl for cab fare. He kissed her and told her he'd see her at her place as soon as he got this cleared up. Then he fell in between the detectives, walking toward the Plymouth with a bounce in his stride that neither of them liked one bit.

The dance in the yellow room began slowly, the way Doyle had planned it. With Jimmy, Sgt. Schroeder and half a dozen detectives watching from the hallway, Doyle offered cigarettes, coffee, soft drinks. Bledsoe didn't want anything. He seemed relaxed. Didn't ask for a telephone or a lawyer, didn't even need to use the bathroom.

Doyle promised he would make this as quick and painless as possible and would do everything in his power to keep his bloodthirsty partner at bay—provided Bledsoe gave him straight answers. Bledsoe nodded. Doyle opened by expressing amazement at how Oakland had managed to piss that ballgame away, and Bledsoe jumped on this, obviously glad to talk about anything but the thing they had brought him here to talk about. Then Doyle asked Bledsoe about his job at Oakland Hills, his Uncle Bob, just letting him know he knew things. Finally Doyle said, "What's with that farmer get-up you wear to the library sometimes?"

"That's what we use to wear when I was with Snick down South."

"Ahh." Doyle guessed Snick had something to do with Bledsoe's civil rights work. Which made this a good time to ask, "How's your book coming along?"

There was no surprise on Bledsoe's face. He said, "Real well, thanks. I just found out that *Ebony* magazine's going to run six chapters of it—like a serial—starting in December."

"Congratulations."

"Thanks." He said it sincerely, with no false pride.

Doyle began to circle closer. "That musta been rough when they picked you and your buddy Walter Mitchell up during the riot."

There was a slight pause, nothing serious. "Guess you heard about that at the fish shack in Algonac."

"That's right. There and in the arrest records."

"Me and my big mouth. Yeah, it was pretty rough, all right."

"That garage still stinks."

"I don't doubt it. I've smelled worse though."

"Where at—Mississippi or Alabama?"

There was no hesitation this time. "Mississippi's definitely got the worst jails. I believe those crackers are proud of it."

Doyle wanted to keep him off balance. "Heard from your brother lately?"

"Which one?"

Nice try. "The only one you got. Wes."

"Yeah, we talked on the phone a couple days ago."

"I understand Wes was quite the war hero."

"Yeah, to hear him tell it he killed a couple hundred Viet Cong with his bare hands—then cut off their balls and sewed 'em in their mouth."

"That must hurt."

"You know it's got to." Bledsoe was smiling, as cocky as he'd been back on Plum Street. Doyle wanted to make that smile go away.

"Did Wes have a good time while he was in Oakland?"

Another pause as the smile vanished and the eyes darted. Then came the falsely cool reply: "He didn't say much about it one way or the other, to tell you the truth."

"Any idea what he was doing out there?"

"Probably selling guns to the Panthers. Isn't that what all the niggers are doing in Oakland these days?"

Doyle was impressed. This was, indeed, a worthy adversary. It was time to find out just how worthy. Doyle reached under his chair and took a bulky reel-to-reel tape recorder out of a box and set it on the table. "Got something I want to play for you, Willie."

"I dig 'Trane and Miles."

"No shit. Me too. You checked out 'Round About Midnight' yet?"

"Picked it up last week. I think it's the best thing Miles's ever done."

"I agree. Well, this isn't exactly jazz, but see if it doesn't sound familiar." Doyle switched on the tape.

"Where you been, bruh? Been tryin to reach you all damn day long," boomed the drunken voice of Wes Bledsoe.

"I been out. What up?"

Bledsoe waved a hand and Doyle shut off the tape. "You don't need to play the rest of that," Bledsoe said. "I already had that conversation. I know how it turns out. That an F.B.I. tape?"

"Maybe."

"Maybe, as in definitely. We got schooled on all that COINTELPRO wiretap shit when I was with Snick. At the time I thought it was just a buncha brothers being paranoid. Naive me, as usual. One thing they taught us is that those tapes aren't admissible in court. They're just one a J. Edgar Hoover's sick little hobbies. Besides, my brother's in Saigon by now, or Bangkok. You gonna go over there and bring him in for questioning too?"

"Maybe. But I don't think we'll need to. Since you don't want to listen to the tape, let me refresh your memory." Doyle reached into his files and took out a typed transcript of the tape recording. "You said to your brother, quote, 'You remember those three guns from the roof of your building, that night during the riot?' Unquote. Which three guns were you talking about?"

Again he didn't hesitate, like he was ready for the question. "The three guns my brother took up on the roof."

"Why'd he take three guns up there?"

"Cause he got beat half to death by some cops at the Algiers Motel and he wanted to see if he could shoot him a cop."

"Did he?"

"I got no idea."

"Did he try?"

"He fired, I don't know, half a dozen rounds. But he was pretty messed up from the beating—plus he was drinking. Tell you the truth, I don't think he coulda hit Ford Hospital."

"Were you on the roof with him?"

"Yeah."

"Why'd you go up there?"

"I wanted to keep an eye on him, make sure he didn't fall off the roof or shoot himself. Like I say, he was pretty messed up."

"You fire any of the guns?"

"Nosir."

"Not even once?"

"Nosir."

"You had to be some kind of pissed-off after spending twenty-three hours in that garage."

"Sure, I was pissed off. But I didn't fire any gun."

"Was it just the two of you on the roof?"

"Yessir."

"A woman in the building told us she heard three men on the roof."

He shrugged. "Maybe she was hearing things. Was just me and Wes."

Doyle flipped through the transcript. "When your brother called from Oakland, he wanted to know why you were asking so many questions about the guns. And you said, quote, 'Want to make sure those guns don't come back to bite us.' End quote. What did you mean by that?"

"Meant I didn't want to get picked up on some bogus weapons charge."

"Bogus? You didn't know those guns were illegal?"

"I don't know legal from illegal. But it's illegal to fire a gun inside the city limits, right?"

"That's right."

"And since I didn't fire any of the guns—or even touch 'em—I didn't want to get picked up on some bogus weapons charge on account of my drunk brother."

It was time for Doyle to play his next chip. "How'd your brother get all those guns from Alabama to Detroit?"

"All what guns?" he said right away, like he'd been expecting the question and had rehearsed the answer.

"Those three guns on the roof of the Larrow Arms, for starters. And the couple dozen guns he sold to black militants all over town before, during and after the riot."

Again Bledsoe shrugged. "I wouldn't know a thing about that. Only time I ever seen my brother handle guns was that night on the roof, and that's God's honest truth."

"That's a goddam lie. Caldwell Petty, the police chief in Tuskegee, told me you and your brother used to blast a shitload of guns in the woods outside of town."

"A shitload? That cracker's got an imagination. That was two deer rifles and a snub-nose .38. All registered in my brother's name. I thought we were talking about guns in Detroit."

"How'd you and your brother get from Alabama to Detroit?"

"I drove him in my old Buick. The one I traded in at Murphy's."

"Your brother ever say anything about smuggling guns back from Vietnam?"

"Only time I heard him mention guns was that phone call from Oakland, when he said he brokered something for the Panthers. Which was probably just more a his bullshit. Man's all mouth."

"Well, your brother might be all mouth, but it so happens we've got some of his best customers in custody. We've also got a lot of the merchandise he moved here in Detroit—including the gun that killed Helen Hull. That name mean anything to you?"

"Nope."

Doyle could see that gears were turning in his head now. A good sign. Bledsoe was trying to figure just how much the police knew, and if they really had his brother's customers in custody, and a murder weapon. The door opened on cue and Jimmy walked in and dropped a stack of photographs on the table. He remained standing. Bledsoe sat up straighter, another good sign.

"Got some good news and some bad news, Willie," Jimmy said. "Which you want first?"

"Your call."

"Okay, here's the good news. We just this morning lifted some razor-sharp prints off the gun that killed Helen Hull—"

"Who's this Helen Hull I'm hearing so much about?"

"Lady got killed by a sniper in a hallway at the Harlan House Motel, just across the Lodge from the Larrow Arms," Jimmy said. "Happened early in the morning on July 26th, that was a Wednesday during the riot, a few hours after Thomas Henderson bailed you and your buddy Walter Mitchell out of jail. Here's what she looked like."

Jimmy slid the crime-scene photograph across the table toward Bledsoe—Helen Hull lying on the hallway floor, eyes open, hands raised, a bullet hole in her chest. Doyle was studying Bledsoe's face, but it was hard to read the expression. Horror, definitely. Guilt, too?

"And," Jimmy went on, "we matched the prints from the gun to the prints on a sixteen oh-zee can a Schlitz malt liquor we found on the roof of the Larrow Arms. That's the building where your brother use to stay."

"I know where my brother use to stay."

"You ready for the bad news?"

"Sure." He actually seemed calm. Doyle was beginning to like him.

"Your fingerprints are a perfect match."

That was supposed to be a kidney punch. That was the moment when most suspects started to blubber and grovel. But Bledsoe's face showed nothing this time, and Doyle felt his first twinge of panic.

"Where'd you get my fingerprints for comparison?" Bledsoe said, cool as could be.

"From the night you and Walter got picked up and booked during the riot."

"Ah."

Jimmy pressed on. "There's more. Lady who lives in the building saw your old Buick—the one you unloaded at Murphy's after you painted it black—she saw it pull up to the building way after curfew, early that Wednesday morning. Saw two men get out and carry a duffel bag into the building. One was big and fat, had a limp, like your brother—the other was tall and thin, like you."

"This lady see the men's faces?"

Jimmy ignored the question. "Few minutes later the woman heard three voices on the roof. Then she heard nine gunshots."

Bledsoe's face still showed nothing. He said to Jimmy, "That's interesting what you say about my fingerprints on the beer can."

"Why's that interesting?" Jimmy was smirking. Doyle was not.

"Cause I don't drink Schlitz malt liquor."

"Never?" Jimmy said, still smirking.

"Nope."

"Not even a sip?"

"Naw, not since college."

"What you got against the Bull?"

"Nothing personal. Too sweet for me's all. Plus the hangover."

"Don't make no difference." Jimmy was admiring the stack of photographs on the table. "All that matters is we got your fingerprints on the murder weapon. That's all the jury gonna hear when we go to trial. I should say if you stupid enough to let this thing go to trial."

Bledsoe still showed no emotion. A sick feeling was taking hold in Doyle's stomach.

"Mind if I have a look?" Bledsoe said, still cool as could be.

"Be my guest." Jimmy slid the photographs toward him.

Bledsoe sifted through the stack. "Which one of these you say's the murder weapon?"

"The one you holding."

While Bledsoe studied the picture, Doyle could see that he was seeing something he liked, and he liked it a lot. Bledsoe said, "A Winchester Model 70."

"Right." Jimmy's smile was getting brighter.

"That a Starlight infra-red scope on it?"

"Sho nuff is." Jimmy turned to Doyle. "Man knows his guns." Jimmy still didn't see it coming.

"My brother had a Navy book with all these guns in it," Bledsoe said. "He studied that thing the way some guys study *Playboy* magazine. Is this Winchester a thirty caliber?"

"Right again."

Bledsoe flipped the photograph onto the table and let out a sigh. There was no mistaking what was in that gesture. It was relief and triumph and, biggest of all, surprise. Doyle realized then that the picture of the murder weapon had revealed something to Bledsoe that even he hadn't realized till now. Bledsoe said, "I never touched that gun before in my life."

Jimmy nearly choked. "Say what?"

"I said I never touched that gun—I never touched any Winchester Model 70—in my life. Never. So it'd have to be some kind of miracle if my fingerprints were on that one."

Jimmy looked stricken, like a man who'd just patted his pockets and realized his wallet was missing.

Bledsoe said, "You sit there and tell me with a straight face that my fingerprints are on some murder weapon, and I tell you I know for a fact you're lying. Same with the Schlitz can. I haven't touched a can a Schlitz in years." He leaned back in his chair. "Time to cut the shit, gentlemen. You going to charge me with a crime or not? If so, let's get it on. I got a lawyer's phone number right here in my pocket."

Doyle knew then that they were dead in the water. Jimmy shot him a look that said he knew it too. They both believed there was a third man on the roof because the prints on the Winchester didn't match Willie Bledsoe's and, based on a set of prints they got from the military police at the San Diego Navy base, they didn't match Wes Bledsoe's either. So they were pretty sure Willie was lying about being alone on the roof with his brother, but they had no lever to pry the truth out of him. Of course it was possible that Wes or Willie had fired the fatal shot, then wiped down the gun, and someone else's prints got on it later. Doyle and Jimmy were hoping that the wiretap and the eyewit and the photograph of the victim and the knowledge that there were people in custody would spook Bledsoe into confessing, maybe into giving up the name of the third man on the roof, at the very least the names of some of Wes's customers. They had gotten signed confessions with a lot less. But Bledsoe was way too cool for that—and while that didn't mean he was definitely innocent, it meant it would be damn near impossible to prove he was guilty, which amounted to the same thing. And Bledsoe seemed to know that the detectives didn't have anywhere near enough evidence to charge him. Doyle knew what Jimmy was going to say next because he always said it when a suspect asked if they were going to charge him with a crime. This time, though, it was the wrong thing to say.

"No," Jimmy said, "we're not going to charge you just yet, but I'd be perfectly fuckin happy—"

Bledsoe held up a hand. Then he reached in his wallet and placed a black and gold business card on the table. Jimmy picked it up. "Look here. Man has Clyde Holland handling his legal representation. Nothin but the best for Mr. Willie Bledsoe." Jimmy's bluster was pathetic, a beaten man trying to save face. He said, "How long you been knowin Clyde the Glide?"

"We met in the bleachers at Tiger Stadium on Opening Day. That's it. I'm not saying another word. Where's the telephone?"

Willie Bledsoe never made the call to Clyde Holland. Doyle rode down with him in the elevator, neither man making eye contact, not a word passing between them. Then Doyle watched him walk across the marble lobby and through the swinging doors onto Beaubien Street. The bounce was back in his stride. It made Doyle almost happy to watch him melt into the night, still a free man. Hadn't Doyle gotten a similar break—possibly an even bigger break—on the night Wilson Lee Pryor died?

Doyle was now convinced Willie Bledsoe was not their shooter. And for the first time he was convinced they would never find out who was.

25

WHEN WILLIE GOT TO THE BOTTOM OF THE STAIRS HE TURNED around and took one last look at 1300 Beaubien Street. Its limestone walls were sooty near the ground, as though rain had stained them with the blackest filth the earth had to offer. Each round-topped window was adorned with a bronze lion's head. They were all sticking their tongues out at the world. Fuck you too, Willie thought. Goodbye and good riddance.

He walked to Woodward and boarded a northbound DSR bus. He would fetch his Deuce from Plum Street in the morning. He hurried to the back of the empty bus and watched police headquarters and the rest of downtown recede. It all shrank quickly, becoming small

293

and insignificant and then disappearing, already a thing of the past, a trifle, nothing.

Here I am again, Willie thought, riding a bus while my life takes another dizzying turn. As the bus moved out Woodward, he realized that the things he'd just learned inside the yellow room may have had the power to free him, but they lacked the power to absolve him of a single thing. That was not how the world worked. Absolution was beyond the reach of most men. All he was hoping for when he'd walked into that yellow room was to save himself and his brother from justice that wasn't just, to survive the myth that one more wrong could somehow make all the other wrongs right. When he walked into the yellow room the only thing that mattered was that he and Wes both remain free. And they had.

When the bus stopped in front of the Seven Seas to pick up a passenger, Willie considered getting off and having a few belts. Even at this late hour the place was still packed with people celebrating Denny McLain's historic win. But he stayed on the bus because he couldn't wait to see Octavia and tell her his good news.

He already knew how his book ended—with that despondent bus ride from Atlantic City to Alabama in 1964. Now, thanks to the two homicide cops, he knew how his story ended, too.

It ended during the riot, on the night Thomas Henderson sprang Willie and Walter Mitchell from jail. When Willie got home that night he must have played Coltrane's "My Favorite Things" fifteen, twenty times. Then he switched to "A Love Supreme." Coltrane had been dead more than a week, but it wasn't until that night that Willie began to appreciate how much he was going to miss him. Lying on the floor of his darkened living room, sweating in the heat, listening to 'Trane and drinking can after can of Stroh's, Willie could hear sirens and gunfire and shouting and he kept hearing the angry woman from the basement garage: *When I get out this hole, The Man gonna* PAY. . . .

As the beer went to work, Willie's body had filled with something he had never felt before. He had felt murderous rage before, on the night that white cop pulled him over, taunted him, humiliated him.

But now he was feeling something far more complicated, something far worse, a mixture of pain and shame and rage that would be unbearable to live with for a single day. He understood that he had to make this thing go away, he had to purge it, or it would be the end of him. But how?

A fist pounding on his door woke him up. He had drifted off to sleep on the floor. His first thought was that the police had come back for him, and he crawled to the door, terrified, not making a sound. When the pounding finally stopped he heard sobbing out in the hall, a man sobbing. "Open up, bruh! It's me, Wes! Open the fuck up!"

At first Willie thought his brother had been shot. Then he saw that there was a wicked gash over his left ear—a piece of skull was visible—and the blood was pouring down the side of his face, soaking his shirt. His pants were wet from where he'd pissed himself. Willie ordered him to take off his clothes and sit in the bath tub, and for the next hour he cleaned the gash and listened to his brother babble about how cops and Guardsmen had busted in on the craps game at the Algiers annex and lined everyone up in the hall and pistol-whipped them and ripped the clothes off the white girls and took people into rooms and shot them. Wes wasn't sure how many were dead. He couldn't stop sobbing. Willie thought his brother was drunk, then he thought he'd lost his mind, but after a while, remembering his own experience, Wes's story started to make the worst kind of sense.

Finally, when Wes's scalp stopped bleeding, Willie bandaged it with gauze and tape. The cut would need stitches. Willie thought of the night at the veterinarian's house in Montgomery, that bandage on the gash on John Lewis's head, the stitches in his own throbbing lip.

Wes took a long hot shower and put on a clean pair of Willie's sweatpants and a T-shirt. Then Willie got two beers from the kitchen and they sat on the living room floor in the dark listening to 'Trane while Willie told the story about Walter Mitchell flying in, about the firemen and the beatings and the filthy garage, about Thomas Henderson bailing them out and the mayor calling to apologize. When he finished telling the story he could see, even in the stuffy darkness, that his brother's eyes were shining.

Wes said, "Where your Buick at?"

"Out back. I was afraid to leave it on the street—thought they might recognize it and come back for me."

"We ain't goin far."

"Wes, the curfew's still—"

"Fuck the curfew. Let's go."

"Where we going?"

"To my crib. Now quit axin so many questions. It's payback time. You don't want a piece a this, then you a stone punk. Gimme the keys to you damn car."

Willie realized then that he was being offered a choice and a chance, a chance to purge the unbearable thing that had come to live inside him. Again he remembered the night the white cop pulled him over, whacked his head with the flashlight. His life had come full circle: The thing he was capable of doing then was the thing he was obliged to do now. It would be impossible to live with himself if he didn't take his brother up on this offer. Right now. He said, "I'll drive."

All the streetlights on Pallister had been shot out. The only light came from a hazy half moon. Willie drove the Buick with its headlights off and his heart in his mouth, just like Mississippi, driving down those country roads in the dark with your lights off and the gas pedal on the floor, praying you didn't see headlights in the rearview mirror, praying with everything you had in you. Now Willie prayed all the way to the corner of Hamilton.

Wes told him to turn left and park the car. Then he told him to open the trunk. When Willie did, he was surprised to see a long, lumpy duffel bag next to the spare tire. "How'd that get there?" he said.

"I put it there," Wes said.

"What's in it?"

"The fuck you think's in it?" Wes picked up the bag. It made a clanking noise.

"How long those guns been in my car?" All Willie could think of was what would have happened if the cops had opened his trunk at the fire station. He'd still be in that garage—with no hope of getting out. Suddenly he was furious. "Wes, how fuckin long have those—"

"What difference it make?" Wes slammed the trunk shut, a noise that made Willie jump. "Let's get off this street fore we get our black asses shot."

"God*dammit*, Wes!" Willie shouted.

But Wes ignored him. He crossed the lawn and started up the steps that led to the front door of the Larrow Arms. Willie had to hurry to catch up with him. Even in the watery moonlight he could see that his brother was limping.

Wes took a key from the mop closet on the building's ground floor, and they went up the darkened staircase tiptoe so as not to wake anybody. They could hear televisions and radios inside some of the apartments. On the fourth floor Wes knocked on the apartment door across the hall from his. The door flew open and there stood Clarence Rawls, a chronically out-of-work autoworker, a part-time car thief and full-time welfare cheat, dressed in a Pistons jersey and cut-off jeans. He had a can of Schlitz malt liquor in one hand and a joint in the other. He was barefoot.

"If it ain't the brothers Bledsoe!" Clarence cried, sucking on the joint. "Perfect timing. I just walked in the door my ownself." He had the curtains drawn. The only light in the apartment came from the color television set, which was showing footage of an orange fire eating a supermarket.

"What you been up to?" Wes said.

"Out lootin, like everbody else. Man, I ain't seen so much inna-gration in D-troit in all my life—white people helpin black people loot, women with they hair up in curlers, everyone havin a big ole time. I swear, some a them ofays is better at lootin than us brothers."

He handed the joint to Wes, who took a deep hit. Willie waved it away.

"What'd you get?" Wes said.

"Nothin much tonight, just some necessaries. Some cigarettes and Del Monte's peaches and a couple fifths a gin. Oh, and I got a nice clock radio for my nephew's graduatin present." He opened the door wider. "Come in the house, gentlemens."

"Later," Wes said. "We got a little bidness to take care of first."

"What kinda bidness?"

"Up on the roof." Wes hefted the duffel bag, that clanking noise again. "You always said you wanted to shoot you a honky, Clarence. Now's your chance. You comin?"

"You knows I is!"

"Bring some beer," Wes said. "I got the key to the fifth floor."

Clarence put on a pair of new sneakers that looked like marsh-mallows—looted, Willie guessed—and he grabbed two more Schlitz tall boys. The three men marched up the last flight of stairs. As he climbed the stairs, Willie understood that his life was about to change forever and he accepted this with a serenity that surprised him. He welcomed what awaited him on the roof, whatever it proved to be. Someone had to pay for what had happened to him and his brother and the people in the garage and so many others. It was his duty to see that someone paid, and he understood that if he didn't do his duty he would not be able to go on living.

They walked across the flat roof, gravel crunching underfoot, and suddenly the city was spread before them. No streetlights burned on this side of Woodward—even the Lodge Freeway was dark—and the carpet of darkness stretched almost all the way to the zoo, miles to the north. The only light came from the moon and the fires, dozens of fires. It looked like a city that had been fire-bombed, Willie thought, like newsreel footage of Dresden or Tokyo, or London during the Blitz. Flames shot into the sky, and Willie remembered how beautiful it had been when he and Walter Mitchell watched the flames jump from that warehouse onto the roof of that pitiful two-story house. Fire had a life of its own.

Wes rummaged in the duffel bag and handed Willie a Remington 700 with a Unertl scope. It was a decent gun, good up to several hundred yards. Then Wes handed a rifle to Clarence and selected one for himself. It was too dark for Willie to tell what kinds of guns the other two were.

As Wes passed out ammunition, Willie thought it was a waste to give any to Clarence. At this late hour he was probably seeing triple. But Clarence surprised him. Willie couldn't find a thing in the Remington's scope while Clarence, crouching on his right, kept saying, "Lookit that! A motherfuckin cop car, big as day! . . . Oooh-wee, a fire truck! . . . Damn, I just missed that Jeep!" And every time Clarence spoke, Willie's right ear rang from the rifle's roar.

Clarence offered the cans of Schlitz. Wes accepted, but again Willie passed. He couldn't stomach that skunk piss. Besides, the adrenaline was clearing his head, and this was no time to get sloppy. He had already decided to select his targets carefully, to go for police cars, fire trucks, tanks, Jeeps, men in uniform—anything that shared responsibility for the nightmares he and his brother had just been through. If vengeance was going to accomplish its mission, it had to be precise, an eye for an eye, no more and no less. To kill randomly would be to cheapen the purity of his rage. He was making the rules now. He was above the law, outside the law. He had finally repudiated the world that made him—he had repudiated America itself—and he felt free, truly free and truly alive, for the first time in his life.

But when he got off a clean shot at a police car speeding out the Lodge Freeway, he was yards behind it.

"Remember what I tole you back in Alabama," Wes said, squeezing off a shot. "Shit. Missed him. Your target's the eighteen inches between the chin and the belt buckle."

Willie got off a shot at a Jeep parked on the far side of the freeway but missed badly again. It drove off while he was reloading.

"Y'all see dat?!" Clarence cried.

Willie and Wes peered through their scopes. "See what?" they said in unison.

"That buildin just past the left corner a the hospital. The one with the tank in front a it . . . three, four floors up . . . a woman standin in the window, lit up like a motherfuckin Christmas tree. Y'all see it?"

"Yeah, I see it," Wes said.

"I see it," Willie said.

What he saw was a dark silhouette—a woman in a dress—lit from behind. The silhouette wobbled and came to rest in the cross-hairs. Willie's face was wet and suddenly he felt cold. He waited. The shape didn't move. He could hear sirens in the distance, the chatter of automatic weapons fire. He felt for the trigger and held his breath, the way his brother had taught him to do in the woods outside Tuskegee.

"All right, muthafuckas," Clarence said. "This is it. We takin the honky bitch down together. On the count a three. One . . ."

The woman moved half a step to her left and Willie's cross-hairs moved with her. He was steady as a stone.

"Two . . ."

A doubt entered Willie's mind. This was no Guardsman or cop in the cross-hairs. It was a civilian. A woman. Somebody's wife, maybe somebody's mother. At this distance it wasn't even possible to tell for sure if she was black or white. No—

"Three!"

Clarence's rifle went off first, a terrifying jolt. Then, a fraction of a second later, the gun to Willie's left boomed. In the instant he decided he was not going to squeeze the trigger, he felt the Remington kick into his shoulder. The woman had disappeared from the window. Willie felt sick. What just happened?

"I got the bitch!" Wes shouted over the ringing in Willie's ears. "I fuckin got the bitch!"

"The fuck you did," Clarence shouted back. "*I* got the bitch!"

"Fuck you, nigger!"

"No, fuck *you!*"

As their ecstatic shouting went back and forth, Willie kept looking at the window through his scope. The woman was still gone. Suddenly the window went dark. Someone started shooting from inside the building, then tracer fire started pouring from the street into the building.

Peering over the edge of the roof, Clarence said, "Here comes a po-lice. Time to split, my brothers."

They hustled down the dark stairs and into Wes's apartment. He drew the curtains and lit a candle and put it on the floor. Willie's hands were shaking as he wiped down the Remington and handed it to Wes and watched him tuck it into the duffel bag. Then he watched Wes wipe down Clarence's gun—a 7.62 millimeter Garand with a powerful Redfield scope that magnified objects to ten times their actual size. No wonder crazy drunk Clarence had been able to spot so many targets. Then Wes wiped down his own gun, a Winchester Model 70 with a Starlight infra-red scope. The murder weapon. When all three guns were zipped inside the duffel bag, Wes stowed the bag in the space he'd hollowed out under the linoleum floor in the kitchen.

And now, riding the bus out Woodward, Willie finally knew how his story ended. He got off the bus at Tuxedo Street and hurried toward Octavia's building. He flew down the sidewalk, so light he thought he might float away. He had gotten away with helping his brother get away with murder, and he didn't regret it. If Wes wasn't innocent, he was a long way from guilty. Willie had gotten rid of his pain and his shame and his rage—those things he could not live with—and the stone of guilt in his guts was finally gone. He hadn't wanted that woman to die, and he hadn't killed her. He was free for the first time in his life. He had no unpaid debts, he had no scores to settle, and he no longer had anything to fear from any man.

26

THE WORLD SERIES BETWEEN THE TIGERS AND THE CARDINALS opened on Oct. 2 in Busch Stadium in St. Louis. Late that morning Anthony Capriati, the dapper little Wayne County prosecutor with watered hair, red galluses, and a loud paisley necktie, told Doyle and Jimmy Robuck something they already knew. He, Capriati, was not going to press charges in the Helen Hull case, not even weapons charges.

"You boys haven't got shit and we all know it," Capriati told them. "Even if you go drag Wes Bledsoe back from Saigon or Singapore or wherever the hell he is, you still haven't got enough to get him to cop to Man One because his fingerprints aren't on the murder weapon. They're on a beer can. Sure, you might be able to prove he sold the murder weapon, but that doesn't mean he was the one who fired the fatal shot. And he might tell you a completely different story from the one his brother told you about the rooftop—and be able to back it up. And you think there had to be a third person on the roof because you've got someone else's prints on the murder weapon, but we all know that a hundred people could've handled that gun in the fifteen months since the shooting took place."

Doyle managed to get in two and a half words. "But Mayor Cav—"

"Don't start in about Jerry Cavanagh again. I don't give a rat's ass how bad Hizzoner wants this thing to go down. I'm up for re-election next month and I'm not taking on a sure loser. Especially not one with this much visibility. Thanks for stopping by, gentlemen."

Doyle drove to the Harlan House because he wanted to break the news to Henry Hull in person. As always, the door to Room 450 was ajar. But instead of the familiar clutter, Doyle was surprised to find tidy stacks of cardboard boxes, bare walls and a spotless coffee table. There were two large suitcases in the corner by the little refrigerator. Henry was sitting alone on the sofa staring at the television set.

"This is terrible!" he moaned when Doyle knocked and entered the room.

"Listen, Mr. Hull. I just want you to know how sorry I—"

"The Cards just scored three runs off McLain—and Gibson's already struck out twelve of our guys!"

Doyle looked at the television set. The volume was turned all the way down and Ernie Harwell's voice was coming out of a transistor radio on the coffee table. The grass in sparkling new Busch Stadium looked even better than the lawn in front of Doyle's brother's house. He watched as Willie Horton let a called third strike zip past his kneecaps.

Ernie Harwell didn't even try to hide his disgust. "Willie just stood there like a house by the side of the road and watched that one go by. Thirteen strike-outs now for Gibson."

"*Thirteen!*" Henry cried.

"Mr. Hull. . . ."

"Have a seat, Frankie." Henry patted the sofa, and Doyle sat next to him, facing the television set. "You don't gotta tell me how it went with the D.A. I had it figured out soon as you told me about having to let that Bledsoe fella go."

Doyle told him about Capriati anyway. Then they watched the game for a while, not talking. The Tigers looked like a bunch of scared Little Leaguers—or maybe Bob Gibson really was that good. During the seventh-inning stretch Henry said, "Look in the fridge, Frankie. Should be some beer in there. Grab us a couple. I need one."

Doyle opened the refrigerator. It contained half a bag of carrots and three cans of Budweiser. He took two. "Budweiser?" he said, wrinkling his nose as he handed a can to Henry and popped one for himself. "Isn't this swill from St. Louis?"

"Quit yer squawkin. It's beer and it's cold." Doyle could tell he appreciated the ribbing. "Cheers," Henry said. They tapped cans as Doyle returned to the sofa.

After a while Henry put his hand on Doyle's knee and said, "You did the best you could, Frankie, you and Jimmy both. The whole department did, and I want you to know how much I appreciate it. You never gave up. Now it's time to let it go. It wasn't meant to be. Case closed."

"The file will stay open till the case is solved, Mr. Hull." It would stay open and it would turn cold and eventually it would slip into the deep freeze. "We never stop working open cases."

Doyle wondered if it was possible that the old bird was feeling the same thing he'd felt when he watched Willie Bledsoe walk out the front door of 1300, a free man. He wondered if it was possible that Henry was feeling a skewed sense of relief now too. No, Doyle told himself, I know more than Henry knows, and he lost his wife. No way Henry was feeling relief.

Yet Henry was willing to let it go. His wife didn't deserve to die, but Henry, like Doyle, seemed to believe that Willie Bledsoe didn't deserve many of the things he'd been through, things no white man in America would ever have to endure. Something had to give. Somebody was always having to pay for the things that went on, for the things that had been going on in this country for hundreds of years. If the cycle of vengeance was ever going to stop, it had to stop somewhere. Why not here? If Henry wasn't exactly relieved, Doyle told himself, maybe he agreed that some sick form of justice had prevailed. Somebody had to be the first one to step off the merry-go-round.

"I said let it go," Henry repeated. He waved at the boxes. "If I can get on with my life, then you can get on with yours. It's time for me and you—and this whole city—to move on."

"You coming back to the old neighborhood?"

"Afraid I can't. There's nothing for me there but memories, mostly bad ones, and I've still got a few good years left in me."

"So what are you going to do?"

"My kid brother's got a place in the U.P., not far from Marquette. He says he needs someone to go fishing with him. His wife passed away last summer too."

"Sounds like a plan."

"How about you? What's next for you?"

"Let's see. I'm cooking dinner tonight for Jimmy and Flo and a gorgeous strawberry blonde. In the morning Jimmy and I'll go out looking for new killers."

"Is it serious?"

"Killers are always serious, Mr. Hull."

"No, I mean the strawberry blonde."

"Yeah, I think it's safe to say we're falling in love."

This perked Henry up. "Tell me about her."

"Well, she's gorgeous and she's sexy and she knows a lot about art and she loved the lamb chops I cooked for her last—"

"Shit!"

Bob Gibson had struck out his fourteenth Tiger batter.

"I'm sorry, Frankie. You were saying about the lamb chops."

"She likes my cooking almost as much as Jimmy does. I'm making chicken *cacciatore* for everyone tonight."

"You say she knows a lot about art?"

"She's getting her master's in art history at Wayne State. She's writing her thesis on the way the Nazis looted art during the War."

"Sounds like an interesting gal."

"She is, she really is. And smart as hell."

"You remember me telling you I was in Patton's Third Army during the war?"

"Yeah, I remember that picture of you in your uniform, the one behind the cash register at the market. Right next to the picture of you shaking hands with President Truman."

"Well, my unit was the one that found the salt mine full of stolen art near Altaussee, Austria. Hitler was going to put the stuff in his museum in Linz after the war. There were hundreds of pieces."

Doyle had forgotten that about Henry Hull, the way he was always surprising you with his stories. It was what made the Greenleaf Market such a lively place. This city was going to miss him.

"So what's your girl's name?" Henry said.

"Cecelia Cronin."

"She from Detroit?"

"Hamtramck. But yeah, she's been here all her life except for a short spell in New York. She's going to move in with me to see, you know, how we work together."

"Sounds pretty damn serious."

"Yeah. . . ." Like any inveterate bachelor, Doyle was anxious about having Cecelia move into his big empty house. Surely her presence would cut down on his front porch chats with his father. And he knew that those buckets of rainwater in the master bedroom would seem romantic to her for only so long. He told himself that this might actually be a good thing, might force him to get off his ass and replace that sieve of a roof before the house fell down. Doyle was much less anxious about their travel plans. "We're hoping to go to Italy together in the spring. My mother made me promise I'd go see the Uffizi and the Sistine Chapel before I died."

"You should go. Go while you can." Henry glanced at the naked walls. "You never know when it's going to get yanked away from you."

They sat there on the sofa like father and son and watched the rest of the game. It wasn't pretty. Bob Gibson broke Sandy Koufax's World Series record by striking out seventeen Detroit batters, and the Cardinals embarrassed the Tigers, 4-0.

When the game was over, Doyle asked Henry what he was planning to do with all the boxes, all the evidence and tips and dead-end leads he'd amassed so painstakingly over the past fifteen months.

"The guys on the motel staff are gonna toss it in the dumpster out back for me."

"I was wondering, Mr. Hull . . . I've got my brother's pickup truck parked out back—had to pick up some topsoil yesterday—and I was wondering if you'd let me take this stuff with me."

"Take it where?"

"Back to my house. For some strange reason I cleaned out my old bedroom last week. It's the only room upstairs that doesn't have any leaks in the roof. I'd like to spread everything out in there as a way of, you know, keeping the case warm."

"I dunno, Frankie. Like I said, maybe it's time to let it go."

"I can't do that, Mr. Hull."

Henry sighed. He sounded older than he'd ever sounded, like a man who was finished with life. "Be my guest then, Frankie. Do what you gotta do."

When the post-game show ended, Henry called the front desk and a bellhop came up to fetch his two suitcases. He was taking a cab to City Airport, then a plane to Duluth, Minnesota, where his brother was meeting him. He wrote down his brother's address and phone number in Marquette and made Doyle promise he would keep in touch. They hugged then, and Doyle stood in the doorway and watched him walk, one last time, down the hallway where his wife died.

When the elevator door closed behind him, Doyle got a porter to help him load the boxes into his brother's pickup. There would be time to smoke a cigar on the front porch before he had to start sautéing the vegetables and the chicken. He wanted to tell his father about the latest developments. The old man would be surprised and saddened that Henry Hull had packed it in. But Doyle had a hunch— he hoped—that his father would be proud that he'd brought all the evidence home and planned to keep the candle burning for Vic #43.

27

On the night before the World Series opened, Willie broke the news to Octavia that he would be leaving Detroit for good as soon as the Series ended. His friend Walter Mitchell had a spare room waiting for him in D.C., a quiet room with a view of Rock Creek Park, and Willie was determined to finish writing his memoir there.

Willie broke this news while he and Octavia were lying in her big four-poster bed, sticky and spent from their most frenzied lovemaking yet. He had dreaded this moment, but he thought she took the news pretty well, almost calmly, almost like she'd been expecting it. "Oh Willie, we so different," she said, sounding relieved to finally be able to admit that this was something they could never hope to overcome.

The next afternoon, feeling subdued but not unhappy, Willie and Octavia watched the opening game of the World Series at the Chit Chat. Erkie sat on the barstool between them, chain-smoking, chasing shots of Old Overholt with Stroh's and sending a torrent of abuse at the overmatched Tiger batters. When Bob Gibson struck out the side in the ninth inning, Erkie bellowed, *"Seventeen* a y'all struck out? Yain't nothin but a buncha born-insecure, rat-soup-eatin, barnyard mutha-a-*fuckas*!" Willie was the only person in that morgue who laughed.

After the game Octavia dropped Willie off at his apartment and he went right back to work at the typewriter. He worked deep into the night, until he finished a rough draft of the story about the night Helen Hull died.

He had to work the lunch shift at Oakland Hills the next day, but his Uncle Bob was the only one on the staff who did a lick of work. All the other waiters and busboys stood along the walls in the packed men's grill to watch Mickey Lolich try to atone for yesterday's disaster. Lolich pitched brilliantly, even hit the first home run of his career, and the Tigers won with surprising ease, 8-1.

There was no game the next day as the teams traveled from St. Louis to Detroit. Willie had the day off and he spent it at home polishing his account of what had happened on the roof of the Larrow Arms. It was already good, but he wanted to make it perfect. Clarence Rawls had moved out West somewhere, but Willie didn't want to give him up, so he'd changed Clarence's name to Tyrone Bell and changed his appearance, moved him into a different apartment. Willie had also decided to make Tyrone Bell the killer. It was a little lie that would preserve a larger truth—that Wes didn't deserve to go to prison.

Late in the afternoon, just as he was getting ready to knock off for the day, Walter Mitchell called from Washington. It was Walter who'd convinced the editors at *Ebony* to run six installments from Willie's memoir—it was going to be called "Death of the Dream"—and now Walter was calling to tell him he'd taken the liberty of slipping the first three installments to Dreyfus Trotter, an editor at McGraw-Hill who used to work at *Ebony*, another Tuskegee man. Trotter wanted to talk to Willie about publishing his entire memoir in hardcover. Walter gave Willie Trotter's phone number in New York and told him to call him immediately. Just before he hung up, Walter said his spare bedroom was cleaned up and Willie could move in any time. Willie told him he would show up right after the World Series. Then he dialed the number in New York.

Dreyfus Trotter didn't sound black. He sounded vaguely English. "Mr. Bledsoe," he began, "from what I've seen so far I'm of the opinion that your story will belong on the same shelf with *Soul on Ice*. In a word, I find it brilliant."

In a word, Willie was speechless.

"Are you still there, Mr. Bledsoe?"

"Yes, I'm right here."

"Have you read *Soul on Ice*?"

"I read it last week, as a matter of fact."

"I edited the book, which, as you're surely aware, Mr. Cleaver wrote while he was incarcerated." He paused to let that credential sink in. "I trust you'll agree with me that the source of the book's power is its candor. Its refusal to pull punches, if you will."

"I agree." Any black man in America who openly admits to raping white women—and calls it an "insurrectionary" act—cannot be accused of pulling his punches.

"I'm assuming you saw Walter's photo essay in *Ebony* about the Detroit riot."

"Of course."

"He tells me you were with him when he was arrested."

"That's correct."

"I'm curious, are you planning to include that experience in your memoir?"

"As a matter of fact I spent this afternoon working on that chapter. I've just decided to make it the book's ending."

"Would you be so good as to tell me a bit about that night?"

Willie realized Dreyfus Trotter was asking to be sold a bill of goods. Willie also realized that Dreyfus Trotter was hoping he wouldn't pull any punches. So Willie told him, as dispassionately as he could, about that horrific night, beginning when he and Walter got arrested, continuing to the moment bloody Wes knocked on his door, and ending when Willie and Wes and "Tyrone Bell" hustled down off the roof of the Larrow Arms while a woman lay dying in the Harlan House Motel. Willie even told Dreyfus Trotter the part he hadn't told Walter yet—about getting taken in for questioning by the detectives and learning the identity of Helen Hull's killer from them. The only thing Willie didn't tell Dreyfus Trotter was the killer's name.

Trotter said, "Do you intend to name the killer in your book?"

"Yes, but I don't want to give it away yet."

Trotter chuckled. "Very shrewd of you."

Willie was thinking, *You got no idea how shrewd.*

"I should very much like to read that chapter, Mr. Bledsoe. Are you planning to include it in your *Ebony* series?"

"No. The current plan is to end the series with the 1964 Democratic convention—you know, when they refused to seat the black delegates from Mississippi—because that was when I dropped out of the movement. The *Ebony* series is about my disillusionment with the civil rights movement, not what happened to me afterwards."

"I'm guessing that the chapter you just described to me—about your arrest and what happened on that rooftop—I'm guessing that's going to be the most powerful passage of the entire book."

"I think you're right. I hope you're right."

"Aren't you worried about possible legal repercussions? Possibly a charge of accessory to a murder?"

"No, because I didn't kill anybody—or help anybody kill anybody. Did they charge Eldridge Cleaver for those rapes he admitted committing?"

"No, they did not." There was a pause, a rustling noise. Then Trotter said, "Could you possibly come to New York, Mr. Bledsoe? Based on what I've read and what you've just told me, I should very much like to talk to you in person about publishing your memoir in hardcover. I think it would be advantageous for us to meet as soon as possible to discuss contract terms."

Willie knew that the World Series would be over by the following Thursday at the latest—if it went to seven games, which seemed unlikely unless Bob Gibson got run over by a bus. He told Dreyfus Trotter he could leave Detroit late next Thursday.

"I assume you'll fly?" Trotter said.

"No, I'm driving." He didn't tell him he'd never been on an airplane and was deathly afraid of the things. He told him he was moving in with Walter in Washington, and could stop in New York on his way to D.C.

"Very well then. Shall we say four o'clock next Friday afternoon in my office?"

Willie wrote down the address of the McGraw-Hill Building. In parting, Dreyfus Trotter got him to promise he would bring the riot chapter to New York and would not show it to the people at *Ebony* or anyone else. As soon as Willie hung up he phoned Clyde Holland and asked him what he should do when he got to New York.

"The one thing you don't do, Alabama, is you don't sign nothin,'" Clyde said. "He offers you a contract you show it to me before you sign it. Got that?"

"Got it."

"Say, I'm glad you called. Du and me got an extra ticket for tomorrow's game. Upper-deck in right field. Ain't the best seats in the house, but—"

"My answer's *hell* yes."

"I'll leave the ticket at Will Call."

Willie's next call was to Dick Kowalski at Oakland Hills, telling him he would not be coming back to work. To Willie's surprise, Simon Legree took the news well, even wished him luck in New York and D.C. After that call, Willie started packing up the apartment.

❖

That Saturday broke crisp and sunny, football weather, and the big barn at Michigan and Trumbull was packed for the city's first World Series game in twenty-three years. When Willie showed up an hour before the first pitch, Louis and Clyde were sitting in the sunshine in the upper deck, passing a silver flask back and forth over the empty seat between them. They both stood up when he came down the row. "Have a taste a this anti-freeze," Clyde said, handing Willie the flask. He took a nip. It was expensive scotch, nice and smooth.

"Got Earl Wilson warmin up," Louis said. "Just like Openin Day!"

Wilson didn't fare any better than he had on Opening Day, failing to make it through the fifth inning. The Cardinals proved to be rude guests, stealing bases at will, blasting home runs and winning with ease, 7-3. The loss did nothing to dampen Louis and Clyde's merriment.

"We done witnessed history," Clyde said, watching the disappointed fans shuffle down the aisles.

"What we done witnessed is a historical *ass*-whippin," Louis said. The three friends whooped and slapped hands and went off to meet Octavia at the Seven Seas.

She was in a funk about the Tigers' loss but she lit up when Willie told her about the call from Dreyfus Trotter, the possible book deal. She smothered him with a hug and a kiss. When their lip-lock finally ended, she whispered in his ear, "Oh Willie, I'm so proud of—I'm so happy for you. . . ."

They watched the next game together on the portable TV at the foot of her bed. They were so busy with each other that they missed most of the game. They didn't miss much. It rained frogs on and off all day, big plump juicy frogs, and Jose Feliciano, the blind folk singer, stood by home plate with his seeing-eye dog Trudy and gave a disjointed rendering of the National Anthem that infuriated the national television audience and embarrassed the citizens of Detroit. To make matters worse, after several rain delays Bob Gibson and the Cardinals splashed out a 10-1 victory and a three-to-one lead in games in the best-of-seven Series. Everyone said it was over. They said the same thing about Jose Feliciano's singing career.

At the packed and raucous Chit Chat the next day, Erkie again sat between Willie and Octavia. Overnight she had become a rabid and highly superstitious fan. She wore a new Tigers cap, and she pulled the brim down low so she could concentrate on the TV screen. She was in a tunnel. She didn't say a word or seem aware of the pandemonium around her. But Erkie was his usual self, spraying colorful abuse at the Tigers, chasing shots with beers, smoking like the stacks at the Rouge. This time it worked. Mickey Lolich came through again, and the Tigers stayed alive with a gritty 5-3 victory. Octavia was convinced her new Tigers' cap was the reason the team's luck had so mysteriously changed, and she vowed to wear the cap and sit on the same barstool for the rest of the Series.

Two days later, her voodoo worked again. Denny McLain got a chance to redeem himself back in St. Louis, and this one was no contest. The Tigers breezed, 13-1, setting up a decisive seventh game.

Willie spent that night at Octavia's and woke up in the middle of the night to find her pacing in the living room, chain-smoking, gnawing her fingernails. She was wearing an oversized T-shirt and her Tigers' cap. He wasn't sure if she was pacing because of their looming separation or because of the enormity of the next day's game. He believed it was the Tigers keeping her up. He hoped it was.

Mickey Lolich, pitching on just two days' rest, faced Bob Gibson in the deciding seventh game. This time Willie would root without a qualm for the white man to beat the black man. Remembering that raucous seventh game of the '64 Series, Willie was amazed how completely his loyalty had shifted in four short years. Back then Bob Gibson's race had meant everything; now it meant nothing. Was this a sign, after all he'd been through, that some small thing had actually changed for the better?

Again Octavia was speechless through the first six innings, which were scoreless. Even Erkie was silenced by the pitchers' superb performances and the mounting tension. With every pitch, the screws got tighter. Willie didn't know it was possible for the Chit Chat to be so quiet.

Then it happened. With two outs in the seventh, Norm Cash and Willie Horton singled. Jim Northrup sent Gibson's next pitch to deep center field. Curt Flood took one step in, seeming to misjudge the ball in the bright sunshine, then he turned and sprinted for the wall. He couldn't catch up with the ball. Two runs scored and the Tigers were on their way to an improbable 4-1 victory that completed their impossible comeback.

The Detroit Tigers were World Champions.

Octavia turned her Tigers cap around backward and gave Willie a ten-minute kiss in the jostling bedlam of the Chit Chat. Then she started dancing with Erkie. Outside, Willie could hear horns honking, firecrackers popping. It was a vast improvement over last summer's soundtrack of sirens and gunfire. The whole city was lifting off.

Izzy Gould declared that drinks were on the house for the rest of the night, but Willie needed to hit the road for New York. When the post-game interviews ended, Willie and Octavia left the Chit Chat and headed for Tuxedo Street in his Deuce and a Quarter. Everything he owned was in the car's trunk.

People were pouring out of barrooms and houses and apartment buildings, yelling, drinking, dancing in the streets. The blare of car horns was like the cry of a delirious animal. The Deuce and a Quarter passed through the spray of fire hydrants and several showers of confetti. Octavia held her hands above the windshield, let the breeze dance through her fingers the way she'd done on the day they drove back from Algonac. Watching her, Willie glimpsed the enormity of what he was about to walk away from.

When the Temptations' new hit, "Cloud Nine," came on, Willie turned up the volume. Finally Motown had gone beyond boy-meets-girl, had released a record that dealt with something from the real world, the urge to get high and check out of those dark times: *"CLOUD NINE . . . you can be what you wanna be . . . CLOUD NINE . . . you ain't got no responsibility . . . CLOUD NINE . . . and every, every, every man is free . . . you're a million miles from reality . . . reality . . . reality . . ."*

"You like that song?" Octavia asked when it was over.

"Love it. Bout time somebody at Motown woke up."

"Said that right."

He pulled up in front of her building and cut the engine. Music was blasting from every window—rock 'n' roll, soul, blues, R&B, Motown, country—a strangely melodious din. He realized he'd parked in this very spot the first time he and Octavia kissed. He leaned over and took off her Tigers' cap and kissed her.

"You wanna come in?" she said. "One last time, old times sake, all that good stuff?" He could see she was trying to smile at least as hard as she was trying not to cry.

"I better get going, baby. Got a long drive ahead of me. Gonna try to make Niagara Falls tonight. Gotta be in New York by four tomorrow afternoon."

She made no move to get out of the car. "I was just rememberin that night you got back from the po-lice station. You remember? The way you ate me up?"

"Course I remember. You liked it?"

"No, I loved it. I remember thinkin I finally met a brother knows how to love a woman right. Guess I was wrong. Again."

"Octavia. . . ."

"I'm sorry, Willie. We both know you doin the right thing. This been fun and all, but you and me got too many differences. You need your wings and I need my nest. I promised myself, that night at my crib when you broke the news, I promised I wasn't even gonna try to convince you to stay in D-troit."

There wasn't a woman—there wasn't a person—on the planet who could convince him to stay in Detroit. He didn't tell her this, though, because he didn't know if it would soften her pain or sharpen it, and he didn't want to do anything to hurt this woman. She is who she is, Willie thought, a sweet sexy woman with a good heart who isn't the one for me. And I am who I am, a man with a story to tell who needs to get far away from this town and never look back.

Octavia brushed confetti from his hair, forced herself to smile. "Hey, Willie, our D-troit Tigers done won the World Series."

"They damn sure did. I'm still not sure I believe it."

"I believe it. D-troit City gonna rock tonight."

"Guess it'll have to rock without me." He could see it now—
Edgar Hudson and Chick Murphy, Sambo and the Surf—both of
them drunk as lords, dancing an impromptu interracial polka right
there on the plush carpets of the Oakland Hills men's grill. Willie
supposed such a dance would have to be considered progress in this
sick country right now.

"You drive safe," Octavia said. She gave him another kiss, a quick
one, a goodbye kiss. Then she screwed her Tigers cap back on. It
looked sexy on her. Everything looked sexy on her. She got out of
the car and said, "Good luck in New York."

"Thanks, baby."

"And write me a letter soon as you get to D.C."

"I promise."

As always, he watched her walk to her front door, the astonishing
back and forth, watched her turn and blow him a kiss. Then she was
gone.

But he didn't leave for New York. When he got to Woodward he
took a left instead of a right and headed north, away from downtown.
He took a left at McNichols, another left at Normandy Street. There
were half a dozen HUMPHREY-MUSKIE posters stabbed into the lawn in
front of the big Tudor house halfway down the block. The lawn had
just been mowed, and Bob Brewer was washing the bronze Deuce
parked on the driveway. There was a HUMPHREY-MUSKIE sticker on its
back bumper. Bob shut off the hose and dried his hands with a towel
as Willie came across the lawn.

"You got time to do mine when you're finished?" Willie said.

"Cost you five dollars."

They laughed and shook hands. Willie fished in his pocket and
handed a set of keys to his uncle.

"What's this?" Bob said.

"Keys to my apartment. Sorry about the short notice, but everything I own's packed in the trunk. I'm moving to D.C. to live with

Walter, stopping in New York on the way. Looks like I've got a book deal."

The surprise on Bob Brewer's face gave way to a smile that was bright but hard to read—relief, pride, maybe both. He took Willie in his arms. "That's great news, Cuz. Can't say I'm surprised—I always knew you had it in you." He released his nephew. He was still beaming and Willie could see that he, too, was fighting not to cry. "So," Bob said, "guess this mean's you're clear with the po-lice?"

"Yeah, they brought me in for questioning, then let me go—cause I didn't do anything."

"How bout your brother?"

"They got nothin on him either. Sides, he's back in Saigon starting a restaurant, or somesuch foolish shit. Looks like we're both home free."

There was no mistaking the relief on Bob's face now. "Thank God. You got no idea how worried your momma and I were about you boys."

"Mary home?"

"No, she's out leafleting." He motioned toward the posters on the lawn. Dedicated Democrats, Willie thought, true believers in the big lie.

"Well, tell Aunt Mary goodbye for me."

"Will do."

"And thanks for everything, Uncle Bob. You been a prince—except for that damn rent."

Bob laughed and they hugged one more time. The last Willie saw of his uncle was in the Buick's rearview mirror. Bob was rubbing his Deuce with a sudsy orange sponge. Willie couldn't tell for sure, but he thought he saw a smile on the man's face.

When Willie drove onto the Ambassador Bridge, the sun was setting off to his right. To his left he could see the empty stadium and, beyond it, downtown, all of it backlit by the fading sun. The river was molten copper. It looked like a postcard of a place he was already forgetting.

Ontario was as flat as a plate. He left the top down, rolled the windows up and cranked the heater on high as the night came down. There were stars, millions of stars, hard and white and pulsing. He stepped harder on the gas—*go ahead and see what she'll do*—and the Deuce and a Quarter carried him at a gallop away from Detroit and into the cold velvet night.

THE END

Acknowledgments

This book was so long in the making that it's hard to remember everyone who helped bring it into the world, let alone thank them properly. But I'll try. Marianne gave me judicious readings, cold-eyed advice, and, above all, repeated reminders that giving up is not an option. Alice Martell is the agent all writers dream of—passionate, dogged, and classy. Jessica Case is that rarest of editors, able to dissect a manuscript line by line without losing sight of the big picture. Copyeditor Deb Anderson and proofreader Phil Gaskill are my heroes, dedicated to doing the thankless, invisible work that every writer needs. People will try to tell you that nobody in America edits books anymore. Don't believe them. It has been a joy to see how much everyone at Pegasus cares about the books they make.

Thanks, too, to my family and the friends who stuck with me through some lean times, including David Newton, Pete Khoury, Loren D. Estleman, Adrienne Short, Danny Fox, Michael Gentile, and my beloved German girls, Katrin and Lotti. I hope the next one doesn't take this long.